DEADLOCK

Colin Forbes, born in Hampstead, London, ⬛⬛⬛⬛⬛ very year. For the past twenty years he has ea⬛⬛⬛⬛⬛ olely as a full-time writer.

An international bestseller, ⬛⬛⬛⬛⬛ been published world-wide, including the U⬛⬛⬛⬛ He is translated into twenty-two languages.

He is an enthusiastic traveller ⬛⬛ visits all locations appearing in his novels. 'It is essential for an author to see everything for himself to achieve vivid atmosphere and authenticity.'

He has explored most of Western Europe, the East and West coasts of America, and has made excursions to Africa and Asia. He lives with his wife in Surrey.

Surveys have shown that his readership is divided almost equally between men and women.

COLIN FORBES

DEADLOCK

Pan Books
in association with Collins

First published 1988 by William Collins Sons & Co. Ltd
This edition published 1988 by Pan Books Ltd,
Cavaye Place, London SW10 9PG
in association with William Collins Sons & Co. Ltd
18 19 17
© Colin Forbes 1988
ISBN 0 330 30311 2
Printed and bound in Great Britain by
Cox & Wyman Ltd, Reading, Berkshire

FOR JANE

CONTENTS

Prologue

Prologue

Breckland. Shrouded by dense fir forest on three sides, The Bluebell pub seemed like a haven from the April storm to the seven villagers drinking inside. Night was a cloak, further isolating the ancient two-storey building. The gale rattled the windows, rain lashed the mullion panes, a single tile was torn from the roof. There was a deathly hush along the drinkers as they heard the clatter of the falling tile. Although death was the furthest thought from their minds.

Outside the pub the distant cottages of Cockley Ford were blurred silhouettes. No lights showed in the tiny Norfolk village. It was eight o'clock.

Ted Jarvis, ploughman, clad in an old check shirt, corduroy trousers tied at the ankles with pieces of string, a shabby windcheater, broke the silence.

'Well, let's get on with it. Are we all agreed? We're having nothing to do with this crazy foreigner and his mad plan. Money isn't everything . . .'

'Now, Edward, there's more to it.' Mrs Rout, postmistress, clutched her glass of port, her voice raucous and domineering as she settled her plump body inside her favourite wooden chair – next to the bar. 'The other villagers – greedy lot that they are – have to be told. And no nonsense. No argufying. Without us they can't do a thing. That's the long and short of it.'

Everyone, including Joel, the barman, nodded. Mrs Rout had spoken and that was an end to it. She drank more of her port. The other four men – Ben, the tractor driver; Eric, the lad who was simple in the head; George, the grocer; and William, the ditch digger nodded again. Mrs Rout drove her point home.

'Then there's that new doctor just come. Portch. Don't

like him. Not one of us. Anyone needs doctoring goes to Ransome at Cockley Cley . . .'

The heavy wooden door slammed open. A weird figure stood inside the doorway. Mrs Rout stiffened. She opened her mouth to speak but only a croak of fear emerged. She had thought it was the gale which had forced open the door.

The figure wore a Balaclava helmet. Over that he wore a yellow oilskin with the hood half-pulled down across the helmet. Rivulets of water ran off the oilskin, dripping on to the scoured wooden floor. In gloved hands he held an Uzi machine pistol.

He stood motionless, the cold eyes behind the helmet slit surveying the room with its smoke-blackened beams supporting the ceiling. The eyes noted the position of each of the seven villagers who looked like frozen waxworks. Then he began operating the gun. In short bursts. A fusillade of bullets swept the room as he arced the weapon.

Rain beat against his back as he stood, steady as a rock, continuing the sweep of the muzzle. Mrs Rout slumped in her chair, her hand knocking over her glass of port. Its contents stained the floor as she lay with her head twisted to one side, her false teeth hanging half out of her mouth. Joel, the barman, tried to duck behind the counter. A hail of bullets hurled him against the shelves attached to the rear wall. He sagged out of sight, bringing down a load of bottles on top of his corpse. A momentary pause in the lethal chatter of the Uzi. The gun moved past Simple Eric, leaving him standing and staring with glaucous blue eyes, staring at the blood oozing from Mrs Rout's lolling hand, blood which mingled on the floor with the spilt port. Ted Jarvis stood up from his chair and the gun chattered again. He crashed back into the chair, broke its back, sprawled behind it. Ben, the tractor driver, a tough stocky man, grabbed an almost-full bottle of beer, hoisted his arm to aim for the killer's head. He doubled up like a jackknife closing, dropping the bottle. It rolled across the floor in another brief pause. The only sound was beer gushing on to wood. Two more brief bursts. George and William crumpled into lifeless caricatures of human beings.

It was all over in twenty seconds. Five hideous corpses in various postures of death furnished the room, the sixth out of view behind the bar. The man in the Balaclava helmet walked into the room as a hawk-nosed man wearing a black wide-brimmed hat and a black coat sodden with rain came in behind him. He had a pince-nez perched on the bridge of his nose.

Balaclava pressed a lever, changing the mechanism to single-shot, then paused by each body. He placed the muzzle tip close to each skull, fired once, then moved on. He was walking behind the bar when the hawk-nosed man spoke as he shook water from his hat.

'Is that necessary?'

'I do a job.'

Balaclava was laconic, spoke English with an American accent. He stooped behind the bar. A last shot rang out. The man with the pince-nez carried a black bag which he placed on the nearest table before bending over Mrs Rout. He pursed thin lips.

'I'll have to dig the bullets out of the skulls,' he complained.

'Your part of the operation, Dr Portch,' Balaclava commented. He stared towards the doorway where another man had appeared, a wide-shouldered countryman with an overlong jaw which gave him a primeval look. 'Grimes, are you coming in to clean up this mess?'

'They're queueing up outside,' Portch answered. 'Best give them a few minutes to prepare them for this. I've been in enough morgues but the place looks like an abattoir. Where is Simple Eric?' he queried.

'Ran right past me,' Grimes replied. 'Hell for leather towards village. Christ! What's that?'

Balaclava stiffened, his first reaction since he had entered the pub. In the near distance, muffled by the torrential rain, a bell began chiming. A slow, dirge-like chime. Portch reacted

11

first, addressing Grimes whose ruddy face had lost colour.

'Ned, it's the idiot. Eric. Stop him at once. We have to clean up quickly . . .'

Grimes ran outside. Villagers stood huddled in pairs, protected against the weather in oilskins and raincoats. Each couple held a makeshift stretcher, carried a plastic bucket and a mop. Inside Portch beckoned to them, calling over his shoulder to Balaclava.

'They'll be all right. I gave each of them a Valium to soothe their nerves . . .'

Grimes pounded along the curving road, head down against the driving rain, heart thudding in his chest, glad of an excuse to get away from the bloodbath. He ran on past the few cottages lining the three sides of the triangle-shaped village green.

His objective was a tiny church perched beyond a wall on a small hill. The church was constructed of flintstone. Attached to the western end of the ancient edifice was a circular bell-tower. The chimes continued, louder now. With trembling hands he pushed open the grille gate in the wall, stumbled up the mossy path to the entrance porch and turned the iron ring handle of the studded door. He paused, then went inside.

At the foot of the bell-tower to his left Eric stood hauling a long rope up and down with both hands. The single rope was tied at intervals into a series of loops like nooses. The solemn, doomful note of the invisible bell – a metal ladder led up to a closed trap-door in the wooden ceiling – rang out again.

'What the hell are you doing?' Grimes demanded.

'Tolling for the dead. Tolling for the dead . . .'

Eric grinned foolishly and then the grin vanished as Grimes hit him a savage blow on the jaw with his clenched fist. The simpleton sprawled on the stone-paved floor, his back against the curving wall as he gazed up.

'No one died,' Grimes told him as though speaking to a child. 'Understand? No one died tonight. They was ill, they was sick. They did die. A few weeks ago. Dr Portch was away. It was too late to save them when he got back. So they was buried. Do *you* understand, for God's sake?' He grasped Eric by the shirt collar and shook him like a dog. There was saliva on his mouth as he bent close to the simpleton's face. 'I said, do you *understand?*'

'*Aaarraagh!*'

Eric was choking, gasping for breath. Grimes realized he had twisted the lad's shirt collar in a vice-like grip, that without meaning to do so he was strangling him. The horror he would have to return to inside The Bluebell had filled his mind. He relaxed his grip, began slapping Eric's face with desperate urgency.

Eric *mustn't* die. Grimes was panicstricken at the thought. They had discussed it the previous day. Dr Portch had said the idiot lad would help to frighten people away from the village. That it didn't even matter if Eric was there when the killing of the objectors took place. No one would believe a word he said. And he never left Cockley Ford. He was an asset to the atmosphere of a tightly-closed off community Portch had created. Only Grimes left the village to collect supplies from Thetford. To Grimes' profound relief, the lad began to recover, sitting up.

'They was sick,' Grimes repeated, hammering the message into the fool's skull. 'They died a few weeks ago. They was buried then. No one died tonight.'

'No one died tonight,' Eric agreed, parrot fashion . . .

Outside in the churchyard in the drenching rain behind the building six sheets of heavy canvas covered freshly-dug graves. In the lee of the church wall, sheltered from the rain, crouched an old man like a guardian of the graves. He leant on a rusty shovel smeared with wet mud, huddled in a sailor's pea-jacket with a hood concealing his head. He would have to wait. He knew that – but that was one thing a gravedigger learnt. Patience.

The outside world might never have heard of the April massacre at Cockley Ford but for a chance happening. A man called Tweed decided to take a rare holiday.

Over a year later.

Part One

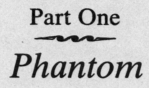

Phantom

1

'It's a super idea – taking this holiday,' Monica said. 'You haven't had one since Noah and his Ark . . .'

'I don't like holidays,' Tweed said mulishly, prowling round his office in Park Crescent. 'I get bored stiff in three days.' He stared glumly out of the first-floor window as the wind bent the trees in distant Regent's Park. 'Look at it. And it's raining. May. Godawful . . .'

'The forecast is sunshine this afternoon,' his assistant said brightly. 'Even the Deputy Director of the Secret Service needs a break. And Bob Newman has loaned you his 280E Mercedes. You will have a whale of a time.'

'It's already afternoon,' Tweed grumbled, cleaning his glasses with his handkerchief. 'And who believes in weather forecasts any more?' He glanced towards the phone on his cleared desk – willing it to ring.

The door opened and Howard, faultlessly dressed in a dark blue suit from Harrods, waltzed in, shooting snow-white cuffs. His chief was in the worst possible mood from Tweed's point of view, exuding an air of bonhomie. He eyed the suitcase standing by Tweed's desk.

'Off on our hols? Good show. Don't delay. We'll keep the home fires burning. Just forget all about us.'

Probably burn the place down, Tweed thought to himself. The second sentiment was more acceptable. Howard thrust his right hand in his trousers pocket and rattled loose change. Another irritating habit. He stooped to brush a speck of dust from his trouser leg as he continued.

'Going somewhere interesting? Barbados? The Seychelles?'

'Clacton,' Tweed said perversely. 'A breath of sea air.'

'No accounting for tastes.' Howard studied the manicured fingernails of his left hand. 'Well, I'd better be off. Just thought I'd pop in, wish you bon voyage and all that. Even if it sounds like a trip round the pier. Clacton has one?'

'No idea.' Tweed sat down behind his desk and Monica frowned. She waited until Howard left the room before she shook her index finger at her boss.

'No more hanging about. Off you go. It isn't Clacton, is it?'

The phone rang before Tweed could reply. Monica lifted her own instrument quickly. After identifying herself she grimaced as she listened.

'He's just going off on holiday, I'm afraid . . .'

'Who is it?' Tweed demanded.

'Paula Grey – calling from Norfolk,' she reported, holding one hand over the mouthpiece. 'She sounds a bit fraught – but I can handle it. I'll tell her you've just left . . .'

'I'll take it,' Tweed said firmly and lifted his receiver. 'I am still here, Paula. How are you? It sounds as though something's bothering you.'

He listened, saying little, grunting, asking the occasional question. At one stage he opened a deep drawer, using his left hand to rifle through a collection of maps of the British Isles, hauled out one of East Anglia and unfolded it as Paula continued talking.

'Got it,' he said, his finger pressed on a section of the map. 'Are you still at your new home in Blakeney? Yes, I have the address in my head. You may see me in the next day or two. It is odd, I agree. One thing, Paula,' he concluded, 'don't go anywhere near Cockley Ford again. Not until I've seen you. Promise? Good girl . . .'

He replaced the receiver, folded up the map, pocketed it, stood up and went over to the stand where his Burberry hung on a hanger. Monica watched him suspiciously as he hastily slipped on the raincoat and picked up his suitcase.

'And what, may I ask,' she enquired, 'is odd?'

'You may ask. I may not tell you.' He changed the subject to soften his reply. 'Howard was just a bit too jaunty – the way he is when he's covering up a problem.'

'It's Cynthia, his wife. There's talk she's on the verge of leaving him . . .' She stopped, appalled, could have cut out her tongue. Tweed's own wife had walked away several years ago – to live with a wealthy Greek shipowner. Rumour had it they were shacked up together in a luxurious villa in South America.

Tweed's face was expressionless. Behind his glasses his eyes showed no reaction. The parting had come as a great shock to him – something he never referred to. Monica, a woman of uncertain age, a spinster who had worked with Tweed for years, began talking rapidly.

'It's office gossip. Probably nothing more. Some people have to have something to natter about in the canteen. About Paula. Something's happened. Suddenly you're in one hell of a rush to leave. Five minutes ago you were like a ship without a rudder.'

'Maybe I've found my rudder . . .'

'Blakeney is on the coast, you mean?'

'A breath of sea air I said earlier. Very bracing – the wind off the North Sea . . .'

'You're not going anywhere near Wisbech, the interrogation centre, I hope?'

'Not a chance. Hold the fort while I'm away. Maybe a holiday is a good idea.'

'Paula might be a good idea for you – now she's on her own . . .'

'You're a wicked woman. I don't know why I employ you.'

On that note he left the room before she could think up a suitable retort.

Tweed sat behind the wheel of the 280E parked in the Crescent, studying the manual Newman, foreign correspondent and trusted confidante, had left with the car. Everything was automatic – you pressed buttons to open the sun-roof, the windows, to elevate the aerial for the radio, and it had a central locking system. Depress the small lever which locked the driver's door and all the other three doors were locked.

He drove out of London and headed for Bedfordshire. The rain continued to pour down steadily. He left the suburbs behind and moved into open country as evening approached. The sky was a low ceiling of slow-moving pewter cloud. He stopped in Woburn for a late tea at the Bedford Arms. When he drove on along the straight road which followed the endless stone wall enclosing Woburn Abbey estate it became almost like night.

On the seat beside him the map of East Anglia was open, his route outlined with a felt-tip pen. He had drawn a large circle round a section marked with one word.

Breckland.

2

He had left the village of Mundford behind. The turn-off from the A 1065 to Cockley Cley was on his left – several miles ahead. Curious, he thought as he gazed down his headlight beams, that there should be two villages so close with similar names. Cockley Cley – and Cockley Ford. To his right the black fir forests of Breckland loomed close to the highway. He reduced speed as the cloudburst increased in intensity.

The windscreen wipers were fighting a losing battle with the floods of water pouring out of the sky. Lakes snaked out on to the deserted highway from the grass verges. No sign of human habitation anywhere. No traffic had passed him for miles when he reached a narrow tarred road turning off to his right. As Paula Grey had told him on the phone, no signpost indicated where it led.

He swung the wheel easily with the aid of the power-assisted steering. The 280E was a dream of a car to drive. Straight ahead stretched a lonely road just wide enough to take the large Mercedes. Tweed, using undipped head-lights, peered through the cascade, hoping to God he wouldn't meet anything coming from the opposite direc-tion.

The wind had reached gale force, hammering the side of his car, threatening to blow its one-and-a-half tons of metal off the road. No drainage. Rivers of water flooded down each side, his wheels sent up great clouds of spray as he pressed his foot down.

Tweed was worried the engine would become water-logged, stopping the vehicle. His increase in speed was an attempt to counter the danger. He stiffened as he saw a flash of light in the distance. A car *was* coming from the opposite direction, a car moving at high speed. He doused his headlights. Approaching a gated entrance to a field, he slowed and swung the Mercedes on to gravel, then waited as the projectile hurtled towards him, headlights still turned full on.

'Dip your headlights, you swine,' he muttered to himself.

It was a Porsche, a red Porsche. Tweed raised a hand to shield his eyes against the glare. As it passed him, the car slowed. He caught a glimpse of the driver and stared. A man in his fifties – with a thick thatch of white hair and prominent cheek-bones. Tweed blinked as the car con-tinued on towards the highway. He couldn't believe it.

Lee Foley. American. Ran the Continental International Detective Agency in New York – CIDA.

Here? In the middle of Norfolk? Had his eyes deceived him? He'd had only a brief glance at the driver. He tightened his lips, recalled snatches of his conversation with Paula Grey on the phone. *I was driving up this country road . . . I'm positive the driver of the car was Lee Foley . . . Hugh pointed him out to me once in a New York restaurant . . . said he was very bad news . . . He damned near drove me into the ditch with his bloody red Porsche . . .*

Tweed had felt sure Paula must be mistaken when she

called him. He'd decided to drive up to see her, to reassure her after taking a look at the hamlet of Cockley Ford. No, he wasn't being honest with himself. He'd wanted to see Paula again.

Rain pounded the roof of his car as he sat thinking of his encounter with Foley two years ago in Berne, Switzerland. The American had gunned down three men, had then escaped via Paris. No clear identification. No case to answer.

He sighed, wondering whether he could manage a three-point turn to go back the way he'd come, decided the car was too big. He would have to drive on, keep to his original plan, have a look at Cockley Ford. Might be interesting . . .

The heavy five-barred gate was open. It hung from a concrete post. Something about it made Tweed stop. He lowered the window, ignoring the rain, staring at the glass eye set into the post. He pressed a button, closing the window, and pressed another button which lowered the passenger seat window. Through the blurred downpour he saw a second glass eye in the opposite post.

Photo-electric cells. Normally the gate was operated automatically with a remote control system. The cloudburst must have put the system out of action. He drove on round a curve, saw an old two-storey building standing back from the road, huddled in the forest. The Bluebell. The local tavern. Beyond it, on either side of the road, a single row of cottages ran away into the distance.

Tweed swung the Mercedes through one hundred and eighty degrees, using the open space in front of the inn, then stopped, switching off the engine, taking out the ignition key. He was now pointed back the way he had come, an instinctive manoeuvre. He sat for several minutes, aware that the curtain over a lower window had moved, exposing lights inside. He was being watched.

Alighting from the car, he locked it and walked to the

inn's front door, which had an iron ring for a handle. He turned it, went inside to a large rectangular room, and stopped. Half a dozen country types sat drinking. Faces turned and stared at the newcomer. The barman stood with a cloth in his hands – stood as still as Tweed. It was like observing a frozen tableau.

'Nasty night,' Tweed commented, taking off his hat and shaking rain on to the mat.

'How did you get through the gate?'

The question came from a broad-shouldered man sitting near the bar. He wore a navy blue pea-jacket with gleaming brass buttons and rumpled grey slacks. Despite their appearance, the clothes looked expensive and his leather boots could have been Gucci. In his late forties, Tweed guessed, his face was weatherbeaten, his complexion ruddy, his jaw overlong, his eyes a cold blue. The accent was Norfolk, the tone unfriendly, demanding.

'It was wide open. I drove straight through. This is Cockley Cley?'

'No. Further up the 'ighway towards Swaffham. Turn off to the left.'

Standing up, the man presented his back to Tweed, leaned on the bar and ordered a large Scotch. Tweed joined him, aware of an atmosphere of hostility he'd never before encountered in a Norfolk village. His stubborn streak surfaced. He waited patiently while Pea-Jacket was served. The barman had a blank expression, a head which was squarish, as though hewn from a chunk of wood.

'I'll have a Scotch, too,' Tweed said pleasantly. 'And a drop of water, please . . .'

The barman was looking over his shoulder. Tweed swung round and caught Pea-Jacket in the act of nodding his head. He turned back to the bar in time to see the barman reaching for an unopened bottle.

'Not that one,' Tweed said quickly. 'I'll take it from the one used to serve our friend here.'

His eyes scanned the rear wall of wood which had been stripped and re-varnished, destroying the aged atmosphere of the rest of the room. Knots of wood appeared to have been inserted at various points. He glanced down at the deep skirting board, which had not been subject to renovation. The barman pushed a glass across the counter and forgot about the water. He shook his head when Tweed tried to pay.

'On the 'ouse. Then you'll be on your way, I s'pose. We'll be closing soon.'

'At this hour! And I insist on paying.'

Tweed pushed a pound coin over the counter. Again the barman looked at Pea-Jacket, who nodded for the second time. Tweed was clumsy with his change, dropping a ten-penny piece on the floor. He stooped to retrieve it, staring briefly at the defect in the old skirting board where it met the bar. It looked uncommonly like a bullet-hole. He straightened up, glanced over his shoulder and addressed Pea-Jacket.

'Excuse my lack of manners. My name's Sneed . . .'

'Ned Grimes,' said Pea-Jacket and then clamped his thin lips shut as though he'd replied too quickly.

'Cheers!' Tweed leant against the bar, raised his glass, took a sip, his eyes on Grimes. 'I seem to have taken the wrong turning. Which place is this? There was no signpost at the turn-off.'

'Cockley Ford,' Grimes said shortly. 'We have a bird sanctuary 'ere – and private zoo. That's why we needs the gate, you see. Public don't come 'ere.'

'Really?' Tweed was at his most amiable as he glanced at the other four seated drinkers. They had hardly moved, hadn't said a word to each other since he entered. 'I'd have thought that people would be visiting a bird sanctuary . . .'

'Private. Not for public.'

'Not the village as well, I imagine?'

He never did get a reply to his question. A vacant-faced youth stood up from a table by himself and giggled idiotically. Tweed noted on his left wrist he wore a Rolex with a gold expanding strap, the kind of timepiece which registered the moon phases and God knew what else.

Grimes swung round in his chair but before he could react the youth spoke. In a sing-song tone which was chilling.

'No one died. No one died tonight. No one was buried . . .'

Grimes turned on the youth, who smiled fatuously. Jumping up, he grabbed him by the arm and propelled him to the door. The rain had stopped slashing at the windows, the storm had worked itself out. Grimes heaved the heavy door open, took the youth by the shoulders and hurled him into the night, slamming the door shut.

'He be soft in the 'ead,' Grimes informed Tweed as he returned to his chair and took a large gulp of whisky. 'Simple Eric we calls 'im.'

'Every village has one,' Tweed agreed.

From outside the inn he heard the faint sound of a car crawling past The Bluebell, moving towards the cottages. He looked at a hard-faced woman, middle-aged and grey-haired with the hair tied back in an old-fashioned bun. She sat knitting, watching Tweed, the only sound inside the pub the click-clack of her needles. *Les triocoteuses*. Why was he reminded of the women who had sat by the guillotine during the French Revolution – watching the heads roll? An absurd thought. Grimes followed his gaze.

'Mrs Sporne, postmistress,' he remarked.

'Good evening to you,' Tweed addressed her.

She dropped her eyes and started counting stitches, making no reply. Two of the male drinkers were now talking in whispers, their eyes on Tweed. Under the surface he sensed something deeper than the animosity he had felt when he first entered the pub. The rank smell of *fear*.

He finished his drink, was about to leave, when something happened which caused the drinkers to freeze, staring at each other in horror. The distant chiming of a bell began tolling. A murderous look came over Grimes' face as the chiming continued. He hastily composed his expression when he saw Tweed watching him.

'Can't be far away that church,' Tweed commented. 'I'm

interested in churches.' He strolled towards the door as the mournful chimes continued their dirge, pausing by Grimes' chair. 'Oh, a couple of my friends may arrive at any moment. SAS men. They drove up with me from London in their own car. We lost each other in Thetford. I gave them the same instructions to find Cockley Cley – the other village. Turn right off the highway. Think I'll just take a look at your church before I go . . .'

'I'm coming with you then. Least I can do – seein' as you're so interested.'

It was pitch-black outside. Rain dripped from the branches of a fir tree which spread out towards the inn like huge hands. Tweed collected a large torch Newman had left in the car, a torch which might be described as a blunt instrument. He turned towards the darkened cottages.

Grimes walked beside Tweed, his boots clumping on the tarred road. By the light of the torch beam Tweed crossed a small footbridge over a gushing stream where the road sloped into a ford. There were lights in the cottage windows behind drawn curtains. One was drawn aside as they passed. A man's face peered out and the curtain closed hurriedly. The road curved again as it climbed and Tweed saw the silhouette of the church raised on an eminence. He switched off the torch to gain night vision. A moment later he stopped.

'Something's wrong?' Grimes demanded.

'It's got a pepperpot bell-tower. I haven't seen one of those except on the coast. At Brancaster, places like that. Never so far inland.'

'Just a church. Seen all you want?'

Tweed didn't reply. He strode to the gate in the flintstone wall, pushed it open and walked along the moss-covered path leading up to the church. Also constructed of flint-stone, he estimated it at hundreds of years old. The chimes were very loud. Grimes hurried after him.

'Don't want to go in there. And those men comin' to look for you. Who be they?'

'Special Air Service. Elite anti-terrorist troops. Very

tough types. They're on leave,' he continued, elaborating the lie, 'on holiday, I mean.'

He went inside.

Tweed stared at Simple Eric, who was hauling on the bell-rope as the chimes echoed weirdly above, sweat pouring down his face. Reaching up to pull the rope, Eric's shirt cuff was rolled well up his forearm and Tweed saw his wrist-watch was definitely a Rolex. Suspended from the wooden ceiling in the circular bell-tower was a naked forty-watt bulb which cast menacing shadows. Grimes pushed rudely past Tweed and swore foully.

'. . . idiot child. Go *home!*'

'Toll for the dead. Toll for the dead. Toll for the . . .'

Eric seemed in a trance as he chanted his chilling litany. He let go of the looped rope as Grimes seized him with his left hand, then struck him a savage blow to the face with his right. Eric blinked. His soiled shirt was drenched with sweat.

'Take it easy,' Tweed advised.

'Go home, I said!' Grimes roared in a frenzy. 'You want me to strap the hide off you?'

Tweed glanced to his right, surveying the tiny church. Seven rows of worn wooden pews stretched on either side of the central aisle towards the altar. He stiffened. The altar was completely covered with a black velvet cloth. Grimes slammed the door shut as Eric ran outside and noticed Tweed's gaze at the altar.

'Crazy loon,' he rasped. 'Best wait outside while I turns off lights. Wait by the gate.'

Tweed left the church. Instead of heading back down the moss-covered path he wandered through the wet grass round the bell-tower to the back of the church. Before him stretched a graveyard hemmed in by the high flintstone wall. He had a trapped feeling but walked on. An old gated railing sealed off a huge mausoleum with steps leading down beyond the gate. He flashed on the torch. The

27

padlock holding the chains on the gate was brand new. He wandered on. Headstones thrust up out of the grass, slanting at different angles. Six were standing erect, close together. He swung the torch beam, examined the engraved lettering on the stones.

Edward Jarvis. Died April 1986. RIP. He swivelled the beam to the next one. *Bertha Rout. Died April 1986 . . . Joel Couzens. Died April 1986 . . . Benjamin Sadler. Died April 1986 . . .*

Altogether there were six people who had died the same year, the same month. He had just examined the last headstone when Grimes ran up behind him. Tweed turned and the villager was panting for breath. When he spoke he was hardly coherent.

'What the hell are you doing?'

'Now, Ned, what have we here?'

Round the end of the bell-tower a tall figure had appeared. Tweed swung the torch beam full on the newcomer. He had a hawk-like nose and a pince-nez was perched on its bridge. The eyes had an odd opaque look in the glare of the torch, were unblinking. He wore a wide-brimmed black hat, a long black overcoat. For a moment, before he doused the torch, Tweed thought he was a priest.

'I am Dr Portch. I heard the bell. Then Eric ran past me in a panic. Has he had another epileptic fit? And perhaps you would introduce me to the stranger, Ned?'

A soft, almost hypnotic tone of voice. Years of practising the bedside manner, Tweed assumed as Grimes replied.

'Mr . . . Now I never was one for remembering names . . .'

'Sneed,' said Tweed.

'That's it. This is Mr Sneed, Doctor. He has two SOS men who come lookin' for 'im.'

'SOS?'

'He means SAS,' Tweed interjected. 'We share a common interest in bird-watching. I took the wrong turning – I was heading for Cockley Cley. I'm glad I had a chance

28

to look at your ancient church. Most unusual in this part of the world.'

'And you are also interested in headstones, Mr Sneed?'

Tweed was trying to place the strange doctor's accent. He detected an undertone of Norfolk burr but it was overlaid with a quite different regional accent. The brown eyes behind the pince-nez stared coldly at Tweed, as though struggling to come to some decision.

'I was curious to see that six people died in the same month,' Tweed replied. 'A heavy toll for one tiny village.'

'Meningitis. Unfortunately I was away for a few days when the outbreak started. Then it was too late. A major tragedy. It started with Simple Eric – the only one to survive. A weak head but a strong body. So often the case in this world, Mr Sneed. Is that your Mercedes outside The Bluebell?'

'Yes.' Tweed switched on the torch, swung the beam full on to the ancient mausoleum. 'That must go back a few years.'

'Ah! Sir John Leinster's final resting place. The last of his line, sadly. He died forty years ago. Now, Mr Sneed, I expect you'll be wanting to continue your journey. Ned, perhaps you'd be good enough to escort our visitor *safely* back to his car. Breckland, Mr Sneed, is a very lonely and dangerous place. So easy to get lost in the forest where feral cats roam.' Portch was almost purring like one of the wild cats he'd mentioned. He asked the question as Tweed was turning away.

'Your two friends. If they turn up do we tell them you have proceeded to Cockley Cley?'

'Yes, please. They're travelling in a large blue Peugeot,' Tweed said, keeping up the fiction.

He almost tripped in a deep gulley. He kept walking, glancing down. Two deep wide ruts were embedded in the grass. At some time a heavy vehicle had been brought into the church yard. He opened the left-hand side of the double grille gate and walked briskly back towards his car, followed by Grimes who hurried to catch him up.

They were passing a giant fir overhanging the road when Tweed glanced to his right. Almost concealed in the undergrowth below the fir was a red snout. The front end of a Porsche.

'I'll be leavin' you here,' Grimes said. 'There's your nice car waitin' outside Bluebell . . .'

He pushed open the garden gate of a cottage, hurried along the path. Tweed heard the slam of the front door and was on his own in the night. He recrossed the footbridge, walking at his normal pace, gripping the torch firmly.

He had the key in his hand when he reached the Mercedes, pushed it in the lock and turned it. Somewhere behind him a thud of running feet came closer. He slid behind the wheel, slipped the key into the ignition, started the engine, turned on the headlights, pressed down the lever which locked all the doors.

In the wing mirror he saw Simple Eric rushing towards the car. Grimes, close behind, grabbed the lad and began wielding a large strap, beating him about the body. Tweed put the gear into reverse, released the brake and backed the vehicle slowly towards the struggling figures. He saw Grimes pause, stare towards him as the car moved closer. Eric seized his chance, broke free and ran, disappearing behind the pub into the dark wall of the forest. Grimes jumped to one side, then grabbed the handle of the rear door, pulling at it furiously.

Tweed changed gear, drove off, pressing his foot down. The acceleration was impressive. He caught a last glimpse of Grimes, thrown off balance, sprawling in the road. Tweed drove on through the gateway and pressed his foot down further, speeding along the straight road. He kept glancing in his rear view mirror, waiting for the headlights of the Porsche. Nothing appeared.

He turned right along the highway and sped along its smooth surface. Within minutes he passed a signpost on his left. Pointing to Cockley Cley. He kept on, heading for Swaffham, leaving behind the forest where feral cats roamed, where a strange doctor seemed to have a village in the palm of his hand. He left behind Breckland.

It was late evening when he reached the Norfolk coast, taking the turn-off for Blakeney Quay, Paula Grey's new home.

3

'Tweed, what a weird experience. Now finish up your bacon and eggs while I natter. You could have had a pork chop . . .'

'This is fine, Paula – no good for my weight but marvellous for my stomach.'

Her tiny house overlooked the harbour at Blakeney just across the road. Which was little more than a wharf at the edge of a creek. Paula Grey was a slim thirty-year-old with a good figure, raven-black hair shaped to her neck, a longish face and strong bone structure. She wore a blue blouse with a mandarin collar and a cream pleated skirt. Sitting in a bentwood chair close to him, she crossed her long legs

'Shouldn't you tell the police – or something?'

'Nothing to go on. Nobody attacked me. I just felt they wanted to. Queer village, that. We'd best forget it. Just don't go near the place again.'

'But someone has been checking up on me here – going round showing a photo of me and asking where I live . . .'

'What?' Tweed paused, his napkin half way to his mouth. 'You didn't mention this on the phone.'

'I didn't want to go into everything,' she explained. 'After you said you'd come and see me.'

'Go into everything now. Start from the beginning – and I need the complete picture, please.'

'Have some more coffee. Now, from the beginning. I was in my car outside this house a few days ago – ready to drive off into the wild blue yonder. No particular destination. Day off from my pottery business – which I'm seriously thinking of selling. Behind me were the docks where a coaster was unloading soya bean meal. They store it in that tall warehouse down the street. I saw this white-haired man – very tall and tough-looking – striding down the gangplank, carrying a case. I began to get curious . . .'

'Why?'

'The coasters normally carry only cargo. And he looked familiar.' She leaned forward, slim hands clasped over shapely knees. 'And a funny little man brought him a red Porsche. Didn't add up – travelling cargo and then the expensive car. I decided to follow him, see where he went. For something to do.'

'Surely he'd spot you quickly?'

'I didn't think so – not in this part of the world. The roads are so narrow. Often it's happened to me. Driving to the factory at Wisbech – another car catches up with you, perches on your tail for miles until it can overtake. See what I mean?'

'Go on.' Tweed drank more coffee and started on the bowl of fruit salad she'd put before him.

'We drove to Fakenham, then he took the A 1065 to Swaffham. Beyond Swaffham he kept on the 1065 for Mundford. We were in Breckland by now. He pulled up suddenly – the bastard timed it perfectly.'

'What happened?'

'I had to stop close behind him – a big truck was coming in the opposite direction. So, when I passed him I was moving slowly. I glanced at him and damned nearly swerved. He was pointing something at me which looked like a gun.'

She shuddered at the recollection and helped herself to coffee. 'He got a good look at me – and I'm sure it was Foley. Afterwards I realized he was holding some kind of camera – a cine job . . .'

'Probably the type with a pistol grip.'

'That's right. Next thing I knew he overtook me and drove alongside. We were both going like bats out of hell. Then the sod deliberately swerved towards me, tried to drive me off the road.'

'Unnerving. What happened then?'

'I've seen that sort of thing so often in films and wondered why they didn't do the obvious thing. I suddenly reduced speed – as much as I dared. He shot ahead and I dropped back.'

'What next?'

'I was flaming. You know – macho girl not going to allow a chauvinist pig to get away with that. I followed him. When he turned left up the narrow road to Cockley Ford I kept after him. Soon he'd gone clear out of sight. That cooled my ardour. Commonsense took over. I came to an entrance to a field and turned the car round. I find Breckland creepy and there have been queer rumours about that village.'

'What kind of rumours? And this fruit salad is some of the best I've ever tasted.'

'Take you to Cockley Cley – the other village. That is, if you will stay on a few days. I've a friend there, a Mrs Massingham who knows all the gossip.'

'There's a hotel in Blakeney?'

'Hotel! I have a guest bedroom. Bit of a box, but you can bed down there.'

'You're tempting me.' Tweed paused.

'Box room for you then.' She smiled. 'It was good of you to come. Have you got your complete picture now?'

'You've missed out a vital bit. Something about someone going round with a photo of you, asking where you lived.'

'That was yesterday. Creepy – like Breckland. A woman friend who lives up the street warned me. Told her some yarn about visiting his cousin and he'd lost the address. Showed her a photo of me. She sent him off with a flea in his ear – but he went on to see Mrs Piggott. She'll tell anybody anything.'

'Any description from your friend?'

'Yes, and she's observant. Short, stocky build, in his forties at a guess. Wears pebble glasses which gives him a sinister look. A face like a lump of dough. Plump. His clothes hanging off him – and messy into the bargain. Spoke English with a foreign accent. Mittel-European, Cathy thought.'

'Observant, Cathy, as you said . . .'

'Oh, and the description reminds me of the man who met Foley with the Porsche off the coaster.'

'*If* it was Lee Foley. I deal in facts. Talking about facts,' he continued casually, 'your vetting for joining the Service came up Al. If you're still interested.'

'That's marvellous.' Her grey-blue eyes glowed. 'I can sell the business at any time for a good price. I held off till I heard the verdict.'

'Hold off a bit longer,' Tweed advised. 'I'd like to think about it a bit longer. The fact that you come from a military family helped.'

'Sounds rather snobby . . .'

'Oh, don't worry. That was just background. We're looking for a different type these days. Excellent linguists. The fact that you can speak French, German and Italian like a native was the key qualification. Let's sleep on it. We can talk more tomorrow – things will look clearer then.'

'Sleep well . . .'

Tweed didn't sleep well. He lay awake in the tiny bedroom at the front, overlooking the harbour. Some time after midnight he heard a great surge of water. The tide was going out. He remembered a remark a restaurant owner had made to him at Brancaster, further along the coast towards King's Lynn. *It's like pulling the plug out – one moment the sea's there, then it's gone. Nothing left but the empty creeks.*

The surging sound ceased abruptly. Tweed fretted about

the Mittel-European who had enquired about Paula's address. Why should they want to know where she lived – whoever *they* might be? The episode had sinister implications. Of course, they'd got her photo from the cine-film taken by the Porsche driver, Foley.

At some ungodly hour he fell into a troubled sleep. He woke suddenly, alarmed. Broad daylight. He checked his watch. 7 a.m. Stupid. He heard the sound of movements downstairs – Paula was up.

He went to the window, pulled back the curtains. Black clouds above. Below, beyond the road, a channel of water vanished to the west, towards the North Sea. Beyond the channel a maze of muddy creeks snaked away between large elevated banks of sour grass. At high water in March the spring tides would submerge the lot.

He was in the bathroom at the back of the house, dressed in pyjamas as he washed and shaved when a hand looped round the door, placed a cup and saucer on a shelf. Paula sounded brisk and businesslike.

'Room service. First cup of coffee. No milk. No sugar. Do I score?'

'Ten out of ten . . .'

He dressed quickly, ravenous for breakfast. He was walking down the stairs when Paula appeared from the kitchen. Looking up, she smiled as she continued towards the front door.

'I've just remembered the fresh milk. The trouble with not being used to having a man in the house. Now, what's this?'

She had opened the front door as Tweed reached the foot of the stairs. She stood quite still for a moment, staring down. As she stooped forward she called over her shoulder.

'Well, who can this be from? Someone's left me a present . . .'

'*Don't touch it for Christ's sake . . . !*'

Tweed ran along the hall, wrapped his right arm round her, hauled her upright and backwards. Her right hand had been on the point of closing over a large plastic carrier bag standing on the doorstep. He propelled her back towards the rear of the house.

'Go into the kitchen, out of the back door and into the yard . . .'

She obeyed without asking a single question. Tweed stared at the bag from which the fronds of a plant protruded. There was a card with writing on it. By the side of the bag stood a pint bottle of milk. He closed the door carefully, ran back into the kitchen as she opened the rear door, holding her handbag. She kept moving as she waved the handbag.

'I've got my passport . . .'

'Is there a way out of this back yard?' he demanded.

'Yes, a gate leads to a side road . . .'

'Move! We have to warn the village. The whole sea front must be closed off. I think it's a bomb . . .'

Panic, confusion, movement took hold of Blakeney for the next half-hour. Tweed sent Paula to warn the villagers, to evacuate houses on the front. It was Tweed who walked on the far side of the harbour road by the deep-water channel past the plastic bag perched on Paula's doorstep to stop all activity where a large crane was unloading a coaster.

Some of the men ran up a side road, carrying the warning; others fled out on to the open marshland. It was Tweed who found a house with a phone in the side street and called the Bomb Squad at Heathrow. He had a few minutes' frustration identifying himself until Jim Corcoran, chief security officer at the airport, vouched for him. He gave curt instructions to a Captain Nicholls, chief of the Bomb Squad.

'. . . you've understood? You fly your team to the private airfield at Langham in a chopper, land, and I'll have two cars waiting. Langham's only a couple of miles from here . . .'

'Understood. On our way . . .'

It was Tweed who then called the American air base at Lakenheath in Suffolk and had a far more frustrating conversation with an American sergeant who thought it was a hoax call. Tweed at last blew his top, shouting down the phone.

'Put me through to your commander at once or you'll find yourself on the next bloody flight back to the States. I said I was Special Branch – our equivalent of your FBI . . .'

The high-ranking officer he was transferred to was equally dubious of Tweed's motives. The Englishman adopted different tactics and spoke with cold vehemence. Eventually the officer responded – to an extent.

'I'll first have to check your identity with that phone number you gave me before I can . . .'

'Check it, for God's sake. But alert your Bomb Squad first.'

'There are procedures . . .'

'Bypass them. Then get moving.' Tweed paused for a few seconds. 'If this is a bomb, if it detonates, if it kills, imagine what the press reports will do to Anglo-American relations. And I wouldn't want to be in your shoes . . .'

He slammed down the phone, insisted on paying the stunned woman who owned the house, thanked her and ran out to check that the danger zone was sealed off.

It was. He found Paula had alerted the local police who had acted quickly. Improvised barriers had been erected, lengths of rope closing off both ends of the front. Uniformed constables stood well back, guarding the barriers. A woman ran out of a house in the main street.

'You lookin' for Paula? You Mr Tweed?'

'Yes to both questions . . .'

'She's in the car park – where you left your lovely Mercedes. Is it a bomb?'

'Quite possibly . . .'

'Terrorist swine. They should castrate them.'

She ran back into the house and Tweed knew she'd be on the phone, reporting the news to her friends. Which had been his intention. He glanced back along the front which looked strangely deserted.

A black-headed gull swooped silently over the front, then glided out over the marshes as though it sensed danger from the unaccustomed hush. The thought crossed his mind that, unlike the white-headed variety, the black-heads rarely uttered nerve-racking screeches. He walked to the car park situated on a slope rising up from the street. Paula, standing by the 280E, ran towards him.

'Are you OK?'

'Sweating like a bull. You did a magnificent job. God! That carrier bag by my car . . .'

'Mine. Or rather that lady's – the one you were talking to. She's a friend. You had no breakfast. Fancy a thermos full of hot coffee and some ham sandwiches? She's a nice old thing, she made them for you . . .'

'For us. Let's sit in the back of the car. Nothing more we can do except wait.'

'Wait for what?' Paula settled herself in the back of the car, sank her teeth into the sandwich Tweed gave her and ate ravenously.

'Bomb Squad. They'll come down this road. Either from Lakenheath or Heathrow.'

She drank more coffee. 'God, I'm thirsty.'

'Dehydration. Delayed shock.' He drank coffee from the chinaware mug she handed him. 'Me, too. I'm parched as the Sahara. Did that woman volunteer the breakfast?'

'Actually, no. I asked her.'

'You really are a practical girl,' he commented. 'And I noticed how you kept your cool back at the house. Good for you.'

'Did you read the card attached to that plastic bag on my doorstep?'

'No.'

'It said, *For Paula. With love.* In strange handwriting.'

4

The Heathrow Bomb Squad arrived first. Tweed climbed out of the Mercedes as the two police cars he'd arranged to wait at Langham airfield drove past the car park. He ran, catching them up as they stopped a few yards behind the rope barrier. A three-pipper in Army uniform alighted, carrying a large box, followed by a sergeant and a corporal.

'Captain Nicholls?' Tweed panted.

The officer, tall and unsmiling and with alert grey eyes turned round. He looked Tweed up and down. 'Yes,' he replied in a clipped tone. 'What is it?'

'I'm Tweed.' He showed his Special Branch folder produced in the documents section in the Park Crescent basement. 'I called you on the phone. I'll show you exactly where it is . . .'

'Any idea how long the thing's been sitting there?'

'It could have been parked on the doorstep any time after ten last night. There's a plant sticking out. A large plastic bag.' They were walking side by side and the Captain grasped Tweed's arm as they reached the rope.

'No need for you to proceed any further, sir. If you'd just locate it . . .'

'Come to the other end of the rope.' Tweed pointed. 'It is parked on a doorstep exactly opposite that lamp-post. The whole immediate area has been evacuated.'

'Then I'd go back and stay in your car, sir. Our job now.'

'I'd appreciate a report on what you find.' Tweed paused. 'Good luck.'

Nicholls stared hard at Tweed. A wintry smile appeared briefly. 'You seem to know a bit about these jobs. Luck *does* come into it. See you later, sir.' On this optimistic note he turned to his men. 'Let's get cracking, lads.'

Tweed returned to the car. Paula would be under pressure. It was important to see how she was coping. He found her with a sketch-pad on her knee, drawing with a felt-tip pen. 'I use this for working out new pottery designs,' she said without looking up. 'Carry it with me everywhere.'

Tweed checked the time by his watch and drank the last of the coffee. Ten minutes later he checked his watch again. Paula closed her book and folded her arm inside his as she asked the question. 'Something's bothering you?'

'Yes. I want to warn you. The police will question you soon. They may be London men from the Anti-Terrorist Squad. Shrewd as a barrel of monkeys. So let's get your story straight. No mention about following that chap who may – or may not – be Lee Foley. Start your story with going to the front door. I was on holiday and you offered me a bed for the night. Then jump to this morning. Tell them how it happened. The way I grabbed you, etc. Keep it simple.'

'They may be curious you spent the night in my house.'

'Who cares?' He hastily corrected himself. 'You mean your local reputation could go down the drain?'

'I couldn't give an "f" for my local reputation. I'll do as you say. I won't let you down. Now answer my question – the one you dodged.'

'Which one?'

'Something's bothering you – something else. You keep checking your watch and your mouth tightened the third time.'

'All right. They've been there over half an hour. If it had been all right – a harmless package – they'd have been back before now. It is a bomb.'

Three hours later Captain Nicholls appeared alone beyond the rope. Ducking under it, he walked to the car park, glanced at Paula and frowned at Tweed. Climbing out of the car, Tweed bent down and spoke to Paula before closing the door.

'Won't be long. I think the captain wants a word with me.'

'Take your time . . .'

Nicholls strolled up to the deserted top of the car park with Tweed. He lit a cigarette and waved the pack before replacing it in his pocket. 'Don't normally use them any more. This one tastes very good.'

'It was a bomb?'

'Forty pounds of TNT. It would have converted that house into a pile of powdered rubble. No hope for anyone inside. Same for the houses on either side. A bit tricky, this one. My chaps are taking the TNT out on to the marshes for a controlled detonation. They'll have to walk miles. Conservation area and all that.'

'Instant detonation if the woman living there had picked it up?'

'Oh, absolutely. She'd have been blown into a million pieces. Bit of a bore, the time we took – but it had been tricked out with all kinds of gadgets. You did say Special Branch?'

Silently Tweed handed over his folder. Nicholls examined the document very carefully this time. He compared the photo with its subject, then handed back the folder.

'What was so special about that bomb that made you double-check my identity?'

'You want the details?' Nicholls took a deep drag on the cigarette.

'The lot, please.'

'First, it had a plate of steel lined with lead facing towards the waterfront. That would create *implosion* – most of the blast would have gone into and up the house.'

'The harbour would have suffered?'

'Not a chance. Second – and this is particularly confidential – it was not the work of *any* kind of terrorist. Absolutely not.'

'How do you know that?'

'The new and highly sophisticated mechanism. Perfected no more than a year ago. Of course, normally the explosive wouldn't be TNT – but it was just right for taking out that house. The one item which could be improved – in my opinion – is the timer . . .'

Nicholls sported a small trim moustache. He fingered it with the nail of his index finger. Apart from the cigarette, Tweed could detect no trace of the enormous tension the officer must have laboured under. The professional had taken over and his tone was full of enthusiasm as he went on.

'Devilish clever device though. Really a weapon of war – for use by saboteurs on major naval targets when the balloon goes up.'

'It sounds pretty heavy – all that steel and lead,' commented Tweed. 'Surely no plastic bag would hold it?'

'Very cunning, these johnnies. Inside that plastic bag was a smaller one. Made of reinforced leather – with a carrying handle. You do have a point. No one could have carried it far. Probably transported by car. Maybe they parked it a few yards back from the target house, then carted it the rest of the way.'

'Or brought it in by boat. The deep-water channel is opposite that house, and I noticed a metal ladder attached to the sea wall.'

'That's something I didn't think of. Yes, it could be brought in that way. This is going to create a stink in high places.'

'Why?'

'Well, you mentioned luck – and we *were* lucky. We would have been plastered all over Blakeney but for Naval Intelligence. They smuggled a sample to us a few months ago. The lab boys took it apart – under the guidance of a naval commander – so we knew what we were doing.'

'Does this naval commander have a name?'

'Well . . .' Nicholls chewed his lower lip, then smiled. 'Seeing as you chappies are concerned with the internal security of the State I suppose it is your business. Though it foxes me why the device was used here. It's main purpose is use as a sea-mine. Commander Bellenger is your man.

My job now is to get the shell – complete with mechanism – back to Admiralty. Anything more?'

'This sounds something entirely new. You said it couldn't be any kind of terrorist. Where was the blasted thing made?'

'Moscow, old boy. Compliments of the Soviet Union.'

5

The bad news came in a telephone call. It so often did, Tweed thought.

Blakeney had returned to normal. Rope barriers had vanished, as had the uniformed police. The Lakenheath Bomb Squad team came and went, relieved that someone else had done the dirty work. The coaster on the front had resumed unloading its soya bean meal.

Tweed stood staring out of the front room window. Low tide. Masted boats were scattered along the creek banks, heeled over in the mud at drunken angles. An elderly man, well-wrapped against the brisk wind, wearing a deerstalker hat with field glasses looped from his neck, walked along the front. Birdwatcher.

'Paula,' Tweed began, 'if you still want the job with me it's available . . .'

'Great,' she said coolly. 'I'll start packing. And I'll call the buyer of my pottery business to clinch the deal . . .'

'Why not delay that?' he warned. 'You'll join on six months' probation. It's the regulation . . .'

'I'll take my chances. I've built that business as far as I want to. I've thought up God knows how many designs for pots for the Californian market. There's nothing ahead but more and more expansion. I want something new – a fresh challenge.'

'Monica might be a problem,' he warned again. 'She

43

could resent the arrival of a younger woman. She's been with me forever.'

'I've talked with her on the phone. She sounds nice. That's my problem – and I'm confident I can handle it.'

'And this house?'

'I'm keeping it on. Somewhere quiet to visit when I can . . .'

The phone rang. 'That will be my buyer,' she continued. 'I gather he's keen as mustard. The profits for the past three years are very good. And don't forget – we have to visit Mrs Massingham at Cockley Cley, get all the gossip about Cockley Ford for you . . .'

She was in the narrow hall, lifting the phone. Tweed stood watching the wasteland, thinking why he'd decided to employ her. Two main reasons. One, the calm, controlled way she'd reacted to the bomb and the later period of waiting. Two, and it was a very secondary consideration – had to be – he liked her.

'It's for you,' she called out. 'Monica. Says it's urgent.'

'Blast!'

'I hoped I was safe here,' were his opening words when he took the call.

'I'm frightfully sorry . . .' Monica sounded nervous. 'But you did say you were going to Paula's. There's a crisis, Major, over a new insurance contract. They're running round in circles since they found you'd gone.'

'Who are "they"?'

'Top management. And Howard is frantic.'

Monica knew she was talking on an open line. Translation: a summons from the PM, no less. Howard in a dither. Something very serious.

'All right.' He sighed audibly. 'I'll be back by nightfall. It was a bloody short holiday.'

'You grumbled enough about going,' she said waspishly.

'I'll be back,' he repeated. 'With a new recruit.'

He put down the receiver before she could ask about that – and immediately felt guilty. Monica was only doing her job. He ran upstairs where Paula was packing swiftly in her bedroom.

'A major crisis back at the ranch. We have to be at Park Crescent by nightfall. Looks as though you're going straight in at the deep end.'

'Best way to learn to swim,' she replied, deftly folding more clothes, laying them neatly in the case. 'That would give us time to call in at Cockley Cley, wouldn't it?'

'I suppose I'd better just check. It was a weird business – and it could just be linked with the bomb.'

'Don't follow . . .'

'The Porsche driver took your picture. Dough-face carried a photo of you when he was tracking down where you lived. So, there's your link.'

Cockley Cley was almost the twin of Cockley Ford. The same grassy green shaped like a triangle, the same huddle of old cottages, the same approach up a long narrow road. But no gate, no inn, no stream.

Tweed let Paula do the talking while he studied Mrs Massingham. Must be close to eighty, a tall, thin woman with grey hair and the face of a golden eagle. Her legs were thin as a couple of sticks but she had a commanding presence, a clear mind. He wasn't surprised to hear she'd been a senior Civil Servant, a Principal.

'Of course,' Mrs Massingham continued, 'there have been rumours that Satanism is practised at Cockley Ford. Don't believe a word of it myself – but the locals are superstitious. And the papers do say witchcraft is on the increase. More tea, Mr Tweed? It *is* Earl Grey.'

'Thank you, yes,' replied Tweed, who hated Earl Grey.

Mrs Massingham, sitting very erect in a chintz-covered armchair, prattled on. She didn't like Dr Portch. He had arrived only eighteen months ago. Yes, she had heard of the outbreak of the disease which had killed six villagers. Peculiar, she thought. No, she didn't know where Portch had come from. He was rarely seen. Come to that, the villagers of Cockley Ford were rarely seen. Portch had on one occasion organized a holiday for most of the villagers in the West Indies somewhere.

'Expensive,' Tweed commented.

Mrs Massingham agreed, remarking that Voodoo was practised in the islands. The natives, of course, were simple-minded – even more so than the local villagers. And then there was the private zoo Portch had installed. Cages full of wild cats and cobras. It all discouraged outsiders from going anywhere near the place.

'We'd better be going.' Tweed stood up. 'I'm Chief Claims Investigator for an insurance company. We've had a belated claim on the life of one of the villagers who died at Cockley Ford,' he explained. 'Can't give you the name. Claimant has just returned from a long tour abroad. I have to check.'

'Oh, I did wonder.' A twinkle appeared in the eagle eyes. 'I mean, what you did.'

'Dr Portch seems to run Cockley Ford like his private estate,' Tweed ventured.

'Yes, I suppose he does. I'd never looked at it like that before.' A frown crinkled her high forehead. 'Very odd . . .'

They were driving through the rolling hillsides of Bedfordshire, heading for Woburn. Tweed was behind the wheel. Paula sat beside him, drawing in her sketch-book – content, Tweed thought, not to keep up a running streak of chatter. Which suited him as he sorted things out in his mind.

He brought up the subject over lunch at the Bedford Arms in Woburn. They were the only diners, which made it an ideal moment and place.

'I'd better tell you the form. I phoned a friend of mine, Bob Newman, while you were finishing your tidying up . . .'

'Robert Newman? The foreign correspondent? Writer of

that blockbusting bestseller book, *Kruger: The Computer That Failed*?'

'The same. That book made him financially independent. Now he works freelance, just takes on the jobs that interest him. He has a flat in Beresforde Road, South Ken. He's agreed you can stay there for a few days until we get you fixed up with living quarters.'

'Won't I be a damn nuisance to him?'

'He won't be there. I want Cockley Ford investigated. I can't do that now something else big has come up. Bob has agreed to do the job for me. You may as well know he's been vetted like yourself years ago.'

'Might it not be dangerous for him? If the bomb is in some way linked with that village as you wondered?'

Tweed smiled. 'He can cope. He's an ex-SAS man. He survived the full course when he was writing a series of articles on how they operate. But I'm still sending one of my men with him – which is something he doesn't know yet.'

'Your expression suggests he won't like that.'

'Bang on target. He's the lone wolf type.'

'Is that why,' she enquired, 'we're going to reach London hours before nightfall as you told Monica?'

'Bang on target. Again. Things to arrange before we arrive at Park Crescent. First port of call after lunch, Newman's flat.'

'Forget your phone call,' Newman said. 'Go over it again for me.'

They were sitting in the very large sitting room of Newman's flat where bay windows looked out on to St Mark's Church. The ceiling of the Victorian room was way above their heads and the original coving of interwoven bunches of grapes had been left in place by the developer.

Newman, a well-built, sandy-haired man in his early forties, lit a cigarette as he watched Tweed who sat on the other sofa. His blue eyes had a hint of humour but the strong mouth and jaw-line were clenched and unyielding. Newman, Tweed, reflected, was a much harder man since his experience behind the lines in East Germany.

Paula was unpacking her case in the large bedroom at the back, deliberately taking her time so the two men could talk alone. Tweed took no more than five minutes to tell him about his experiences at Cockley Ford and Blakeney. As he sipped at the coffee Paula had made for them Newman stood up and began strolling round the spacious room.

'It doesn't add up,' he decided. 'It's a mystery without any key. The two separate incidents *do* link up. The photo Dough-face peddled round Blakeney to pinpoint Paula's address *had* to come from the cine-film the Porsche driver took. And you saw a red Porsche which must have come from Cockley Ford the night you arrived. Paula saw Foley come off that coaster and drive off in a Porsche, later turning off up to the village. OK?'

'Agreed so far.'

'That means an *American* was involved in the planting of the bomb on Paula's doorstep. But this Nicholls character later tells you the bomb is of *Russian* origin. And a new device perfected recently. The Kremlin isn't going to be handing out a thing like that to anyone. But no one. OK?'

'Still with you.'

'So, it doesn't add up – any of it,' Newman repeated. 'Why would the Soviets cooperate with the Americans, using their latest secret development – weapon of war, Nicholls said – to kill a girl who isn't – or wasn't at that moment – even a member of the British Secret Service?'

'Makes no sense,' Tweed agreed again.

'It gets more mysterious. If Paula had been on your staff why would the Kremlin join hands with Washington to do this? They wouldn't is the answer. So, what the hell is going on?'

'That's what I want you to find out . . .'

'Thanks a bundle. Incidentally, the name Portch rings a

bell. Something in a paper. About eighteen months ago. Tucked away on a back page . . .'

'Eighteen months ago is when Portch moved to Norfolk from God knows where according to old Mrs Massingham – and she's a lady with all her marbles where they should be.'

'Before I head for Norfolk I'll go sweat it out in the Reading Room at the British Museum, find that item.'

'Ball's in your court,' Tweed stood up. 'I'm grateful . . .'

'I'm intrigued . . .'

'What I was going to say,' Tweed went on casually, 'was I want you to take one of my people with you . . .'

'Not on. I work on my own. You know *that*.'

The two men faced each other like terriers bracing up for a dog fight. Tweed compressed his lips. Newman, wearing a polo-necked sweater and well-creased grey slacks, scowled and shook his head.

'It's essential,' Tweed insisted. 'The groundwork is laid. I told them a couple of SAS men were coming looking for me – perfect cover for you to penetrate that strange village.'

'And who, may I ask, did you have in mind?'

'Harry Butler,' Tweed said promptly. 'You've been with the SAS. Harry is built like one of them. You both talk the same language. You'll lead the team. You know Harry – he'll follow that lead. He's cool, resourceful, a good man to go into the jungle with. Unless you don't trust him,' he added artfully.

'Crap! Harry's OK in a tight corner. And now you're being wily. Give me one good reason why I should agree.'

'The bomb. Made in Russia. That concerns my outfit. It concerns me. And I'm up to my neck in God knows what. I don't even know what this new crisis is all about – but it's something pretty big for them to drag me back off the first holiday I've had in years. I need your help, Bob.'

'That's better.' Newman grinned and folded his arms. 'I'm going in. For one reason only.'

'Which is?'

'I smell something pretty strange and sinister.'

6

The next few hours passed in a flash for Tweed. Everything came at him at once. He became very calm and absorbed a tremendous amount of data. It started the moment he walked into his office at Park Crescent. He'd left Paula at Newman's flat.

'Best you arrive later when things have cooled. I'll call you . . .'

Howard was waiting in his office with Monica, striding round the room, unable to keep still. An expression of relief crossed his face as Tweed came in.

'Thank God you've got here. The world has exploded . . .'

'I didn't hear the bang. If I could just take off my raincoat.' He walked to the other side of his desk and sat down, clasped his hands in his lap. 'I'm ready.'

'Reports are filtering in from all over the continent that some great terrorist outrage is planned.'

'Anti-Terrorist Squad,' Tweed said. 'Their job . . .'

'The PM doesn't think so in this case,' Monica intervened before Howard could resume his torrent of words. 'You have to go and meet her at 5 p.m. if you were back. I'll call and confirm you can make it.' She picked up her phone.

'Fill me in then,' Tweed suggested. 'Don't understand this at all. Why us?'

'Because of who it isn't,' Howard explained. 'It's not the IRA. It's not the Shi-ite fanatics. It's not the Red Army Faction. All our contacts confirm this . . .'

'Baader-Meinhof relic?' Tweed queried.

'Not them. That's what I'm trying to get into your head. It is not any of the known groups. No one can pinpoint a single clue. The Paris lot are mystified. So is Bonn . . .'

'Then what's all the fuss about?'

'The Russians are worried, too. And our Yankee cousins. The Deputy Director of the CIA is talking about flying over here. God help us. You'll see him, of course?'

'You never did like Cord Dillon.' Tweed smiled amiably.

'Who does? The man's impossible. Can't imagine how he ever got the job . . .'

'Because he's efficient, skilled, never gives up. Like a dog with a bone. The aggressiveness you take in your stride . . .'

'*You* take it in *your* stride,' Howard interjected, determined to avoid the American at all costs. He took out his display handkerchief, flicked something off his razor-creased trouser leg, carefully refolding the handkerchief before tucking it back in his breast pocket.

'We have a new addition to the staff,' Tweed remarked. He chose this moment when he was not alone with Monica. 'She will be along here later this evening. Paula Grey. As you know, her vetting was top-flight.'

'Splendid!' Howard showed unusual enthusiasm. 'A most welcome addition to our little family.' Tweed winced inwardly at the patronizing phrase as Howard continued. 'I know her pretty well – she could do her first term at school with me. I need someone extra.'

'You hardly know her at all,' Tweed told him. He was watching Monica who looked anything but pleased. 'And since I did the spadework I'm attaching her to my office. There's plenty of room in here.'

'If you insist. Sometimes I wonder who's running the outfit. And I could have gone along to see the PM in your absence . . .'

'Except that the PM specifically asked for Tweed,' Monica said tactlessly, working off her indignation at the news of the new recruit.

'The lady always does. You might at least send Paula in to meet the nominal head of the SIS when she arrives.' On this piqued note Howard stalked out of the room.

'Isn't there somewhere else in the building Paula could

work?' Monica asked. 'We're very cramped already in here . . .'

'Cramped!' Tweed stared round at the empty space. 'And you once liked her.'

'Paula in Norfolk is one thing, Paula taking up residence in this office quite another. It will never be the same again – our talks together about work, I mean.'

'She won't be here every minute of the day,' Tweed said irritably. 'And I've taken the decision. I've got enough on my mind without domestic problems. Wouldn't you agree?'

Monica checked her watch. 'Time you left for your appointment at No. Ten. You know how you hate rushing.'

Tweed stood up and silently went to the clothes rack, put on his Burberry. Monica fidgeted with her pen, drawing meaningless lines on her notepad. She spoke in a subdued, conciliatory tone.

'I wonder what all these alarming rumours are about?'

'Maybe I'm about to find out,' said Tweed and walked downstairs.

As arranged over the phone by Tweed before leaving Beresforde Road, Harry Butler arrived at Newman's flat on the dot of 6 p.m. To Newman's surprise – and annoyance – he was accompanied by a second man.

'Pete Nield, you know him, of course,' Butler explained. 'Tweed decided on the phone this Cockley Ford is an unknown quantity – that we could do with back-up. Pete's brought his own transport – even managed to find a parking slot half a mile away . . .'

'The two of us could do this job,' Newman informed him.

'That's what I like,' Nield broke in. 'An enthusiastic reception. An immediate acceptance of the team spirit.' He grinned.

Newman stood in the living room, studying the two men. Butler was about his build and height, in his thirties, clean-shaven and his expression controlled. He wore an old check sports jacket, blue denims, carried a windcheater over his arm. Just the type of gear an SAS man on leave might choose. He used his left hand to smooth his darkish hair, staring straight at Newman.

Pete Nield was a different personality and build. Lighter weight, slim, a few years Butler's junior, he had black hair brushed neatly, a small trim moustache. His clothes were smart; a navy blue suit, striped blue shirt, dark blue polka dot tie. His manner was easy, he moved more quickly than the immobile Butler. Newman had observed previously they worked well together as a team.

'Welcome aboard, gentlemen,' he said, looking at Nield. 'What are you drinking? Then we can get straight to the planning stage.' He indicated a map of East Anglia spread out over the long Regency dining table. 'We're driving up to King's Lynn tonight. I've booked two rooms at The Duke's Head. I'll call them again to reserve one for you, Nield.'

'King's Lynn?' Butler was studying the map as Nield joined him when they'd decided on drinks. 'Excuse me putting my oar in – you're the boss – but wouldn't a hotel in Blakeney be a better operational HQ?'

'No.' Newman had climbed the two steps into the kitchenette, was pouring drinks. 'That's where the bomb was planted. Whoever left the offering may be watching the place. At King's Lynn we can maintain the traditional low profile . . .'

'Christ! Why didn't I think of that?' Butler was appalled. 'You make us look like amateurs at our own game.'

'Amateurs is not the word I'd use about you two,' Newman remarked, fetching the drinks. 'Cheers! Here's to a successful partnership. I wonder what we'll find at Cockley Ford?'

'Something's terribly wrong. I can tell . . .'

Monica, feeling contrite for her earlier behaviour, stared at Tweed as he slowly looped his raincoat over a hanger.

He winked at her, went to his favourite place, the swivel chair behind his desk, sank into it.

'Good job other people can't read me the way you can – I am not supposed to reveal anything by my expression.'

'We have been together a long time. What has happened? Can you talk about it? Want some coffee?'

'Something has happened. I can talk about it – but only to you. It's extremely confidential. Coffee later. The PM has stunned me. I'm not even sure it's a good idea. And Paula is on the way – phoned her from a call-box . . .'

'What idea?'

'You won't believe it.'

'Try me . . .'

'The PM,' he said very deliberately, 'wants me to fly to a secret meeting with General Vasili Lysenko, Head of Soviet Military Intelligence, the GRU.'

'My God! You're not serious?'

'She is. Very. Gorbachev has been in touch with her – and he was the one who suggested the meeting.'

'What on earth for?'

'I'm not sure,' Tweed confessed. 'Apparently the Kremlin is worried stiff about the rumours of a gigantic terrorist outrage being planned.'

'Normally they'd welcome it. Their attitude doesn't add up. I don't believe a word of it. And surely the PM doesn't?'

'She was told something in complete confidence by the General Secretary – something she couldn't break her word by telling even me. I get the full details only when I meet Lysenko.'

'And where is this rendezvous? It could be a trap . . .'

'Hardly.' Tweed turned to stare at the large map of Western Europe attached to the wall. 'The rendezvous is Zürich. The Swiss already know about it. They're busy laying on security at this moment. Security for protection. Security to ensure total secrecy. They're pretty good at that.'

'It's amazing. I thought I'd heard everything. When are you supposed to fly there?'

'Tomorrow. That's when Lysenko is flying in direct from Moscow. Any idea of flight times? It has to be Swissair . . .'

'Starting early, depart Heathrow 8.30, 9.50, then 13.50. I've left out BA flights.'

'Swissair will be more anonymous. I'll travel under the name Johnson. Lysenko is due to touch down at Kloten at three in the afternoon, local Zürich time. I'll catch the 9.50 – get there ahead of him.'

'I'll book it. What about the actual rendezvous, the place where the meeting will be held?'

'No idea. That's been left to the Swiss. They'll find somewhere quiet. Not too far from Kloten Airport would be my guess.' Tweed's mouth tightened. 'Charming. I'm to meet my old enemy for the first time face to face – with no idea of the agenda.'

'Not to worry. You think like chain lightning on your feet.'

'Trouble is, we'll probably be sitting down,' he joked.

'Not a word to Paula, I assume?'

'She can know I'm flying to Zürich. But not why. And she should be due here soon,' he said, checking his watch. 'I see you've had a desk and chair brought in for her. That was thoughtful. She's completely under your jurisdiction, of course. On probation. For six months.'

Monica glanced at the desk against the wall, placed so when the new member was sitting she faced both Monica and Tweed. 'I thought I'd put the welcome mat out for her. She'll need help to pass with flying colours.'

'Up to you,' said Tweed. 'Not perfect timing – with the Zürich thing imminent.'

'And when has the timing ever been perfect?' Monica asked.

Paula came into the office and closed the door, then waited for instructions. Tweed introduced her to Monica who, he noticed, eyed Paula up and down as she walked with her to the new desk.

She had dressed cleverly for her baptism of fire. A severe dark blue two-piece suit, a blouse with a mandarin collar and plain beige tights. No little squirrels running up her shapely legs. She sat down.

'I'll make coffee,' said Monica, who had phoned Heathrow and booked Tweed's flight.

'Please let me do that.' Paula jumped up immediately. 'I'm the probationer. If you'll just tell me where everything is.'

'I'm afraid we keep it in the top drawer of this filing cabinet,' said Monica. 'Instant, too. Milk and sugar in the same drawer with the crocks.'

'How does everyone like it?' Paula was taking out equipment when Howard strolled in without knocking. He stopped in mid-stride at the sight of Paula. Checking the knot of his tie, he smiled broadly.

'Just starting class? Good show. I'm Howard . . .'

'The Director,' whispered Monica.

'I'm pleased to meet you, Mr Howard,' Paula said with no particular expression, holding out her slim hand.

'May I call you Paula? Don't stand on ceremony here. Just so long as everyone does their job.'

Oh, Christ, thought Tweed, he's trying to be charming and pompous at the same time. Howard held her hand a shade too long, then turned to Tweed.

'Maybe Paula could pop along to my office for a few minutes – give us a chance to get acquainted and all that?'

'I could come in a few minutes, Mr Howard,' Paula said quickly. 'I have a job to finish first.'

'When you're ready, my dear. When you're ready . . .'

He left the room and Paula arranged the coffee things on a tray. Monica told her where she would find the stove and waited until Paula had left the room before she made her remark.

'She doesn't like Howard.' She smirked. 'He's on the prowl and she guessed. He's looking for compensation now Cynthia is going her own way – one in the eye for his wife is what he's looking for. And he rather likes the idea. And!

56

Did you notice how she was determined to make our coffee before she went near him?'

'Yes,' said Tweed and busied himself with a file. Monica already approved of Paula. He'd never have believed Paula could solve the problem so quickly. Now he could concentrate on Zürich – and the unknown spectre which had risen up in his face.

7

Tweed peered out of the window of the Boeing 737, staring south at the spectacular view as the machine approached Zürich. The sky was cloudless, to the south the vast panorama of the Bernese Oberland range stretched. Even in May the wave of world-famous peaks were snowbound. Silhouetted against an azure sky, the light was blinding. The Jungfrau, the highest peak amid the chain of other giants, stood out like a monarch of mountains.

The aircraft began its descent towards Kloten. He forced himself to relax. He had no idea who would meet him. 'A Swiss who will certainly recognize you,' he had been told. Highly informative.

As he descended the mobile staircase he glanced round at the fir forests surrounding Kloten. One of his favourite airports in the world – quiet, well-organized, peaceful. But this was Switzerland. A familiar figure waited at the foot of the steps, a plump-cheeked man with a ruddy complexion, quick movements, dressed in a navy-blue business suit. Arthur Beck, chief of the Federal Police.

'Welcome,' said Beck, not using Tweed's name. He took him by the arm, guided him towards a black stretched Mercedes with tinted windows parked near the main building. 'A pleasant flight, I hope?'

'Yes. Good to see you again, Beck. What's happening?'

'Straight to business. You haven't changed.' Beck glanced back, saw they were out of earshot of the trail of passengers alighting from the aircraft. 'I have transport – this car. I'm driving you personally to the rendezvous . . .'

He opened the door of the front passenger seat, closed it as Tweed settled himself, put Tweed's small case in the back and sat behind the wheel.

'We travel as we did for our earlier arrival, General Lysenko. No motor-cycle outriders, no fuss, nothing to draw attention to ourselves . . .'

'Lysenko has arrived in Zürich? He wasn't expected until this afternoon.'

Beck nodded, a gleam in his grey eyes under bushy brows. 'So we thought, too. We had thirty minutes' warning that he was aboard a regular Aeroflot flight coming in. But I was ready for him – waiting at Kloten. I came here from Berne yesterday. I know the Russians.'

'Where's the rendezvous?' Tweed asked.

'Not far away. A small village called Nürensdorf. I chose it because it is near Kloten, because it is a sleepy place – no chance of either of you being spotted by reporters. The actual location is a nice old hotel, the Gasthof zum Bären. My old friend, Rosa Tschudi will see you are well fed. She is a superb cook. I go there myself when I come to Zürich if I can.'

'How many in Lysenko's bodyguard?'

'None. He travelled by himself as an ordinary passenger.'

'You've spoken with him?' Tweed probed.

'Through his interpreter, yes. Where is yours?'

'Don't spread it abroad. I speak Russian myself now.'

'Really?' Beck looked surprised. 'There is no end to your talents, my friend. And you are wondering what kind of a mood our visitor from the East is in? I thought so. Very preoccupied. My guess is he is a very worried man . . .'

They said no more until they arrived in a small attractive village. The Gasthof was an old three-storey building with a steeply-sloping roof and dark red shutters. Beck parked the car in a space at the side, paused before getting out.

'Officially the hotel has been taken over for a convention. The only people here – apart from Rosa, who won't have any idea who her guests are – are my people. Men and women. Take a deep breath, we will go inside if you are ready.'

'Let's get on with it,' said Tweed.

8

A large room overlooking the front, furnished with stripped pinewood cupboards. A large table stood in the centre, four wooden chairs, two easy chairs by the window, masked with a heavy net curtain against the outside world. A sideboard with a large array of bottles and glasses. Tweed had asked for coffee downstairs.

General Vasili Lysenko stood at the far side of the table in civilian clothes, hands clasped behind his back. A stocky man with a heavy Slavic face, clean-shaven, his greying hair trimmed *en brosse*. From under bushy eyebrows he stared back at his old enemy. For both it was quite a moment.

A third, thin-faced, studious-looking and younger man stood a few paces behind the General. Lysenko indicated him with a gesture of his thick-fingered right hand, speaking in Russian.

'My interpreter. Where is yours?'

'We won't need his services,' Tweed replied also in Russian.

Lysenko couldn't keep the surprise out of his expression. He smiled wintrily. 'Our files are out of date. I thought I knew everything about you . . .'

'Welcome to Switzerland.' Tweed held out his hand, taking the initiative. Lysenko grasped it in his paw-like hand, peering closely at Tweed. 'Younger than I'd been led to believe. A present from Moscow . . .'

He lifted a large white porcelain bowl off the table, handed it to Tweed, gesturing for the interpreter to leave them. 'Beluga caviar. We know you like it – that *is* in your file.'

'Thank you.' Tweed waited until one of Beck's girls, wearing a dove-grey two-piece suit, came in, laid a tray with his coffee on the table and left them alone. He balanced the bowl in both hands, watching Lysenko closely as he spoke.

'Not a cleverly designed bomb, I trust?'

No trace of wariness in the slate-grey eyes. Tweed was thinking back to the bomb at Blakeney. Lysenko showed a moment of surprise, then grinned, exposing lead-coloured fillings.

'I'll leave you to wonder about that when you come to sample it. Shall we start?'

'At once. I've come to listen,' Tweed commented as they sat facing each other. He was glad to see the Russian pouring himself a glass of vodka when Tweed shook his head. Built like a block of wood, it was the only hint of nervousness the GRU chief showed.

'We have a potential catastrophe facing us,' Lysenko began.

'Who is "we"?'

'You and I. All we say under this fine old Swiss roof is totally confidential. Not to be ever revealed to anyone but your Prime Minister – and maybe two members of your staff, very senior staff. The Americans must never know. Agreed?'

'Not until I have some idea of what this is all about. You will have to rely on my discretion . . .'

'So!' Lysenko's tone was aggressive. 'We are fencing already. That is not good.'

'I still have to listen first.'

'You always were a stubborn bastard, Tweed . . .' He pronounced it *Twaad*. 'But we will proceed. I have my instructions from the very top. We had a near-genius in our apparatus, Zarov. Igor Zarov. But we just call him Zarov.'

'His real name?'

'Yes. He comes from the South. Father Georgian, mother Armenian. Like mixing vodka and brandy. The fiery, independent, ruthless Georgian, ruddy-faced. The smooth, cunning Armenian. A formidable combination, this man. Only thirty-four years old. He could set Western Europe aflame. One man, Tweed . . .'

'Surely an exaggeration?'

'Wait!' A stubby index finger pointed at Tweed's chest, a mannerism a Soviet defector had described to Tweed. 'This man has been trained in every aspect of my work. He was marked for the highest promotion. He might even have taken over my job one day. But he couldn't wait. He is greedy for power and money, a vast sum of money. He disappeared two years ago from East Germany.' He paused. 'I've been instructed to be frank. He disappeared when he was operating in West Germany. At first we thought he'd gone over to the Americans – but that would have been out of character. Now we know he never went near the Americans.'

'How can you be sure of that?'

Lysenko drank more vodka, gave Tweed a quizzical look. 'Now you don't expect me to give you a list of contacts in Washington? Take my word. I wouldn't be here talking to you unless we were certain.'

'I suppose not.' Tweed's expression was blank, but he was growing interested. 'Go on.'

'We have a very dangerous man loose in the West, planning some enormous outrage to obtain a fortune. We have heard rumours. If Zarov is caught after the catastrophe occurs the Americans will make the most of it – at a time when the General Secretary is moving heaven and earth to build a new détente.'

'That's twice you've used the word catastrophe. What makes the man so very dangerous?' He saw Lysenko pause and pressed home his point. 'I need to know far more about him. How come he was able to operate in West Germany? What is his history which makes you so worried?'

'First, he is a natural linguist – the Armenian coming out. He speaks fluent German, French, Italian, English and American. As you know, there *is* a difference in how the last two races speak the so-called common language. He was brilliant at everything he undertook.'

'Such as? I do need to know if I'm to trace him – which I presume is your hope?'

'That is not my hope, it is my prayer.'

For the first time Tweed began to half-believe him. He drank more coffee, a dozen angles flitting through his mind.

'He may simply be dead,' he suggested. 'Operating in West Germany he'd be using false papers. He could have been knocked down by a tram in Frankfurt . . .'

'Except that he was seen in Geneva four weeks ago.'

Tweed was stunned. His expression remained the same. Now they had got talking in the same language – plus for Lysenko the vodka – the earlier stiff atmosphere between the two men was more relaxed. Tweed still remained guarded as he spoke.

'Seen by who?'

'Yuri Sabarin, member of a United Nations organization in Geneva. Sabarin happened to work closely with Zarov at one time in Moscow. He is observant and cautious. He has made a positive identification under the most gruelling attempts to shake him. Here is his telephone number.' Lysenko produced a white card from a brief-case by his side, handed it across the table. No address. Just a phone number.

'Sabarin has been instructed to meet you, to tell you what happened. You only have to call . . .'

'We'll see.' Tweed slipped the card into his wallet, drank

more coffee, watching Lysenko. The Russian wore a drab grey sports jacket made of a hairy fabric. Linked with his hairstyle, the bristles protruding from his short nose, he reminded Tweed of a wild boar. And boars were dangerous and cunning creatures.

'So Zarov *is* alive – and in Europe,' Lysenko insisted. 'I am certain at this moment he is planning a catastrophe to obtain his fortune. He is a lone wolf, he simply decided he would have to wait too many years in the Motherland for the high places.'

'That word again. Catastrophe. Why?'

'All right.' Lysenko sighed. 'I was instructed to tell you certain things I would not have thought wise. But . . .' He splayed his hands. '. . . I was brought up in the old school – total secrecy. Tell the West nothing. Now we have a quite different chief – a man who has broken some of the moulds revered since 1917. Zarov was the most brilliant pupil at the Planning School. Always we went for the daring scheme – and concealed it from the enemy with a clever smokescreen. He came out top of the class. Again. A superb organizer.'

'Fluent in several languages, you said earlier,' Tweed reminded him. 'But could he pass for a German, a Frenchman, an American, and so on?'

'With the greatest of ease. He is a natural actor. Also, if it is of interest he is a great charmer of the ladies. They are putty in his hands.'

'I still don't see it. Tell me more about the catastrophe thing.'

'His theory was that to succeed in a major operation a great shock should be delivered to the enemy. A catastrophe so enormous it would stun the opposition, make it incapable of reacting. "Terror is the ultimate weapon" was his favourite maxim.'

Tweed shook his head. 'There's something you're not telling me. He couldn't do all this on his own.'

'True.' Lysenko paused again. Old habits died hard, Tweed thought. 'During his postings to the West he made it his business to build up contacts in the various underworlds. The Union Corse in France, and so on. They never knew who he really was, of course . . .'

Tweed pounced, seeing his opening at last. 'These postings to the West. Where exactly was he – and when?'

'I have to be careful here . . .'

'And I need the data – or I'll forget the whole thing,' Tweed snapped. 'I must have somewhere to start *if* we decide to look for this ghost.'

'You will find he is just that,' Lysenko warned, reaching for a pale green file in his brief-case. He opened it and began reciting in a monotone. 'Brussels, 1982 – with brief trips to Luxembourg City to observe the EEC units there. Paris in 1983. Bonn in 1984 . . .' He looked up. 'Don't you wish to take notes?'

'Not so far . . .'

'Ah! Your phenomenal memory. The UN in New York, 1984. He went on to London, 1985. He returned to Moscow and was sent unofficially to West Germany in 1985. From that mission he vanished. Not seen again – until Sabarin's sighting in Geneva . . .'

'You've missed something out.'

'I don't understand . . .'

'Switzerland. When was he there before he disappeared?'

'In 1983,' Lysenko admitted.

Tweed blew up. 'Listen to me, General. I need the complete history or it's no go. What's this so-called unofficial mission to West Germany in 1985?'

'Classified. I have no authority to . . .'

'All right. Let's try something else. These official postings – Brussels, Bonn, Paris, London and so on. Now, was he attached in each case to the relevant Soviet Embassy? Don't waste my time . . .'

'Yes, he was.'

'Under his own name? Zarov?'

'I feel you are interrogating me . . .'

'I am doing just that. You're forcing me to. Now, answer my question, for God's sake.'

Like getting blood out of a stone he mumbled half under his breath but still audibly. Lysenko flushed, glared at Tweed who stared back. The animosity which would always divide the two men was surfacing.

'I am in a very difficult position,' the Russian growled and returned to checking his file.

'It's not a piece of cake for me – being asked to look for a man you've lost and with nothing to go on. Answer my question, please.'

'No, he was never posted to an embassy under his own name.'

'Then I'll need the names he used . . .'

'Classified.'

'If there's nothing else I can't – and won't – take action.'

'But there is. Very grim information.' Lysenko had calmed down, closed the file, returned it to the brief-case, clasped his hands on the table and began talking.

'Zarov was born in Sevastopol in the Crimea. At one period he was in charge of security at a certain military and naval depot at Sevastopol. He returned there on holiday just before being sent to his final posting in West Germany. The depot stored advanced equipment – including at that time powerful explosive weapons . . .'

Tweed felt his stomach muscles tighten as Lysenko paused and, away from the disapproving eye of Moscow, drank more vodka. He was coming to the key to the whole unprecedented meeting. Tweed waited, careful to keep silent.

'A consignment of sea-mines and bombs went missing from the depot while Zarov was in the Crimea. A large truck arrived late one night with a signed stamped order for this consignment. Zarov, I should mention, was at one time attached to a highly secret documentation centre in Moscow. He showed great skill in mastering the system – as he did with all he undertook. We had the highest hopes for him.' Lysenko sounded wistful, a side of his character Tweed found surprising. Clearly he had liked Zarov.

'He was an explosives expert, too?'

Tweed awaited the answer with trepidation.

'Ah! He was an expert with explosives – and with weapons. I've never had such a promising pupil.'

'What happened to this truck?' Tweed demanded. 'And please don't tell me that's classified . . .'

'It was driven – with the correct movement order papers – to the Turkish border along the Black Sea coast. Two days later at midnight the driver of the truck crashed the border at a weak point and disappeared inside Turkey. They also took a lot of sophisticated equipment.'

'Such as?'

'I cannot give technical details. That you will understand. Equipment for the detonation of the sea-mines and bombs by remote control from long distance . . .'

'How far? What kind of range?'

'Thirty or forty kilometres.'

'I see,' Tweed replied, concealing the shock he felt. 'You must have made enquiries through your contacts in Turkey,' he pressed. 'About what happened to the truck . . .'

'We found nothing. Eastern Turkey is a remote area – very thinly populated. The only city of any size is Erzurum, which I have no doubt the truck by-passed.'

'What about Istanbul? The Golden Horn harbour?'

'We checked that, too,' Lysenko admitted. 'We estimated as far as we could when the truck would arrive there. A Greek freighter, the *Lesbos*, sailed for Marseilles at about the right time. It never arrived. It disappeared into thin air. There was an unpleasant sequel – which was what focused our attention on Istanbul. All this is totally confidential, you understand?'

'We've been through that bit.'

'The driver of the truck was an Armenian called Dikoyan. We think now he was one of the few dissidents, a member of the Free Armenian Movement bandits. Zarov

is clever. He probably persuaded Dikoyan the huge consignment of explosives was to help the dissidents.'

'And what happened to this Dikoyan?'

'The Turkish police fished him out of the Bosphorus
shortly after the *Lesbos* sailed. His throat was cut from ear
to ear.'

'Unpleasant, as you said.'

'I told you Zarov is ruthless . . .'

'That consignment of sea-mines and bombs. How big is
it?'

Lysenko paused. Tweed could almost hear the wheels
whirring in his brain. *How much more dare I reveal?*

'The explosive is very special.' Lysenko was phrasing his
reply carefully. 'It's enormous power bears no relationship
to the size – or weight – of the sea-mines and bombs.'

'How many did they get out of that Sevastopol depot?'

'Thirty sea-mines, twenty-five bombs. It was a big truck.'

'Give me some idea of their explosive power – what we
face.'

'They have the potential to wipe off the face of the earth
a city the size of Hamburg.'

9

Tweed was subdued and businesslike for the remainder of
their meeting. He asked for a photograph – several if
available – of Igor Zarov. Lysenko shook his head and
Tweed jumped on him before he could speak.

'Oh, come on, you must have God knows how many
pictures . . .'

'*Had.* I told you Zarov was a wizard with documentation.
At one time he trained in our documentation centre . . .'
Tweed knew what he meant – the centre where false
passports and papers were prepared for agents travelling

abroad with new identities. Driving licences, library memberships, medical cards. All the bureaucratic paraphernalia of modern life.

'Before he left for his posting to West Germany,' Lysenko explained slowly, 'he removed from the files every single photograph of himself in existence. He even erased his image from the Central Computer – and substituted another man's.'

'Formidable, as you said,' Tweed agreed.

'I took a precaution before I set out on this trip.' Lysenko reached into his brief-case, produced a large sheet of paper. 'I had an Identikit picture drawn with the aid of the three associates who had known him well. Ruddy-faced, like his father.' He handed over the sheet. 'That is the best I can do . . .'

Tweed studied the head and shoulders portrait which, as far as he could tell, had been drawn in charcoal and then photocopied. The image was blurred but the tremendous force of character of the subject came through.

Thick dark hair, a high forehead, hypnotic eyes beneath thick brows, a long nose, prominent cheekbones, a thin mouth, strong jaw. The shoulders were wide, suggesting a man of considerable physical strength. It was the eyes Tweed kept returning to, eyes which held a hint of irony as though Zarov regarded the whole world cynically.

'If that's the best you can provide,' Tweed said eventually.

'It's a good likeness. I can vouch for that . . .'

'So, what exactly do you hope we can do – assuming we agree to do anything?'

'Track him down, hunt him, eliminate him. Before he can put into operation whatever catastrophe he is planning – for which we could be blamed. Especially by the Americans.'

'You've presumably tried to do the job yourselves – assuming always he is alive?'

'With no success.' Lysenko became vehement. 'Do you not see our difficulty? He knows how we operate, which areas to avoid, which people to avoid. You understand?'

Tweed understood only too well. Zarov knew not only the Soviet agents in the West – he'd also know their secret contacts, men and women who passed on information to Moscow for money – who had no traceable connection with the East. Lysenko continued.

'But we regard your network as the best in the world. That he doesn't know about . . .'

'Because you don't know yourself?' Tweed said quizzically.

'No comment. Will you help? It is in your own interests – the rumours multiply of some entirely new organization being built up in Europe. We believe Zarov is the mastermind. We have not been able to locate one source that really can give us a hard fact. Something in Europe is in great danger – think of that consignment of terrible explosives.'

Tweed pushed his chair back from the table. 'Is that everything?'

'I give you this second card. It has a special phone number in Moscow where you can always reach me. The operator will put you straight through if there is a development. I will expect to be kept fully informed.'

'You'll be disappointed then.' Tweed stood up. 'I don't work that way. Even assuming I take any action at all. That is not my decision.'

'Tweed!' Lysenko had now stood up. 'This I will always swear you invented if repeated.' His rough voice trembled with emotion. Tweed watched him closely. Was this man a far better actor than he had been told? 'It was Gorbachev himself – after reading your file from beginning to end – who told me you were probably the only man in Europe who could find Zarov and deal with him.'

'I repeat, it is not my decision.'

Tweed ended the conversation on that note and then witnessed an extraordinary scene. Lysenko filled his glass to the brim with vodka, swallowed the contents in one gulp and hurled the glass across the room, smashing it against the wall.

'To your success, my friend!'

It was mid-afternoon when Tweed's flight headed back for London. After Lysenko had left, Tweed had sat down and enjoyed the best meal he could remember provided by Rosa Tschudi at the Gasthof. He was grateful for the lunch because now he could think about all he had been told.

Images tumbled through his mind. The blurred picture of Zarov which could not disguise his burning eyes. A large truck crashing the Soviet–Turkish border from Armenia. The body of Dikoyan floating in the Bosphorus, the throat slashed from ear to ear. The Greek freighter, *Lesbos*, slipping its moorings in the fabulous Golden Horn harbour, sailing to oblivion.

Was any of it true? The GRU had concocted some fairytales in its time: Tweed, of all people, knew that. If so, they had excelled themselves. For what motive? Park Crescent had never had even the hint of the existence of an Igor Zarov. Did he even exist? If so, had Yuri Sabarin really seen him in Geneva recently? All he had was the word of Lysenko, a man who made lying a way of life.

I'm inclined to discount the whole bloody story, he thought. So what new manoeuvre was it intended to conceal? For the first time since he had joined the Service Tweed felt at sea, completely baffled. And he didn't even know what opinion to express when he arrived back. He had never felt so frustrated. Maybe something would happen to bring the mystery into focus. He doubted it.

10

It was mid-afternoon in Marseilles when the man called Klein stood in the shadows of the entrance to the ancient church. Notre Dame de la Garde is perched high above the city like a fortress guarding the great seaport spread out far below. A vast stone terrace spreads away west of the entrance, a terrace surrounded by a low stone wall. Lara Seagrave perched her backside on the flat-topped wall, aimed the Leica camera equipped with a telephoto lens, took more pictures of the harbour and its approaches. There was no one else on the great platform.

Below the wall the ground fell sheer towards the rooftops. Mid-afternoon, the sun at its highest point, beating down ferociously with a burning glare. It was well over 80° in the shade. Lara looked up from the camera and gazed round.

The harsh limestone – of which Marseilles is built – stood out from the bleak, treeless ridges and bluffs which encircle the city. The heat radiated off the rock, a heat haze shimmered, the Mediterranean was a blinding blue, the islands – including the famous Chateau d'If – vague silhouettes.

Lara loved the heat, soaked it up. Twenty-one years old, the step-daughter of Lady Windermere, she revelled in her freedom, in the excitement of the adventure. This was the moment when Klein, tall and thin-faced, wearing a suit of tropical drill, strolled into view, casually walked to a point close to her by the wall and raised a monocular glass looped round his neck.

'What do you think?' he asked in perfect English, staring out to sea, giving no hint to a watcher that they knew each other.

'Doesn't seem right for hijacking a ship,' she replied.

'And why not?'

'The harbour entrance is too narrow. It's like a snake the way it winds about. No easy escape route inland either if things go wrong. See how crammed together the old buildings are. The traffic jam in the streets. I feel it's not what you're looking for.'

She spoke in her upper crust accent, hardly moving her lips as she, also, gazed out to sea. She forced herself to stay cool, although the nearness of this man always excited her. Mustn't show it, she reminded herself. He doesn't approve of that.

'I'm inclined to agree with you,' Klein said. 'Best have a look at the next port. Le Havre.' His voice was cold, remote, his pale features contrasting strongly with Lara's sun-baked complexion. She was probably that colour all over, he mused. She loved sunning herself in the nude – one aspect of her sensuality.

'I'll leave tonight then?' she suggested.

'No. Tomorrow. And by train. From the Gare St Charles. I don't trust airports. Too easy for the security people to check each passenger. Go to Paris. I've reserved a room for you at The Ritz. Take another train from there to Le Havre. I'll meet you in five days' time. Friday – in the restaurant at The Ritz for dinner. You have enough money?'

'I've got over three thousand pounds left. Plenty . . .'

'I'll see you then.'

'What about the photographs I've taken? I never expected to see you up here.'

'Destroy them. Wait five minutes after I've gone, then you can leave here . . .'

He drifted away like a ghost. Despite the heat she shivered with anticipation. For Paris. She hadn't even looked him in the eye. *I never expected to see you up here* . . . Klein always did the unexpected. Ever since that first meeting at a party in a flat near Harrods. She'd seen him watching her across the room. When he came up to

72

her she didn't trust her luck. The other guests babbling away were crashing bores. This man was not only good-looking; he was intelligent, amusing, made her laugh.

'I'm Reinhard Klein. Consultant for a German armaments firm. A bit hush-hush – what I do.'

'You sound so English,' she'd remarked.

'Who says I'm not?' He'd grinned and she threw her normal caution to the winds. He could charm the birds out of the trees. And he had certainly charmed Lara. 'The Germans like to think they're dealing with one of their own kind . . .'

'You mean . . .'

'I mean I'd like to take you out to dinner. Send you home as soon as you've had enough . . .'

That was how it had started. She had learned practically nothing about his background, and this air of mystery intrigued her. Klein had – by the end of the evening – heard the story of her life.

She'd endured the usual débutante-style education. After prep school it had been Roedean. She whipped through her exams, got high marks, hated the whole childish business, simply couldn't wait to get out into the real world.

'I was good at languages,' she had told him. 'I went to a perfectly awful finishing school at Gstaad in Switzerland. To pass the time I became fluent in French and German. The other girls chased stupid men . . .'

'You don't like men?' Klein had probed.

'Not the kids – the twenty-year-old lot. They're callow, can't talk about anything except Henley and Glyndebourne. And bedding girls. I prefer older men. And I want to make a lot of money while I'm still young enough to enjoy it . . .'

Klein had showed interest in that remark – and her ability as a linguist. He'd tested her, chatting in German and French. She'd told him how her mother had died young, killed in a car crash. Then her merchant banker father had married Lady Windermere.

73

'He's not very bright about women,' she'd explained. 'I didn't like my mother. All she thought about was mixing with so-called high society. My step-mother turned out to be a disaster area as far as I was concerned. Wanted me out of the way.' Lara had mimicked her: 'My dear, the duty of an attractive girl in your position is to find some wealthy young man with prospects. Love doesn't come into it. You can get that elsewhere later. If you must . . .'

'An absolute bitch,' Lara had continued. 'Having endured a basinful of school, I was packed off to St James's Secretarial College in South Ken. I found the same empty-headed lot there. I passed top of the course and was supposed to get some job as PA to an executive type, preferably a bachelor. I rebelled . . .'

'You're politically aware?' Klein had asked.

'You must be joking.' She'd blown cigarette smoke into the air between courses. 'I'm aware politics is a bloody bore. Just a pack of self-seeking second-raters trying to ingratiate themselves with the voters – and the people higher up who could lift them into a good position. My grandfather was right.'

'Your grandfather?'

'On my father's side. The brains ran out after that. He used to tell me on the quiet, "Lara, go for the money. Don't marry for it. That way lies misery. Find out what you can do well, be unorthodox, travel, get to know the world outside this tight little island. An opportunity will crop up. Trick is to spot it when it does."'

'Your grandfather was right,' Klein had agreed. 'Maybe one day I'll be able to show you that opportunity. We'll keep in touch. Time to send you home now . . .'

Lara had asked how she could contact him. He'd drawn back from that one. The other way round, he said. He would contact her one day. She'd given this marvellous man her address in Eaton Square and her phone number. He'd kissed her on the cheek before leaving her at the entrance to her apartment block. No attempt to fondle her.

She'd finished her secretarial course, never ceasing to despise the empty chatter of her fellow pupils. Her coming-out party, insisted on by Lady Windermere, had been pure agony.

'This occasion,' the tall handsome step-mother, had remarked, 'is where you may find the right man. Do put yourself out to attract a few prospects.'

'If you say so . . .'

Of course, it was Robin, Lady Windermere's son by her previous marriage to Lord Windermere – killed in a car crash – who got all the attention. His mother was very ambitious for Robin, the present Lord Windermere. 'With a lot of luck, a bit of judicious seduction at the right moment, he'll land an American heiress.'

Oh, my God, Lara thought, that went out with Henry James. For a few minutes, in the privacy of her bedroom at Eaton Square, she'd looked critically at herself in the mirror. The image staring back was of a slim girl, five feet seven, a good figure, shapely legs, and her crowning glory – thick shoulder-length auburn hair. A girl who stood erect and with a rather aggressive stance. What does *my* future hold, she wondered?

Pictures of her appeared in *The Tatler* at parties she hated, always with some idiot man grinning foolishly. Lady Windermere glowed each time. 'You're getting known. It won't be long now . . .'

You just want to get rid of me, Lara thought. To sever the last link my simple-minded father has with the past. My presence is a bloody nuisance to her – because I always outshine bloody Robin. I really must get away before this atmosphere suffocates me.

Klein kept in touch with occasional phone calls. 'I'm in Brussels,' he would say. 'Saw your picture in that magazine . . .' He'd chat on, and always closed with, 'I'm moving on tonight. Don't ask where. Be in touch . . .'

Two years passed since her first meeting with Klein. She got away from Eaton Square by taking secretarial jobs on the continent in Switzerland and Germany. A small legacy from her grandfather when he died gave her some financial independence, but she was still looking for the big money which would take her away from Eaton Square for ever. Then the call came from Klein, followed by a registered envelope containing an air ticket for Paris and some spending money. The conversation stunned her.

'Like the chance to make a quarter of a million pounds?'

At the Hotel Crillon in Paris Klein explained. He needed a girl above suspicion who could travel. He was going to hijack a ship. There would be no casualties. Tear-gas would be used to put the crew out of action.

'No more details than that,' he told her. 'This envelope contains the equivalent of four thousand pounds in French currency. That's for expenses. It won't be subtracted from the quarter of a million.'

Over dinner they had been speaking in French. Klein was checking her fluency before he put his proposal to her – and was impressed with her command of the language.

'What do you expect me to do for my fee?' she had asked coolly, talking as though it were an everyday occurrence.

'Travel to Marseilles. By train. Buy a good camera, learn how to use it, take pictures of the port, check out security. Go there tomorrow,' he had instructed. 'Stay at the Sofitel. I will contact you . . .'

After dinner he suggested they went to his room. She had no hesitation in accepting the invitation. They spent the whole night together. By morning Klein had no doubt Lara was his, body and soul.

All this history of her relationship with Klein drifted across Lara's mind as she waited in the inferno of the heat-laden terrace of Notre Dame de la Garde. Waited for five minutes until Klein was well gone.

A large modern liner appeared through the haze, heading for the docks beyond the fishing harbour. One of the big jobs coming in from Oran, Algeria. One of the passenger ships which plied regularly between Marseilles and North Africa.

To give herself something to do, she raised the camera, adjusted the focus, and took a dozen shots as it loomed larger and larger. She realized suddenly she had run out of film, checked her watch, let the looped camera fall alongside the field-glasses also looped round her neck and left the terrace.

Leon Valmy stepped out of the shadows beside the church, walked slowly after her. A small, spare Frenchman, he had a nose like the beak of a parrot. In fact, his colleagues often referred to him as The Parrot behind his back.

Lara started the long walk down the steep road leading back to the city, watching her step on the uneven paving blocks. The last thing she needed now was a sprained ankle. In the blazing heat of the afternoon there was no one she could see as she continued the descent. Marseilles gradually came up to meet her, a solid mass of shabby, red-tiled rooftops.

She passed an old tank complete with a long gun parked where the street widened. Some memorial to the American landing in the south of France in 1944. She passed it without any interest in reading the plaque. The Parrot, making no sound in rubber-soled shoes, followed a hundred metres behind.

Arriving at the harbour at long last, she walked past the landing-stages where a forest of masts rose, climbed the hill to the Sofitel, a concrete block, collected her room key On the way to the bank of lifts she paused to look at a huge cactus sprouting from a giant pot.

Behind her, The Parrot whipped out his smaller Voigtlander, aimed it, took three shots of the girl. In case she had seen him out of the corner of her eye, he then swivelled the camera and took three more shots of other pots. When he looked again she had vanished inside an elevator. He walked quickly to the bank, checked the lights. She had got off at the second floor. He returned to the reception counter and spoke to the girl behind the counter.

'The manager. It's urgent . . .'

'Can I help? He's off duty, taking a siesta.'

'I said it was urgent. Wake him up. Do it. Now!'

She stared resentfully at the small man who wore a pair of dark-tinted glasses. Something about the way he stared back bothered her. She picked up the phone, spoke a few words Valmy couldn't catch, then replaced the receiver.

'He will be here in a minute.'

A portly man, wearing a linen suit, brushing back his hair with his hand, appeared from behind a door. The girl gestured at Valmy.

'What is it?' the manager asked.

'DST.' The Parrot showed him a folder. *Direction de la Surveillance du Territoire.* Counter-Espionage. 'You have a girl staying here. Early twenties. Auburn hair. With a room on the second floor. I need to see a copy of her registration slip.'

'That is Miss Lara Seagrave. An English girl,' the receptionist said.

'Leave this to me,' the manager snapped. 'Go and get a cup of coffee. Come back in five minutes . . .'

He had been sorting through a card index box. He brought out a printed form and handed it to The Parrot, who noted the details in his book. He handed back the form, staring hard at the manager.

'I have never been here. Warn your girl. If she opens her mouth she'll be charged with an offence against state security.'

The Parrot walked back down the hill and round the harbour to the infamous Canebière, the street where a German woman had been robbed of thirty thousand francs crossing it the day before on her way from a bank to Cook's. At five in the afternoon the city was like an oven.

The Parrot had taken up station at Notre Dame de la Garde out of pure chance. Rumours were rife about a plot to hijack a ship. And Miss Lara Seagrave had taken an awful lot of pictures of the harbour from the best vantage point in Marseilles. She'd also studied it carefully through her binoculars.

He mused over the idea until he reached his hotel. It would give him something to report to the rue des Saussaies in Paris. They liked reports – it showed their superiors the agents in the field were active. Then it would be filed away. Forever.

After a meal which took ages to serve, Valmy went up to bed. The heat persisted throughout the night. He had trouble sleeping, rolling from side to side, covered in sweat. That girl came back into his mind. Why?

After breakfast he phoned the manager at the Sofitel. It was the same man. Still feeling it could all be a waste of time, he made his request.

'If Lara Seagrave checks out, I'd like to know – here is my phone number . . .'

'But she is leaving soon, sir. She has called down for the bill to be made up.'

'Thank you . . .'

The Parrot slammed down the phone, grabbed his bag which he kept packed, went down to the lobby, paid his own bill, rushed out of the hotel and jumped into his hired Deux-Chevaux. It was too early yet for heavy traffic and ten minutes later he parked in the drive to the Sofitel. He was just in time. Within minutes he saw her, carrying a suitcase, climbing into a cab. He followed.

She alighted at the Gare St Charles. He walked after her to the ticket counter, queued behind her. He had changed into a lightweight shabby blue suit and no longer wore his tinted glasses. She bought a one-way ticket to Paris and headed for the platform.

Valmy was careful. The Paris express was not due for another fifteen minutes. He bought a ticket for the first place that came into his head. Aix-en-Provence. Then he strolled on to the platform, standing close to a woman with a child.

Lara slipped the ticket into her purse and casually

glanced round, checking the other passengers. A family of three, one man and woman with a child, several men carrying brief-cases, four women on their own. No one she had seen before.

The express arrived, people boarded the train. Lara waited, checking her watch. She glanced round again. Valmy was out of sight, standing by the wall of a waiting room, watching her through the window. Just before the express left, he saw Lara leap aboard, slamming the door behind her. Curious.

He was walking back to his car when he saw the phone box and took his decision. He called rue des Saussaies, identified himself, then the stupid operator went off the line. A new and familiar voice answered. René Lasalle, Chief of the DST.

'Who is it?'

'Leon Valmy . . . I didn't ask for you . . . the girl . . .'

'Now you've got me, what is it?'

Valmy explained, keeping his story short. Lasalle couldn't stand wafflers. Terse and decisive, the chief believed words were to communicate information. He listened, thinking there wasn't much to all this.

'What made you phone?' he asked eventually.

'A hunch. Nothing more, Chief,' Valmy said apologetically, wishing now he hadn't made the call.

Hunch? Lasalle was instantly alert. It was a hunch of The Parrot's which had elevated him to his present position. He reached for a railway timetable, telling Valmy to hang on, then checked the time by the wall-clock.

'That express arrives in Paris at 1650 hours. Assuming she stays aboard, doesn't get off en route . . .'

'She did book through to Paris . . .'

'We'll take a chance. Get to Marignane Airport fast, catch a flight to Paris. You'll beat her to it. We'll have a car waiting at the airport, take you to the Gare de Lyon – you'll be here in time to identify her.'

'I'd better rush . . .'

'Do that.'

11

Klein was also up early. He had stayed overnight at the Hotel Roi René in Aix-en-Provence. Never linger at the same place for more than twenty-four hours. That defeated the system of hotel registration the French employed – with the police calling for their copies of the registration form during the night.

He drove off at six for his appointment in Cassis, the small resort east of Marseilles. He arrived at the iron grille gates of the luxurious villa overlooking the sea at 7.30 a.m. A guard checked his passport, then operated the mechanism which opened the gates. Who would dream that the head of the local Union Corse lived in a place like this?

Emilio Perugini was waiting for him in a lounging chair by the side of the obligatory status symbol, a swimming pool. A large Alsatian swam in the water, heading for a rubber ball the small fat man in the chair had thrown.

'Sit down, Mr Klein. What can I do for you?'

'Find me a specialist with very specific qualifications. For a fee.'

Klein handed the fat envelope containing two hundred thousand French francs to the tanned man with brown hair and a face like that of a cadaver. Perugini opened the envelope, made a quick flip through the banknotes, dropped the envelope on the table as though it were nothing.

'What qualifications, Mr Klein?'

'Someone you can spare for several months. An expert with a hand-gun, an automatic weapon, a knife, also,' he added as though an afterthought, 'a first-rate scuba diver.'

'You don't ask for much, do you?'

'I pay quite a lot. It's a while since we last met – but you will have what I need, I know.'

'The hand-gun, the automatic weapon, the knife. He is a hard man you're wanting?'

Dressed in a white shirt open at the front and shorts, Perugini reached for a bottle of red wine, Klein shook his head and the Union Corse chief refilled his own glass. He patted his fat belly, sprawled short thick legs under the table as the Alsatian dropped the ball by his side.

The animal stared at Klein, bared his teeth and gave a snarl. Klein turned and gazed straight at the animal. He pushed his chair back a few inches. 'César doesn't like you,' Perugini remarked. The dog backed away when Klein half-rose from his chair, gave a low yelp and flopped some distance away.

'Yes, a hard man,' Klein said, sitting down again. 'And he needs to have experience with explosives . . .'

Perugini threw his bony head back and laughed contemptuously, a weird cackling sound. 'All that for two hundred thousand francs! And my man is out of action for several months? You must be joking . . .'

Klein took out another fat envelope, tossed it on the table, waited. Perugini regarded it without touching it, drank more wine.

'How much in there?'

'Another two hundred thousand . . .'

'Double it and I may help . . .'

'Nonsense time is over.'

Klein's tone was cold, bleak. He reached forward under the low table, wrenched something attached to the under surface and produced a miniature tape recorder. His long fingers tore out the recorded tape reel, he turned to the dog and hurled the reel far out into the pool. César dived in, swam underneath, came up with the mangled tape in his teeth.

'You shouldn't have done that,' Perugini snapped. 'I only have to flick my fingers and a couple of my boys come out that villa.' He waved a hand across the beach. 'The sea is wide and deep. A weighted corpse stays down forever . . .'

'Except that neither of us would be around for it to happen.'

'What does that mean?' Perugini asked, his eyes hooded.

'See those wooded hills behind your film-star villa?' Klein waved his own hand. 'Four men are up there, two watching us with field-glasses ever since I arrived. The other two have rocket launchers. We'd end up as jelly.'

'You're bluffing.' Perugini sounded uncertain, glanced up at the woods.

'Want to risk it?'

'OK.' Perugini had reached his position of power by taking fast decisions, by never taking unnecessary risks. 'You get your man – for the fee on the table. Louis Chabot. He is based in Marseilles. Here is the address.' He produced a crumpled notebook from his back pocket, scribbled on it, tore out the sheet and handed it to his guest. He was anxious to get rid of Klein. Something about the man's eyes disturbed him. He checked the second envelope, tossed it back on the table.

'Is that it, Klein?'

'Not quite. My fee buys absolute silence. See that rock sticking up out of the sea?'

Klein stood up, raised his right hand, dropped it in a chopping movement. There was a *whooshing* sound. Then a loud bang. Perugini stared at the rock where the explosion had happened. The top half had vanished, splinters of rock splattered the sea.

'Don't ever threaten me again,' Klein said and left.

Klein climbed the worn stone steps of the evil-smelling tenement building behind the Old Port to the first floor. The plaster was crumbling between the stonework. He paused outside the old heavy wooden door to Number Eleven. No sound from inside.

Using the phone number Perugini had scribbled on the

scrap of paper with the address, he'd called Chabot, made an appointment for 11.30 a.m. It was now eleven o'clock. Klein liked to arrive early. You sometimes learned important things about a new recruit by catching them off guard. He rapped loudly on the door.

'Who the hell is it?' a man's voice called out in French.

'I phoned you earlier . . .'

'And you're early.' The door had opened on a thick chain, a swarthy, heavy-jowled face peered out. Naked to the flat waist. Trousers hastily thrown on. The man called to someone over his shoulder. 'Get dressed, get out . . .'

'No names,' Klein warned as the man unfastened the chain, gestured for him to come inside. 'You are Louis Chabot?'

'That's me.'

'You'll know who I come from then.' Klein handed him the scrap of paper when Chabot had relocked the door, glanced round the room.

'The mark at the bottom tells me.' He turned to the girl who had recently scrambled out of the bed against one wall. She'd had time to slip on her skirt, but like Chabot she was naked above the waist and had a pair of firm, rounded breasts. She stared saucily at Klein as she reached for a sweater, then pulled it over her head and slid her bare feet into shoes.

'This is Cecile, my new girl,' Chabot introduced.

Her presence disturbed Klein: she'd had a good look at him, but he said nothing. Apart from the bed, which Cecile was hastily making up, the room was unexpectedly clean, neat.

Chabot put on a fresh striped shirt, buttoned it to the neck, then donned a linen jacket hanging over the back of a chair. On his instruction, Cecile took dirty glasses into the kitchen and washed them. She was a bottle blonde with a pretty *gamine* face and kept glancing at Klein when she was in the room.

He stood with his back to her, staring out of the window. It overlooked a jumble of ancient roofs on the far side of a narrow street. Lines of washing hung on makeshift clothes lines on flat rooftops, drying in the morning sun. Klein remained quite still as Cecile left.

'See you soon, dear,' Chabot called out to her. 'Don't do anything I would . . .'

'That's going to be a hell of a lot of fun.'

Then she was gone. Klein swung round, studied the Frenchman as he locked the door. About thirty, thick brown hair with brows to match, a hooked nose, pale blue eyes which didn't waver before his visitor's scrutiny, a brutal jaw. Heavily built, Chabot moved lightly on his small feet, his legs and arms long, his hands large, powerful-looking. Strangler's hands, Klein thought.

'Seen enough?' Chabot demanded. 'Want a drink?'

'Coffee.' He followed the Frenchman into the small kitchen. 'Who is that girl?'

'Cecile Lamont. Hangs out at a bar along the street. The Wolf.' He was preparing café filtre. Klein said no milk, no sugar. 'It's our first week.' He glanced at Klein. 'If you have in mind what I think you have, she performs well. But only if she likes you. She likes you. Now, what's this all about? Do I measure up? You've been working that one out ever since you came in.'

'Know much about explosives?'

'Everything. Handle with care. Never trust them . . .'

'How did you get the knowledge?'

'Working in a stone quarry. Blasting rock. Everything I know I've learned legit. That way you don't get a police record.'

'Ever been inside?'

'Not a chance. Coffee's ready. Let's go into the other room, make ourselves comfortable . . .'

For ten minutes Klein grilled Chabot. At the end of that period he was convinced Perugini had not lied: this Frenchman had all the qualifications he needed. He nodded, his head turned slightly to the right.

'You'll do. On conditions . . .'

'Not so fast, Klein. What do I have to do. Kill a few people?'

'Maybe quite a lot . . .'

'You mean that?'

Klein didn't answer. With hands clad in white cotton gloves he had worn since leaving Aix, he took out an envelope, dropped it in Chabot's lap. 'Ten thousand francs. That's just for starters. And expenses.'

'What comes later?' Chabot was counting the banknotes.

'Two hundred thousand. Used notes, of course.'

'What's the job?'

'That's part of the two hundred thousand. You don't get any more information until you need to know. And we work in cells of no more than three people. There will be a lot of cells – it's a security precaution. Which also protects you.'

'Does make it safer. You seem well organized.'

That was the moment when Klein knew Chabot was hooked. But the swarthy-faced man had one more question. 'It isn't political?'

Klein smiled grimly, a smile which did nothing to soften the coldness of his personality. He shook his head, gave his final instructions.

'I said there were conditions. You vanish. From Marseilles, I mean. No goodbyes to old cronies . . .'

'I don't have them. And if you're worried about Perugini – I work freelance. He hires me as bodyguard from time to time. At least six people want to take over from him, know the only way they can is to bury him. He told you I was freelance?'

Klein nodded. Perugini, the bastard, had omitted that interesting item – to push up his fee. Klein told Chabot to start packing while he completed the instructions. The Frenchman hauled a case out of a cupboard, began neatly packing clothes as Klein continued.

'You travel by train today to Luxembourg City. Second-class. Go via Lyon, then Mulhouse – where you pick up the express for Luxembourg City.' He tossed another envelope across to Chabot who caught it deftly and waited for Klein to finish. 'Inside that envelope you'll find the route I outlined typed out. Plus a phone number. Call that number from Mulhouse. Ask for Bernard. Tell him what time your train reaches Luxembourg City. Nothing else. It's a Hotel Alsace you'll be calling. Bernard will phone the time through to the man who will meet you on the platform at Luxembourg City. Inside that envelope you'll also find a Cook's label. I've written on it, Brussels Midi, and circled it twice. You put that label on your case only when you board the express at Mulhouse. The label will identify you to the man waiting to meet you.'

'Wouldn't it be quicker to travel via Geneva and Basle – then straight up to Luxembourg?'

'Yes. But Swiss security is good. We'll avoid them. And the route I've laid down is all inside the Common Market. No checks.'

'Name of the man meeting me?'

'He'll know you.' Klein checked his watch. 'You've got thirty minutes to catch the train for Lyon. And that's it. No more questions. I hope?'

'Only one.' Chabot shut the case, snapped the catches closed. A man who didn't waste time. 'Curiosity,' he went on. 'Why wear those gloves in this bloody heat?'

'Because I have eczema. I dislike unsightly hands.' There was a pause. Klein's tone hardened. 'And curiosity in this game can kill you.'

'Truly.' Chabot glanced at Klein, saw his stone-faced expression, looked away. 'I'll remember that. I'm off now . . .'

Klein left the room without a word. Perugini had not commented on the gloves. He'd known the reason why. To avoid leaving Klein's fingerprints on the envelopes. But that was why Perugini was living in a luxurious villa at Cassis, while Chabot occupied a tenement behind the harbour.

Klein returned to his car, drove slowly along the street until he passed *Le Loup*, the bar where Cecile hung out.

That gave him one more little task to attend to before he left Marseilles.

Eleven o'clock at night. Well after darkness had fallen. The bar, *Le Loup*, was packed with customers. Klein knew because earlier he'd peered through the bead curtain at the entrance. Cecile Lamont was perched on a bar stool, chatting to some man. He'd returned to his car parked a few metres away, climbed behind the wheel, and waited.

He was used to waiting, much as he hated it. It was 11.30 when Cecile came out, wobbling a little, and on her own – as he had hoped. He started the engine, drove after her and slowed alongside her.

'Cecile, care for dinner? Maybe a fun night? Up to you.'

He had his head poked out of the window and she recognized him instantly, which showed how wise he'd been to take this precaution. She jumped in, slammed the door, and he was driving off before she noticed how he was dressed.

'Why are you wearing that white coat?'

'Some fool in a bar spilt half a bottle of wine all over my best suit. Looked dreadful. The owner of the place loaned me this to cover up the mess. I'll change into a fresh suit at my apartment before we go on for dinner.'

'Where is this apartment?'

She lit the Gauloise after offering him the pack which he refused. They drove round the harbour and up the hill in the direction of Cassis. She looked at him when he didn't reply. He was a handsome bastard.

'Near Cassis,' he said eventually. 'I'm taking a short cut. Then we can get off to the restaurant . . .'

'I'm not too hungry yet – if you want to linger in your apartment.'

'We'll see.'

He swung off the main route on to a side road he'd explored earlier in the day. The car bounced about over the rough road, the wheels grinding over rocks. He came to the quarry which had been abandoned long ago, stopped the car.

'Got a present for you in the boot.'

Flowers, she thought. He's a gentleman, thinks of things like that. Unlike Louis. She followed him in the deserted night, thinking it was very quiet. He had opened the boot. She bent forward to see what was inside. Klein slipped the knife out of his sock, grasped her round the shoulders and slowly cut her throat from left ear to right. She gurgled, her blood spurted over his sleeve, down her front. He felt her go a dead weight. He lifted her and folded over her body the canvas sheet laid on the floor of the boot.

Half an hour later he dumped the canvas bundle in the sea, threw the screwed-up butcher's overall he'd worn after her. It had taken him three hours to find a shop where he could buy the overall to protect his suit. He drove back to Marseilles. He would continue north – towards Geneva. He felt satisfied. The problem of Cecile was dealt with. Never leave behind loose ends.

12

Gare de Lyon. Lasalle of the DST checked his watch. The express from Marseilles was due in Paris. 10.50 p.m. He stood close to the exit barrier. A tall, heavily-built man in his forties, his eyes were half-closed under thick brows, behind horn-rimmed spectacles.

He wore a camel-hair coat against the night chill and a narrow-brimmed trilby, a motionless figure, hands thrust inside his pockets. By his side The Parrot looked even smaller, despite his crash helmet, goggles and motor-cycle gear.

'I'm surprised you came yourself, Chief . . .'

'Something about the way you described Lara Seagrave.

What she did down there south. A check has come through from London. Step-daughter of Lady Windermere. High society stuff.'

'Sounds an unlikely terrorist,' The Parrot ventured.

'The rumours report an entirely new organization being built up. Don't like that. Our normal sources have no inside track. She could just be a new type. Better get back. Here it comes . . .'

The express came slowly inside the vast concourse, stopped, doors were thrown open as impatient passengers alighted. Lasalle had two more men standing further back. His eyes blinked. This girl, carrying one case, smartly dressed, fitted Valmy's description. He glanced towards The Parrot who nodded once and then vanished outside where his motor-cycle was parked.

Lasalle took a newspaper out of his pocket, opened it, crossed to where his other two men stood, engaged them in conversation, pointing to the paper. Attractive, Miss Lara Seagrave; walked erect even though she must be tired. She passed out of the concourse, heading for the taxi rank.

'Rue des Saussaies,' Lasalle snapped. 'Then we wait. For The Parrot's report . . .'

Gare Centrale. Luxembourg City. The express from Basle, Switzerland, which had travelled via Mulhouse, came to a stop at just about the same time. 11 p.m. Among the passengers who alighted was Louis Chabot, carrying a case which bore a Cook's label. On the label in large printed letters were the words *Brussels Midi*, circled twice.

Chabot walked slowly along the platform, trailing behind the few other passengers. Without appearing to do so, he glanced everywhere, looking for his contact. Klein was so bloody careful – he didn't even know the contact's name or sex. Still, security like that protected him as well.

'Mr Louis Chabot?'

The odd-shaped figure had appeared from nowhere.

Chabot studied him, kept walking as the hatless man trotted by his side. Small, running to fat, a clean-shaven face the colour of lard. His eyes were blank of expression, his clothes nondescript. A grey two-piece suit, the trousers crumpled, the wide shoulders slumped.

'Yes, I'm Chabot.'

'Our mutual friend, Mr Klein, arranged for me to meet you. Outside I have a car waiting. We go into the country. A peaceful village . . .'

'Strangers are noticed in villages. You have a name?'

They were talking in French, but his escort spoke it with an odd accent. Chabot had already taken a strong dislike to the placid little man. More like a servant. Not what he had expected. A nobody.

'I am Hipper,' the little man said. 'We will be working closely together. We go up in this lift. And no one will know you are at Larochette.'

'Where?'

'The village. Twenty-five kilometres north of Luxembourg City. I am in charge,' Hipper continued in the privacy of the ascending lift. 'You will stay underground until the operation begins . . .'

'What operation?'

'Only Mr Klein knows that. You are explosives expert?'

'Yes. You're not French.' It was a statement.

'I am Luxembourger.'

God, Chabot thought, how long am I going to be hanging round with this creep? Hipper had a habit of sneaking sidelong glances at the Frenchman and never looked him straight in the eye. Luxembourgers. A hybrid race. A mix of French and German – with all their vices and none of their virtues.

'You are explosives expert,' Hipper repeated as the elevator stopped and just before the doors opened. 'When the timer devices arrive you will have a chance to practise your expertise.'

*

'Valmy here . . .'

'Yes?' said Lasalle, leaning back in the swivel chair inside his office at the rue des Saussaies. He frowned at the two officers to stop them chattering.

'The subject is occupying a room at The Ritz. Room 614. She registered, went straight to bed. The registration form gives an address of Eaton Square, London . . .'

'I know all about that. Did she make a phone call after she'd arrived?'

'No,' The Parrot reported. 'I checked. What next?'

'Stay there. If she leaves in the night, follow . . .'

'The reservation was made for six days. In advance.'

Lasalle leaned forward. 'By her? Do you know?'

'The reservations manager who took the call – it was late in the evening – thinks it was a man. But can't swear to that. He has taken so many calls since.' The Parrot paused. 'I need back-up. There are two exits from the Ritz.'

'I'll send someone. And you'll be relieved by a fresh team before morning . . .'

Lasalle put down the phone, pursed his thick lips and thought. He looked at the two officers, obviously waiting to go off duty. It was almost midnight.

'The Lara girl is at The Ritz,' he said eventually. 'For six days. Reservation booked earlier by a man. Perhaps. The significant thing is she phoned no one before retiring for the night. That suggests she's waiting to meet someone. And at Notre Dame de la Garde in Marseilles a man stood alongside her for several minutes on the terrace. The Parrot couldn't get a picture of him – as he did of her. Had the feeling the man would have spotted him. Interesting, that last bit. Maybe we'll find out who he is when he arrives at The Ritz.'

One of the officers chuckled. 'Sounds like a liaison. A married man having it off with this Lara Seagrave.'

'Since you find it so amusing,' Lasalle informed him, 'you can get your backside over to The Ritz now. Liaise, so to speak, with The Parrot . . .'

*

Chabot gritted his teeth, refused to show any fear. Hipper was driving the Volvo station wagon like a madman. Leaving Luxembourg City behind, they turned up a side road into a dense forest. The damned road curved viciously, Hipper was driving at a hundred kilometres an hour, skidding round the bends.

On his side great rock outcrops protruded into the road. Chabot estimated they missed the rocks by millimetres, almost scraping past. It was black as pitch, the undipped headlight beams swung round another hairpin bend, flashing over great limestone crags. They had not, thank God, met another vehicle since leaving the main highway. Chabot was constantly waiting for the sight of headlights coming the other way.

Hipper crouched over the wheel, enfolding it with his shoulders, his pudgy hands clutching the rim near the top. They began to descend, they passed an old stone cottage, falling to pieces. Hipper grunted.

'Larochette . . .'

Silhouetted against a moon which had appeared, the relics of an ancient castle perched on a hilltop. In the gaunt walls were window spaces, like skeletal eyes. Buildings appeared on either side. No lights. No sign of a human soul. Like a village abandoned by villagers who had fled from a plague.

'We are here. The Hotel de la Montagne.'

An ancient stone structure standing back from the road with a wide drive leading up to the entrance. Chabot frowned. The shutters were closed. Some windows were boarded up and the headlights showed a layer of moss on the drive.

'What is this bloody place?' Chabot demanded.

'The Montagne. Closed for renovation. No staff. We look after ourselves. You stay inside during daylight hours. If you must walk you go out after ten at night. Klein's instructions . . .'

'For how long?'

'Who knows? You will have plenty to occupy you when

the timer devices arrive. The most sophisticated in the world.' Hipper drove the Volvo round the side, straight inside a vast shed. When he switched off the engine the only sound Chabot could hear was the oppressive silence of a dead village.

Klein was driving through the night, the autoroute far behind, heading for Grenoble which he planned to pass through before dawn. He would hand back his hired Renault in Annecy. Driving into Switzerland was not a good idea.

At Annecy he would catch a train. Eventually he would cross the Swiss frontier and alight at the small Swiss station of Eaux-Vives in southern Geneva. Security took very little interest in travellers arriving by train. And Eaux-Vives was a backwoods station.

Seeing a lay-by ahead, he checked his rear view mirror again. No traffic in sight. He slowed, swung into the lay-by, stopped. Taking out a notebook, he inserted a piece of cardboard under a sheet and began to write, leaving no impression on the sheet below.

Timers. Scuba divers. Marksman. Lara. Explosives. Banker.

Like other lone wolf characters, Klein had a habit of talking aloud to himself, but was always aware of what he was doing. It helped to concentrate his thinking. He began now.

'Timers. Let's hope Gaston Blanc has them ready. A genius with miniature instrumentation. The only problem is after he hands them over. No loose ends . . . Scuba divers. Luxembourg swarms with them. Marksman? Paris. The Englishman would be ideal. Lara . . .'

The problem with Lara was to keep her occupied until the time came for her to play a role she had no idea – fortunately – she was destined for. A member of one of Britain's most distinguished aristocratic lines. Again, ideal. He'd send her on more wild-goose chases, Klein decided.

The last two items were all organized. It took money to persuade people to cooperate in an unknown operation – a lot of money. Well, he'd already obtained that.

Klein reckoned he'd calculated the amounts just right. Four thousand for Lara. With the promise of a quarter of a million pounds. Four thousand was not enough to tempt her into walking away. Not with a fortune dangled in front of her.

Louis Chabot had been a different proposition. A professional. Ten thousand francs for starters. The promise of two hundred thousand, the equivalent of £20,000. More money than Chabot had ever earned before. Not too much, not too little – that was the delicate balance.

Greed. That was the motive force. Estimate the level of greed with a man – or a woman – and you had them in the palm of your hand. A compulsive checker, Klein looked at his list again. *Explosives.* In place. *Banker.* Everything arranged.

Whichever way he looked at it, Klein felt sure he had overlooked nothing. Already rumours about the hijacking of an unknown vessel were spreading. The essential smoke-screen. You couldn't recruit people on the scale he was operating at without whispers reaching the authorities. So, give them something to chew on, the wrong thing.

Of course there would be casualties. Hundreds of them. But you couldn't mount the biggest operation since World War Two against the biggest target in Western Europe – without casualties. You couldn't make an omelette without breaking eggs – a two hundred million pound gold bullion omelette.

And, Klein, a careful man, thought, as he used a lighter to set fire to the sheet from his notepad, then dropped the blackened remnant into the ash-tray, he hadn't left a single clue behind. Who in the world was there to stop him?

13

Tweed returned to Park Crescent at 7 p.m. Howard and Monica were waiting for him in his office. They looked up expectantly as he walked round his desk, sank into his chair.

'Well,' Howard pressed, 'what did the PM say?'

'I have to investigate the Zarov thing. Sheer waste of time, I'm sure . . .'

'You didn't tell her that?'

'Of course I did. She's frank, expects frankness. But I have to check it out.'

'How on earth are you going to do that?' Howard crossed his well-creased trousers carefully and drank more of the coffee Monica had supplied. 'Not a damned thing to go on,' he continued. 'Doesn't she realize that?'

'It's that conversation she had when Gorbachev phoned her. I don't think she's told me everything that was said. I'll just have to get on with it.' Tweed waved a hand in the air. 'A search for a phantom.'

'With not a damned thing to go on?' Howard repeated.

'Not quite true.' Tweed fingered his tie, a sure sign to Monica he wasn't happy about the situation. 'First, there is Yuri Sabarin, the Russian in Geneva who swears he saw Igor Zarov a few weeks ago.'

'What about him?'

'I'm flying to Geneva tomorrow to interview him. Grill him, if you like. He'll probably back-track under pressure . . .'

'And what else is going for you?' Monica asked. 'Like some coffee? Yes, you look fagged out. I'll make a fresh pot.'

'Thank you. While I'm in Geneva I'll also start checking

my personal contacts. Then go on to Paris. Check with someone who knows everything that happens in the quiet streets . . .' A reference to the quiet streets which house Soviet embassies. 'Then,' he continued, 'I may go on to my contact in Brussels.'

'Why those cities?' Howard asked.

'According to Lysenko this Zarov was stationed in them at various times.' He reached inside his brief-case he'd dropped beside his desk, extracted the photocopy of Igor Zarov, put it on the desk facing Howard. 'That's who I'm supposed to track down. If he's still alive . . .'

'You sound doubtful,' Howard observed as Monica returned with a tray and began pouring coffee.

'I am *very* doubtful – despite the PM's views. I'm also wary.'

'Wary?' Monica queried. She looked at the picture. 'That's him?'

'Wary and suspicious. Lysenko could be up to something. The only thing is he seemed genuinely worried – even frightened.' He pushed the picture towards Monica. 'Get the Engine Room boys in the basement to run off two dozen copies. It will be tricky – making copies from a copy. Then send one to Chief Inspector Benoit of the Brussels police, René Lasalle in Paris, Otto Kuhlmann in Wiesbaden and Arthur Beck of the Swiss Federal Police in Berne. I'll draft a letter to them later to go with the photocopies.'

'Why so many policemen?' asked Monica. 'Instead of all the Intelligence chiefs?'

Tweed showed wry amusement, watching Howard. 'Oh, didn't I tell you? The PM has given me a temporary appointment as a Commander of the Anti-Terrorist Squad. And, Monica, check all the files on Soviet embassy personnel over here for the past three years . . .'

'Ye Gods!'

'Yes, it will take awhile. But Zarov was in London, 1985. The point is this – Lysenko told me his postings, but not the names he worked under. Undoubtedly not Zarov. He'll have been a commercial attaché officially, something like that.'

Howard sat with a stunned look. 'You did say you've been given a special attachment to Scotland Yard? Your old stamping ground?'

'Youngest Superintendent, Homicide Squad,' Monica said with relish. 'After he left Military Intelligence, before he came here.'

'I was just lucky,' Tweed commented.

'I still don't understand it,' Howard protested. 'That's never been done before. A split allegiance – to the Service and to Scotland Yard.'

'Nonsense!' Tweed waved a hand. 'I didn't ask for it. The PM's idea. It will give me more clout with the police on the continent.'

'I don't like it,' Howard said stiffly. 'She should have consulted me.' He stood up to leave.

'Send her a memo,' Tweed suggested.

Howard glared, shot his cuffs, and walked out of the room. He closed the door very quietly behind him. Monica giggled, refilled Tweed's cup. 'He's hopping mad again. He'll be impossible for days . . .'

'I won't be here for days. There's something else. That bomb at Paula's house in Blakeney. A Captain Nicholls and his team defused it. Nicholls said it was a new type – he'd been shown a sample obtained by Commander Bellenger of Naval Intelligence. Call Admiralty after I've gone home – try and get Bellenger to come and meet me here before I have to catch the flight for Geneva.'

'Will do.' Monica frowned. 'Funny isn't it? A Soviet bomb is planted in Norfolk – then the Kremlin asks for assistance finding this mysterious Zarov character. And you were told by Lysenko a huge cargo of sea-mines and bombs had gone missing from their Sevastopol depot. Doesn't make sense.'

'Maybe it will after I've talked with Bellenger. Any word from Newman out in Breckland?'

'Not a dicky bird. You know Bob – he'll go his own way, only report in when he's got something.'

'True.' Tweed had put on his Burberry, was about to go home when he made the casual remark. 'Where is Paula now?'

'Where do you think? Working in Howard's office. He invented some French documents he wanted translated. She's pretty cool about the whole idea . . .'

'Not to worry. Just get two air tickets to Geneva. One for me, one for Paula.'

'And what's your excuse?' Monica asked frostily. 'Sorry,' she added hastily, 'that must have sounded bitchy . . .'

'You said that, I didn't.'

'Why do you need her? Sheer curiosity on my part. I suppose I get ticked off again?'

'Not at all. Paula speaks French and German. And Yuri Sabarin, who must speak French to be posted to Geneva, may be susceptible to women.'

Paula came back to the office half an hour later, her expression blank, followed by Howard, who strolled in, staring around. Monica spoke first.

'If you're looking for Tweed he's gone. For the night. Paula,' she went on rapidly, 'you're travelling to Geneva with Tweed tomorrow. Thought I'd warn you – so you could pack a bag.'

'I keep one packed for an emergency departure – just like Tweed. But thanks for the warning. Which flight?'

'Best be ready by eleven tomorrow morning.'

Monica was watching Howard who had slumped into an easy chair, one leg lolling over an arm, hands clasped behind the back of his neck. He watched Paula, who busied herself at her desk, sifting through files.

'Tweed still doubtful about the whole business?' he enquired.

'You heard what he said,' Monica replied cautiously.

'The PM is probably right, you know. It ought to be checked. All these rumours about some new outfit hijacking a ship. It might turn out to be one of ours . . . '

You bastard! Monica was thinking. You're covering yourself in case any of Tweed's comments get back to No. 10. She eyed him, playing with a pencil before she reacted.

'I wouldn't have thought something like that was our concern.'

'The PM thinks it might be, that's enough for me.' He smiled with an air of self-satisfaction. Monica saw through him instantly. He'd expressed support for the official view and had two witnesses to back him up – if push came to shove. 'And,' he went on, 'there's that business about the peculiar character who may – or may not – exist. Has to be checked.' He glanced again at Paula, her raven-black hair bent over the files. At least, Monica thought, he'd had the sense not to mention Zarov by name in front of the new recruit.

Howard stretched out his long legs, checked his watch, stood up and stretched. He thrust both hands in his trouser pockets and stared at Paula.

'What about a spot of dinner? You've worked well today. You need fodder to keep you going. I know a place where the fodder is rather good.'

'Thank you. Sir,' she added as an afterthought. She was sitting still crouched over the files, looking up at him. 'But it's an early night for me. I must be fresh for the flight tomorrow.'

'There's always another night. Have fun in Geneva. I hear the fodder is pretty good there. Tell me all about it when you get back. All right?'

'Good night. Sir,' replied Paula. She waited until they were alone. 'I'm looking forward to my first mission abroad,' she told Monica.

'Things happen when Tweed arrives somewhere. Baptism of fire.'

*

Commander Alec Bellenger arrived at Park Crescent late in the afternoon of the following day, which caused Tweed to put off his flight to Geneva until twenty-four hours later. A phone call from Admiralty had warned he was delayed returning from abroad.

Mid-thirties, Tweed estimated, Bellenger was a tall heavily-built man with thick brown hair. Ruddy-cheeked, a strong jaw, ice-cold blue eyes, he carried himself with the easy assurance of a man accustomed to command.

He listened in silence as Tweed related the bomb incident at Blakeney, his eyes never leaving Tweed's. He's weighing me up, Tweed thought. Fair enough. He finished speaking and Bellenger crossed his large hands in his lap, then reacted.

'Nicholls, that Bomb Disposal officer, came to me afterwards. Brought the shell and innards of the infernal device. It's a Cossack, all right . . .'

'Cossack?'

'Code-name for the sea-mine we smuggled out of Russia. Can't tell you how. Came out by submarine. Period.'

'Understood,' Tweed assured him.

'Apart from the hydrogen bomb it's the most devilish device invented since World War Two. Don't mind telling you the thing scares the living daylights out of me.'

'Why?'

'First the explosive the sample we purloined contained. We've called it Triton Three. Its power is roughly midway between TNT and an atom bomb.'

'Just supposing,' Tweed said casually, 'we were talking about thirty of these sea-mines – plus twenty-five bombs – and they were all armed with this Triton Three. What effect could that lot have?'

Bellenger stiffened, leaned forward. Monica, who was watching him from behind her desk could have sworn the naval commander lost colour. He took his time replying, like a man recovering from shock.

'Take out Birmingham,' he responded. 'The whole city. Three miles radius from impact point. Level every building. No survivors. Inside that three-miles radius . . .'

'Jesus!'

Tweed let slip the blasphemy involuntarily. He stared at his visitor, who stared back. Bellenger straightened up, steepled his hands.

'Is this theoretical? You chose very precise numbers.'

'Oh, completely.' Tweed smiled and drank some coffee. Inside the office the atmosphere was electric. He took his time over drinking the coffee – to defuse the tension. His hand was very steady as he replaced cup and saucer on desk. His tone was offhand when he spoke.

'What is so special about Cossack – the mechanism?'

Bellenger glanced over his shoulder at Monica. Tweed repeated the assurance he'd given when Bellenger arrived – that Monica had top vetting. 'In fact, if anything happened to me, she'd have to carry on.'

'Delayed action detonation for one thing. A saboteur could carry an object no larger than the smallest pocket calculator, stand thirty miles from the mine – or bomb – press a button and *bang!* The most advanced form of the old World War Two magnetic mine we've ever encountered. For one thing . . .'

'And for another?'

'It's size – in ratio to its appalling destructive power. It is quite small. About one foot in diameter. And it's death to any sizeable naval vessel. Take a submarine. They drop it within thirty miles of one of our subs. Our chaps are dead – that means they're so many fathoms under, all engine power switched off. No one even drops a spoon. Cossack homes in on them, even comes up to the hull, attaches itself like the suckers of an octopus with a revolutionary magnetic system. Someone presses the button. Our sub splits in two, is blown out of the water in a million bits.'

'How does it home in if everything is switched off and silent.'

'The men inside have to breathe,' Bellenger said grimly.

'So?'

'Cossack has an ultra-sensitive chemical probe which picks up carbon dioxide – even through a hull of sheet steel. How much carbon dioxide do you imagine a sub's crew breathes out?'

'Sounds a bit diabolical.' Tweed sipped more coffee. 'But the men who despatch the mine or bomb – from a plane, another sub, whatever. They *breathe* . . .'

'I see where you're heading,' Bellenger commented. 'Cossack's sensitivity to carbon dioxide is controlled. The pocket calculator device again. Press another button and the carbon dioxide probe comes into action. We've no defence as yet. All that – and the Triton Three. Only the timer device is second rate.'

'I think,' Tweed said, checking his watch under the level of his desk, 'you've put me into the picture.'

'And now you can put me in the picture. How did that bomb in Norfolk get there? Admiralty only let me come in the hope you'd give me a lead on that.'

'I simply have no idea, no lead, no clue. I'm sorry.'

'But you'll let me know if you unearth one?'

Bellenger was standing up. Not a man to waste time. Either Tweed didn't know or wasn't telling. For the moment. Bellenger recognized a man who couldn't be talked into saying anything he didn't want revealed. They shook hands, Tweed saw him to the front entrance, came back to his office.

'Now do you believe Lysenko?' Monica asked vehemently.

'No. I'm still dubious . . .'

'For God's sake. After listening to Bellenger – and Lysenko telling you about the theft from that bloody Sevastopol depot?'

'Lysenko would know someone had obtained a sample as Bellenger so quaintly puts it. They'll keep careful checks on the numbers of Cossacks they have. It would embroider his story – make it sound more convincing when I found out, as he knew I would.'

'So you think it's a wild goose chase?'

'I may know more after Geneva.'

14

La-Chaux-de-Fonds, centre of the Swiss watch-making industry, lies high up in the Jura Mountains near the French frontier. The modern buildings are white, antiseptic-looking blocks, the streets laid out on the American grid system, forming perfect rectangles. Set amid rolling green Alpine pastures, the place had an unreal atmosphere – like some vast laboratory, Klein thought.

Behind the wheel of the Mercedes hired in Geneva, he drove along the rue de la Paix, home of the watch-making factories. 12.55 p.m. The street was deserted. He drove slowly past a three-storey edifice, headquarters of Montres Ribaud, one of the leading watch-makers.

Pulling in at the kerb beyond Ribaud, he checked the time, kept the motor running. It is doubtful whether Louis Chabot, hidden away in Larochette, would have recognized him. Klein wore dark-tinted wrap-round glasses; a soft hat concealed his black hair; a polo-necked sweater made his lean jaw seem longer.

Promptly at 1 p.m. Gaston Blanc emerged from the Ribaud building, carrying a large case. Klein watched him approaching in his rear-view mirror. Then – as arranged – he drove slowly on, turned down an equally deserted side street and stopped.

Gaston Blanc was a small, plump-faced man. He wore gold-rimmed spectacles and stooped as he walked. The result of years of bending over a work-bench, Klein guessed. Blanc was Ribaud's Director of Research, reputed to be the most brilliant in Switzerland.

Klein had the front passenger door open when Blanc arrived. The Swiss deposited his case on the back seat, climbed in beside Klein, who drove off immediately without any kind of greeting.

'I will give you route instructions,' Blanc said in French. 'We don't talk until we are outside the town.'

They drove along the ruler-straight main street, reached the end of the small town at a place called Les Eplatures. Following Blanc's directions, Klein swung left over a concrete bridge spanning the railway and climbed up a green Alp. They had the world to themselves as Klein turned off the road, stopping the car behind a copse of dark firs.

'You have the timers, the radio-control systems?' he asked.

'In the case behind us. Sixty timers, five control systems. You will approve the merchandise. The timers are completely waterproof. As requested,' Blanc continued in his soft sibilant voice. 'One delicate matter. Payment . . .'

'I have it in my pocket. It's yours – once I'm satisfied with what you've produced. Have you met the specification?'

'Oh, yes. Of course.' Blanc sounded smug. 'Your specification was clever, very clever. I've never been asked to design anything so sophisticated. It was quite a challenge . . .'

'Let's get on with it.'

Blanc unzipped the case. Neatly packed inside was a collection of white cardboard boxes. Blanc opened one, took out a tissue wrapped package, handed it to his client. Klein produced a pair of chamois gloves and slipped them on before taking the box.

'Very wise,' Blanc commented. 'No fingerprints. I prefer dealing with professionals . . .'

Half an hour later Klein was satisfied. The instrumentation was an engineering work of art. The plastic control boxes – no larger than small pocket calculators – enabled a man to detonate the timers over distances varying from one to fifty kilometres.

The timer devices were equally good, fitted with magnetic clamps. Once attached to a bomb, Blanc explained, they were immovable. The control boxes worked over the long distances through the medium of an ultra-high frequency radio wave.

'You understand how the system works?' Blanc asked.

'Perfectly. Now, payment. Here you are.'

Still wearing the chamois gloves, he leaned across Blanc, opened the compartment facing the Swiss, took out a thick envelope and handed it to him. He waited until Blanc had closely examined the bearer bond.

'As you know, a bearer bond is untraceable, the most negotiable form of money.'

'I know that.' Blanc stared at the man beside him. 'This is for only half a million Swiss francs. The agreed fee . . .'

'Was one million,' Klein snapped. 'You still have to make the delivery. You get the second bearer bond when you've completed the job. You have made the arrangements, I hope?'

'Of course. My contact with Transportation at the Glasshouse was most cooperative . . .'

'The Glasshouse?'

'It's the Vevey locals' name for the Nestlé chocolate headquarters building. As you know, the chocolate *usine* – where they make the stuff – is at the small town of Broc north-east of Vevey. This evening, precisely at six the case is handed to the Turkish driver of a certain truck. He has a consignment for Belgium – so he can personally deliver the case in Larochette on his way. He will have no trouble crossing the border . . .'

'We arranged this before. You have a car? Good. What make?'

'A Renault station-wagon. Why?'

'Because I want you to fetch your car now, taking that case with you. You then come back here and drive to Broc. I'll follow you. Once the case is aboard the truck the second bearer bond is in your hands.'

'You didn't tell me this before . . .'

'Don't argue. You want the money? And the Turk will know you presumably. We do it my way . . .'

Gaston Blanc didn't like it, didn't like it one bit as he drove his Renault through Neuchâtel and along the lakeside to Yverdon. From there he headed due south for Lausanne and the autoroute near the shore of Lake Geneva.

He kept glancing in his rear-view mirror and always Klein's black Mercedes was one or two vehicles behind him. Blanc disliked any change of plan. And he had no idea why Klein had done this to him.

His feelings about Klein were mixed. He knew nothing about the man except that he'd approached him weeks ago with a letter of introduction from a previous client. It was the money which had tempted Blanc. One million francs! Never before had he earned so much from what he quaintly termed in his own mind a 'freelance' job. Which meant he used his company's facilities to produce equipment paid for privately, money tucked away in his secret bank account in Geneva.

He drove through Lausanne, heading for Vevey. He glanced once more in his mirror. Klein was immediately behind him. Those eyes! They seemed to stare into the very depths of a man's soul. Cold as ice. Yet, on other occasions, Klein had shown an amiable side, encouraging Blanc to talk of his problems with his wife. He had even told him about his mistress in Berne . . .

Klein, his gloved hands on the wheel, checked his watch. They would arrive in Broc early. That mustn't happen. He had always planned that Blanc would carry the case of timers. That eliminated the outside chance that they would be intercepted by a routine patrol car check. If that happened Klein would simply drive on, leaving Blanc to explain.

He glanced in his wing mirror, saw the highway was as

empty behind as it was ahead. Pressing down his foot, he overtook Blanc, slowed, gestured with one hand for him to pull in at the lay-by. Alighting from his stationary vehicle, he walked back to the Renault.

'What is it?' Blanc asked irritably, poking his head out of the window.

'We're going to be early at Broc.' Klein opened the door, sat himself in the front passenger seat, shut the door. 'I drove over this route and timed it in sections. We don't want to hang around at Broc. Get there in time for you to hand that case to the Nestlé truck driver and leave immediately. Here is the exact address he has to deliver the case to . . .'

Blanc sat with hands clasped in his lap, made no move to take the card with a typed address. 'I've done what you asked me to,' he went on, not looking at Klein. 'You take the case – and give me my second half-million.'

'It's not going to happen that way.' Klein was relaxed, his hands clasped behind his neck. 'You wouldn't want me to make a phone call – to police headquarters in Berne. They'd be interested to hear about the terrorist groups you've supplied in the past . . .'

'You wouldn't . . .'

'Then there's the managing director of Montres Ribaud. He'd be intrigued to hear about you. To say nothing of your wife. Then you'd never use your secret funds to buy that villa you covet in Cologny – where you'd live happily ever after with Yvette from Berne. After you'd dumped your wife. How do you propose to dump her?' Klein asked in the same conversational tone.

'I have no idea,' Blanc said, his voice faint.

'Buy a Doberman – one of those fierce guard dogs. Train it to be loyal only to yourself. Teach it a word which means "Attack!" Then use the word when you are alone in the apartment with your wife. It will rip her to pieces. Who could blame *you*? The dog went mad. I won't even charge you for the idea.'

'It's quite horrible – your idea . . .'

Klein glanced sideways. He could see Blanc was already thinking about it. Klein sat in silence, watching the clock on the dashboard. He also kept an eye on the highway, but traffic was light. And no patrol cars.

'Time we moved,' he announced. 'You lead the way. As before.'

Blanc drove automatically for the rest of the journey, turning away from the lake at Vevey, heading north for Broc. He was stunned. All idea of forcing Klein to take the case had vanished from his mind.

How the devil did Klein know about his desire to live in Cologny? Cologny was the millionaire district on the southern shore of the lake just outside Geneva. A place where world-famous racing drivers lived, where Arab sheiks owned villas with grounds patrolled by guards and fierce dogs.

Dogs? The Dobermann idea wouldn't leave him alone. It seemed foolproof. Even the Swiss police would never suspect anything. He'd create an alibi for himself – so everyone would think the dog had killed her while he was away . . .

He slowed down as he approached the rendezvous, a lonely part of the road not too far from the Broc *usine*. Behind him the Mercedes was a hundred metres away. Blanc crawled to the bend, stopped, peered through the windscreen. The Nestlé truck was parked on the grass verge, also about a hundred metres ahead.

Blanc switched off the engine and proceeded in his precise way. First the card with the address for delivery which Klein had dropped on the seat. *Hotel de la Montagne, Larochette, Luxembourg.* He slipped this inside the envelope containing a one-thousand franc note – the driver's fee. About £350. Then he left the car, carrying the case, and walked to the truck.

Klein had watched all this through a monocular glass he had taken from his pocket. Once Blanc was out of sight he moved. He ran light-footed to the bend, peered round it. Blanc was climbing inside the cab of the Nestlé vehicle, a Ford truck with its body painted cream and a large red band above the chassis. At the rear was a heavy door with a large handle. A VD registration plate, showing it was registered in the Canton of the Vaud.

Klein lifted the bonnet of the Renault, reached in with his gloved hand, took out the distributor arm and hurled it over a hedge into the nearest field. Closing the bonnet, he returned to his Mercedes and waited.

Blanc reappeared within minutes, climbed inside and tried to start up the Renault. Klein waited until the Swiss had made six efforts to get the engine going, then drove alongside. He got out, leaned inside the window.

'It's gone dead on you. Leave it here. I'll drive you to Vevey station. Catch a train to Geneva . . .'

'I can't just leave my car here . . .'

'You can't hang around. I thought you said the bank would stay open to accept your bearer bonds.'

'It will . . .'

'Not all night. Takes ages to get a pick-up truck. By the time you get back to Geneva the bank will have given up – closed its doors.'

Blanc was in a dilemma. He didn't want to leave the car; even less did he want to carry around a million francs in negotiable bonds. If his pocket was picked anyone could cash the bonds in any bank in the world.

'I can't wait much longer,' Klein pressed. 'Do you want a lift or don't you?'

'Who at Montres Ribaud might have seen you making the timers?' Klein asked as he drove back to Vevey through growing dusk.

'Absolutely no one . . .'

'Why so confident?'

'Because I always worked on them late into the night. The building was empty.'

'But surely that is unusual? Someone belonging to the firm might have seen a light in your office if they passed it?'

'They would think nothing of it,' Blanc insisted. 'Often I work late for the company's work. You can concentrate – no interruptions from staff or phone calls. When do I get the balance of my fee?'

'Now.'

Klein drove with one hand on the wheel. The other slipped inside his pocket, took out a bulky envelope which he gave the Swiss. He watched with amusement as Blanc produced a pencil torch and closely examined the bearer bond for half a million francs.

'Satisfied?'

'I will be when I have deposited it with the bank. Can't you drive any faster?'

'Not in this treacherous light. Want to end up in hospital and have someone find those bonds?'

Klein was watching the dashboard clock without Blanc realizing it. He timed it so they arrived at Vevey station just after a local had left for Geneva. Blanc would have to catch the express coming up from the Valais. In fifteen minutes. Klein had memorized the timetable in his head. He pulled in by the station.

'Haven't you forgotten something?' Klein asked.

'Oh, the blueprints I made for the devices. I was worrying about my car. Here they are. Now, I must catch my train . . .'

'The express isn't due yet. Wait a minute.'

Klein opened the envelope, took out the folded contents. Two blueprints. He borrowed Blanc's pencil torch to check them, then handed it back.

'Satisfied?' enquired Blanc, mimicking Klein's earlier query.

There was a hint of smugness in his tone which made Klein look at him quickly. Then he guessed the Swiss had been playing a little game with him. For the first time he misunderstood the plump little man. Blanc reached for the door handle.

'Two more things,' Klein said. 'I may have a similar job for you later,' he lied. 'Another million francs . . .'

'I'd have to think about it.'

'A million and a quarter.'

'Get in touch when you're ready. There was something else?'

'Yes. Travel first-class to Geneva. Remember what you have in your pocket. It will be safer. Train travel can be dangerous.'

'You are probably right. Good night . . .'

It was a relief for Blanc when he boarded the express. He had worried in case Klein suggested driving him back to Geneva. This was the last thing Klein thought of as he drove the Mercedes into a parking lot near the station.

Unlocking the boot, he took out a large hold-all bag, relocked the car and walked into the hotel facing the station. The toilets led off from the public restaurant. Keeping an eye on his watch, Klein worked quickly. He was just in time to buy a first-class ticket to Geneva as the express came in. He watched Blanc board a first-class coach and ran to board the train himself moments before it departed.

Blanc sat in the non-smoking section – divided off from the smoking area by a door with a window in the upper half. The express had left Lausanne. The next stop, Geneva, was about twenty minutes away when Klein saw what he had hoped for.

The Swiss was the only passenger in his part of the coach – as was the case with Klein. Blanc, suffering from nervous reaction to his recent experience, stood up and made for the lavatory. It was situated in the exit, between his coach and the next one.

Inside the toilet, Blanc relieved himself and at once felt

the tension draining out of his system as he washed his hands. He used a tissue to clean his glasses. He wasn't at all sure he would ever accept another commission from Klein.

What really worried him was that Klein seemed to know everything about his most intimate life – whereas Blanc knew nothing about Klein. Where he came from. His nationality. What he was up to. It was not the way Blanc usually undertook his 'freelance' assignments. The trouble was the million francs had proved too tempting.

At least I've got them, he thought as he straightened his tie, checked his watch. Not long before he arrived in Geneva. He would take a cab to the bank. Safer. Klein had been right on that point. He opened the door and froze.

It took him a few seconds to recognize the man in the waterproof hat who stood apparently waiting to use the lavatory. He also wore a long dark blue waterproof coat which came to below his knees and was buttoned to the neck. Klein . . .

'You! What is this?'

'Keep your voice down. Something has gone wrong . . .'

Klein eased himself inside the toilet before Blanc recovered from his shock and re-locked the door. He was carrying the large hold-all bag and spoke again rapidly.

'There is something wrong with one of those bearer bonds. I have to come to the bank with you – so I can countersign it.'

'Why? A bearer bond doesn't need . . .'

As he spoke he reached a hand inside his breast pocket for the two envelopes. Klein glanced down, swore, remarked that his shoe-lace was undone. Dropping the bag, he bent down to attend to it. He stood up again suddenly. His right hand gripped the knife he had plucked from the sheath strapped to his leg. His left hand pushed back Blanc's jaw, exposing the throat. With one swift movement Klein slit it from ear to ear. A second hideous red mouth appeared below Blanc's chin.

113

Blood spurted, gushed, splashing Klein's coat. Blanc uttered a brief moan-gurgle and sagged back on the lid of the toilet seat. Klein wiped the knife on Blanc's suit, shoved it back inside the sheath. Blanc's head had slumped sideways, his eyes wide open behind the gold-rimmed spectacles which hung askew. He looked almost ridiculous, except for the growing lake of dark red spreading down his shirt front.

Klein reached inside his pocket with his gloved hand, took out the envelopes. No point in throwing away a million francs. He checked his watch. Four minutes to Geneva's Cornavin station – where the train ended its journey. He examined himself in the mirror. Only the coat was stained.

Stripping off the coat, he folded it inside out, extracted a plastic bag from a local department store from the hold-all. There was a spot of blood on his right glove. He dropped both gloves inside the plastic bag which was already weighted with stones.

He slipped the screwed-up plastic bag inside his jacket pocket. Next he put the folded coat inside the hold-all and zipped up the bag. The train was slowing down. Too late for anyone to be waiting to use the lavatory. He counted off precisely two minutes on his watch after the train had stopped. All passengers would have disembarked.

Taking a small leather pouch from his other jacket pocket, he selected a tool like a small screwdriver. Picking up the hold-all, he opened the door, peered out. Not a sound. Emerging into the deserted exit area, he glanced in both directions and fiddled with the closed door, sliding the notice to *Occupé*. He was the last passenger to leave the express as he strolled towards the exit hall.

The next job was to get rid of the hold-all, the blood-spattered coat which had protected his suit. The coat had been bought in Harrods, London, over a year before. Untraceable. And several sizes too large. Its eventual discovery would give the police no idea of his true measurements.

Walking to the baggage container section, he chose one at random, opened the door, shoved the hold-all inside, adjusted the mechanism to a twenty-four hour period, fed in coins, locked it and took away the key.

At the station canteen he bought a doughnut, asked them to put it in a paper bag and walked off. Ten minutes later he stood on the footbridge crossing the Rhône near the Hotel des Bergues. With one hand he fed pieces of bun to swooping gulls, with the other he dropped the plastic bag into the tumbling current. A pair of gloves could give information about the size of his hands – and one was spotted with blood. The bag sank into the torrent, was followed by the baggage container key.

Klein walked straight back to Cornavin Gare. Shutting himself inside a phone booth, he dialled the number of the Hotel de la Montagne. Hipper answered almost at once.

'Klein here. The delivery is on the way, should arrive before dawn.'

'I shall be here to receive it,' the soft pedantic voice replied.

'Don't forget to give the driver his *reward*. I shall be there sometime tomorrow.'

'Our friend from the south has arrived . . .'

'I'll see him . . .'

'He is restless . . .'

Klein broke the connection without comment. Short phone calls were a strict maxim with him – even from a public call box. He returned to the baggage container section, took out another key and collected the Samsonite case he had deposited earlier. He checked his watch. He'd have to keep moving.

He carried the case to the men's lavatory, locked himself inside a cubicle and perched the case on the toilet lid. Ten minutes later he came out again. He had entered the cubicle dressed like a businessman. He emerged looking like a holiday-maker.

He was now wearing a windcheater and a pair of clean blue denims. Horn-rimmed glasses completed the transformation. He bought a second-class ticket to Basle and was just in time to board the express. When a girl came along with a trolley he bought a carton of coffee as the train left Geneva far behind. He enjoyed the drink. It had been thirsty work. And once again he had the satisfaction of not having left a single clue behind.

Half an hour after the Basle Express left for northern Switzerland a woman cleaner noticed the toilet in the stationary express at Cornavin which said *Occupé*. It bothered her – a passenger could be ill inside. She called a guard.

The guard produced a bunch of keys, chose a flat ended instrument and eased back the lock. Taking a deep breath, he pushed open the door and the cleaning woman peered inside. That was when she began to scream and scream and scream . . .

15

'We may well be chasing a phantom, a man who doesn't exist any more,' Tweed told Paula as the Swissair machine continued its descent.

'Has this phantom a name? Or am I asking the wrong question? I do realize I'm very much the new recruit.'

'Igor will do. Another Russian based in Geneva swears he saw him in the city four weeks ago. I have to decide whether he's right or not. More I can't tell you. Yet . . .'

He had given Paula the window seat and she was peering out of the window as the plane completed a right-angled turn and headed straight down the centre of Lake Geneva. They were due to land at midday.

'What a marvellous view,' she enthused. 'Those mountains over there. What are they?'

'The Jura.'

The aircraft was half-empty in first-class. The seats behind and in front were empty, so they were able to talk freely as the descent continued. Paula looked at her Swiss watch.

'I wonder where this was made?'

'Probably at La-Chaux-de-Fonds. A town up in those Jura mountains. Funny place. None of your old-fashioned Swiss chalets with window-boxes. More like a child's town built of bricks – then enlarged to normal building size. A bit stark.'

'Do I get to meet this Russian? The one who says he saw this phantom? He knows you're coming?'

'I'll see him first. And no, he doesn't. I'm hoping to catch him off balance.'

He glanced at Paula who was staring out of the window again. She was dressed perfectly for the occasion. A classic two-piece suit with pleated skirt and a pussy bow at the neck of her blue blouse. Would he have to unleash her on Sabarin he wondered? He doubted it. Bloody waste of time, the whole trip. He looked glum as the aircraft descended on the final run-in to Cointrin Airport.

Yuri Sabarin agreed to come immediately to the Hotel des Bergues when Tweed phoned the number Lysenko had given him. Which made Tweed even more sceptical. The Russians normally took their time – to emphasize their self-importance, to show how busy they were. Paula waited in her own room while Tweed paced back and forth in his bedroom. The second surprise was when the Russian arrived on time. The third was his opening remark after he met Tweed.

'This is an appropriate place for our discussion. It is here where I saw Zarov.'

'Actually in this hotel?'

Yuri Sabarin was a small, wiry, lean-faced and energetic man who, Tweed estimated, would be in his thirties. He was also dressed smartly in a pale grey suit, blue-striped shirt and a pale blue tie. One of the new breed Gorbachev was using? His command of English was excellent.

'No, outside this hotel,' Sabarin smiled. 'If we could go downstairs to the small restaurant I could show you exactly – Le Pavillon.'

On the spur of the moment Tweed changed his mind, phoned to Paula, asked her to come to his room. Sabarin was not what he had expected. He introduced Paula and they went downstairs in the elevator. Sabarin led the way through the reception hall and into the restaurant Tweed knew well.

It faced the street with windows overlooking the Rhône beyond. 'Watch to see if you think he's telling the truth,' Tweed whispered as they followed the Russian who seemed at home in one of Geneva's best hotels. The PM had allocated a generous budget for what Tweed still felt was a useless exercise.

Sabarin made for an empty window table. They were almost the only customers at three in the afternoon. The Swiss eat early and get back to their desks, abhorring the long business lunch. He pulled out a window chair for Paula and Tweed intervened.

'Why are we sitting here?'

'Because I was – when I saw him . . .'

'In which chair?'

'This one.' It was the chair he had offered Paula. Tweed shook his head. 'Then I want you sitting there – so we can reconstruct exactly how it happened . . .' He heard himself speaking and it reminded him of his days back at the Yard in the days when he was investigating a murder case. 'Paula can sit opposite you,' he continued. 'I will sit alongside –

so I get a similar view. Ah, here is the waitress. Coffee for everyone. Good, that's settled.'

He sat alongside Sabarin and looked out of the window without speaking for a short time. The sidewalk was immediately beyond the window and passers-by walked close to the glass. He kept up his silence, wanting to unsettle the Russian, to undermine some of his confidence. Thankfully, Paula followed his lead, saying nothing as she also stared out towards the swift-moving waters of the Rhône. Tweed waited until coffee had been served.

'It was after dark when you think you saw him?' he suggested.

'No! It was just about this time of day. That is why I wanted you to come down.' Sabarin checked his watch. 'He walked past this window at 3.10 p.m. exactly.'

'How do you know the time so precisely?'

'Because I looked at my watch before I jumped up and rushed outside. Through the main exit. I was too late. He had disappeared. I came back in here . . .'

'Wondering whether you'd been mistaken?' Tweed pressed.

'No! It was him. Igor Zarov. There's only one.'

'How was he dressed?'

'Dark blue two-piece suit, blue-striped shirt, plain blue tie. No hat . . .'

'Colour of shoes?'

'No idea,' Sabarin responded promptly. 'Couldn't see.'

Which made sense, Tweed thought. Even sitting by the window, passers-by walked so close you couldn't see their footwear.

'One thing was different from when I last saw him,' Sabarin continued. 'His face was chalk-white. He used to be ruddy-complexioned – that's the Georgian side coming out. For a second that did make me wonder, but only for a second.'

'When did you last see him?' Tweed fired at him.

'About two-and-a-half years ago. In Moscow.'

That fitted in with what Lysenko had told him, Tweed

thought. *He disappeared two years ago from East Germany.* That was what the GRU chief had said. Sabarin was talking volubly.

'I knew him well. You see, we worked together for a year in a certain section. We went out drinking in the evening. He was a strange chap . . .'

'What did he drink? A heavy drinker?'

'Vodka, like me. No, one glass was enough. He said he was giving up alcohol. It muddled his brain.'

'A strange chap – strange in what way?'

'First, he was a brain-box. We all knew that. He had a very mixed personality. He could charm any woman.' Sabarin looked at Paula. 'You would have fallen for him. But at other times he was as cold as ice. He frightened all of us when he was in that mood. We felt that if we got in his way and he could have eliminated us with a flick of his fingers, he'd have done just that.'

'When he walked past this window,' Tweed asked, 'do you think he saw *you*?'

'Definitely not. He was walking in a trance, his mind fixed on some problem . . .'

'Walking fast?' People hurrying past the window came and went in seconds.

'No, he strolled past, very erect, staring ahead . . .'

'I'd like to try an experiment. Both of you wait here. I'm going to stroll past that window myself. He did come from that direction?'

'Yes. Towards me as I was sitting here – towards the rue du Mont Blanc.'

Tweed left the restaurant by the entrance which leads direct on to the street. He paused outside until an elegant woman walked past towards the window, a woman wearing a cream suit, carrying a fur over one arm, a single string of pearls round her shapely neck. He strolled after her.

As he reached the window he deliberately glanced inside where the Russian was sitting. Even strolling you had to make a deliberate effort to look inside Le Pavillon. He

120

came back through the main entrance to the hotel, sat down again.

'Someone passed this window just before I did. Tell me what they looked like, what they were wearing.'

'A stunning brunette. Wearing a two-piece cream suit. She had a single string of pearls round her neck. Oh, yes, and she carried a sable fur over her right arm.'

'How do you know it was sable?'

'Please!' Sabarin made a dismissive gesture. 'I am Russian. I have attended the fur auctions in Moscow. I certainly know sable when I see it!'

Paula intervened for the first time. Giving Sabarin her most encouraging smile, she asked the question quickly. 'When this man passed you were eating a meal?'

'No. I only came in here for coffee. Why?'

'I just wondered,' she said, and left it at that.

'One more question,' Tweed said, 'and then I think we are done. Oh, your English is very good . . .' He brought a brief-case up on to the table, took out an envelope. The Engine Room crowd down in the Park Crescent basement had been busy – photographers as well as their Identikit artist.

'Thank you for the compliment,' Sabarin replied. 'I have spent time in London. I used to go into pubs, buy a pint and listen for colloquialisms – how the English of different classes talk. What have you there for me?'

'Four different Identikit pictures.' Tweed looked round the empty restaurant. The waitress was cleaning the counter some distance away. He handed the envelope to Sabarin. 'Are any of them remotely like Zarov?'

Sabarin extracted four large photocopies. The Engine Room had used the same paper, the Identikit artist had drawn three portraits from imagination. The Russian handed the fourth back, inserted the others inside the envelope.

'That's him.'

He had chosen the picture Lysenko had provided at the Gastof zum Bären. Tweed stared at the sketch. By some

121

curious technical trick the eyes were horrifically life-like – almost bulging off the paper.

'It's an excellent likeness,' Sabarin continued. 'Better than a photograph, oddly enough. It has captured his personality. Maybe you can see now why he frightened us when he was in one of his Arctic moods. Ruthless and ferocious as a wild boar. I wonder where he is now?'

'Well, did you believe him?' Tweed asked as they crossed the footbridge over the Rhône.

'Yes, I did,' said Paula, using one hand to stop her skirt flying up. A strong wind was blowing down the lake from the east. 'So the phantom, this Zarov, may be for real?'

'I'm still dubious. Sabarin could have been trained in how to react to my grilling. Why the question about was Sabarin eating at the moment he saw Zarov – if he did?'

'Because a man eating his lunch is less likely to notice what is going on outside the window.'

'Very true. You handled yourself well back at Le Pavillon.'

'Is that why you're telling me a bit more about what's going on?'

'Yes,' Tweed admitted. 'And the man we're going to see is Alain Charvet, an ex-policeman and a contact of mine. Never to be mentioned back at Park Crescent. Charvet, using his old police connections, runs a profitable information consultancy. He knows a lot about what's happening underground in Western Europe.'

'And that man, Beck, who called while we were in the restaurant and thought you were out. Do I get to know about him?'

'Bad news,' Tweed replied as they reached the far bank and turned along the waterfront. 'Arthur Beck. From the Taubenhalde in Berne. Chief of the Federal Police. God knows what he wants – or how he knows I'm here.'

'When we came through Passport Control at the airport I noticed an officer took a long hard look at your passport, then checked it against a list of names before he handed it back.'

'Beck can wait. And you can bet on one thing. He'll be back. At the moment we have other fish to fry. Alain Charvet.'

'Where are we meeting him?'

'His favourite rendezvous. The Brasserie Hollandaise in the Place de la Poste. It's old-fashioned and rather nice. Let me do the talking.'

La Brasserie Hollandaise was almost empty at four in the afternoon. Paula looked round the large room and thought it very Dutch. A quarry-tiled floor, the windows screened by heavy lace curtains, leather banquettes along the walls topped with brass rails. The place was illuminated by large milky globes. Tweed walked towards a corner banquette where a thin-faced man in his early forties sat nursing a beer.

'Alain Charvet,' he introduced. 'This is my new assistant, Paula Grey.'

Charvet stood up, formally shook her hand, his eyes staring straight at hers. Yes, she thought, you'll know me should we meet again. They sat down, Tweed ordered coffee for two, and handed an envelope to Charvet containing a one-thousand franc note.

'Is anything happening? You can talk freely in front of Paula. Fully vetted.'

'What are you looking for?' asked Charvet. 'Not like you to be so vague.'

'I don't really know,' Tweed admitted, heard himself say the words and inwardly cursed the futility of this enterprise. 'Even rumours might help,' he added.

'Rumours are all I have. You know I keep in touch with my friends in France. They keep mumbling about rumours of some huge operation being mounted. Sometimes it's about the hijacking of a ship. I ask you! Then they refer to someone nicknamed The Recruiter. All hot air.'

He was speaking French. Paula was fascinated by the way he used the language. So different from Parisians – but it was said the most perfect French was spoken by the Genevoises. Charvet made a quick gesture as he went on.

'As for this country, there was the big gold bullion robbery two months ago in Basle. Two banks in one night. They got away with twelve million francs of gold.'

Twelve million. Paula did a quick calculation in her head. Over four million pounds. She sensed Tweed's awakening interest as he leaned forward closer to Charvet.

'Both banks in Basle, you mean?'

'Yes. You know the city, of course. They were both near the Bankverein tram stop on the way to the railway station. No clue as to how they moved the gold, but the police have called the robbers The Russian Gang.'

Tweed sat drinking his coffee, absorbing the information. He had a faraway look Monica would have recognized. He was trying to link up this new development with the meagre data he already possessed.

'Why The Russian Gang?' he asked eventually.

'It was the UTS lot, which is surprising. Load of cranks.'

'You mean the Free Ukraine movement?' Paula asked. 'Those pathetic people who were born in the Ukrainian Republic and escaped to the West. They still believe that one day they can bring about a Free Ukraine state – independent of Russia. Mostly they operate out of Munich, pursuing their dream.'

'Yes.' Charvet looked surprised, addressing Tweed. 'Miss Grey has a lot inside her head. Most people have never even heard of the UTS.'

'How do the police know?' Tweed asked.

'One of them was dragged out of the Rhine shortly after the robbery, his throat slit from ear to ear. He carried papers which soon led Arthur Beck to Munich – to identifying him. Presumably they organized the bullion theft to finance their activities.'

'Presumably . . .' Tweed had drifted off into another bout of silence. 'I don't think it's what I'm looking for,' he said eventually.

'Of course not,' Charvet replied. 'I'm just reporting whatever comes to mind. I know I'm not being very helpful.'

'That man your French friends have nicknamed The Recruiter. I don't understand why?'

'Oh, he's supposed to be paying out huge sums to build a team of villains – top specialists in their fields. No one tells me anything specific. You have to realize some of my contacts do spread pure gossip rather than say they have nothing.'

'And that's it?'

'I am very much afraid so.' Charvet peered inside the envelope Tweed had given him. 'This is far too much for rubbishy gossip.'

'Keep it,' Tweed said as he stood up. 'On account of another day.'

'I'm sorry,' Paula apologized as they made their way across the footbridge in the dusk. 'It must have sounded as though I was showing off when I babbled on about the UTS.'

'Quite the opposite. Charvet was impressed. That's good. One day I may want you to come and see him if I'm tied up. Now he will talk to you. And he will never let another soul know you exist.'

'Was it all a waste of time?'

'I think so. Charvet makes his living dealing with *facts*. He has a reputation to keep. That's why he kept emphasizing he was passing on rumours – gossip.'

'What about this gold bullion robbery in Basle? You did seem intrigued by that news. It's the first I've heard of it.'

'Me too. But the Swiss won't want to broadcast a thing like that. Their banks have a reputation for being the safest in the world. One thing puzzles me. Brr! It's getting chilly. I'll be glad to get back inside the hotel.'

'And what puzzles you?'

'That a ramshackle outfit like the UTS could organize not one – but two – successful robberies. And from Swiss banks!'

'What's the answer?'

'No idea. Here we are. Let's dive inside. Come along to my room when you're ready. We'll talk about it a bit more.'

Tweed had taken off his lightweight Burberry, wishing he'd worn a heavier coat, had a quick wash, when he decided to call Charvet at his apartment.

'Alain, Tweed here again. That chap, The Recruiter, does this character have a name?'

'More like a ghost than a real person. It's all gossip like I told you . . .'

'But does he have a name? It is a man, I assume?'

'So the grapevine says. Which is about all it does say. And yes they do toss around a name. Common enough in a number of countries. It's Klein.'

16

Klein was the first passenger to get off the train at Basle. He hurried to the French station, which is attached to the main station. A curious city, Basle. Three countries meet here – Switzerland, France and Germany. Only a short train ride away is Basle Bad Bahnhof, the German station.

He used French francs to buy a single first-class ticket to Brussels. The express was waiting and he settled himself in an empty compartment. As the train began to move through the night he checked over in his mind a list of the tasks he had accomplished.

Timers. They were on their way aboard the Nestlé truck bound for Larochette. By using trains Klein would arrive there before the truck. Gaston Blanc had been eliminated.

And no one could connect Klein with that episode. He had bought a single ticket from Geneva to Basle. Now he was travelling with another single ticket to Brussels. That severed the link with Switzerland.

But the day's work was not yet finished. There was still the problem of the Turkish driver bringing the timers. A problem he would solve soon. Klein settled back to sleep. He had an alarm clock inside his head, could always wake before he reached his destination . . .

Fifteen minutes before the express arrived at Luxembourg City, Klein woke, checked his watch. He extracted from his case a small slim black box, shoved it in his pocket and made for the toilet. He seemed to spend half his life inside lavatories he thought with macabre humour as he opened the box.

Among other articles in separate compartments in the velvet-lined box were a tube of foundation cream, a container of light-coloured face powder, cottonwool and a small brush. He worked quickly, rubbing into his face a little of the foundation cream with his fingers. He then applied some of the powder, brushing off the surplus with the complexion brush. He studied the effect in the mirror.

That make-up girl in the closed city of Gorky had taught him a thing or two. 'Most people don't realize,' she had said, 'that a man's complexion – especially someone with a high colour like yours – is one of their most distinguishing features.' Mind you, later he had taught her a thing or two stretched out on the leather couch.

The stark white image stared back at him. It gave him a somewhat sinister appearance. Intimidating. Satisfied, he packed his equipment back inside the box and returned to his compartment after taking a pee.

Again he was the first passenger off the express when it rolled into Luxembourg City. The Volvo station wagon was parked outside the station where Hipper had left it earlier, taking a cab back to Larochette.

Klein unlocked the car with the key Hipper had provided, slid behind the wheel, inserted the ignition key and drove off. Reaching the turn-off from the main highway, he pressed his foot down. Klein moved along the crag-walled winding road at even higher speed than Hipper had driven. Louis Chabot would have been terrified.

It was close to midnight when Louis Chabot returned from his walk through the deserted village and along the winding gorge where, Hipper had told him, the old railway had once run. My God, it was good to get away from that mausoleum, La Montagne. From the rooms with furniture covered with sheets. Only the kitchen was modern and in use.

He heard the car coming from the same direction he had been driven and stepped back inside a narrow alley. The Volvo braked suddenly, swerved into the drive in front of the hotel, sending up a shower of pebbles.

'Bloody maniac,' Chabot growled.

He remained hidden as the driver got out after dousing his lights. The figure was no more than a pale silhouette in the shadows as he disappeared round the side to the rear entrance. Chabot decided to wait, lit a Gauloise. He was good at waiting. Sometimes he'd had to wait hours for the target he'd been commissioned to kill.

He might learn something. Which was more than he ever would from that Hipper who was as informative as a wooden Indian. Half an hour later the Nestlé truck arrived, pulled in by the side of La Montagne. Chabot went on waiting. There were some things it might be better not to know. And Hipper *had* let slip a cargo of timers was expected.

Klein was amiable with the Turkish driver after he had handed over the case containing the timers. He poured him a glass of red wine in the kitchen, illuminated by a harsh fluorescent tube, then perched his buttocks on a table as he chatted to the driver in French.

'You are heading for Brussels now, I understand?'

'Yes . . .'

The greasy-haired, swarthy-complexioned Turk's command of the language was limited. Klein spoke slowly, kept it simple.

'There's been a landslide of rocks on the direct route. I will take you to Clervaux.' He produced a map folded to the right section, showed the driver. 'From there you can drive on to Brussels. You will never find the way on your own – at night it is easy to get lost in the Ardennes.'

'How you get back – from this Clervaux?'

'Easy. My friend here will follow in his car and bring me back. After I have taken you through the difficult bit.'

'You make me pay money for this?'

'God, no! The consignment of drugs you have brought is so important I am glad to see you safely on your way.'

A more intelligent mind might have wondered why such dangerous information had been revealed. But Klein had judged his man well. The Turk's Swiss work permit expired in two months and would not be renewed. He didn't worry about that. He'd be glad to get back to his family, to his wife, in the village a few kilometres outside Ankara.

He had saved a lot of money, sending it back home. But never before had he received so much for one simple job – a thousand-franc note. He had never even seen one before. He readily agreed to Klein's suggestion. He was standing up, finishing off his glass of red wine when Klein bumped against him, spilling wine down the Turk's front.

'I am so sorry . . .'

'It is nothing. Should we go now?'

Klein led the way to the truck, climbing up into the cab on the driver's side behind the wheel. The Turk stood looking up with a puzzled expression as Hipper ran to the Volvo.

'Get in the passenger seat,' Klein called down. 'I know the way. There are few signposts this side of Clervaux.'

The Turk shrugged, walked round the front and joined Klein. As the truck came out of the drive, heading away from Luxembourg City, followed by the Volvo, Chabot watched from inside his alley.

He didn't understand what was going on. Had the Nestlé truck delivered the timers? He peered out of the alley, saw the red tail-lights of the Volvo turning left, driving north. He went back to La Montagne.

He found the open bottle of red wine in the kitchen, poured himself a glass, drank it, then began his search for the timers. He searched all three floors, using a torch he had taken from his case, which was still packed. Chabot had a feeling he might want to leave Larochette quickly. But he didn't find the timers.

It was still the middle of the night when Klein stopped the truck. He had turned off the highway up a side track – in the headlight beams the Turk could see straight ahead a thin copse of pine trees. He looked in the wing mirror on his side. The headlights of Hipper's Volvo had stopped a few metres behind.

'What is happening?'

'I have to take a leak.' Klein patted his crotch. 'Now you can take over the wheel. You back the truck the short distance we came off the highway and continue north. You are near Clervaux. And I will pay you the rest of the money in a minute . . .'

More money? The Turk kept his face expressionless. He'd understood at Vevey he'd be paid one thousand francs. Had this man not known he had already been paid? The prospect of another one thousand franc note filled him with joy. He would buy his wife a present . . .

'Here you are.'

Klein had suddenly opened the other door, climbed up into the passenger seat. He held an envelope in his left hand. His right hand grabbed the Turk's long hair and jerked his head back. The Turk felt certain the hand couldn't hold his slippery mane. He lunged forward. Which was exactly the reaction Klein was expecting. His hand

130

opened, the palm shoved the head forward with all his force. There was a thud as the Turk cracked his skull on the wheel and lay still. Klein checked the neck pulse. Nothing. He nodded to Hipper who stood outside the foot of the passenger door, holding an inflated plastic bag.

'Dead.'

Klein spoke the single word as he jumped down from the cab, leaving the door open. He walked cautiously to the copse he had found a week earlier, looking for the right place. Beyond the sapling pines the earth dropped away sheer into an abyss.

'Let's get on with it. We have to get back to La Montagne. See what Chabot's been up to. He must be a marathon walker.'

Hipper went round to the driver's side where the Turk slumped over the wheel. He would never see Ankara, his waiting family again. Hipper perched on the edge of the cab, reached over, turned on the ignition. Klein had taken a small sachet of cocaine he'd bought on the Paris streets for an absurd sum, ripped the packet and scattered the contents inside the cab. Something for the forensic fanatics to think about – assuming any traces of the stuff survived.

Hipper waited while Klein checked the plastic bag of petrol the Luxembourger had handed him. A fuse protruded from the neck of the bag. He'd have to act fast. He took his lighter out, nodded again to Hipper standing in the cab. He really was a very small man.

Hipper adjusted the gear, jumped to the ground and grasped the brake. Klein nodded a third time as he lit the fuse. As Hipper released the brake and slammed the cab door shut Klein threw in the bag, slamming his own door shut. The vehicle was already moving down the slope.

There was a *whooshing* sound and light flared inside the cab. The truck trundled on downhill as Klein followed. It brushed aside the feeble trees, upended and vanished. Klein and Hipper ran to the edge. The truck plunged straight down the abyss past the rock face, went down a good hundred feet and hit the rocks at the bottom with a distant thud. For a few seconds it was very quiet. Then the base of the abyss exploded with a dull roar. Flames flared. Smoke drifted in the windless night up the side of the precipice. Klein sniffed. Smelt like burning flesh and petrol fumes.

His precautions were a waste of time. Inside the inferno the Turk was incinerated into almost a blackened skeleton.

'Better get back,' Klein commented. 'Another loose end dealt with. I'll drive.'

17

Tweed, like Paula, was an owl. Both were at their most alert when most of the world was going to bed. They had a late and leisurely dinner in Le Pavillon, talking about Alain Charvet, about why they were there.

'I just can't get a grip on a single hard fact,' Tweed complained. 'Maybe there isn't one to get hold of.' He drank more coffee, called for the bill and signed it.

'Why didn't you show Charvet the picture of Zarov?' Paula enquired.

'Because the fewer people who see it the better. That is, until we have something concrete to go on. The odd thing,' he ruminated, 'is I have used the word phantom several times – which shows I don't really believe in his existence. Then on the phone when I called Charvet to ask if the so-called Recruiter has a name, Charvet himself used the word ghost. You see?'

'See what?'

'Phantom. Ghost. Neither of us really believe in the existence of a mysterious mastermind. Zarov.'

'If he was really brilliant wouldn't he set out to make you think just that?'

Before he could reply the concierge from reception came to the table and whispered in Tweed's ear. 'Thank you,' he said. 'Tell him we'll be out there very shortly.' He waited until they were alone. 'Blast the man!'

'What's the matter now?'

'It's Arthur Beck again. Chief of the Federal Police. Waiting in the lobby to see me. At this hour. I suppose we'd better take him up to my room. Although what he can want I can't imagine.'

Seated on a couch by herself in Tweed's room Paula studied Beck. Not a bit like my idea of a top policeman, she thought. Dressed in a light grey business suit, a blue-striped shirt, a blue tie which carried a kingfisher emblem woven into the fabric, he looked more like a clever banker. Plump-cheeked, his most arresting feature was his alert grey eyes beneath thick dark brows the same colour as his thick hair. In his mid-forties, she guessed, his complexion was ruddy, that of a man who spent as much time as possible outdoors.

His movements were quick and he fiddled with a silver pencil as he watched Tweed, who had already made introductions. He showed rare surprise when Tweed spoke.

'I should tell you, Arthur, that I'm now a commander with the Anti-Terrorist Squad at Scotland Yard. Here is my warrant card.'

'I don't believe it.' Beck stared at the card and handed it back. 'You mean you've left the Service?'

'More complicated than that.' Tweed was mildly pleased with the shock he'd given his old friend. 'I also still hold my position with the Service. I'm working on a weird investigation. What I would like to know is why you took the trouble to fly from Berne to see me. And how you knew I was here.'

'Answer to first question, I didn't. I'm working on a murder case. A bit grisly.' He glanced at Paula. 'Answer to second question, the Passport Control man at Cointrin

133

thought your name rang a bell, checked it against his list, called me.'

'What murder case?' Tweed enquired. 'You don't get many of them here.'

'Well . . .' Beck smiled slightly. 'Seeing as you're now also with Scotland Yard means I can talk to you about anything.' Again he glanced at Paula.

'You used the word "grisly",' she said. 'Not to worry. I've a pretty strong stomach.'

'Funny business. Murdered chap discovered in a train at Cornavin which had finished its journey. Cleaning woman finds a lavatory locked, calls guard. He opens up. Inside, parked on the lavatory seat lid is this body of a man. Small and fat, head lolling to one side, mouth open . . .' He was looking towards Paula again. '. . . his throat slit from ear to ear, blood all down his shirt front . . .'

'Like a butchered pig,' Paula said, looking straight back at him. 'Like some more champers? Of course you would . . .'

'Why champagne?' Beck asked.

'To celebrate the company of such an agreeable guest,' she said, still gazing at him when she'd refilled his glass.

My God, Tweed thought, she's got him eating out of the palm of her hand. Arthur Beck! He saw the Swiss' hand rise from his lap and fall again. He'd been going to check his tie was neat, had stopped himself just in time.

'Any identification?' Tweed asked for something to say.

'Oh, yes. Which doesn't help. Research Director of Montres Ribaud, one of the top watch manufacturers up at La-Chaux-de-Fonds. Most brilliant watch designer in the country – the inner workings, I mean. A great loss.'

'Any clues?'

'Not yet. Only happened yesterday. Had a one-way first-class ticket in his pocket from Vevey to Geneva. That in itself is odd. No one at Ribaud can guess what he was doing in Vevey. The only thing there is the Nestlé Group HQ. We may know more tomorrow.'

'Why?'

'He had a private safe in his office. No one else knows the combination. I've got one of my chaps working on it now.'

'Got any further with the Russian Gang?' Tweed asked casually.

'Hell's teeth. How do you know about that? We've done a job keeping it out of the papers.'

'Someone told me. Can't reveal their identity. I also heard the UTS mob were the culprits. Strikes me as strange. What do you think?' Tweed asked.

'I thought the same thing,' Beck admitted. 'It was a highly skilled operation – not what you would associate with freaks like the UTS crowd. A free Ukraine! What a hope. A good idea, of course – it would enormously weaken Russia. A lost cause, though. Another thing about those two bank robberies. A special explosive was used to blow open the vaults.'

'What explosive?'

'No idea. One victim was the Zurcher Kredit Bank – and they have one of the so-called safest vaults in Switzerland. We put an army explosives expert on the job – happens to be a director of the Zurcher, and a colonel in the reserve. Tomorrow I fly to Basle by chopper to hear his report. Want to come with me?'

'Not in a chopper.' Tweed grimaced. 'Dislike the things. But we could go there by train, meet you in Basle.'

'That's arranged. Where can I contact you?'

'At the Hotel Drei Könige. What time of day?'

'Late afternoon, if that suits,' Beck replied. 'I'm waiting for Blanc's safe to be opened. Gaston Blanc, the murdered man found in the train. I have little hope.' He finished his second glass of champagne and stood up, thanking Paula profusely, shaking her hand as he smiled warmly. He threw the question at Tweed without warning.

'Why are you on my patch? Investigating what?'

'Rumours circulating Western Europe about some huge criminal operation being planned.'

'Really?' Beck looked surprised. 'Pure gossip. I wonder

that they send someone of your rank on a wild goose chase.'

'I wonder that myself,' Tweed confessed.

'Oh, one more question, you mentioned staying at that hotel in Basle as though you'd already decided to go there.'

'I had. Those robberies intrigue me.'

Tweed accompanied Beck in the lift, saw him to the front exit of the hotel. The Swiss turned to him as a driver opened the door of a parked car.

'I like your new assistant, Paula.' His eyes twinkled. 'You will have trouble concentrating on your job with her around.'

'The relationship is strictly professional,' Tweed replied.

'Oh, really? That's a new version.' He dug Tweed in the ribs, said he could be contacted at the local police HQ and climbed into the back of the car.

Explosives. The team. Finance. Tweed handed Paula the short list he'd scribbled on a hotel pad. 'Make anything of that?'

'Not a thing,' she said after studying it. 'Stop playing cat and mouse with me.'

Tweed eased himself more comfortably into the armchair. 'Let us just suppose there is something behind these rumours. The first item – explosives . . .' Without mentioning Lysenko he told her about the truck of explosives which had crashed the Turkish border and then disappeared. About the Greek ship *Lesbos* – which had left the Golden Horn and also disappeared. About the Armenian dragged out of the Bosphorus.

'I still don't get it,' Paula said eventually, 'I must be more than a bit thick.'

'Hardly. You're organizing some very big operation. You have the explosives. Next you need the team – to hire a bunch of cutthroats – professionals. All that costs *money*. Where is the finance going to come from?'

'A major gold robbery?'

'It's just possible. No more than that.'

'How would the organizer convert gold bullion into cash – he'd need to do that to pay the members of the team.'

'I have no idea,' Tweed admitted. 'Also, you heard about this murder of Gaston Blanc, found with his throat cut from ear to ear? That was how the Armenian truck driver who brought out the explosives into Turkey was killed. Then Charvet tells us they dragged a member of the UTS gang out of the Rhine – with his throat slashed from ear to ear.'

'Could be sheer coincidence.'

'You're right.' Tweed used a box of hotel matches to set light to his list, watched it burn in an ash-tray, emptied the relics down the toilet and flushed it. Paula was waving the empty champagne bottle when he came back.

'Like me,' Tweed said. 'Nothing in it. I admit frankly I really am floundering – just checking anything that catches my attention. We'd better get some sleep – see what the morning brings.'

The morning brought Arthur Beck, a grim-faced Beck. Tweed and Paula, who had just finished breakfast, took him up to Tweed's room. Beck planted his brief-case on a table, let Paula take his coat, said yes, he'd love coffee and sat staring at the brief-case.

'You'll never guess what we found inside Gaston Blanc's private safe – what's inside that brief-case.'

'So I won't try,' Tweed replied calmly.

'What do you think these are? Paula, you can look, too.'

He brought out a sheaf of six photocopies, unfolded them and laid them on the table. Paula covered them with a newspaper as room service arrived with coffee. When they were alone Tweed examined the diagrams carefully, then looked at Paula.

'Doesn't mean a thing to me. Some kind of engineering blueprints.' He looked at Beck. 'I give up.'

'So did I. Until I showed them to an inspector over at police HQ – who is an explosives expert. He says they are incredibly sophisticated bomb-timers.' He picked up two sheets. 'He says these are probably the control boxes. I'm taking this lot with me to show Colonel Romer this afternoon.'

'Who is he?'

'The bank director I told you about. The one who's providing me after two months with his report on the explosive used to blow the vaults. He's a demolition expert. He can bring down a mountain.'

'Basle could be interesting,' Tweed said quietly.

'More so than you might think. I had a phone call from the police chief there. They've just dragged out of the Rhine a second body – another member of the Russian Gang. Found in the weirdest place – the barge harbour on the north bank. A dredger hauled him out by chance.'

'How do you know who he is? There'd be decomposition after all this time in the water. You think he was shoved in from the harbour?'

'No. The current would naturally take him in there under certain conditions – if he was dropped in higher upstream. He's been there right under our noses. Identification? He had his papers inside one of those waterproof wallets. We checked his name with Munich. In case that's not enough, guess how he was murdered. His throat was cut . . .'

'From ear to ear,' Tweed completed.

'Do you think it's going to work?' Klein asked.

'Of course,' Chabot replied. 'This is my job.'

The question was the first sign of nervousness Chabot had seen Klein display. No, not nervousness. Excitement. A kind of mad exhilaration. The reaction disturbed the Frenchman.

The two men sat round the kitchen table in La Montagne, a table Chabot had scrubbed clean before starting work. One of the assembled timers lay inside its white metal box.

Chabot had used a watchmaker's glass (he always carried one) to handle the small pieces of precision metal, following the blueprint Klein had given him.

Klein had been fascinated to watch earlier how Chabot's stubby fingers had handled the bits and pieces with such delicate care. Now the only item missing from the timer was the detonator.

There had been a furious argument as to where Chabot should work. When Klein had returned with Hipper in the Volvo they had unlocked a cellar door and led Chabot down into the wine cellar, a stinking subterranean hole of tunnels which smelt of must. A rat had slithered over Chabot's foot. He had made no bones about it. He wasn't working in that hell-hole. Besides, he needed better lighting. The kitchen was the obvious place.

'You could be seen – working on the equipment,' Klein had objected.

'Shut it, for God's sake!' Chabot had burst out. 'Look at the window. Ten feet above the ground. And it faces that rock face. Who's going to see me in here? This is where I'm working '

Now they were waiting for the experiment to be completed. Hipper had taken a control box and was driving the Volvo a distance of approximately ten kilometres. He would stop the car in an isolated spot, take the control box and press the button Chabot had indicated.

'He's taking too long,' Klein complained. 'I hope to God he hasn't crashed, had an accident . . .'

Which was pretty rich, Chabot thought – considering the way I saw you driving that Volvo when you first arrived. He lit a Gauloise and relaxed back in his chair. Despite his impatience Klein noted the Frenchman's aplomb. It boded well for a man who was going to handle a mountain of high-explosive.

Click!

Klein almost jumped. Chabot checked his watch. He'd synchronized it with Hipper's before the Luxembourger had left, emphasizing he must also check the time at the moment he pressed the button. Only in that way could Chabot be sure detonation was instantaneous.

'It works!' Klein said, his voice highly-pitched.

'Of course.' Chabot took another drag at his cigarette, then took a sip of beer from the mug on the table. 'Now all I have to do is to assemble fifty-nine more of them. It won't happen overnight. How long do I have?'

'Time enough. Just get on with it. And keep down your nightly walks to the minimum. Hipper will get you food and drink.'

'Don't forget to leave me the cellar key. We'll keep the case down there – but I work up here. And I don't want to be asking Hipper's permission every time I want to take a pee. If you get my meaning.'

But Klein was leaving the kitchen, on his way upstairs to put on a businessman's suit, to pack a case. His mind was working ahead. Next on the list, as always. He had to arrive in Paris as soon as possible. Two important tasks.

To occupy Lara Seagrave's time with some convincing mission. And to hire the finest marksman in Western Europe.

18

'Let's take a tram,' Tweed said as they walked out of Basle Bahnhof into the sunshine. 'I seem to remember it's a Number Eight we want. Drops us almost outside the Drei Könige.'

'I like trams – but why?' asked Paula. 'You have a reason, I sense. You know Basle well, it seems.'

'Spent a month here once. There's the tram stop over there. Yes, I have a reason. One stop en route is Bank-verein. I want to see where those robberies took place.'

Less than a hundred yards from the ancient façade of the Bahnhof, they waited on an island between streets busy with traffic. Tweed checked with the driver he was right and they boarded a Number Eight. It trundled off and Tweed chose a seat on the right-hand side facing the way they were going.

The green tram curved along its track between venerable old buildings. Tweed told Paula many of them were erected between 1100 and 1200 AD. The loudspeaker system announced the next destination before they reached it. In a few minutes they heard the driver's voice again. *Bankverein.* The tram stopped. Tweed peered out.

'There's the Zurcher Kredit Bank,' he whispered. He looked round as passengers alighted, got on board. More heavy traffic. Just as he remembered it. Then the tram was on the move again.

'It beats me,' he said.

'What does?'

'Twelve million francs of gold bullion. How they got away with it. This is the centre of the city. Unless it was on a Sunday. The streets are deserted then . . .'

They got off a few stops further on and Paula saw The Drei Könige, The Three Kings, another ancient building. As they crossed the street Tweed pointed out the Rhine to her. Trams were cruising across a bridge over the wide river. Unlike Geneva, which had an air of excitement, Basle secmed peaceful despite the traffic.

The message was waiting for them in the room allocated to Tweed.

'Saucy,' Tweed said when Paula came along to his bedroom ten minutes later. He indicated a spray of flowers with a message written on a card. 'Those are for you – as though we're sharing a room.'

'Maybe he thinks we should,' Paula said after reading the note. *Welcome to Basle, Paula. Tweed, call me at this number . . . Arthur Beck.* 'The flowers are beautiful. Isn't that nice of him? And you've got the same marvellous view I have.'

She went across to the window which led on to a balcony. The Rhine flowed immediately below beyond a narrow walled walk for pedestrians. More trams rumbled over the bridge as a barge chugged under one of the spans, heading downstream. A great canvas cover masked the hold and the wheelhouse was close to the stern.

'I once spent a holiday with a boyfriend on a barge – smaller than that,' Paula said wistfully. 'We cruised down the Canal de l'Est from Dinant in Belgium on through France via the Canal de la Marne au Rhin – and emerged on to the Rhine itself just south of here. When are you going to call Beck?'

'I've called him.' Tweed stood beside her, watching the barge slide past without really seeing it. 'He'll be here any moment. And he's bringing Colonel Romer with him – the chap who lost the largest share of gold bullion in the robbery. Boss of the Zurcher.'

'Should I make myself scarce when they . . .'

The phone rang. Tweed shook his head as he went to pick up the receiver. 'You might as well stay. You could spot a point I miss.' He spoke rapidly in German, put down the receiver. 'As you probably gathered, they're on their way up.'

Beck ushered in a tall, well-built man with a trim moustache and wearing a navy blue business suit. His thick hair and brows were grey and he carried himself with a military stance. Beck made introductions. 'Commander Tweed . . . His assistant, Miss Paula Grey . . .'

Romer stared hard at both of them, decided they were trustworthy, plunged straight into the topic. 'You've heard we lost twelve million? That is, with the other bank. Chief of Police here is baffled. Are you?'

'What day was the robbery?' Tweed asked.

'Sunday. Middle of the night.' He laid a brief-case on one of the tables.

'How might they have got away with that weight of gold?'

'Put your finger on it,' Romer said crisply, sitting down at Tweed's invitation. 'Local police first thought they used the airport. A Fokker Friendship aircraft took off. They worked out the timing. It seemed right if trucks transported the gold. Seemed right at the time.'

'But not now?'

'Seemed right,' Romer continued, 'because the Fokker had a flight plan to fly to Orly, Paris. Never arrived. The manifests were checked, proved to be forged. Vanished into thin air. Literally. The aircraft.'

'A Fokker could have carried that weight in gold?'

'Put your finger on it again.' Romer's tone expressed confidence in Tweed. Behind his back Beck nodded to Paula: the Colonel was not an easy man to impress. 'I had that point checked myself,' Romer went on. 'No Fokker could have taken the whole load. I think it was a smokescreen – to divert our attention from how they did move the gold.'

'How would a gang like that dispose of the gold? You're a banker . . .'

'Good question. Asked it myself times without number. A crooked banker – or bullion merchant – is the only answer. Mind you, they wouldn't get anything like the twelve million – the robbers. Eight if they were lucky – and had the right contacts. You'd find the answer in Luxembourg City or Brussels. Better still, in London. I'll give you a name.'

He extracted from his wallet a blank white card, wrote on it rapidly in neat script, handed it to Tweed. 'Mention my name. For obvious reasons it's not on the card. He'll phone me for confirmation, then talk to you.'

'Who would buy the gold – the ultimate customer, I mean.'

'Russia,' Romer said promptly. 'At the head of the list. I probably overdid it when I said the bastards who took the bullion would get eight million. Six more likely. The go-between wants his cut. Then Russia – if it was them – gets four or five million francs for nothing. Hard currency for nothing when they sell it again.'

'I don't know much about bullion,' Tweed persisted, 'but I understood each bar of gold is stamped with its origin?'

'Quite so. So, the go-between has it melted down, destroying the distinguishing mark, then cools it, resolidifies it. No trace of origin left. Of course, he'd need all the facilities. That chap in London will know more.' He opened his brief-case. 'Now, Beck tells me you want to know about the explosive used.'

'It would help?'

'Not much, I'm afraid.' He handed Tweed a sheaf of typed papers. 'It's in English – for your experts. It's a new type of explosive. That's really all we can say. There's a lot of chemical analysis stuff there that doesn't mean a thing to me. All our chaps had to go on was smears taken from flashpoints inside the vault. Oh, the mechanism of the bomb was a bit diabolical. Caused implosion – if you know what that means.'

'Designed so the whole force of the explosion goes in one direction . . .' Tweed glanced at Paula who had lost colour. 'Took ninety per cent of the vault door,' Romer went on, 'nine inches of cold steel . . .' He took a slim executive case out of the bulky brief-case, handed it to Tweed with a key.

'Inside is a plastic bag containing pieces of debris our boffins scraped off the floor of the vault. Maybe your people can make something of it. God knows they've had enough experience with the IRA crowd. I think that's it.'

Beck produced an envelope, handed it to Tweed. 'Copies of the blueprints found inside Gaston Blanc's safe at Montres Ribaud. Colonel Romer says they are designs for timers – and control boxes. Take them, too. Just about all we can do now.'

'There is one more thing,' Tweed said. 'I'd like to look at that barge harbour further down the Rhine where you dragged out a second body . . .'

'Let's all go,' Romer said. 'In my car.' He glanced at

Beck. 'Your friend, Tweed, has that look in his eye.'

'What look?'

'A bloodhound. Never gives up.'

Romer led the way, followed by Tweed and Paula, Beck brought up the rear as they picked their way over a complex of rail tracks. The barge harbour was protected from the Rhine by a peninsula on which stood several large silos. Behind them oil storage tanks reared up like large white cakes.

Barges were moored three abreast alongside the river. There was a stench of oil and tar and resin Tweed associated with waterfronts. Romer paused, called back to Paula to join him. 'You've charmed the Colonel, too,' Tweed whispered.

'Phooey!' She went ahead and Romer took her arm. Using his other hand which held a baton he pointed across the oily, gliding river. 'That's France over there on the far bank.'

'And over there?' She pointed eastward. 'Germany?'

'On the nose, as you say. The dredger is still at work, I see . . .'

Tweed and Beck joined them near the tip of the peninsula. On the other side of the entrance to the harbour a line of cypresses screened a factory complex. Workmen in stained boiler suits trudged steadily about their labours.

'The dredger which hauled up the second body?' Paula asked.

'Yes,' said Romer.

He was watching Tweed who stood, hands in his coat pockets, staring fixedly at the dredger. Its dragline emerged dripping from the water, carrying a load of rocks. Nearby a barge was heeled over, its bow partly submerged. Men were working, attaching fresh cables to the stricken vessel.

'This harbour is drained regularly for silt?' Tweed enquired. 'The entrance is very narrow – and the Rhine flows past it.'

'Good Lord, no!' Beck explained. 'That barge carrying rocks capsized. Hence the dredger working – to haul up the cargo, clear the depths. Pure chance the first thing the dredger brought up was the body. Not a pretty sight. Bloated to an extraordinary size after long immersion.'

'And normally the harbour is never dredged for silt?' Tweed asked again.

'No. Look at the current. Sweeps straight past. So, no debris to fetch up.'

'Then how did that body drift in here?'

There was a long silence before Beck replied. Paula noticed Romer was watching Tweed closely, tugging at his moustache. A habit of his when he was intrigued, she suspected.

'We assumed it must have done,' Beck said eventually. 'The local police put that in their report . . .'

'And where was the other body dragged out of the river?'

'By the Rhine Falls at Schaffhausen. A long way upstream. So the natural assumption was the second body had floated down to here. Both were UTS men, both had street plans of Basle with the two banks marked.'

'The corpse recovered here was identified because he had his papers in a waterproof wallet. What about the one at Schaffhausen?'

'Same thing. He also had his papers in a new waterproof wallet . . .'

'*New?*'

'Yes. Purchased in Munich. We even traced the shop.'

'Didn't that strike you as odd?' Tweed suggested. 'That the killer should leave both wallets on his victims? He could so easily have taken them away – then no connection with the UTS would have been made.'

'Yes, it did,' Beck admitted. 'We couldn't think of an explanation . . .'

'The killer wanted the connection with the UTS established – in case the bodies surfaced. To point you in the wrong direction – and away from the real reason the bullion was stolen.'

'That's an assumption,' Beck pointed out.

'And a very valid one, I'd say,' Romer intervened.

'Where exactly was this corpse found here in the harbour?' Tweed asked.

'Under the very lee of that far side of the harbour. The very first time the scoop was sent down it brought up this body and one large rock. We were lucky – the dredger must have scooped up the big rock first, then lifted the body. Had it been the other way round the corpse would have been smashed to a pulp – maybe never even noticed. You see the rocks it is bringing up being dropped into the barge alongside.'

Paula turned away, as though examining the inner harbour. She had a sudden vision of a corpse bloated to at least twice its original size, the huge rock smashing down and bursting it like a pricked balloon. She swallowed, took a deep breath. Beck had changed the subject.

'I don't suppose it means anything, but a bloodstained coat was discovered in a luggage locker at Cornavin Gare. Probably worn by the man who killed Gaston Blanc. Forensic have estimated his probable height and weight. Giant of a man. Here are the details.'

He handed Tweed a folded sheet which Tweed tucked in his wallet without looking at it. 'Time to go?' he suggested, still watching the dredger, the barge alongside.

'Nothing more here for us,' Beck agreed. He talked as he joined Tweed in the walk back to the car while Paula chatted to Colonel Romer behind them. 'You like all the bits and pieces, I know. Gaston Blanc's car was discovered abandoned by the roadside near Broc, the place where the Nestlé factory is. God knows why!'

'Interesting,' remarked Tweed.

'Is it? Oh, a final titbit. My assistant who sorts reports before I see them is on holiday. I've got a fool of a girl who dumps everything on my desk standing in. The titbit? A Nestlé truck and its Turkish driver has gone missing en route to make a delivery to Brussels. Big deal, as the Americans would say.'

'I think we'll fly back to London tomorrow,' Tweed said, stretching out his legs in the armchair in his bedroom. They had enjoyed a good dinner and Paula had joined him for a final chat.

'You still think we're chasing phantoms and ghosties?' asked Paula.

'I've moved into a neutral zone, but there are connections which keep bugging me.'

'Such as?'

'Four men now with their throats cut ear to ear. Dikoyan, the Armenian who crashed the explosives truck into Turkey. Then two members of the UTS dragged out of the Rhine. Same method. Including dumping them in water. The fourth, Gaston Blanc – who made timers and control boxes . . .'

'You don't know he'd made them. He might have just been going to start making them.'

'True. But why was he murdered before he'd done the job?'

'That's the lot?' Paula asked.

'The explosive technique used on the bank vaults. I saw your expression when Romer used the word *implosion*. Took you back to Blakeney, didn't it?'

'Yes. It's a long way, though, from Basle to Blakeney. And I wonder how Bob Newman is getting on?'

'We'll hear when he's good and ready. One question bothers me more than any other. I feel it could be the key to the entire conspiracy – if there is one.'

'What's that?'

'We may know more after Bellenger has examined those

pieces of debris in the executive case Romer gave me . . .'

'You can be the most annoying man. What was the question?'

'How the gold bullion was smuggled out of Basle – and what was its ultimate destination?'

Waiting for Paula, who was collecting the air tickets for the return to Heathrow, Tweed sat staring out of the window at the sheen-surfaced Rhine, watching the occasional barge glide past. She returned when he was dialling the number of the Zurcher Kredit Bank, calling Romer.

'Colonel, Tweed here. One more question I'd like the answer to. You seem *au fait* with all the action the police took the night of the robbery. I presume they set up road-blocks?'

'The moment they were alerted. The gang cut out the alarm system – but missed one box. Of course it had to be the defective one – reacted half an hour after it activated. It was tested by experts and did the same thing. Went off a half-hour after activation.'

'And the road-blocks?'

'Set up immediately. They reckoned they missed the large truck later found abandoned at the airport – with traces of gold on the floor. That's why they were so sure the Fokker Friendship plane took out the bullion.'

'What I want to know is how far out they set up their road-blocks?'

'Oh, on the outskirts of the city, of course. Ten to fifteen kilometres from this bank, I gather . . .'

'No road-blocks were set up closer in, then? Near the centre of the city?'

'No. It seemed pointless. A Sunday night, the streets deserted, a half-hour start.'

'Thank you.'

Tweed put down the receiver and explained the conversation to Paula as she handed him his ticket. Paula listened, then frowned.

'I don't get the significance of your question.'

'It's odd,' Tweed responded dreamily. 'I find myself thinking like a detective again. All the old training, the experience comes back. A weird feeling . . .'

'You didn't answer my question,' Paula pointed out.

'I don't believe I did. But I'm like a man wandering through a fog – seeing silhouettes I can't identify yet.'

'And you can be the most maddening man to work for.'

'Monica would agree with that. Next stop, London . . .'

19

It was eleven o'clock at night when Klein came back to La Montagne. In the kitchen Hipper stared at him in surprise. He hadn't expected Klein to return for days. But it was typical of Klein: you never knew when he was going to turn up without warning.

'How is it going?' Klein asked Chabot.

The Frenchman took the watchmaker's glass out of his eye and gazed back. Spread across the table was a whole mass of the precision pieces of metal Gaston Blanc had patiently manufactured in his workshop.

'Ten of the devices are ready,' he said.

'You are working faster than I expected. Fifty more and you are finished.'

'I'm familiar with the mechanism now. So I work much more quickly. The whole lot? Three days from now.'

'I am packing them in the special case,' Hipper interjected. 'I pack them as he completes a set of five . . .'

'And all of them tested – like the first one?' Klein demanded.

In the fluorescent light his lean face seemed whiter than ever. More like a mask than the face of a human being. He loomed over the table as Hipper replied.

'Oh, yes. We test them five at a time. Well after dark – and the locals know I wander about on my own, so there is no risk. They don't like me, which helps.'

'I have a question.' Chabot lit a Gauloise. 'I have been thinking . . .'

'A dangerous habit,' Klein suggested in his cold voice.

'I have a question,' Chabot repeated, 'and I want an answer before I assemble one more device. I calculate that with this number of timers – and the five control boxes – there must be enormous explosive power involved. Don't forget, I'm an expert. What exactly is the job? And how many other men are involved? I'm working in the dark no longer.'

Klein studied the Frenchman, who kept staring straight back at him, showing not a hint of fear. A very hard case, Klein was thinking. Well, that's what we'll need. Someone not nervous of spilling a lot of blood. He'll have to be told something. He made one last attempt to stall Chabot.

'We are working on the cell principle. Only three men know each other. I insist on the tightest security. The success of an operation of this magnitude depends on it.'

'What operation,' Chabot persisted.

'Thirty people in the team altogether,' Klein replied. 'We have them in place now. All except two. I am hiring these two key personnel as soon as I leave here.'

'What operation?' Chabot asked again.

'We are going to hold up the gateway to Europe. We are going to threaten to close down a whole continent . . .' His voice was rising in pitch, he punctuated his statements with a curious chopping movement of his right hand as he went on. 'We are going to give a demonstration of the terrible explosive power at our command. There will be casualties to show we are not bluffing. We shall demand – receive – an enormous sum of money. That gigantic fortune is already available – although those who hold it have no idea what it is really for. Now! No more talk. Get on with your job. I shall collect the timers in three days. Someone will be waiting to move them to the target. *Wiedersehen!*'

Klein gestured to Hipper to join him, left the room. Chabot paused in his work for a few minutes. As he'd spoken the eyes of Klein had bulged hypnotically, had seemed to change colour. It must have been the fluorescents Chabot decided.

He was shaken by the vehemence of Klein's outburst, by the details of his plan. Then he shrugged. For two hundred thousand francs he should worry about the spilling of some blood. But of one thing Chabot was sure. Afterwards all hell would break loose in Europe. What a good job he had decided to leave France forever once he had his hands on the big money – to emigrate to Quebec. They'd never find him there.

'All the Luxembourg scuba divers you recruited are hidden away in Holland,' Klein told Hipper in answer to his question. 'We must have hired every thug in your tiny country.'

'Holland?' Hipper queried. 'The target is there?'

'You know better than to ask questions like that. Holland is a good staging post.'

'Ten foreigners are a lot to hide. Won't they be noticed?'

'We have taken over a camping site. They are housed in campers. Only the two who speak Dutch leave the site to fetch in supplies. It is foolproof.'

Klein omitted to mention the number hidden away on the site was larger than ten. He sensed the little man was becoming nervous, keyed up. It was a problem he had foreseen. He had to keep them all occupied until the moment for the great assault came.

'What about Chabot?' he added. 'When I spoke to you on the phone, warning you about the delivery of the timers, you did say he was restless. I don't like that.'

'He is absorbed in his work at the moment. As long as he takes his midnight walk along the gorge where the railway once ran he is manageable. How much longer do we have before the operation is mounted?'

'As long as it takes.'

20

'Action at last,' said Pete Nield, sitting in the back of the Mercedes 280E as Newman pulled up, then turned into the car park near the Blakeney waterfront. As he turned off the ignition he had no idea he was close to the spot where Tweed had parked the same car while he waited for the Bomb Disposal team to do its job.

A brisk breeze was blowing off the sea into Norfolk and the village had a deserted look. Harry Butler, seated beside Newman, replied to Nield over his shoulder.

'Patience is what you need a little more of in this job – I've told you before. Newman knows what he's doing.'

'Don't dispute it – but hanging round in King's Lynn for days got on my wick.'

'Sorry about that,' Newman commented, adjusting the field-glasses hanging from a loop round his neck. 'I had to go to Brighton to check up on Dr Portch – that's where he came from before he bought the practice in Cockley Ford. We'll be going there to look around tonight. I'm going along to chat with the skipper of that coaster. Why don't the two of you pop into the bar on the front, have a jar. I want to appear to be on my own . . .'

The coaster, moored next to the tall silo, was unloading a cargo of soya bean meal. Newman could see faint white dust rising as the dock crane worked. He had been to Blakeney the day before, had learned a lot chatting to the barman in the pub facing the small harbour.

He wore a deerstalker hat, a windcheater, corduroy trousers tucked into rubber knee-length boots. Standard gear for a bird-watcher. The coaster's skipper, a certain Caleb Fox, was leaning against the sea wall, taking a swig from a hip flask. He hastily pocketed it when Newman arrived.

'Gusty sort of day,' Newman remarked. 'What's the weather going to do?'

'Piss down this afternoon. We'll be unloaded by then – God willin'.'

'Bob Newman.' He held out his hand. The skipper took hold with slithery limp fingers. Like shaking hands with a fish. There was the smell of brandy on his breath.

'Caleb Fox,' he said after staring sideways at Newman. Fox. The name suited him. A small, wide-shouldered man, he stooped like a man accustomed to dipping his head aboard ship and his eyes were foxy. 'Them's pretty powerful binoculars,' he observed. 'Mighty expensive, I reckon. The camera, too.'

'You need good equipment for bird-watching. Soya bean meal your main cargo?'

'Sick of the sight of the stuff. Runs a shuttle, we does. Across to Europort, Rotterdam, pick up our ration from one o' the big container jobs comin' up from Africa, then back here.'

'Sounds a bit boring.'

'Bloody borin'. But when you're past fifty and shippin' is in a bad way, you takes what you can get. I used to sail a ten-thousand-ton freighter. Those were the days. Dead and gone, they are.'

'How big is the coaster?'

'Seven hundred tonner.' Fox spat over the wall. 'A pea-boat compared with what I once 'ad. A man needs money, a lot of it to be 'appy in this vale of sorrows.'

'You live alone?'

''Ow did you know that?'

Sudden hostility, suspicion. The foxy eyes closed to mere slits, stared at Newman for a few seconds, then looked away.

'I didn't. You just sounded lonely.'

Newman had the impression it was the brandy which was talking, that had he come along earlier Fox would not have said a word. Now he was wondering whether he had talked too much. About what? Fox's right hand reached towards his hip, then withdrew and rested on the wall. Something odd, Newman felt.

A man needs money, a lot of it . . . Newman could have sworn Fox had brightened up for a few seconds when he uttered the words. The skipper, reassured by Newman's reply, started talking about his favourite topic. Himself.

'You're right, lives on me own. Got a small place at Brancaster. That's along the coast – towards King's Lynn. You look well fixed, Mister, if you don't mind me saying so.'

There was a question behind the statement. Fox darted another sidelong glance at his visitor. Newman replied carefully.

'I'm a writer. I've been lucky. Brings me in a good income.' He changed the subject. 'What's that funny rattling noise?'

Fox pulled at his greasy peaked cap. 'It's the wind shaking the riggin' against the metal mast of that boat over there, the one beached on the sandbank. Rubbish they are, rich men's toys. All fibreglass and aluminium. Not real boats at all.'

'Well, I think I've changed my mind about pushing off across the marshes,' Newman remarked. 'Don't like the look of those clouds coming in.'

'Told you, didn't I? Goin' to piss down . . .'

Newman retraced his steps back to the waterfront pub. Butler and Nield sat at a window table, two glasses of beer in front of them. Newman walked to the bar, ordered a small Scotch, downed it, glanced at the two men and made his way back to the Mercedes.

His two companions came strolling along five minutes later, climbed back into the car. Nield again occupied a rear seat and spoke as Newman turned on the ignition.

'Found out something interesting talking to the landlord. That skipper you were chatting with is a pal of – guess who? Dr Portch from Cockley Ford.'

'I know,' Newman said as he turned out of the car park and left Blakeney Quay behind. 'He told me the same thing yesterday when I came here on my own. Not a popular character, Dr Portch. Except with the skipper of that coaster, Caleb Fox . . .'

'Why did we come to Blakeney?' asked Harry Butler.

'Because of Tweed's experience up here. There were two places where things happened. Blakeney and Cockley Ford. And that barman told me yesterday the coaster was due in here today from Rotterdam with another cargo of that soya stuff. Also that the skipper knew Dr Portch. Obvious conclusion: have a look at Caleb Fox.'

'And our next move?'

'Visit the other place this evening, Cockley Ford. You and I, Harry, had better get kitted up before we pay the village a call. Denims and windcheaters. We're going in as two SAS types, the couple Tweed invented for protection when he went there.'

'You can play the part,' Butler pointed out. 'You had SAS training when you did that series of articles on them. But what about me?'

Newman glanced at his passenger's sturdy frame, tall build. 'You won't have any trouble looking the part. Box and Cox. I'll be the gabby one, do the talking. You play the silent partner.'

'And where do I come into this?' Nield called out.

'You come into it all right. You'll follow us in Tweed's Cortina parked back at Tuesday Market. Give me one of those compact walkie-talkies you brought, carry another yourself. You park half-way up the side road leading to Cockley Ford. If I call you come like a bat out of hell. Flash that fake warrant card in your wallet. You're police. Special Branch.'

'Sounds as though you're expecting trouble,' Nield commented hopefully.

'I just don't know what Harry and I may be walking into. When Tweed first mentioned Dr Portch the name rang a bell. I checked the newspapers two years ago in the

British Museum reading room. Then, as you know, I went to Brighton where Portch came from. I was right. And that Caleb Fox made a mistake.'

'Which was?'

'The sort of mistake Tweed is good at spotting. The *absence* of something. During our whole conversation he never once mentioned that bomb placed on Paula Grey's doorstep. Funny, that. While I was in that bar the locals were talking about nothing else.'

'And Dr Portch? You said you were right about him,' Nield recalled.

'He could be a two-time murderer – who got away with it in both cases.'

Newman drove back along the coast road – the A149 – towards King's Lynn. Nield, studying the map of Norfolk, pointed out it would be quicker to cut inland via Fakenham.

'I know,' Newman agreed, 'but I want to take a *shufti* at the place where Caleb Fox hangs out, Brancaster.'

The wind was rising, beating against the side of the Mercedes. A nor'easter coming in off the sea. The cloud bank had blotted out the sky and it was half-dark when the rain began to hammer down. Newman turned off the main highway to the right down a wisp of a road.

A winding road, it stretched across a flat area of sedge-land, wild and desolate. Beyond the sea was a dark belt flecked with white-capped rollers. They hadn't seen a soul since leaving the highway as they arrived at a crude car park, no more than a rectangle of flattened earth. Newman stopped the car. Close to the sea was a large isolated two-storey building. Two men with golf bags over their shoulders ran for shelter.

'While I remember,' Newman said, 'slight change of plan for this evening. Nield, you take my Mercedes – Tweed arrived at Cockley Ford in it that night he had his weird visit there. It might look funny if Butler and I turned up in the same car. So, we'll take the Cortina. Now, raincoats

157

on. Time for us to stretch our legs, Harry. Pete, you stay dry and watch the car.'

'Suits me. You're going to get soaked.'

He was right, too, Newman thought as he walked with Butler towards the building and the sea. The nor'easter had increased in fury, forcing them to push against it as rain drenched down.

'What's this in aid of? Not that I mind a bath,' Butler enquired.

'Trying to find someone I can ask about Caleb Fox. Should be someone who knows inside that building. It's a golf clubhouse . . .'

The rain stopped as suddenly as it had started but the wind continued to buffet them. They reached a board-walk which ran past the clubhouse down a slope to the edge of one of many creeks snaking away to the dark and distant belt.

'Sea's one hell of a long way out,' Butler shouted against the howl of the gale.

'And I should leave it there if I may make a suggestion,' an upper crust voice said.

A tall, distinguished-looking man with a white moustache had appeared round the side of the clubhouse. Wearing a waterproof hat and a dark blue raincoat, he carried a walking stick and his complexion had a weatherbeaten look. He gestured towards the building.

'Got a moment for a chat? We'll be out of the wind in the lee of the clubhouse.'

As they stood together Newman took off his hat and shook it free of some of the rain. The tall man stared hard at him.

'You look uncommonly like Robert Newman, chap who wrote that bestseller novel *Kruger: The Computer That Failed*.'

'That's right,' Newman admitted reluctantly.

'Terrific book. Kept me up all night. Never thought I'd get the chance of thanking you for so much pleasure.'

'Glad you liked it.'

'Meant what I said about not walking out there.' He pointed his stick seawards. 'Look at the notice over there.'

The warning notice reared up close to the board-walk. *Don't walk out to wrecks – incoming tide very swift.* Newman gazed out beyond the slope which was covered with large pebbles. Dry creeks snaked in and out amid sand-banks, then vanished. It reminded him of Blakeney but here the creek system looked more insidiously complex. Blurred in the distance rose two hump-backed objects, one much further out. The shipwrecks.

'I'm Timms,' the stranger went on. 'Ex-Inspector of Coastguard stations.' He produced his wallet, extracted a card and handed it to Newman. Ronald Timms. Followed by a Brancaster address and phone number. 'If you've ever got a spare half-hour you'd always be welcome to drop in, have a drink.'

'Very good of you.'

Newman slipped the card into his own wallet, made a mental note to throw it away later. Too many cards in his wallet already. Timms went on, again pointing with his stick.

'Those two hulks are magnetic – and dangerous – attractions for children, especially. You walk out towards them and the tide comes in. Behind you. By the time you realize it you're marooned and it's too late. The tide covers all those sandbanks.'

'Thanks for the warning.'

'See that far hulk?' Timms persisted. 'Bit of a mystery. It ran aground one storm-ridden night. I strolled out to have a look-see one day – with my camera. Bit of an amateur photographer. Got to pass the time somehow at my age. I found someone had changed the original name of the vessel. Came up when I'd developed the pictures I'd taken. Fishy business. But by then the insurance had been paid so I left it alone. They don't like you trying to reopen a case once the claim is settled. If it turned out they'd been wrong someone would say they hadn't checked properly in the first instance. Desk wallahs for you.'

'I did want to ask you a question,' Newman said quickly before Timms resumed his monologue. 'I'm looking for a Captain Caleb Fox who lives in Brancaster. He runs a coaster shuttle between Rotterdam and Blakeney . . .'

'Rotterdam. Europort. That's something to see. Biggest port in the world. Handles half the freight which keeps Europe going. Food, oil, you name it . . .'

'Caleb Fox,' Newman repeated.

'Never heard of him. Mind you, Brancaster spreads out a bit. Sorry, can't help you . . .'

'I think we'd better get back to the car,' Newman interjected, looking up at the sky. 'I think another squall is on the way.'

'Well, good to meet you. Don't forget my invitation . . .'

'Very kind of you. Hope to see again. Goodbye.'

The rain began to pound down again as they made for the car. They ran the rest of the way. The wind was so strong Newman had to heave at the heavy door of the Mercedes to get it open. He flung his raincoat on the rear seat beside Nield and dived behind the wheel as Butler joined him.

'I said you'd get soaked,' Nield told them. 'Was it worth it?'

'Not really. We bumped into an old boy who talks the hind leg off a donkey,' replied Newman.

'Thought he'd never stop,' Butler agreed.

'He's lonely,' Newman said as he started up the engine. 'He made that remark about passing the time somehow. I was worried he'd start talking about my book again. I never know what to say when people do that. Now, straight back to The Duke's Head, a good lunch, a bit of a rest, and we'll be ready for our SAS attack on Cockley Ford – whatever that may hold for us.'

Part Two

The Long Pursuit

21

Tweed plunged into furious activity the morning he arrived at Park Crescent. Monica was away with flu, so he put Paula in her place. He decided to tell her everything that had taken place in Switzerland – including his interview with General Lysenko.

Sitting at her own desk – she refused to sit at Monica's – she listened, her thick eyebrows furrowed with concentration. Tweed had warned nothing must be put down on paper. Except the special Moscow phone number Lysenko had given him.

He was relieved to find that Howard was away – also with the flu – and that the PM was visiting the North-East. For the moment he had the show to himself. He handed her the sheet Beck had given him with the details Geneva Forensic had provided of the probable height and weight of the killer of Gaston Blanc.

'Convert those decimals into feet and inches, stones and pounds. I never did like it when we went decimal.'

'One hundred and ninety centimetres,' she read out. 'Weight a hundred and ten kilogrammes. The man is a giant, as Beck said. Will do . . .'

'Take these,' Tweed continued, pulling sheets of paper out of his brief-case and a plastic bag. 'You remember Colonel Romer said the sheets were chemical analyses of the explosive used to blow the vaults in Basle. The bag has debris collected from inside the same vaults. The lot goes urgently to Commander Bellenger of Naval Intelligence. You'll find his number in Monica's red card index box, top right drawer. Here's the key she left in my drawer. Don't tell Bellenger where I got them from – I just want to know if he can tell me the explosive used.'

'Will do . . .'

'Call this chap, Jacob Rubinstein, gold bullion merchant. Mention Colonel Romer's name. Make an appointment for me to see him today. Tell him I'm Special Branch. Give him my phone number if he wants to call back to check. Tell him fifteen minutes of his time will be enough if he tries to delay the appointment. Oh, ask Bellenger to send a courier to collect that stuff. It's top secret.'

Tweed paused, realizing he'd been firing instructions like a machine-gun. Paula's raven mane was bent over her desk, hand flying across her notebook as she made shorthand notes.

'I'm sorry,' he said. 'You're new and I'm piling it on a bit.'

'Are you?' She looked up and smiled. 'You've forgotten – I ran my own pottery business. Often I'd have two phone calls on the go at once – a buyer from San Francisco wanting urgent delivery, the Wisbech factory on the other line so I could give immediate information. The Americans like that.'

'Just as long as you can cope . . .'

She had continued writing in her notebook as he spoke. Now she looked up again. 'I've converted those decimal figures. A giant of a man. Height six foot three, weighs seventeen stone.'

'Doesn't sound like Zarov. I'll call that Moscow number. No, leave it to me. You deal with the other jobs . . .'

The Moscow girl operator asked him to wait after he'd given her the number. To Tweed's surprise Lysenko came on the line within thirty seconds.

'Something you missed giving me on Zarov,' Tweed told him. 'His height and weight.'

'Let me check the file. That was a bad omission on my part.'

Tweed cupped the mouthpiece with his hand, speaking to Paula. 'The Bear is friendly. Because he wants something. That is, he wishes to give me the impression he wants something . . .'

He broke off as Lysenko came back on the line. 'Ready? I have the data. Height one hundred and eighty-three centimetres, weighty seventy-eight kilogrammes. Has there been a development?'

'Absolutely nothing. One thing else I wanted to know. Are your own people still searching for him?'

'Of course. But with no hope of success. I told you, Tweed. The devil knows our organization, the people and places to avoid. I understand you interviewed Yuri Sabarin. You have been active. Was Sabarin a help?'

'He did his best. But it didn't take me any further. Thank you for the data. With the Identikit picture it gives me a more complete picture of Zarov. If he's still alive. I am still very doubtful.'

'We have heard more disturbing rumours – that the Americans are behind the planned catastrophe . . .'

'Somebody was short of material for a report. That's pure idiocy. Where did the report come from?'

'Paris,' Lysenko said after a brief pause. 'And you will be reporting progress to me?'

'I told you before I work in my own way. You've dropped this in my lap – leave it there. Goodbye.'

Tweed cut the call before Lysenko could reply. Paula was watching him. She hadn't understood a word because they had spoken in Russian. Tweed clasped his hands behind his head, shook it.

'Zarov is a hundred and eighty-three centimetres tall, and weighs seventy-eight kilogrammes. Translate that into English for me.'

She scribbled in her notepad. 'Six feet tall, twelve stone in weight. As opposed to Beck's six foot three and seventeen stone.'

'There you are. Not the same man at all. I thought it was stretching to assume the same killer dealt with Dikoyan, the Armenian driver found in the Bosphorus, plus the couple of UTS corpses dragged out of the Rhine, plus Gaston Blanc. Back to square one.'

'Are you sure?' Paula tapped her pen between her small

white teeth. 'Surely Beck's people got these measurements, estimated the killer's likely weight, from the blood-stained coat they found in a locker at Geneva Cornavin.'

'Yes. So?'

She doodled on her pad as she talked. 'That had to be a pretty audacious, smart and well-organized killer who murdered Blanc on the express. Wouldn't you agree? He must have even been carrying a suitcase – something like that – to shove the blood-stained coat inside while he was still in that lavatory.'

'Agreed,' Tweed said thoughtfully, watching her closely.

'And when he dumped the case with the coat inside that locker he'd know the police would find it sometime. Beck probably found it faster than he anticipated.'

'Go on . . .'

'We've agreed he's very clever. Clever enough to foresee the Swiss police's forensic experts would come up with an estimate of his height and size – from that coat. So, maybe he wore a coat several sizes too large. Perhaps he *was* six feet tall, weighed twelve stone. Back on stage, Mr Igor Zarov?'

'I slipped up there.' Tweed gazed at her in admiration. 'I could have done with you in my days at the Yard. You think like a detective.'

'I'd better make my phone calls now. Rubinstein first, then Bellenger.'

Her hand was reaching for the phone when it rang. She spoke briefly, her tone businesslike, then gestured towards Tweed's instrument. 'It's Bob Newman for you.'

'Tweed, a brief report,' Newman said crisply. 'Butler and I are going in to Cockley Ford this evening. I've found out . . .'

'Where are you calling from?' Tweed broke in quickly.

'A public phone box, of course.' Newman sounded irked. 'You think I've lost my marbles?'

'Sorry, a lot is happening here . . .'

'One or two things are happening up here, too. As I was

saying, I've found out interesting data on the background of the good Dr Portch. Tell you when I come in.'

'Be careful at Cockley Ford. The place has a peculiar atmosphere. When do I see you?' Tweed asked.

'Tomorrow. Early afternoon at a guess.'

'Good. I want your company on a trip – to Paris. OK?'

'If you say so. 'Bye.'

'Paris?' Paula repeated as she wrote down phone numbers. 'Do I get to know why? Or is that indiscreet?'

'Not at all. I'm flying over to see another of my private contacts. Can't give you his name – even Monica doesn't know. I have a string of them, built up over the years. They expect me to respect their secrecy. I'll be staying at the France et Choiseul, rue St Honoré . . .'

'I reserve two rooms? For you and Bob. For how long?'

'Two days, I think. Details of the hotel are in a file Monica keeps, bottom right-hand drawer. I may then go on to Antwerp – again to meet a contact. I'll phone you when I know.'

He broke off as the phone rang. 'One of those days, I can sense it,' he muttered as Paula answered, then looked at him, hand over mouthpiece.

'A René Lasalle of the French DST wants to talk to you . . .'

'Tweed here. How are you, you old ruffian?' Tweed asked in English.

'Fine. I'm not sure I'm calling the right person . . .' In the pause Tweed could almost see Lasalle shrugging his shoulders. '. . . but it is a delicate matter. I know you will handle with the *finesse* . . .'

'René,' Tweed interjected, 'does it help if I tell you I've been appointed a temporary Commander of the Anti-Terrorist Squad?'

'You have! Back to your old days. And you are still . . .'

'I still hold my old position. This is on scrambler?'

'Of course . . .'

'Hold it!' Tweed pressed a button on his instrument. 'Go ahead, we're both on scrambler.'

'There are growing rumours throughout all France of a major outrage being planned . . .'

'I know. Look, I happen to be flying to Paris tomorrow – why don't we meet? I'll be at my usual hotel. At least I think so. My new assistant, Paula, who is helping Monica, will call later and confirm the booking.'

'Excellent. We will have much to discuss. But one thing. There is a girl, English, Lara Seagrave . . .'

'Hold on again, if you don't mind . . .' Tweed called out to Paula. 'A girl called Lara Seagrave. I've heard that name somewhere. Just briefly.'

'Lara Seagrave. Step-daughter of Lady Windermere. Good background, but wild. Bit of a rebel. Does her own thing. On bad terms with Lady Windermere. Used to appear in the society papers. Balls, parties. But not lately – as far as I know. Gutsy type from her pictures.'

'Bit of a rebel, you said. Drugs and drink?'

'Not Lara. Has her head screwed on . . .'

'Thanks.' He resumed his conversation with Lasalle. 'I was getting information on her. What about Lara?'

'I'll tell you more when you come. You sound busy. I'm having her watched night and day. She's staying at The Ritz. She's mixing – possibly – with the wrong people. Could just be a lead, although I doubt it. See you, my friend. *Revoir.*'

'And that,' Tweed said as he put down the phone, 'makes a trip to Paris even more important. Meantime, try and set up an appointment with Lady Windermere if she's in London . . .'

'Eaton Square. If she's at home. I remember reading that in *The Tatler*. Who are you for this meeting?'

'Same as for Jacob Rubinstein. Special Branch. No mention of Lara.'

'Will do. Still think Zarov is a ghost?'

'Probably, yes. But we'll check a bit more.'

*

Klein phoned Lara from the Hotel Georges Cinq. He had never stayed at this Paris *de-luxe* hotel before. It was just after breakfast time and she answered immediately when he was put through to her room.

'Lara, listen carefully. We are going to play a trick on your husband . . .' Which was for the benefit of any nosy switchboard operator who might be listening in. 'First, we synchronize our watches. I make it 9.12.'

'I'm adjusting mine. Just a second. Done it. Go on.'

'My Volvo, registration . . . will be parked in the rue de Rivoli, close to the Place de la Concorde at precisely 9.30. Can you leave in a couple of minutes? Good. Stroll along the rue de Rivoli. Look in a few shops. Time it so you reach me at 9.30. Dive into the passenger seat and if your husband is following we'll give him the slip. Understand?'

'Yes. I'd better get ready now. See you.'

Klein, already wearing a dark coat and hat, put down the phone and left the hotel. He had no reason to suspect Lara was being followed. Why should she be? But he never ceased taking precautions. Always assume the worst. Another of his favourite maxims.

Lara stood in front of the mirror, wrapped the Gucci scarf round her long auburn hair, parted in the centre. She fixed the scarf so it concealed her hair completely, framing her oval-shaped face. That made her look different.

She also had no firm reason to think she was being followed, but Klein had earlier trained her to be careful. And during her train trip to Le Havre she thought she'd seen the same small man with the funny beaked nose twice. Once aboard the express, the second time when she was photographing the harbour.

She left The Ritz by the side entrance leading into the Place Vendôme, pausing on the sidewalk of the eight-sided square to glance round. By the kerb, a short distance from the entrance, a motor-cycle was parked. A small man wearing crash helmet and goggles bent over the machine, fiddling with something.

She frowned. He seemed vaguely familiar. She walked quickly out of the Place, crossed the rue St Honoré, continued down the rue Castiglione and turned right on the rue de Rivoli, the Fifth Avenue of Paris. Slowing down, she strolled along the wide pavement, stopping briefly to glance in a shop window, checking her watch.

Behind her The Parrot swore. He had almost missed her coming out. He was used to recognizing her by that long auburn sheen of hair. And she was dressed differently. A blue two-piece suit he hadn't seen before.

The Parrot was almost exhausted. Flu had struck down half the staff at the rue des Saussaies. He'd had to work without sleep for longer than he cared to recall. Lasalle himself, who cared for his men, had come to the Place Vendôme to apologize, to ask him whether he could carry on a while longer.

'Of course,' The Parrot had replied, cursing himself the moment he had said the words.

He pushed the machine across the rue St Honoré, straddled it in the quieter side street and kicked the starter. At least the scarf on the girl's head showed up. He cruised slowly, turned into the rue de Rivoli. Out shopping, it seemed. Still, he'd be relieved at lunchtime.

He was also worried about following her to Le Havre yesterday. His reflexes had not been too sharp and twice he'd wondered if she'd spotted him. The traffic was heavy and he kept in close to the kerb. Once she looked back after looking in a shop window. He pulled up behind a parked car and she went on, nearing the Place de la Concorde.

The traffic roared past him like an armoured division – the lights were green at the entrance to the vast square of Concorde. The Parrot blinked, his eyes twitching with fatigue. She was walking faster now. Afterwards he cursed himself for not being alerted by her increase in pace.

The lights were still green when she suddenly crossed

the pavement, dived inside a parked car, slammed the door shut. Volvo. He tried to turn into the next lane but there was no gap. Couldn't see the registration plate. The lights turned amber. Good . . .

The Volvo shot forward, swung left into Concorde. And the lights turned red as The Parrot spurted forward. He braked. '*Merde!*' He'd lost the bitch. And it had looked to him like a deliberate manœuvre. He hadn't even seen the driver of the Volvo. '*Merde!*'

Klein roared round the Place de la Concorde in the thunder of traffic, swung up the Champs Élysées. In the distance perched the massive hulk of the Arc de Triomphe. The sun shone brightly, which added to the drivers' zest for speed.

'Any chance you were followed?'

'It's just possible,' said Lara and described the events at Le Havre, outside The Ritz, and the precautions she had taken wearing a different outfit.

'Probably that lively imagination of yours,' Klein replied jocularly. He was in a good mood. Driving at speed, and an attractive girl by his side. Pity she had to play the ultimate role when the time came. Couldn't be helped – a key part in his plan.

He drove on to La Défense, the high-rise complex where a lot of multi-nationals had their headquarters. Pulling in by the kerb, he fed coins into the meter – no point in the police getting to know him. Top criminals had been known to go down neglecting the tiniest detail. He leant back behind the wheel.

'Le Havre? What do you think?'

She was peering up out of the window. They were hemmed in by the towers of concrete and glass. It reminded her of films she'd seen of New York.

'Le Havre didn't look right,' she replied. 'Sorry to be so negative – after Marseilles. But the objections are the same. French security is tough. No obvious and easy escape route inland. Here are the pictures I took – plus a chart I bought from a ship's chandler.'

She handed him a thick envelope. Klein, in his turn, gave her a slim envelope. 'Another thousand pounds – in francs – to keep you going for a few days. Don't go and spend the lot at Valentino.'

'Where do I try next?'

'I'll want you to stay in Paris a bit longer. Another week at least. I've extended your reservation at The Ritz.'

'And how do I fill in my time?'

There it was, Klein thought. His universal problem – keeping the whole team occupied. The men in Holland were kept busy training – out in the wilds of the northern coast. Lara was getting impatient.

'Sometime during the week, check Cherbourg. It's quite a port. You can get there by train, of course. Let a few days pass, then make the trip. Now, wait here for a few minutes. I have to pay a call on someone.'

'I still haven't any idea of what I'm going to be asked to do later,' she reminded him.

'None of the others have either. Security. Worth the boredom, isn't it? A quarter of a million pounds? See you.'

Lara sat thinking as he disappeared down a walk between the buildings. Why was she doing this? She held the envelope in her hand. Another thousand pounds. Handed out like confetti.

It was her bitch of a step-mother, she decided. She wanted to show her what she could accomplish on her own. Life had been absolute hell since Lady Windermere arrived in her life. She'd done everything possible to drive her out of Eaton Square – so she could get a stronger grip on her new rich husband. In the end Lara had walked out in a flaming temper. Later she'd called her father and said she wanted to explore the world a bit. He'd approved of her wishing to make her own way.

And it was her sense of adventure. She knew the enterprise she'd undertaken was dangerous. Plus the fact that at first I couldn't keep my bloody hands off Klein, she thought. To take her mind off thoughts which didn't please her, she explored the back seat of the Volvo. Maybe find a clue as to what Klein was up to. Under a pile of newspapers she found a white pastry-cook's box. Some firm in Dinant, Belgium. The box had been opened. She lifted the lid.

Couques! Hard gingerbread baked in moulds which were often little masterpieces of woodcarvings. Shaped into cows, small houses, churches, other animals. She chose two of the little houses, closed the lid and replaced the box carefully. Klein wouldn't miss two – he'd already had a good go at the box.

Extracting a packet of large Kleenex tissues from her tote bag, she wrapped each *couque* and slipped them inside the bag. It was half an hour before Klein returned along the deserted walk. He climbed inside, closed the door, wrapped an arm round her, pulled her towards him and they kissed passionately. She was lost again. Almost.

It was the previous evening when Newman drove the Cortina up the narrow side road to Cockley Ford. Beside him Butler sat in his denims and windcheater, which made his frame look very bulky. Nield followed behind in the Mercedes.

As he passed the gated entrance to a field Newman slowed, waved a hand out of the window, drove on. In his rear-view mirror he saw Nield turn off the road, park the car at the entrance. Driving on, he used one hand to pull up higher the zip on his windcheater, to pat the pocket which held a walkie-talkie.

'Gate's closed,' Butler said in his laconic way.

'Tweed told us about that. And it's some electronic control system.'

'Not to worry.' Butler was taking a leather pouch out of his pocket as the car slowed, stopped. 'I've brought along a gadget which ought to fix it . . .'

Newman stared round as Butler walked to the gate,

examined it, then checked the fence on either side. Inside two minutes he was pushing the gate wide open, walking back to the Cortina.

'I neutralized the alarm system, too. Funny business at the entrance to a village. You'd think it was Fort Knox.'

'Don't forget Tweed called himself Sneed when he was here,' Newman warned.

It was still daylight, a bright sunny evening as Newman drove round a bend lined with tall rhododendron bushes, saw The Bluebell on his left and pulled up in front of the pub after turning the vehicle through a hundred and eighty degrees.

'Set for a fast getaway,' he remarked as he turned off the engine, climbed out, locked the car and walked with Butler to the entrance.

Inside the large old-fashioned room there were four people. A long-jawed countryman sitting at a table drinking from a spirits glass; an unpleasant-looking woman with grey hair tied in a bun at the back who was knitting; an oddly faced youth, and the barman.

Ned Grimes, Mrs Sporne – postmistress – and Simple Eric, he guessed from Tweed's descriptions. Followed by Butler he marched aggressively up to the bar. A chair scraped on the wooden floor behind him and he glanced over his shoulder as he leaned his elbows on the counter. Grimes was standing now.

''Ow did you two get in 'ere?' Grimes rasped.

'Drove in, of course,' Newman snapped, turning back to the barman. 'Two small Scotches. Water. No ice.'

'You can't 'ave.' The broad-shouldered Grimes moved closer to Newman, his thin lips working. 'You can't 'ave,' he repeated. 'Gate's closed.'

'I said two Scotches, please,' Newman addressed the barman again. 'Shake a leg there. We haven't got all night.' He turned round, perched both elbow tips on the counter and stared at Grimes. 'Calling me a liar, mate? Who the hell are you?'

'Ned Grimes. Not that it's any of your business . . .'

'It is when you start talking stupid. Your ruddy gate is wide open. Why shouldn't it be? This a village or some kind of private club you're running?'

'Better watch it, chum,' Butler suggested mildly. 'My pal has a short fuse.'

'All right, all right . . .' Grimes backed away several paces. 'Just interested to know 'ow you found this place. Folk don't come here much.'

Newman was paying the barman. He handed Butler his glass, picked up his own, raised it in a brief salute. 'Down the hatch.' He turned his full attention on Grimes who was hovering between his own table and Simple Eric's.

'A friend of ours, chap with horn-rim glasses called Sneed, told us about this place. Satisfied now?'

'Sneed? That was the chap with a German car. Posh job. That was days and days ago.'

'What's that got to do with anything?' Newman demanded.

'You isn't sayin' you're lookin' for this Sneed 'ere? And you be Army men – some special unit I forgot the name of. That's who you are, ain't it?'

Newman stood up slowly from the bar, hands hanging loosely by his side. He whipped up one hand, pointed his index finger at Grimes like the barrel of a pistol.

'Anyone ever tell you you ask too many questions? And you may like to know – since you seem to want to know a lot – that one of my ancestors was Sir John Leinster. Sneed told me his tomb is in the churchyard. That's what I've come to see. Any more questions?'

Grimes stood quite still. Newman could see the indecision in his bony face. That was when the youth suddenly let out a whoop. 'Any more bodies? Any more bodies tonight?'

'*Shut your face.*' Grimes spaced out the words, then went up close to Eric and whispered something. He raised his voice. 'And do it *now!*'

'Harry,' Newman decided, 'time to go and look at that church.'

As he marched towards the exit he glanced at the grey-haired woman who was eyeing him savagely. She was knitting a Fair Isle pullover and the colours were hideous. 'Knitting for a baby elephant?' he asked amiably. The needles began click-clacking at a furious rate, her expression became venomous. Simple Eric had run out of the pub and when they emerged into the fresh air he had disappeared – in the direction of the cottages, Newman guessed.

Marching in step with Butler, Newman took the lead when they crossed a footbridge alongside a ford through a small stream. He heard Grimes' Gucci boots clumping across the planks behind them but didn't look back. They passed several cottages but there was no one about. More like a deserted village.

The church perched on its eminence was close when a tall man came out of the last cottage. Behind him Simple Eric was jumping up and down, flapping his arms as though he was an aircraft. The tall man hurried to catch up. Under his black wide-brimmed hat a hawk-like nose protruded and a pince-nez was perched on it. He wore some kind of dark cloak and reminded Newman of a bloody great crow.

'One moment, sir,' he called out as he caught up, walking alongside Butler, 'I am Dr Portch. I gather there was a misunderstanding at The Bluebell. You must realize, sir, the villagers are simple souls. May I ask where you are going?'

'Here.' Newman opened the right-hand side of the double gate at the entrance. He veered off the mossy path, making for the back of the church, glancing down. In daylight he could see very clearly the deep ruts impressed in the grass Tweed had seen. A wide tyre span, indicating a heavy vehicle. The grooves wound their way round the back of the church, ending at the entrance to the mausoleum erected to Sir John Leinster.

'A distant ancestor of mine, Sir John Leinster,' Newman remarked, his hands on the closed gates leading to the large stone building. The new padlock Tweed had spoken of had been replaced by a heavy ancient version.

'Oh, really?' Dr Portch commented in his bland voice. 'I find that strange. So far as I know he left no issue.'

'My family tree – drawn up by a professional genealogist – says different.'

Some of the moss down the centre of the steps leading to the tomb was shrivelled and brown. It gave the impression it had been disturbed, then replaced. Newman turned suddenly and stared at Dr Portch. Grimes stood behind him.

'Have you seen all you want to, sir?' Portch was smiling but the smile did not reach the glazed eyes. He adjusted the cloak and shuffled his feet.

'They be friends of that stranger who came here. Sneed,' said Grimes.

'Dr Portch,' Newman remarked. 'A most unusual name. I seem to have come across it before. Not recently. In the newspapers could it have been?'

The glazed eyes became opaque. Portch stood motionless. Newman lit a cigarette and waited. In no hurry. Then Portch smiled again, clasped his hands in front of him. Like a priest. 'I hope you've enjoyed your visit to our little community.'

'Time of my life. Harry, getting dark. Time to push off.'

He walked off without a backward glance at a brisk pace. He kept it up, Butler alongside, until they had reached the car. Unlocking it, he got behind the wheel, fastened his seat-belt, started the car as Butler fixed his own belt, drove off round the curve and through the open gate.

'Gave him a bit of a turn,' Butler remarked.

'Which was the idea.'

Glancing in the wing mirror, he saw the road behind was empty as he pulled up alongside Nield waiting in the Mercedes. He opened the window and called out.

'Pete, drive after us until we hit the highway. Then find a place where you can watch the exit from this side road. If a car comes from Cockley Ford, follow it . . .' He gave a description of Dr Portch and drove on.

*

Nield had opened a gate leading off the highway, backed the Mercedes into a field, and ten minutes later saw the lights of a car coming from Cockley Ford. He'd spent his time in checking his map of Norfolk and now all the routes from this area were impressed on his mind.

The Vauxhall emerged on to the highway, turned right and moved at speed north along the highway. 'You're headed for Swaffham, matey,' Nield said to himself, keeping well back as he followed. At this speed he guessed the Vauxhall would be keeping on the main highway for some distance. He was right.

At Swaffham the Vauxhall stopped, a man got out, leaving the motor running, went into a pub. Nield nodded to himself. Dr Portch. Fitted the description perfectly. Portch came out carrying a squat bottle, climbed back into his car, took a swig. 'Brandy, I'll bet,' Nield whispered. 'You're all shook up, you are. Could be interesting, this . . .'

Portch followed the highway through the night to Fakenham. Here he turned on to the B1355. A sports car flashed past Nield, inserted itself between the Mercedes and the Vauxhall. Useful camouflage. The three cars whipped along the winding road, turned west on to the A149. The coast road.

Nield recognized the road from their journey along it from Blakeney that morning. He had an excellent memory for any route when he'd passed over it once. 'You're heading for Brancaster, my friend,' he thought. 'Yes, this could be interesting, very interesting indeed.'

The outskirts of Brancaster was a line of isolated cottages separated from each other by hedges. The sports car overtook as Portch turned into a drive. Nield went on past the drive, found a grass verge, parked, walked back.

He had trouble reading the lopsided sign outside the cottage where Portch had parked. The cottage looked tumbledown, the garden was knee-high in uncut lawn, the paved path a mass of weeds between the stones. He had to use a torch to make out the lettering. *Crag Cove.*

178

Lights were on in the front room behind drawn curtains. He walked along the highway past two cottages and went up to the front door of the third. Knocking on the door, he stood well back in case it was a woman who lived alone. It wasn't. The door was opened by a middle-aged man wearing a rumpled pullover and uncreased slacks.

'Very sorry to bother you at this time of night,' Nield began, 'but I'm lost. I have to deliver an urgent package to an address in Brancaster. Trouble is the address is smeared. Looks like Crag Cove but I can't read the name.'

'Oh, him.' The man's tone was indifferent, almost hostile. 'Keeps himself to himself, he does. Crag Cove? Three doors up to your left at the end of my path. Seaman type called Caleb Fox. Got it?'

'Yes, indeed, I have got it,' said Nield. 'You have been most helpful.'

22

The marksman known as 'The Monk' drove just inside the speed limit as they headed through the night towards Rheims. Klein sat beside him, still smarting under Marler's insistence that he would drive.

But Marler had the reputation of being the finest killer with a rifle in Western Europe. He was 'credited' with the shooting of Oskar Graf von Krull, the German banker who had helped finance an army of private informants to track down Baader-Meinhof.

Another of his kills had been an Italian chief of police at the behest of the Mafia. And always he had an unbreakable alibi. He was officially in France every time he carried out a 'commission'. His fees were enormous but he guaranteed results.

Klein studied the Englishman as they approached

Rheims. His researches into the Englishman's background had proved difficult. Plenty of rumours through underworld contacts but nothing concrete. Klein didn't know as much about him as he would have liked – but that was a tribute to the man's ability, and he was an independent-minded bastard.

Marler was in his thirties, a slim man of medium height, clean-shaven with a determined jaw. His smooth face was frequently creased in a half-smile which did not reach his brown eyes. His hair was flaxen-coloured, but seen from the back he had a small bald patch over his pink crown. Hence his nickname, The Monk.

He spoke with a public school accent, his voice light in tone. He always appeared calm and under complete self-control. He had proved himself a crack shot at Bisley – Klein knew that much. There had been talk of an embezzlement, which had shut out the world of business to him.

His father – now dead in a road accident – had been a famous racing driver. The nationality of his mother was obscure. He had a flair for speaking foreign languages – which was probably why he had settled in France. He seemed to have no permanent residence, flitting from one country to another.

'He is what they call a soldier of fortune,' a Corsican in Paris had told Klein. 'A man who will do anything for money. He has expensive tastes. He likes expensive women, I hear.'

Klein's careful preliminary investigation before approaching The Monk only told him Marler had a short-term lease on a good apartment in the upper-class Parisian district of Passy. Discreet enquiries revealed he spent very little time there.

The Corsican had provided Klein – for a fee – with a phone number. A girl had answered, had asked a lot of questions. He had been forced to give her his room number at the Georges Cinq. 'He may call you back,' the girl had said and rung off.

Later Marler had called him, instructing him to meet him at a grotty *pension* called the Bernadotte on the Left Bank. It had been a very clandestine meeting and Klein had choked at the requested fee. Five million francs.

'Take it or leave it,' Marler had told him. 'And I need one million in advance. Cash. Used notes. The usual thing . . .'

All these thoughts ran through Klein's mind as they passed Rheims in the early hours. He told Marler to make for Sedan next. There had even been an argument as to who would drive. 'I'm not yammering on about the point any longer,' Marler had informed Klein. 'I like to be in control.'

That remark had jarred on Klein. *He* liked to be in control. And it was already clear Marler was not in the least frightened of him. Klein was a man who liked to reinforce his authority by intimidating members of the team he had recruited.

'It's not Germany, is it?' Marler asked.

'I told you no before . . .'

'Sometimes,' Marler continued amiably, 'people attempt to trick me. Not a wise procedure, I assure you. Where are we making for?'

'The Ardennes. The Belgian province of Luxembourg.'

'Oh, that's all right. As I told you, I never undertake a commission in any country more than once – which rules out Germany, Italy, Spain, Greece and Egypt. Had the devil of a job hiring a Citroën with a rack fitted on the roof. A practice shoot, you said. Why the rack?'

'You'll see. When the time comes it will be a moving target.'

'We're approaching the Franco–Belgian frontier,' Klein said. 'You have the rifle well concealed?'

'Strapped with tape under the car.'

'You also brought a shovel?'

'Wrapped in a sack inside the boot. I am reputed to be efficient. Here's the border coming up. You might leave me to do the talking,' he snapped in French. They had used the language since their first meeting.

In the dark the headlight beams showed up a striped pole across the road, a small hut alongside it. There were low hedges with fields beyond on either side. Marler pulled up, lowered his window. 'Give me your passport,' he said as a French Customs official plodded towards them with a heavy tread.

'Papers . . .'

Marler showed a British passport. The official made a dismissive gesture and yawned. He saw Klein's German passport and made the same gesture.

'Why are you going to Belgium?' he asked in a bored tone.

'On holiday,' Marler replied.

'Push off!'

'I think we woke the poor devil up,' Marler commented as he drove on.

'A good hour to cross the border. And our passports are both Common Market. Keep straight ahead . . .'

The flat character of the countryside they'd passed through changed. Forested hills dropped sheer to the road which wound its way through deep defiles. Klein pointed to a sign-posted side turning.

'The road to Bouillon. I leave you at the Hotel Panorama on the way back. A room is reserved in your name. I take this Citroën. Hire yourself another car. You stay in Bouillon until you hear from me – or a man called Hipper.'

'What about my fee – the advance payment?'

'You get that after you've shown me you can shoot.'

It was wild and lonely Ardennes country where they stopped the car. An abandoned stone quarry yawned before them in the dawn light – like a vast amphitheatre with sheer walls on three sides. The ground was scattered with stones and rocks across its sandy surface. Marler stood with Klein in the treacherous light – difficult for aiming. A long way off he heard two sharp reports. Marler jerked up his head.

'Rifle shots.'

'They're hunting boar. Anyone who hears you will assume we are doing the same. Let's get on with it.'

From the boot Klein took the large sack and the shovel. He proceeded to fill the sack with a mixture of sand and small rocks. Marler crawled under the car, removed the adhesive tape, emerged holding a high-powered rifle and a telescopic sight which he attached to the weapon. He wiped the infra-red lens of the sight with a silk handkerchief, pressed the rifle stock into his shoulder and swept the top of the quarry.

Klein perched the sack jammed full of rocks and sand on top of the Citroën. He produced a length of rope, attached it to the neck of the sack. He then secured the sack at both ends, tying the rope to the bars of the rack.

'What's that in aid of?' Marler enquired.

'You climb to the top of the quarry. The left-hand side is the easier route. Get up there as fast as you can – before the light improves. Wave to me when you're ready. I shall then drive this car at speed round the base of this quarry. Your target is the sack, which will be bouncing about. I am taking a risk – I will be behind the wheel . . .'

'No risk at all,' Marler drawled. 'I get it now. And by the time I get up there the light will be really tricky – how many shots?'

'Would six be all right? We'll see how many you get on target.'

'Anything you say. Let me check that sandbag first.'

He fetched a pair of driving gloves from inside the car and put them on. Placing the rifle gently across the boot, he began punching the sandbag like a boxer. He punched at it from all angles. Then he tossed the gloves back into the car.

'Tighter than a girl's pantyhose. We don't want you delivering the car hire outfit a vehicle with bullet-holes in the roof.' He paused. 'Or in your head. You've got guts, Klein – doing this. I'll give you that.'

Marler walked away and Klein watched his silhouette in the gloom. Carrying the rifle in both hands he went up the steep path like a mountain goat. At the summit he looked down. The dawn was now a weird amber light. Klein stood waiting by the Citroën.

Marler aimed the sight straight at Klein, then adjusted the sight and checked again. He took his time. In the heavy silence which lay over the forest behind he heard a faint sound. The impatient shuffling of Klein's feet. Let the sod wait. He adjusted the sight a fraction, stared into the lens, waved his hand.

He waited while Klein drove the Citroën three circuits as fast as he could round the floor of the quarry, sending up great clouds of sand. That was going to be a great help. Klein drove deviously, stopping suddenly, skidding, accelerating, following a different course each circuit.

Marler raised his rifle, squinted through the sights, pulled the trigger of the automatic weapon rapidly. Inside the car, above the noise of the engine, Klein heard the thump of the heavy slugs hitting the bouncing sack above him. He swung the Citroën into a vicious turn, skidded sideways, losing control for a few seconds. The thumps continued in swift succession. When he'd counted six he slowed, stopped, waited a moment to show Marler he had stopped, opened the door slowly and got out.

When Marler reached him after slithering down the path there was a pallid glow reflecting off the quarry walls. Klein was using a torch to examine the sack. Marler brushed rock dust off his trousers, held the rifle loosely in his right hand as he spoke.

'Well?'

'Six out of six. Quite remarkable. You are a crack shot.'

'That's why you hired me, wasn't it? A moving target, you said. And presumably I'll be operating from high up – hence the firing position at the top of the quarry. That much I need to know.'

His voice was cold, his last remark a demand. A different voice from anything Klein had heard before.

'Yes, you will be firing from altitude.'

Klein used a pen-knife to slice through the rope – he had no intention of letting Marler see the knife sheathed and strapped to his right leg. Opening the neck of the sack, he emptied the sand and rocks on the ground. Then he held out the sack with six punctured holes and the rope screwed up inside. 'You have the can of petrol?'

'At the back of the boot under a pile of rags.'

'Take this sack to the base of the quarry and burn it. I'll collect the bullets . . .'

'Burn it yourself.' Marler fetched the can, handed it to him. 'I'll find the bullets. You're not my boss, I'm not your servant.'

Klein tightened his lips, accepted the can and walked to the wall of the quarry. Marler searched the ground, picking up the slugs until he'd found all six. Walking to the fringe of the quarry, he hurled each bullet deep into the undergrowth, varying direction for each throw.

The sack flared in the distance, a brief incandescence of red flame which settled down into a coil of smoke. Marler watched Klein using the shovel to spread sand and stones over the relics, then crawled under the car to attach the telescopic sight with adhesive tape. Klein was looking down at him when he crawled out.

'What are you doing?' he demanded. 'I told you, I'm driving the Citroën back to Paris. You have the papers I need to hand in the vehicle?'

'Waiting for you on the driving seat. The rifle is in the back in full view. You said they hunted boar round here. But it is eighty kilometres back to the turn-off to Bouillon. I checked the odometer. If a patrol car stops us, the rifle is OK. Shooting country. The infra-red sight they might wonder about. I'll remove it when we're near Bouillon. You know, Klein, you must watch your security. And the car was hired in my name. How do you handle that?'

'I say you've been taken ill. If they get their car back and the balance of payment they're happy.'

'Which is more than I'll be until I get my advance – a million francs.'

Klein put on a pair of chamois gloves, reached into his pocket, handed Marler an envelope. 'A bearer bond – for one million. It's as good as cash, easier to carry. Plus something extra for expenses.'

Marler made sure the rifle was securely tucked behind his suitcase on the rear seat, climbed behind the wheel and drove back the way they had come.

'I would like some idea of what you have planned,' he remarked.

'For the money you're getting you should appreciate how much security is involved.' Klein decided it was time he asserted himself. 'And what would you have done if I'd decided that you were not the man I needed and driven off?'

'Oh, simple. I'd have put a bullet through your head.'

23

Tweed sat in the large, high-ceilinged living-room on the first floor of the house in Eaton Square. Lady Windermere had placed him on a low couch while she occupied a Regency high-backed wooden chair, which meant she looked down on him.

'Lara is in some trouble, I presume? Otherwise you wouldn't be bothering me.'

'Why do you presume that?' Tweed asked.

She was a tall thin woman of about fifty, her face was long and thin-lipped, her nose aristocratic, her manner arrogant, her tone that of someone addressing the lower orders. She was smoking a cigarette in a long ivory holder.

'Well, is she or isn't she? You must realize this is all a great nuisance. My son, Robin – by my previous marriage – is getting married soon. Can you imagine the number of important things I have to attend to?'

'Supposing I told you Lara could be in some danger?'

'If she's got herself into some silly scrape she'll jolly well have to get herself out of it. At the moment, Mr . . . Tweed, isn't it? . . . Robin's marriage takes precedence over everything. He's marrying a most suitable girl who will, in due course, provide a son and heir to carry on the line.'

'I see.' For a moment Tweed was stunned. He had heard of women like this. In certain mannerisms Lady Windermere reminded him of his own wife, now living it up with a Greek shipping magnate in Brazil. 'I don't think I've made myself very clear,' he persisted. 'It's just possible that in all innocence your daughter . . .'

'*Step*-daughter. She came with Rolly. She was wished on me . . .'

'But you knew that when you married your present husband.'

'Mr Tweed, I regard that as a piece of impertinence which I'm not prepared to overlook.'

'I regard it as a fact of life,' Tweed said mildly.

'And innocence has nothing to do with Lara. She goes her own disgusting way, mixing with the wrong sort of people. Is it any wonder she's got herself into trouble. Is she pregnant, by the way? I might as well know.'

'You might as well,' Tweed agreed. 'To the best of my knowledge, she has no problems in that direction. In fact, I have been told she is a very resourceful and independent girl who simply wanted to live her own life. She is, after all, over the age of consent. Now can we get down to brass tacks? When did you last see her? Did she give any indication that she might be going abroad? Perhaps to look for a job?'

'Am I being interrogated? If so, shouldn't I have my lawyer present?'

'Not with Special Branch,' Tweed said grimly. 'I need some lead about her present activities. I may even be able to protect her . . .'

'Protect her! My God, you'll have your work cut out . . .'

'Why?' Tweed flashed back.

'Because she's one of these so-called rebels . . .'

'We have no information suggesting she is mixed up with anything remotely political.'

'Is there going to be publicity about this?' she demanded. 'That simply isn't on – not with the wedding coming up.'

'I can't keep anything quiet unless you stop thinking about this wedding for five minutes and try and help me. Has she any particular friend she might have gone to abroad – man or woman?'

'Oh, I'm sure it would be a man . . .'

'Lady Windermere, I'm asking you to be specific – to answer my questions. If you won't, we'll have to go about things in a quite different way – which could involve widespread publicity.'

'Is that a threat?'

'Another fact of life. If you want someone present while we talk why not ask your husband to be here? Preferably today.'

'Oh, he wouldn't help at all. Rolly's far too wrapped up in his merchant bank. In any case, he's also too soft with Lara. Ask your questions.'

Too soft? Lara was Roland Seagrave's daughter, Tweed thought. Perhaps he should have gone straight to him. No, he'd come to find out Lady Windermere's attitude.

'Where is Lara now?' she asked.

'Somewhere in France,' Tweed replied vaguely. 'Now, had she any particular friend, close friend, she might have gone to see?'

'She was positively infatuated with some foreigner. I never knew his name, anything about him – except he could have been a diplomat. She met him at a party, I gather. And she did get phone calls from abroad. I answered one call and the man at the other end wouldn't identify himself. Just insisted on speaking to Lara.'

'Any photographs? Of Lara with this man?'

'No, I've looked . . .' She paused, then spoke aggressively. 'I did feel it was my duty to try and find out what she was up to.'

Which meant, Tweed thought, you went through her things while she was away. Sheer curiosity. Maybe something even worse – in the hope of finding pictures which would discredit Lara with her father.

'What jobs, if any, did she take abroad? She's good at languages, I understand.'

'Yes. And that's not always a good thing. It means she can strike up acquaintances with the wrong types. She had one job in Geneva two years ago. With one of the UN outfits, I think.'

'Could you be more specific? Which outfit?'

'No, I couldn't! I lead far too busy a life to keep an eye on an errant step-daughter. She moved on to another post in Luxembourg City – again with some UN organization. I do think that's it. No, just a minute, she was also in Paris afterwards. Don't ask me with whom. Now, you said Lara was in some sort of trouble . . .'

'No, Lady Windermere – you asked me if she was. I said she might just be in danger.'

'She'll squirm her way out of it. Now, if that is all?'

'For the moment.' Tweed stood up. 'I may have to come back if the situation develops the wrong way . . .'

'I'm relying on you to see it doesn't. She's a British citizen, you are Special Branch.'

'I'll do my best. No guarantees . . .'

'And no publicity of any kind.'

'Again, no guarantees . . .'

She fired her last shot. 'You must realize Lara is the most self-centred person. She thinks only of what she wants and gives no consideration whatsoever to other people's feelings.'

189

'Goodbye.'

And that, Tweed mused as he descended the front steps, was a perfect self-portrait of the woman I've just interviewed. He took a deep breath of fresh air, gazing up at the trees in the centre of Eaton Square. God, what a relief to get out of that house.

Timers. Scuba Divers. Marksman. Lara. Explosives. Banker.

After leaving Marler at the Hotel Panorama in Bouillon Klein had phoned Hipper from the Hotel de la Poste. 'Yes, the consignment was now ready for collection,' Hipper had assured him.

Driving to Larochette, Klein had collected a heavy case packed by Louis Chabot which contained the sixty timers and five control boxes. Driving on north to Clervaux – near where the Turkish Nestlé truck driver had perished – he swung west, heading for the Belgian town of Dinant on the river Meuse. He had stopped at an isolated spot in the Ardennes and written out his list again. He sat looking at it now, satisfied with the progress he had made.

The timers. In the case behind him, ready for delivery via a means of transport safe from any Customs inspection. A means of transport already tested by the movement of the gold bullion stolen from the two banks in Basle.

Scuba divers. The whole team recruited and hidden away on two camping sites in Holland. And Grand-Pierre – Big Pierre – Dubois would keep them busy with training programmes. The whole assault team had carefully been chosen from French-speaking nationals – Belgians, Frenchmen and Luxembourgers – so they shared a common language. Essential for liaison when the operation was put in motion.

Marksman. The Monk, despite his arrogance, was the finest shot with a rifle available in Western Europe. Now he was in place in Bouillon. Not too long a drive from the target.

Lara. She'd be kept happy exploring Cherbourg until he returned to Paris. And the extra thousand pounds he'd dropped in her lap would keep her even more happy. No trouble from that direction.

Explosives. Again in place where they would never be found. And again not far from the target.

Banker. The key to the whole operation. And he had already arranged for the huge sum to be available. After despatch of the timers Klein would call again on the banker, make the final arrangements.

Klein ticked off the last item mentally, took out his lighter, set fire to the scrap of paper, dropped it into the ash-tray. He'd empty the curled and blackened remnants later into one of the many streams coursing through the Ardennes. Yes, he was satisfied he'd dealt with everything – and left behind no trace.

But the banker. That was the last knot to tie up before he launched the vast operation.

'Special Branch?'

Jacob Rubinstein, bullion merchant with headquarters in the City of London, studied the card. Sitting on the other side of his large mahogany desk Tweed studied Rubinstein. Small and neat, in his early sixties, Tweed estimated, Rubinstein had thinning brown hair tidily brushed above his high forehead. His eyes were alert under hooded lids, his complexion rosy, his face plump with a small moustache, his manner relaxed.

'You do realize, Mr Tweed,' he began in his quiet voice, 'I have an obligation to maintain discretion in my business? You might say my company's reputation is its major asset – if that doesn't sound pompous.'

'I understand completely,' Tweed agreed. He'd foreseen this was going to be difficult. 'But you might say my own organization is based on the same principles. Secrecy. I need information.'

'I feared that.' Rubinstein handed back the card, smiled, waited.

'I'm looking for a dealer in bullion – or a banker – who may not have the same ethics as yourself. Someone who cuts corners – to make a profit.'

'You mean in this country, Mr Tweed? I couldn't possibly point the finger at a member of my profession.'

'In this country just possibly. More likely on the continent.'

'We do a lot of business with Europe.' Rubinstein's tone was apologetic. 'The same ethics would apply.' He paused, rubbing his hands together. Probably the nearest he ever came to showing disquiet. 'Unless, of course, something of a definitely criminal nature was involved.'

Tweed sighed inwardly with relief, seeing his opening. 'Now I have to ask you to practise the same admirable discretion you have displayed so far about your colleagues. Nothing I'm about to say must be revealed to another soul. I know I can count on you.'

Rubinstein cocked his head to one side, clasped his pink hands. 'You can rely on me. Please go on.'

'What I'm trying to find out is whether some vast terrorist outrage is planned. Not the people you'd immediately think of. Maybe something far more deadly. There were two bullion robberies in Basle a while ago. The gold has never been found. It could have been used to finance this gigantic operation. I've very few leads. If I could get a clue as to the banker – or bullion merchant – who handled that gold I might be in time to locate the gang involved. It's my only hope. A banker willing to take over that gold, provide a percentage of cash in return. You know such a man?'

'I might.' Rubinstein stared at the ceiling. Tweed kept very still, silent. 'The go-between is the man you're seeking?'

'Exactly.'

'I don't think you're a man who would exaggerate, Mr Tweed.'

Rubinstein had reached inside a small box, taking out a blank white card. He wrote on it slowly, lips pursed, then handed it to Tweed. 'I know you will never reveal where you obtained that information from. It is the best I can do for you.'

Tweed read the writing on the card. *Peter Brand, Banque Sambre. Brussels and Luxembourg City*.

'Sounds English,' he commented.

'He is. A brilliant banker – who also deals in bullion. He married the daughter of the man who founded the Banque. He has run it for a number of years. Only about thirty-five or so. He has complete control and has shown a spectacular rise in profits.'

'But surely the Banque belongs to his wife?'

'It does. She is only interested in enjoying herself. What I believe you would call a member of the jet set. Spends a lot of time in the Americas.'

'Which leaves Brand free to run things any way he wishes.'

'Quite right – so long as he provides her with the princely income she needs for her way of life. Which he does. An arrangement which suits both partners. I seem to be gossiping a lot, which is not my habit.'

'Gossip can underlie truth. And Brand deals in bullion, you said?'

'Yes. A brilliant man, as I said earlier. He has every talent you could wish for. Fluent in several languages. His personality is magnetic, a great charmer with the ladies, so I hear. Among the clients he has dealt with are the Russians.'

'Nothing illegal about that.'

'Except that the Kremlin is greedy for hard currency from the West. What better way of getting it than through obtaining large quantities of cut-price bullion.'

'Which makes the origin of the bullion suspect?'

'You said that, I didn't. On the other hand, I don't recall contradicting you.'

Tweed stood up, held out his hand. 'I'm very grateful

for your help. You might just have supplied the break-through I've been searching for.'

'I just hope I've done the right thing.'

'I'm beginning to think I'm involved in a race against time.'

'Let's hope you're not too late, then.'

'As Wellington once said, it could be the nearest run thing.'

24

Paris, rue des Saussaies. Headquarters of French counter-intelligence is situated in a narrow winding street off the rue du Faubourg St Honoré, close to the Élysée Palace. The entrance is a stone archway leading to a cobbled yard beyond and nothing outside indicates its occupants.

Tweed and Newman sat in Lasalle's cramped office, drinking coffee, very strong and bitter. Lasalle had listened in silence while Tweed recalled his conversation with Lady Windermere.

'Sounds a monster,' he commented. 'Why did you see her?'

'One reason only. I wanted to find out whether she knew where Lara was. She doesn't.'

'Why did you want that information?'

'It's a part of the vague picture building up in my mind.'

Lasalle looked at Newman, shrugged, waved his large hands in a gesture of resignation. 'He's playing it close to the chest. As always.'

'Is Lara still at The Ritz?' Tweed asked. 'Because if you still have tabs on her I want to fake a chance meeting with her.'

'Then you might like a brief report from the man who has been watching her. One of my best men. Leon Valmy.

We call him The Parrot behind his back. You will know why when you see him.' He pressed a switch on his intercom, gave a brief order and a minute later The Parrot entered.

'I want you to tell these two gentlemen from England all you know about Lara Seagrave. They both speak French . . .'

'I must first apologize for messing up my job,' The Parrot began. 'Losing the girl when she jumped into that Volvo near the Place de la Concorde was sheer carelessness . . .'

'You hadn't had sleep for God knows how long,' Lasalle told him. 'Now, tell them your story. Start with Marseilles . . .'

The little man with the funny beaked nose sat down at Lasalle's request and began. Tweed leaned forward, watching him intently. Again he felt himself back in his old Scotland Yard days. Some policemen could spend twenty years in the force and learn nothing from experience. The Parrot was a very different kettle of fish.

He spoke precisely, always explained why he had taken certain action. His opening words impressed Tweed. 'There were these rumours of a strange new organization being built up for some great operation. Maybe the hijacking of a ship. In Marseilles the best viewpoint for a terrorist to check the layout is Notre Dame de la Garde. I had been waiting there – on a hunch – for five days before this girl appeared . . .'

He ended with his losing her when she dived into the Volvo. A colleague had taken over the watch on The Ritz. Lara had returned to the hotel two hours later, walking down the rue St Honoré, entering by the main entrance.

'One question,' Tweed said eventually. 'When you've had many years' experience tracking people you get a feeling about your target. What is your feeling about Lara Seagrave?'

'Oh, she is highly suspect. She even watches to see if she is being followed. Professionally, too. She uses shop

195

windows as mirrors. She varies her pace. She has been trained.'

'Does she follow any routine?'

'Only one. She goes each day to Smiths' bookshop tea-room on the first floor – except when she visited Cherbourg. She arrives at 4 p.m. Has tea and a cake.'

'Thank you.' Tweed glanced at Newman. 'I think I shall be having tea at Smiths' at four this afternoon.'

He manœuvred it carefully. The tea-room was filling up. Lara was pulling out the chair of a corner table when Tweed appeared, performing the same action opposite her. Pausing, he spoke in English.

'I do beg your pardon. I didn't notice you. I was dreaming.'

Lara studied him for a few seconds, then smiled. 'Oh, do come and join me. I'm on my own and getting so bored. It will be nice to have an Englishman to chat to over tea. I've spoken French non-stop ever since I arrived in France.'

'Thank you. After a while one gets homesick.' He picked up the menu. 'I see they have a selection of teas. I want something normal . . .'

'Try the Darjeeling. That's my tipple.' She smiled, offered him her pack of cigarettes and when he refused lit one for herself after asking his permission. 'And if you're hungry, they do a very good toasted tea-cake. English marmalade as well. All home comforts!'

'Paradise,' he responded. 'I'll have the same.'

She ordered for them both and he was careful not to ask any direct questions. 'You like Paris?' he enquired. 'By the way, my name is Tweed.'

'Lara Seagrave.' She extended her slim hand. 'Now we're friends.'

She was enormously attractive, he was thinking – with her long auburn hair, her excellent bone structure, the devil-take-the hindmost tilt of her chin, repeated in the humorous glint in her blue eyes.

'You look as though you enjoy life,' she remarked.

'I suppose I like my job. You'll think it frightfully dull. I'm in insurance.'

'What exactly do you do? Sell insurance? You don't look the type, if I may say so.'

'I'm chief claims investigator. Someone dies, a huge sum is at stake. The statistics show it's a most unusual way for a man to die as he did – a ten thousand-to-one chance. I have to check it. I know the wife benefits, I find she has been having an affair with a man who is a confidence trickster. I launch a full-scale investigation. That's an extreme case.'

'Sounds exciting, like being a detective.'

'I was once.'

They ate their tea-cakes, Tweed said she had good judgement. She poured more tea in both cups, then felt around inside her tote bag, producing two articles wrapped in tissue and handing him one.

'Something extra if you've still got space. *Couques*. They come from Dinant on the Meuse, just across the border in Belgium.'

Tweed unwrapped the tissue, examined the small gingerbread house. 'Quite remarkable. I've never seen anything so well-designed.'

'They're scrumptious.' She ate hers and watched Tweed wrapping his up in the tissue again.

'If you don't mind,' he said, 'I'll keep mine for later. I get peckish about six in the evening – well before dinner. You have a job here in Paris?'

'*Had*.' Her blue eyes held his. 'Now I've switched from being a secretary to research. It brings in a lot more money. It gives you independence. I want to show my family I can make it on my own.'

'I applaud the idea.' Tweed frowned. 'Lara Seagrave. I've heard that name somewhere. Probably I'm wrong . . .'

'Probably you're right,' she said with an ironical twist of her full lips. 'If you ever read the bloody *Tatler*. I'm the

197

step-daughter of Lady Windermere. She's queen of the bitches.'

'She is the one you want to show you can make it on your own, then?' he suggested.

'You're so right.' She paused and studied him afresh. 'It's funny, I'm talking to you about things I've hardly ever said to anyone else. You're a good listener. I wouldn't like to be questioned by you if I'd committed a crime.'

'No crime in wanting to upstage an unpleasant step-mother,' he said amiably.

She looked at her watch. 'Glory! I'm expecting a phone call. Would you think me rude if I rush?'

'Only if you refuse to allow me to pay for the tea.' He lifted his hand. 'No argument. I was lonely, too.'

She stood up, held out her hand. 'I do hope we meet again, Mr Tweed. Four o'clock here will find me for the next few days. Now, I really must go . . .'

Tweed rose to his feet. Out of the corner of his eye he saw The Parrot, who had paid his bill early, leaving his table to precede her down the stairs. He looked quite different in a beret and a dark overcoat.

'Tell me again about Dr Portch and Norfolk,' Tweed said to Newman as they sat in the lounge area of the Hotel de France et Choiseul.

'I checked old newspapers in the British Museum reading room for starters. I found what I was looking for two years ago – the story which rang a bell when you mentioned the name Portch. He had a practice in Brighton. Was very popular with the old ladies. Had a number of them as patients. Two died, left him legacies in their wills. A cool ten thousand pounds altogether. People began talking. At the coroner's inquest, it was touch and go whether he was indicted for murder. The coroner was not too bright, retired shortly afterwards. Natural causes was the conclusion.'

'Why the doubt in your opinion? We didn't have too

much time to talk about it before we rushed for the Paris flight.'

'I'd left Butler and Nield in King's Lynn for the day while I drove down to Brighton. I poked around, for the police inspector in charge of the case. He also has retired. He was cagey at first. After a few Scotches at his bungalow he suddenly blew up. Said Portch should be behind bars for life. An Inspector Williams. The coroner's verdict stalled his investigation. Both the old ducks died of overdoses of barbiturates. Williams reckons the coroner was senile, and a woman-hater to boot. But it finished Portch in Brighton.'

'How?'

'Rest of his patients voted with their feet, left him. He had to sell the practice for a pittance. Which explains, I suppose, why he ended up taking a backwater position at Cockley Ford. They probably hadn't heard of the case there. The Portch case wasn't widely reported – there was a lot of international news at the time. It only made one national daily – on an inside page.'

'So someone in London who wanted a man like Portch to take over at Cockley Ford could have read the story?'

'Yes. Who are you thinking of?'

'No one in particular. You'll enjoy tomorrow – Lasalle is taking us to meet a Corsican gang leader here in Paris.'

'What for?'

'He knows something about a man the underworld calls The Recruiter.'

At Dinant in the Belgian Ardennes, just north of the French border, a massive cliff rises above the town, topped by a citadel which looks down on the river Meuse. Klein drove the Citroën over the Pont de Charles de Gaulle and headed for the barge moored further upstream.

Aboard the vessel, the *Gargantua*, its Belgian owner, Joseph Haber, watched the car coming and froze. Haber wore a pair of thick blue serge trousers and an old pea-jacket. A man of forty, he was short and thickset with black hair half-concealed by the peaked cap he habitually wore. He went into the wheelhouse at the rear of the barge and slammed the door as Klein pulled alongside the *Gargantua*, switched off the engine.

Climbing out of the car, carrying a case, he looked round the deserted waterfront and crossed the gangplank linking the barge to the shore. He pushed open the door and entered the wheelhouse. Haber spoke at once.

'I'm not doing any more for you Don't care what you offer to pay me.'

'Clean up your mortgage on the Rhine barge and leave you a fortune in the bank . . .'

'Get off my barge. I don't want to see you again. One job was enough. You paid me. I did it. That's it.'

'I think not.' Klein was amiable. 'For a start there is the problem of the *Gargantua*. There could be traces of the bullion left down in that hold. I warned you about that at the beginning.'

'I'll have her cleaned out. I'll pay for that myself . . .'

'Really, you don't seem to understand.' Klein was patient, as though dealing with a not too bright child. 'Very fine grains of the bullion could be discovered by police forensic experts. We can't risk it. The barge must go – as we planned. You can get the insurance on it afterwards. She has to be sunk where we arranged, Haber. And I have something for you to transport aboard your other barge, the *Erika*. Nothing so bulky or troublesome, this time. In fact, the case I am holding. I really must insist . . .'

'And I told you last time enough was enough. So bugger off . . .'

'Haber, you have a longer trip to make this time with this.' Klein put the case down on the wheelhouse floor, his manner calm and confident. 'And I see your partner, Broucker, is on board the *Erika* further downstream. He must come with us on our trip to Les Dames de Meuse. When we have got rid of the *Gargantua* we then drive back here and I'll tell you your new destination.'

'I said get off my barge . . .'

'Really, you must think of your family. The charming Martine, your wife, and your young son, Lucien.' He dropped a brooch on the ledge of the wheelhouse.

Haber stared at it in horror. The horror turned to fury as he lurched forward, grabbing for Klein's throat with both hands. 'What have you done with them, you bastard? If you have harmed either . . .'

'They are both in a safe place.' Klein grasped Haber by his wrists, forced him to sit down in the captain's chair. The grip felt like a vice of steel. 'Now quieten down. You are going to make a lot of money. I know you're ambitious. You will be able to buy a fleet of barges. Please keep still – we don't want anyone to see us struggling, do we? Not if your family is to remain safe and well-fed . . .'

Inside the wheelhouse aboard the *Nantes*, a third barge upstream from the *Gargantua*, Willy Boden turned to his wife, Simone. 'I think Haber is having an argument with that peculiar chap, Klein. No, don't stand up or they'll see us.'

'I don't like the look of that Klein,' Simone replied, stroking her long hair. 'I think he's trouble . . .'

'It's Haber's business, not ours. Let's finish our meal.'

Half an hour later he wiped his mouth with the back of his hand and peered towards Dinant. 'That's funny,' he remarked. 'The *Gargantua* is leaving. Moving upstream towards the French border and Les Dames de Meuse. Haber was loaded up with gravel. And Broucker has closed the hatches of the *Erika*. He's joined Haber aboard the *Gargantua*. Why would he do that? Why would Haber sail upstream when he always takes the gravel downstream to Liège?'

'What about that man, Klein?' Simone snapped.

'He must still be on board. His car is parked by the mooring they have left.'

'I think something is wrong. My intuition tells me . . .'

'If we steered this barge by your intuition we'd hit the bank ten times a day. I told you, it's none of our business.

And Haber does not like interference. We forget it. The deck is in need of a wash-down . . .'

Further upstream the *Gargantua* proceeded towards the citadel towering above Dinant. Klein was satisfied all was well and no one had noticed his confrontation with Haber.

'This is Sampiero Calgourli,' Lasalle introduced.

Tweed and Newman made no attempt to shake hands since the Union Corse chief remained seated when Lasalle had told him their names. They followed Lasalle's example and sat down in the dark room cluttered with old-fashioned furniture.

Calgourli's headquarters was an apartment near the meat market in the southern area of Paris. Swarthy-faced, the Corsican had very wide shoulders in proportion to his lack of height. His neck was thick, his hair dark and greasy, his moustache curved round the corners of a cruel mouth.

'Who are these people?' Calgourli demanded.

'Mr Tweed is a very powerful man in England, Mr Newman is his protector. Both – like me – are interested in everything you can tell us about the man known as The Recruiter.'

'And why should I tell you anything – even if I knew about this man?'

'Look here, Calgourli . . .' Lasalle leaned forward. His manner was transformed. All hint of good humour had gone. His expression was grim, his tone tough. '. . . One day you will need a favour. I make a good friend – and a very bad enemy. I could get the idea into my head it would be an idea to investigate your Italian connection.'

'Please, my friend!' Calgourli spread his gnarled hands and he smiled, showing bad teeth. 'I merely ask a simple question. I like to know where I stand . . .'

'The Recruiter,' Lasalle repeated.

'Not a man I would do business with. He tried though – this Klein.'

'Excuse me,' Tweed intervened in French. 'You say his name is Klein?'

'That is the name he uses. You think that is his real name? He probably has half-a-dozen. He comes here with an introduction from a man in Marseilles. Little does he know I am no longer a friend of this man. I think Perugini has a perverted sense of humour.' He made a dismissive gesture. 'No doubt he extracted a fee for the introduction from Klein.'

'What did Klein want from you?' Lasalle snapped.

'To recruit one of my associates. A man who is an explosives expert and a scuba diver. Now, Mr Lasalle, where would I find a man like that?'

'In five minutes on your doorstep – if you wanted to. What was your reply?'

'I told him to go fishing – something like that. Perhaps I was a little crude . . .'

'How did he react to that?' Lasalle pressed.

'Very calmly. He is a very cold man. I do not mind admitting I was glad I had a friend with me. Klein is a man who would carve up a corpse if he thought the corpse had pearls in its belly. And he laid down absurd conditions for his fee.' Calgourli stirred himself, rang a bell on the table by his side. 'Maurice! Bring wine.'

Lasalle watched as a thin young man with blank eyes came in, laid a tray of glasses and a bottle of red wine on the table. Calgourli poured wine, offered a glass to each of his guests. Tweed sipped cautiously. *Vin ordinaire.* Very ordinary. He loathed red wine but thought it best not to disturb the atmosphere. The old ruffian, he felt certain, could be explosively touchy.

'I trust,' Lasalle began, 'that Maurice is not listening in to this conversation.'

'If he was I'd cut off an ear.'

'What were these absurd conditions?' enquired Tweed.

'That the man he hired should leave Paris that night, that he should tell no one he was leaving, that no one should know his destination – including myself! I do not work in such ways – even had he asked for someone I could have supplied.'

'How much?' Lasalle asked laconically, not touching his wine.

'Pardon?'

'Oh, come on, for God's sake. I'm losing patience with you. What fee did he offer you?'

'Fifty thousand francs – with a second payment of the same amount when my man had left Paris.'

'Could you please describe this Klein?' Tweed asked.

'About a hundred and eighty centimetres tall, about eighty kilogrammes in weight. Colour of hair – no idea. He wore a black beret and a silk scarf which covered the back of his neck. I didn't like his eyes.'

'What colour?' Tweed continued.

'No idea. He wore those wrap-round tinted glasses . . .'

'Then why didn't you like the eyes – if you couldn't see them?'

'This man is a policeman?' Calgourli asked Lasalle.

'Answer his question.'

'I could only see the eyes vaguely, but all the time he was in this room they stared at me from behind those tinted lenses. Ah, yes, and his face was white as death – a death mask.'

'How did he take your refusal?' Lasalle asked.

'He seemed amused.' Calgourli's lips tightened at the memory. 'He said if I didn't want to do business that was it.' Calgourli paused, looking at Lasalle. 'I can tell you one thing which would greatly interest you – if you would regard it as a great favour. You know what I mean?'

'Let me be the judge of that.'

'He has hired The Monk, the deadliest marksman in Europe.'

'Amazing,' Lasalle remarked as he settled himself behind the wheel of his car beside Tweed with Newman in the

204

back. 'The old villain was actually scared of this Klein. Never before have I heard of anything scaring him.'

'At least we have a name – Klein,' Tweed remarked. 'And one of my contacts in another country used the same name.'

'And what use is that?' Lasalle asked as he started the engine and drove off. 'It is a common enough name. Have you any idea how many Kleins there are in France, Belgium, Luxembourg and Germany?'

'A check on the Interpol computer here might be worth while,' Tweed persisted. 'And I didn't like the news that he has hired The Monk. I've heard of that man – a shadow which passes in the night. Leaving behind a body.'

'So shadowy no one has been able to pin anything on him,' Lasalle remarked. 'But it's very bad news. What kind of hellish operation can this Klein be planning? Hijacking a cruise liner?'

'If something is planned I don't think so,' Tweed said. 'I fear it could be something much bigger. Don't ask me what. But Calgourli did provide at long last what I've been looking for. Some *facts*.'

'Such as?' asked Newman.

'Explosives, scuba divers, and a top marksman. The Monk.'

'Come to check up on me?' Marler asked cheerfully. 'Making sure I was still in Bouillon?'

'I came to reassure you on our mutual friend's instruction,' Hipper said as they wandered through the streets of the small town. 'To tell you we should be ready soon now. It is very important you remain available at the Panorama . . .'

'I'm not staying hemmed in by the four walls of a hotel bedroom day after day. If you phone and I'm out, call back.'

'That is not entirely satisfactory . . .'

'Nothing in life ever is.'

'I will leave you here. Go straight back to your hotel.'

'On the double. Sir.'

Marler gave the Luxembourger a brief mock salute, turned and disappeared round a corner. He ran to where he had parked his newly-hired Volvo, unlocked it, got behind the wheel and started the engine. Ramming a black beret on his head, he perched a pair of dark glasses on his nose and drove to the corner where Hipper was just getting into a Peugeot station wagon.

He followed Hipper past the castle relic which loomed over the town and settled down to keeping the Peugeot in sight. They had left him marooned in the nowhere place of Bouillon. Not good enough. He needed some idea of where Hipper was based. You couldn't know too much about your employer in his line of business.

Hipper drove north through the Ardennes, then turned west. Marler had managed to avoid being spotted when Hipper arrived in Givet, the small French town just inside the frontier and south of Dinant.

Marler drove across the bridge over the river Meuse, turned on to the Quai des Fours, and realized he'd lost Hipper. He parked the Volvo and went into a café overlooking the waterfront for some coffee. 'Can't win them all,' he thought as he gazed out of the window.

A barge was gliding past, moving steadily upstream after passing through the lock. The *Gargantua*. Marler never gave it a second look as he finished his coffee and called for the bill.

In Paris Lara Seagrave came out of the public phone box and walked to Smiths' tea-room for morning coffee. She looked round after ordering to see if Tweed happened to be there. He was nowhere in sight. Well, she was used to drinking her coffee alone.

*

'I have a call to make,' Tweed told Newman after Lasalle had dropped them at the France et Choiseul. 'From a phone box. Only take a minute. There's one up this street.'

'I'll wait outside then,' Newman replied. 'Take your time. I've plenty to think about. I have an idea I've forgotten to tell you something significant.'

Tweed entered the booth, dialled his Park Crescent number. Paula came on the line immediately. Only a brief greeting, then she came to the point.

'Jacob Rubinstein called you. Said he had something urgent to report. He'll only talk to you. Have you his number?'

'Yes. I'm still in Paris. I'll phone him when I've finished this call. There may be a call from someone calling themselves Olympus. Like the mountain in Greece . . .'

'They called fifteen minutes ago. Is it a man or a woman?'

'Can't tell you that.' Tweed sounded anxious. 'What was the message?'

'The voice was muffled – like someone talking through tissue paper. Couldn't tell whether it was a man or a woman. I got them to repeat the message. It's very short. *It's the Meuse, the river Meuse.* That was it. OK?'

'Very,' said Tweed.

Noticing Tweed's absorbed expression Newman kept quiet until they were inside Tweed's room at the France et Choiseul. He waited again until room service had brought the coffee Tweed ordered.

'I haven't remembered the significant bit, but I have recalled a couple of other items I didn't tell you. I must be slipping.'

'You didn't have much time after you arrived at Park Crescent. Then you drove me to Heathrow. The plane was full, so we couldn't talk then. And Lasalle met us at Charles de Gaulle. What are the two items?'

'First, checking Portch's movements after he left Brighton I found there was a six-month gap before he took over at Cockley Ford. The barman whose place overlooks the harbour at Blakeney told me Portch arrived with his

207

furniture, found there was some cock-up in the timing, and went to Holland for about six months.'

'Probably took a locum job.' Tweed was studying a Michelin map of the general area of the Meuse he'd purchased at Smiths' bookshop. 'What was the other thing?'

'You said there were six new graves of villagers who died during the meningitis epidemic. I didn't have much chance to take a good look – Portch and that thug, Grimes, were breathing down my neck. But I'm sure there were *seven*. Could you have miscounted?'

He had Tweed's full attention now. Tweed pursed his lips in an effort to think back to his night at Cockley Ford. Such a lot had happened since.

'I can't be sure,' he admitted. 'But we can't worry about it now. We have to split forces. I have to take the express to Brussels to check on that banker, Peter Brand. And damnit, I forgot to call Jacob Rubinstein. I'll do that on our way out to get a quick snack. Here it's a full-dress effort, will take too long.'

'You said we have to split forces . . .'

'Yes. I want you to hire a car and drive to Dinant on the Meuse just across the border in Belgium. Klein may have made one mistake. Which is what I have been waiting for.'

'What mistake?'

'This.' Tweed opened a drawer, took out a tissue-wrapped package and handed it to Newman. The foreign correspondent unfolded the paper and stared at the small gingerbread house. He looked at Tweed and shook his head.

'A *couque*,' said Tweed. 'A speciality type of ginger-bread – and one of the local industries of Dinant. When you arrive, find a bargee, see if this Klein has ever been seen in the area. Follow it up in any way you like. And if you want to get in touch with me quickly call this number.' He wrote on a page from his notebook, handed it to Newman. 'That's the number of Brussels police head-quarters off the Grand' Place. Chief Inspector Victor

Benoit is an old friend of mine – and a very tough police-man. Now, let's get moving.'

'Hold on a sec. Why this interest in barges?'

'I may have been thick. A chance remark Paula made while we were back in Basle at the Drei Könige came into my mind before I fell asleep last night. That bullion I told you about – the big haul stolen from those two banks in Basle – may just have been transported from under the noses of the Swiss police. By barge down the Rhine, then maybe via the Canal de Haut Rhin and north to Dinant.'

'That's a long shot,' Newman objected as they stood up to leave.

'The whole business is a very long shot . . .'

Tweed used the same phone box he had called Paula from to contact Jacob Rubinstein. The bullion merchant came on the line and Tweed announced his identity.

'Could you tell me, first, what you were wearing the day you came to see me? If you don't mind . . .'

'I applaud your caution. Navy-blue serge suit, white shirt, polka dot tie, a Burberry . . .'

'I won't mention names on the phone, Mr Tweed. I am referring to the man whose name I gave you. Do you understand?'

'Perfectly. Please go on.'

'In my business we hear things. We are on the phone daily to most of the world financial centres. We hear rumours – sometimes very unusual ones. We get so we can sort out the wheat from the chaff, to discount nonsense. Regarding the man we spoke of, I have just heard he has arranged for a truly enormous amount of bullion to be held available by the Deutsche Bank in Frankfurt. It is supposed to be for a loan to some unnamed South American country. I find it peculiar – the amount combined with the urgency.'

'How much bullion?'

'Two hundred million pounds' worth.'

'Thank you for informing me, Mr Rubinstein. It may or

may not be significant. I thank you anyway. Goodbye.'

Tweed hurried out of the box. 'Back to the hotel. You'll be able to get a meal later. I'll get dinner aboard the Brussels express.' He was striding out along the pavement, checking his watch.

'A development?' Newman enquired.

'Peter Brand, the shady banker, has just arranged for bullion to the value of two hundred million pounds to be held ready for swift delivery at the Deutsche Bank in Frankfurt. That could be the ransome amount Klein – Zarov if it is him – will demand for the West to avoid a major catastrophe. Lysenko told me Zarov wanted to make a fortune while still young. If so, we could be running out of time. He may be ready soon to launch his operation. Drive like hell for Dinant.'

They had almost reached the hotel when Newman realized Tweed *had* been listening to him earlier.

'If you're right, I wonder who is occupying that seventh grave at Cockley Ford?'

25

Eighty miles east of Paris – beyond Rheims – Newman's hired Peugeot broke down in the middle of nowhere. There was no other traffic in the middle of the night, no sign of human habitation for miles.

He slaked his thirst with water from the plastic canister he always carried on motor journeys, made himself as comfortable as possible, and slept through the rest of the night.

The driver of a passing car the following morning promised to phone the nearest branch of the car hire firm. It was still midday before a breakdown truck arrived accompanied by a Citroën. Newman took over the Citroën and drove on to the nearest town where he had a leisurely meal – leisurely because the service was so slow.

It was early evening before he drove into Dinant. Parking the car, he wandered round the town huddled beneath the pinnacle of rock with the citadel at its summit. He chose the Hotel de la Gare because it was anonymous and up a side road away from the main part of the town.

After dark he continued his wanderings, calling in at several bars. He chatted to barmen, excellent sources of local knowledge. He found the shop which sold *couques* near the Pont de Charles de Gaulle.

He was adopting his normal reporter's technique on arrival at a new place, getting his bearings, studying life along the Meuse waterfront. He slept like a dog that night, had an early breakfast, and strolled along the river bank to where a barge was moored. The *Nantes*.

'Good morning,' he called up to a thin-faced man with dark eyes who was watching him from inside the wheelhouse at the stern of the vessel. 'May I come aboard? I have a favour to ask . . .'

With some reluctance the bargee gestured for him to cross the gangplank. Newman walked slowly on to the deck. He would have only one chance to get the man talking. What was the right approach? Chance lent him a hand.

A woman appeared, climbing the few steps which he took to lead to the living-quarters. About forty, she was slim with long dark hair and the look of a hard worker. She also looked worried. She stopped at the head of the steps and Newman smiled.

He explained he was writing a series of articles for the Brussels paper *Le Soir* on Belgian waterways, their importance as a means of transport, the neglect of the government in appreciating their importance.

'Tell him about it, Willy,' the woman urged. 'You won't tell the authorities. Tell him. And tell him who you are. Have you forgotten your manners?'

'I'm Willy Boden. This is my wife, Simone.' The bargee

extended a wiry hand, still watching Newman cautiously. 'You won't mention my name if we talk to you? The authorities can make life difficult for us if they think we're interfering.'

'No names,' Newman promised. 'Not even a mention of Dinant – just a Meuse bargee. Who would identify you from that?'

'I have your word on that, Mr Newman? And why would an Englishman work for a Brussels newspaper?'

'It's an exchange system,' Newman said, making it up as he went along. 'One of *Le Soir*'s reporters spends six months with my outfit in London, I come over here. Is there something worrying your wife?'

'No, of course not. Why should there be? We had better go down into the saloon. No one will see us talking there.'

They were seated in the cramped saloon on long banquettes with a table between them when his wife started again on her husband. She had a strong face, alert eyes.

'Tell him – or I will. I sense we can trust Mr Newman . . .'

'You and your feminine instincts . . .'

'Then I'll tell him.'

'Oh, all right. Leave it to me. I saw what happened. And our guest would like some coffee, I'm sure. So would I – I was up at five this morning,' he explained to Newman as Simone went to a tiny galley at the for'ard end of the saloon. From where he sat with his back to the river bank Newman could see through a porthole a barge passing upstream. Boden followed his gaze.

'That's what Simone is talking about . . .' He was having difficulty getting started. Bargees lived in a closed community, didn't talk easily to outsiders, Newman thought.

'I see,' he remarked, although he didn't.

'Do get on with it, Willy,' Simone called out from the galley. 'Tell him about Haber and the *Gargantua*. Then about the *Erika*.'

'Joseph Haber is a friend,' Boden began. 'Not a close

212

friend. He keeps to himself. He's an ambitious man. Nothing wrong with that, I suppose.'

'Can lead to problems sometimes,' Newman commented.

'That's what I tell him. He won't listen. He wants to be the King of the Meuse – that's how he puts it. Sounds funny, but he's quite serious. He wants to own the biggest fleet of barges on the Meuse. He owns three already . . .'

'No, he doesn't,' Simone snapped as she served steaming coffee in large mugs. 'He owns one – the *Gargantua*. The other two have large mortgages on them. Come to think of it, I'm sure he hasn't fully paid off the *Gargantua* yet.'

'Where is he now?' Newman asked as Simone joined them by her husband's side.

'That's the point,' Simone answered, taking over. 'Two days ago he had the *Gargantua* loaded up with gravel – for delivery to Liège. But when he sails he goes upstream – away from Liège – towards the French frontier and Les Dames de Meuse.'

'What's that?' Newman asked and sipped the scalding liquid.

'A very lonely section of the river deep in the Ardennes. It winds about a lot and the woody hills come right down to the water's edge. It's on the far side of the French frontier – beyond Givet where you pass Customs.'

'I still don't see why you're worried,' Newman remarked. He was beginning to think he was wasting his time.

'He's got to know a very peculiar man,' Simone went on. 'Another man who says he is a writer – a writer of books. And a bit of a businessman. A man called Klein . . .'

Newman's face showed no reaction. He took a long drink from his mug. He had been on the verge of thinking of some excuse for leaving this couple. It could be a coincidence, of course. Lasalle had pointed out Klein was a common enough name.

'Can you describe this Klein?' he asked. 'I know someone with that name.'

'About Willy's height and weight,' Simone said. 'Six feet tall. Wears hunting clothes. His complexion is ruddy.'

Doesn't sound like the same man, Newman thought. In Paris the Corsican, Calgourli, had emphasized his chalk-white face. He felt a pang of disappointment. Then Simone spoke again.

'It's those eyes of his I don't like. I was walking along the bank when he passed me on the way to Haber's barge a few weeks ago. Very strange staring eyes. I felt he was looking into my soul when he glanced at me . . .'

'Stuff and nonsense,' growled Boden.

'He scares me,' Simone persisted. 'He isn't human. And Willy saw him having this violent quarrel with Haber before they took the *Gargantua* upstream.'

'What quarrel?'

Intrigued again, Newman listened while Boden described the scene he'd witnessed inside Haber's wheel-house. The brief struggle between the two men. Followed by a long conversation prior to Haber slipping moorings and sailing upstream.

'You mean Klein travelled aboard?' Newman asked.

'Oh, yes, and Broucker, too. That was really queer.'

'Who is Broucker?'

'Haber's employee. He mans the second barge, the *Erika*. It was left moored here while they sailed south. Never known that to happen before.'

'Tell him what happened later,' Simone urged.

'I'm not sure this is any of our business . . .'

'Tell him! Or I will.'

Boden explained that normally there would be nothing strange about Haber taking his barge upstream. He travelled across the border to a landing near Fumay, a small quarry town in France where he took on board gravel. He then returned downstream past Dinant to Liège and other destinations to make delivery.

'But,' he explained, 'this time he already had a load of gravel aboard. So why return upstream? Why take Broucker, who should have stayed to look after the *Erika*? And why was this Klein aboard? It's weird.'

'It's weirder than that,' Simone broke in. 'Late the following day, close to dusk, Willy saw the *Erika* leaving its mooring. We had been into town to collect supplies. Willy came back first – just in time to see the *Erika* disappearing downstream, heading towards Namur and Liège.'

'What's weird about that?'

Newman had earlier unfolded his Michelin map of the Meuse and was making notes on it. He scribbled in shorthand the sequence of events Boden was describing.

'We haven't seen the *Gargantua* since it sailed south. The barge has disappeared.'

'It could have sailed back without your seeing it and continued north towards Namur,' Newman objected.

'It is impossible,' Simone said vehemently. 'We are not thick. Either one or both of us have been here since it departed upstream.'

'But you said you went into town to purchase supplies . . .'

'From shops in Dinant on the waterfront. The *Gargantua* could not have passed without us seeing it.'

'Maybe after dark?'

'Barges don't travel after dark,' Willy told him. 'It hasn't come back.'

'Then maybe it broke down . . .'

'In that case,' Simone broke in again, 'Broucker would stay with it to give a hand. But we told you – we saw the *Erika* sailing downstream. Broucker's barge . .' She looked at her husband as he cocked his head. A ship's hooter was tooting. He went up on deck, followed by Newman and Simone.

Newman was glad of the interruption. It gave him a chance to get away from the barge. He still saw nothing significant in their anxieties. Thanking Simone for the coffee, he was about to disembark, when Willy grabbed his arm. 'Wait.'

The hooter had been sounded by a large two-deck cream power cruiser gliding downstream. A short thickset man wearing a navy-blue blazer and grey slacks stood on deck staring at the barge through a pair of binoculars. He waved and Willy gave a brief wave back as the slow-moving vessel turned inshore aft of the barge.

'He knows Klein, too,' Willy said. 'He's another Englishman. A Colonel Ralston. Lives on that boat with his girl friend. Cruises along all the canals. Dead drunk most of the day.'

Newman watched as crew members jumped ashore at a landing stage and made the vessel fast. A small wiry man waited until the gangplank was in position, wheeled a bicycle across it and rode past the barge along the towpath towards Dinant.

'Think I'll go and have a word,' Newman said.

Seen close up, standing at the head of the gangplank, the owner of the *Evening Star* had a brick-red complexion, iron-grey hair and a moustache of the same colour. He stood with hands in blazer pockets, a thumb protruding.

'Who the devil are you?' he greeted his visitor.

'Robert Newman. I'm interested in the Meuse. I gather you know it well?'

'Well, don't just stand there. Come aboard!'

A very upper crust voice, a clipped military-style tone, the manner of a man used to obedience. Newman followed him down a companionway into a spacious saloon. Walls of mahogany, chairs covered with expensive fabric, and at the far end a well-equipped cocktail bar.

Ralston laid a stubby-fingered hand on the polished counter. He swung round and stared at Newman with blue eyes. Small red veins showed on his pugnacious nose. Sign of a hardened drinker.

'Care for a sundowner? And sit.'

'It's a long time before the sun goes down,' Newman remarked. 'Coffee would be welcome, if available . . .'

'Alfredo!' roared the colonel. 'Coffee for our guest. On the double!'

A slim dark-skinned man appeared behind Newman, walked behind the bar and disappeared beyond a doorway. Ralston would be in his early sixties, Newman guessed, his short stature compensated for by the force of his personality; he was close to being a caricature of the military officer. But there was nothing amusing about the cold blue eyes. He poured himself a whisky into a cut glass, added a splash of soda from a syphon, downed half the glass, ran his tongue over his lips.

'That's better. You're the foreign correspondent chappie. Recognize you from your photo. Back of the jacket on that bestseller you wrote. What's your game?'

'I told you . . .'

'Playing it close to the chest? Want to see some of the Meuse? Have a berth aboard the *Evening Star*? Cost you – I'm not running a charitable institution.'

'How much?'

'Twelve thousand francs. Belgian.'

Newman had seated himself on one of the banquettes lining the sides of the saloon. A gleaming mahogany table was close enough for him to take a pile of francs from his wallet, lay them on the table, keeping his hand on top of the pile. Twelve thousand Belgian francs. About £200.

'What do I get for that?' he asked Ralston who still stood by the bar; his favourite position Newman suspected.

'Grand tour of the river up to Namur. Then Liège. On the way, maybe a brief call on one of our eminent bankers. You know Belgium well?'

'Not really,' Newman lied.

'Here's your coffee. 'Bout time, Alfredo. Chopchop . . .' He continued in the style of a brisk lecture. 'The Frogs all swim like lemmings for their hols to the French Riviera. Most people don't know about the Belgians. They've got their own riviera – in the south of their country like the French. On the Meuse, in fact. So Million-aireville is just north of here . . .'

'Millionaireville?'

'Riverside mansions of the rich. Estates running down to the Meuse. At Profondeville – where the banker is – and further north at Wepion.'

'Who is this banker?'

'A Peter Brand . . .'

Newman removed his hand from the pile of banknotes. Ralston had been eyeing them as he talked. Newman had the impression his two passions were drink – and money. Nothing in his expression had shown at the mention of Peter Brand.

The *Evening Star* was sailing slowly down the Meuse. Wooded bluffs of the Ardennes rose on either side as Newman drank fresh coffee, left alone in the saloon for a short time. He had met the wiry weatherbeaten man who had cycled past the Bodens' barge.

'My ex-batman, Sergeant Bradley,' Ralston introduced. 'He keeps the whole shooting match moving. Watches the crew and all that. Don't stand for any backsliding, do you, Sergeant?'

'Not my way, sir,' Bradley replied. 'Got to keep them up to scratch.' He turned to Newman. 'Just like the Army. Keep on their tails or they slack off. Same the world over.'

'You must have seen something of the world,' Newman commented to Ralston who was pouring a fresh whisky. He picked up a silver cup inscribed with wording. 'Your unit?'

'Seventh Highlanders. Best regiment in the Army. The times we had in India, Egypt and Italy.' Ralston gazed into the distance. 'Seems an age ago. Now we cruise the canals. Always on the move. Just like the old Army days.'

'You go back to England much?' Newman had ventured.

'Never! Don't pay a penny tax in any country. Advantage of having a floating home. Never stay in one country more than five months. Bradley keeps the log. Ready to show any bloody snooping tax inspector. I can spit in their faces

– often feel like doing just that. Have to excuse me. A lock coming up. A bit tricky the navigation sometimes. Like to skipper my own tub . . .'

Left alone, Newman thought it was a queer set-up. Almost as though Ralston was trying to perpetuate his old Army atmosphere. A tall slim girl with a good figure, wearing a formfitting red dress with a mandarin collar, came into the saloon, sat beside Newman.

'I'm Josette. If I wait for his lordship to introduce me we will never meet.'

'You spend a lot of time aboard?' Newman asked.

'I live on the boat. It's like that. You do realize why he invited you aboard?'

'You tell me.'

'To keep an eye on you, of course. He wonders what you're up to. Brand asked him to keep a lookout for strangers,' she whispered. 'Brand pays him a fee, of course. He's mean over money, the colonel. Except with drink. He's never drunk and never sober. I don't think I'm staying with him much longer.' She pulled at her dark hair, staring straight at Newman. 'Do you need a friend?'

'Let me think about it.' Newman paused. Was this a trap? Had Ralston sent her to get him to talk? He didn't think so. They were inside the lock now. Beyond the portholes concrete walls loomed.

'Ever met a man called Klein?' he asked.

'Yes. A friend of yours?'

'Never met him.'

'He's creepy. He's travelled with us several times. And he was very interested in the bargees – and their craft. Asked the colonel a lot of questions. Especially about one called Joseph Haber. Was he married? Did he have a family?'

'And is Haber married – and has he a family?'

'Yes. A wife who lives near Celle, a small village up in the Ardennes. They have a son called Lucien, I remember. It seemed odd to me why this Klein should be interested in things like that.'

'This Klein just travelled back and forth with Ralston?'

'Not all the time. He spent several days at the home of the millionaire banker, Peter Brand . . .'

'Change the subject,' Newman whispered as Sergeant Bradley marched in from the opening behind the bar.

Josette had good bone structure, a well-shaped face and her expression was dreamy, but she was quick-witted. 'I think the Meuse is the loveliest of all the rivers,' she said in a normal voice. 'You really should see the section in France called Les Dames de Meuse . . .'

'Colonel wants you on deck,' Bradley told her. 'He's just noticed you'd disappeared.' He poured more coffee into Newman's cup. 'Next stop Profondeville, sir. We dock there and call on Mr Brand's place.'

26

Tweed missed catching the express to Brussels as he'd planned. He made one last phone call to Lasalle to tell him he was leaving Paris. The Frenchman said he had further information and could they meet?

Inside the DST chief's office Tweed sat drinking coffee while Lasalle explained.

'After our interview with that Corsican villain, Calgourli, I checked with the police chiefs of all major cities. I wanted data on any unusual happenings. I may have come up with something in Marseilles.'

'That's a long way south . . .'

'Wait, my friend. You recall Calgourli referred to his rival in Marseilles, Emilio Perugini? This is confidential – we have a snout inside Perugini's organization. A man called Klein visited Perugini at his Cassis villa – these rats live high. Through Perugini Klein hired a very hard case called Louis Chabot. Freelance type . . .'

'What type?'

'Bodyguard, killer – you name it. The Marseilles police report Chabot has disappeared from his normal haunts. Vanished into thin air was the phrase used. And he's an expert on explosives, also a professional scuba diver. The qualifications Klein laid down to Calgourli.'

'Sounds like a member of the team Klein is forming.'

'Wait!' Lasalle repeated. 'There's more. Chabot had a girl friend, a bar girl called Cecile Lamont. Her body was dragged out of the sea. The screws of a large liner sailing for Oran sliced her clean through the middle . . .'

'You think Chabot . . .'

'No, I don't. He was fond of the girl – and his record has no trace of him ever attacking a woman. The post-mortem showed how she died – before she was thrown into the sea. Her throat was cut from ear to ear.'

Tweed sighed. 'That's getting to have a familiar sound. And it sounds like Klein. He's a ruthless bastard,' he said with feeling. 'You can see the pattern. He never leaves anyone alive who could help us. Did you check with Interpol – get them to put Klein through the computer?'

'Yes. Result, a blank. I asked my colleague for any other recent murders. I don't think this is relevant, but they've found a Swiss Nestlé truck driver dead in the Ardennes near Clervaux. Turkish driver on his way to Brussels with a delivery from the Nestlé factory at some place called Broc . . .' He paused, seeing Tweed's expression. 'What's the matter?'

'This Klein is a ghost.' He took a map from his pocket of Western Europe. 'Can we spread this out on your desk? I'd like to see if we can track this ghost . . .'

Tweed talked as he made crosses on the map, starting with Broc in Switzerland, moving on to Geneva, Basle and Clervaux as he explained the events in Geneva and Basle. The murder of the Swiss research genius in watch-making, the bullion robberies in Basle.

He made more crosses on Marseilles and Paris. Then he drew a route line through the crosses, with off-shoots to

Marseilles and Paris. Standing up, he tapped the map with his felt-tip pen.

'You see?'

'He appears to be moving north, always north. Where the hell is he heading for? And why the cross on Dinant. That takes us into Belgium.'

'My thanks to you there – for putting me on to Lara Seagrave.' Tweed produced a tissue-wrapped package from his coat pocket, showed Lasalle the *couque*. 'Lara gave me that in Smiths' tea-room. Speciality made in Dinant. I think Klein has reached the Meuse. I've sent Bob Newman to poke around in that area. And I think the bullion stolen from Basle travelled this route aboard a barge . . .' He traced a route south of Basle, along the Canal de la Marne et Haut Rhin, continuing up the Canal de l'Est, crossing the border with Belgium and stopping at Dinant.

'That gold,' Tweed went on, 'I'm convinced was the money which originally financed Klein's operation. You heard what he offered Calgourli. Now, I need the fence who handled the bullion – converted it into hard cash for Klein. I may know who the fence is. What I need now is a link between the fence and Klein.'

'What's the significance of the Nestlé truck and its Turkish driver? The Belgians are convinced it was murder. They've asked for the assistance of Chief Inspector Benoit in Brussels since the Belgian capital was its ultimate destination.'

'Like you, Benoit never gives up,' Tweed mused, studying his map. 'Any idea where Lara Seagrave is now?'

'Antwerp,' Lasalle said promptly. 'While she was here The Parrot followed her to Cherbourg. Same procedure as down in Marseilles and Le Havre. She took a lot of photographs of the harbour area. I'd have arrested her, grilled her by now if you hadn't asked me to hold off.'

'Thank you. She could just be our only lead to Klein. How do you know she's in Antwerp? North again. And it's beginning very much to look like Belgium.'

'The Parrot followed her when she took a train to Brussels, then another to Antwerp. I've already called Benoit to tell him. After all, The Parrot is on foreign soil. Benoit was very cooperative, has permitted The Parrot to continue tracking Seagrave. He's given my man back-up. What the blazes could be the target? We've had these persistent rumours of a hijack of a ship.'

'I happen to know Klein may be skilled at throwing out a smokescreen to cover his real operation. We'd better watch it. Under Klein's instructions – if she is – Lara could be leading us astray.'

'Don't follow that.'

'She could already have visited the target – in France. I'm suspicious she may now be pointing us in the wrong direction. Further north than the real target.'

'I tell you something in confidence,' Lasalle replied. 'We have sent out a general alert to all ports from Marseilles up the Atlantic coast to Le Havre. Two more things which may be of interest. Lara Seagrave is staying at the Plaza Hotel in Antwerp. And Interpol told me a number of known hard cases have disappeared from Luxembourg City.'

'Interesting. You know one of the Luxembourger's favourite sports?'

'Tell me.'

'Scuba diving. And Luxembourg is close to the Meuse.'

They had eaten an excellent lunch of salmon steak aboard the *Evening Star*. Newman was getting the hang of the set-up on the vessel. Alfredo was a skilled dogsbody – he acted as cook as well as barman and general factotum. Sergeant Bradley did little except give orders to the crew. Josette did damn-all except look beautiful and listen to Ralston's pronouncements.

Under the surface he sensed an atmosphere of tension. He put it down to the colonel's sudden choleric outbursts of temper when something displeased him. Finishing off

223

his lunch at the head of the table with a couple of cognacs, he was in a good humour as he stood up and beckoned to Newman to follow.

On deck he extended one short thick arm towards the right bank. The boat had changed course, was heading diagonally across the river as the hooter sounded continuously, warning other craft that might lie behind a nearby bend.

'Brand's estate at Profondeville,' Ralston barked. 'Ten acres he's got – and land here costs gold dust.'

'Being a banker maybe he's got plenty of gold bullion,' Newman remarked casually.

'What's that you said? Plenty of?'

'Gold bullion. After all, you said he's a banker.'

'Don't know a thing about his business. Except his HQ is in Brussels – with a branch in Luxembourg City. Lives in a fabulous mansion in Brussels on the Avenue Franklin Roosevelt. Park Lane of Brussels. Here he comes.'

The sun was shining out of a clear blue sky as Bradley ran about issuing orders. The cruiser was approaching a landing stage at the foot of a vast sloping green lawn. Spaced out across the trim green were shrubs sculpted in the shapes of various animals. There were life-like boars, stags, leopards and lions. A tall slim man wearing white flannels and holding a tennis racquet stood waiting on the landing stage.

'Christ!' Ralston burst out. 'Damn helmsman is bringing her in at the wrong angle . . .'

He bounded up the steps to the bridge. Inside the wheelhouse Newman watched him push the helmsman aside, take over the wheel himself. He'd drunk a whole bottle of red wine with lunch, preceded by two double Scotches, to say nothing of the cognacs. Head like a rock.

The cruiser slowed, its course changed a few degrees, then it glided in, bumping the stage gently. Crew members leapt off holding ropes fore and aft, expertly looping the ropes round bollards. The man in flannels remained quite still, erect.

Ralston led the way once the gangway was in position. Shaking hands, he introduced his guest.

'Peter, brought a passenger. Robert Newman. Foreign correspondent chappie.'

'I don't normally permit reporters on my property.'

Brand's expression and tone were sardonic as he shook hands. Pale eyes under thin dark brows studied Newman, who took an instant dislike to the banker. In his thirties, a long lean face, a thin aquiline nose, a mobile mouth, he'd be a wow with a certain kind of woman who went for the matinée idol type. His voice was a stretched out drawl, his movements slow and easy.

Plenty of intelligence, Newman thought – and he'd know that. Not a man to underestimate, but maybe too clever by half.

'You've had a bad experience?' Newman responded. 'An interview that went wrong?'

'Something like that. It's the women who are the real bitches. Well, since you're here, you'd better come up to the house for a drink, I suppose.'

'Only if I'm welcome,' Newman said neutrally.

'Wouldn't have asked you had it been otherwise.' They had left the landing stage, were walking up a gravel path towards a two-storey white-walled mansion. The path was wide but on either side beyond the gravel Newman noticed deep wheel ruts in the lawn.

'Something's spoilt your grass,' he remarked, walking alongside Brand. Ralston was stumping ahead, doubtless in need of more liquid refreshment.

'That's what I mean,' Brand replied in his slow careful tone. 'Reporters are always noticing things, remarking on them.'

'Must have been a heavy vehicle,' Newman persisted.

'Jesus!' Brand slapped his leg with the racquet. 'It's a machine I have for levelling the gravel. Its axis is too wide. Obvious solution, widen the path. Which I'm going to have done. Any more questions?'

'Know a man called Klein?'

'Several. Common name on the continent. What's his first name?'

'Oscar,' Newman invented.

'No. Friend of yours?'

'I've been asked to interview him. He's an authority on the Meuse.'

'Is he now? I think we'll have drinks on the terrace. The Colonel makes himself at home, as you'll see.'

The terrace was raised up and a central flight of steps led up to the elevation which ran the full width of the mansion. To the left of the building Newman saw a tennis court. A large swimming pool with a blue tile surround occupied the centre of the terrace. Garden chairs were placed round it and Ralston was helping himself from a decanter on a table laden with bottles and glasses.

'What are you drinking – if anything?' Brand enquired in a bored tone, throwing down the racquet on a swing couch.

'A Scotch. Water. No ice. Nice little place you've got here.'

Brand flashed him a look as he reached for the decanter. The hostility between the two men crackled like static electricity. Newman had no intention of touching his fore-lock to this sarcastic sod. And if you needle a man long enough he sometimes says more than he wishes.

'I'm glad you like my *pied-à-terre*,' Brand responded as he poured the drink, planted the glass on the table and plonked a heavy jug of water beside it. The jug, Newman noted, was the finest Swedish glass. 'You should,' he went on, mixing himself a drink, 'it cost four million.'

'Francs?' asked Newman innocently.

'Christ no! Pound sterling.'

Ralston sat down, crossed his chunky legs. He had sensed the animosity and his eyes studied Newman who occupied one of the garden chairs.

'Newman,' he told Brand, 'is interested in whether your outfit handles gold bullion.'

'Is he now?' Brand swallowed half his drink before he

replied. 'May I ask the reason for your interest? Thinking of tucking away some of your book profits in a few bars the tax man will never find?'

'Oh, I'm just intrigued in how the other half lives. Could I use the loo?'

'Round that side of the house. Second door on the left and straight ahead. You can't miss it. I hope . . .'

Newman grinned amiably, walked along the rim of the swimming pool and round behind the house. He looked down as he walked. The wheel rims of the heavy-tyred vehicle had continued from the lawn up the gravel but were fainter. As though someone had brushed the gravel to eliminate the traces.

He walked on past the second door. The wheel impressions continued past the house across the front drive. They only disappeared where they met a tarred road which wound its way past more millionaire-style mansions behind trim hedges.

He returned quickly to the house, checking the mullion-paned windows. There was no sign of life, no sign that anyone had seen him. He walked inside the house in search of the toilet. A tall slim girl in her twenties, hair the colour of golden corn, dressed in tennis blouse and shorts, met him, coming the other way down the corridor.

'Looking for the loo,' Newman said.

'That door at the end of the passage.'

She pulled strands of her long hair, tucked them in her red-lipped mouth, stopped and stared at him. 'You look English. Are you?'

'Robert Newman. And yes, I'm pretty English.'

'Thank God for that. I'm sick of speaking French. Peter insists it's the polite thing to do. He plays a mean game of tennis – hates to lose, especially to a woman. Great sportsmen, these bankers. He plays a mean game at everything, come to think of it. God, you've no idea how boring the rich are. I think I'm going to cut and run.'

'Your decision,' Newman said breezily.

She lingered, studying him. Over her shoulder Newman

227

gazed through a half-open door into a study. A teleprinter machine was quietly chattering away, mouthing out a spool of paper.

'I'm Carole Browne,' the girl went on. 'Maybe we could meet in Brussels – or some place?'

Newman took out his visiting card, tucked it inside a pocket of her blouse. The firmness of her breast pushed against his hand.

'Ever heard of a man called Klein?' he asked.

'Yes. Friend of Peter's. Some friend. He's spent several nights here. They spend their time behind the closed door of the study . . .'

She broke off as Newman heard steps crunching the gravel outside. He winked at her, spoke rapidly. 'I agree this is a lovely part of the world. Riviera is the word for it . . .'

'And what the hell do you two think you're up to?' Brand's voice asked behind him. 'I thought you were on your way to the loo.'

'I am.' Newman half-turned. 'This young lady has just told me where it is. You need a map for this maze of a house.'

'And who, if I may ask, left that study door open?'

'I was just going to close it,' Carole snapped, 'when I bumped into your friend. Here is the paper you asked for.' She handed him a copy of *The Times* which she produced from the tennis bag she carried. Newman saw from the front page it was one of the issues containing a series of articles he had written on revolutionary methods for tackling the terrorist menace – complete with his picture. Carole showed no sign of being intimidated as she continued talking to Newman.

'Since you admire the scenery go to the tennis court on the far side of the house. You get the most marvellous view up the Meuse.'

'And I,' Brand said in his most upper crust tone, 'would be frightfully grateful if all my guests would assemble by the pool.' He slammed the study door shut and Newman heard an automatic lock click into place. 'The key,' Brand demanded, extending his hand. No *please*, Newman noted. Carole delved into a pocket, handed him a key. 'Come with me now,' he told her, 'while Mr Newman is making himself more comfortable.'

After relieving himself, Newman stepped into an empty corridor, walked briskly to the exit door, turned left, marched round the front of the house and down a side passage. The tennis court was elevated on a small plateau. A pair of powerful binoculars were slung from one of the posts supporting the net.

He picked up the field-glasses and peered through them into the distance. The view of the Meuse with its sweeping bends was spectacular. He found it interesting that the focus of the glasses picked out the landing stage and the river beyond clearly.

Assumption? Brand had seen Ralston's cruiser approaching, had recognized him on deck – or thought he had. Hence his demand for the copy of *The Times*. He'd been going to check the photograph if the girl had brought the paper in time.

Back at the pool Brand's mood had changed. He greeted Newman affably, handed him a fresh drink, took him by the arm and sat him in the canopied swing seat next to Carole.

'He's at his most charming,' Carole whispered as Brand relaxed in one of the chairs. 'Better watch out.'

'I hear Ralston is taking you up to Namur,' Brand remarked. 'If you're really interested in the river you should later reverse – go south across the French frontier to the Dames de Meuse. Really beautiful stretch.'

'I think I might do that tomorrow. Why do they call it that?'

'Legend hath it that centuries ago three unfaithful wives in that region were turned to stone by divine power. My God, nowadays the area would be littered with stone wives. Including my own . . .'

'Do we *have* to go into that now?' asked Carole.

'While you are eating my food and imbibing my drink, my dear, you sit and listen while I hold forth on any subject which takes my fancy.' He stared at Newman. 'Lilyane is at this moment in New York having it off with a Wall Street broker – one of the advantages of having excellent world-wide communications. There's a titbit for you.'

'I'm not a gossip columnist,' Newman replied mildly.

'Oh, I thought you chaps would use anything that brought in a few quid . . .'

'I think maybe we'd best get back to the boat,' intervened Ralston.

He had stood up rather stiffly, his movements rather like a robot's, his voice husky. But he still walked steadily to the flight of steps as Newman said goodbye to Carole and followed.

'I'll be in touch, Peter,' the Colonel called out from the head of the steps.

'Give me a buzz on the blower.'

'Thanks for the hospitality,' Newman said amiably.

Brand didn't reply, staring at his departing guest with a brief look of hatred.

Brand unlocked his study door which was padded on the inside. He closed it and went straight to his desk, picked up the phone and dialled the number of La Montagne in Larochette. Klein answered and spoke immediately.

'La Montagne Hotel. I'm afraid we're closed for the season.'

'It's Peter. Something which needs attending to has happened . . .'

'Which is?'

'A Robert Newman turned up at my riverside place. *The* Newman, the foreign correspondent. He mentioned you by name. And he is interested in writing a story on gold bullion.'

For a moment Klein was stunned. His mind flashed back, recalling events of the past few weeks – months. Nowhere had he left a clue. How on earth could Newman, of all people, have linked him with the Meuse?

'My friend, the Colonel, brought him on his cruiser. I made a reference to Newman he ought to see the Dames de Meuse. I think he'll go there tomorrow. I have a picture of him in *The Times*. Can you send someone to meet him? We are so close to concluding the business deal.'

'I'll send Hipper to your villa this afternoon to pick up the picture. I'll arrange for someone to meet Newman. Stay in your villa until Hipper arrives.'

Klein broke the connection. He sat in a first-floor room at La Montagne with the lights on; the shutters were closed over the windows. He sat for a moment, tapping his long fingers, then dialled the Hotel Panorama in Bouillon.

They had to fetch Marler from the sitting area downstairs. The Englishman paused before he lifted the receiver. Hipper checking up on him again? He'd give him a mouthful.

'Lambert here.'

'You know who I am. A newspaper photograph will be delivered to you later today. You know the area the Dames de Meuse?'

'I do.'

'Be there tomorrow. You have to use your professional skill to conclude a deal with Robert Newman, the foreign correspondent. I do mean conclude.'

'Understood. You do realize the Dames de Meuse covers a pretty large stretch of the river?'

'That's your problem. You do grasp what is required?'

'Got wax in your ears? I said understood . . .'

27

Tweed flew back to Heathrow late that afternoon. He changed his plan to go to Brussels after his meeting with

Lasalle. Before he left Paris he phoned Paula, told her to call what he termed a 'council of war'.

Harry Butler met him at Heathrow and drove him straight to Ten Downing Street. 'The PM called Paula,' he told Tweed. 'When she heard you were flying back she said she wanted to see you earliest . . .'

Tweed emerged half an hour later from Number Ten, grim-faced. He told Butler to get him to Park Crescent urgently. On the way Butler filled him in on Norfolk.

'I left Nield to watch things up there. I called Park Crescent to report, heard you were returning, decided to drive back and tell you personally. Dr Portch has returned to the village – Cockley Ford. Nield stays overnight at The Duke's Head in King's Lynn – to avoid being conspicuous. Daytime he spends at Blakeney, mostly with the barman at the place overlooking the waterfront. He's developing a reputation for being a hardened drinker . . .'

Tweed listened to Butler's terse report in silence until they arrived at Park Crescent. He ran up the steps, up the staircase to his office, opened the door and Paula looked up with an expression of relief.

'Thank God you've arrived. Newman called from Namur in Belgium. He's established a connection between Klein and some banker called Peter Brand . . .'

'Where is he at this moment?'

'At a hotel in Namur. Tomorrow he's visiting the Dames de Meuse section of the river. I remember it. Very lovely – but very lonely . . .'

'Why?'

'This man, Brand, drew his attention to it . . .'

'You have Newman's hotel number in Namur?'

'Yes . . .'

'Call him. Tell him to move at once to a hotel in Liège. When he gets there he's to let you know the name and number. He's to stay there until he hears from me. I'm flying to Brussels tomorrow. Tell him that. And I'm giving him an order.'

'Why?'

'I sense a trap. Klein eliminates anyone who can provide a clue as to what he's planning. His next intended victim could be Newman.'

'Can I tell you something else first?'

'Yes. Anything. For five minutes. Then call Newman.'

Tweed had taken the marked map he'd shown Lasalle in Paris and was pinning it up on a wall. He put a cross on Antwerp, the last known destination of Lara Seagrave. Paula went on reporting.

'Howard is waiting in his office for your council of war. And Commander Bellenger of Naval Intelligence called. Wants to see you very urgently. The results of his analysis of the bombs used to blow the bank vaults in Basle are ready – plus expert opinion on the photocopies we got from Arthur Beck – the ones found in the watchmaker's safe.'

'Call him first – ask him if he can come over right away. He'd better sit in on our meeting. Then Newman. I'd like the meeting to start in half an hour . . .'

'I'll get people moving now. Something's happening?'

'Something pretty horrific is imminent.'

Five people sat round the table. Tweed, Howard, Bellenger, Butler and Paula. Tweed had obtained the PM's permission to reveal everything – excluding her contact with Gorbachev and Tweed's secret meeting with Lysenko in Switzerland. They were listening as Bellenger, looking very solemn, gave his report.

'The debris collected from the vaults in those two Swiss bank raids has been analysed. It's Triton Three – the same explosive found in the sea-mine we smuggled out of Russia, the same casing used for the bomb left on Miss Grey's doorstep at her house in Blakeney. Tweed, you quoted to me certain figures you said were theoretical – thirty sea-mines and twenty-five bombs. Are they theoretical?'

'No. They were stolen from a Soviet depot, brought out of Russia into the West.'

'Christ! Where are they now?'

'That's what we're trying to find out – before they can be used.'

'They could annihilate a huge city – I checked with my experts, without revealing the source of my information. I hope they aren't in the UK?' Bellenger asked.

'I don't know . . .'

The phone rang. Paula reached for it as Tweed frowned. 'I said I didn't want any calls.'

'You'll want this one,' she said after listening for a few seconds and handed the instrument to Tweed.

'Yes?'

'Lysenko here. We're on scrambler?'

'Yes. What is it?'

'It has been decided . . .' Pause. '. . . at the highest level that further information should be provided if you haven't tracked Zarov yet. Have you?'

'No. And I'd have liked the lot at the beginning.'

'It was a policy decision . . .' Lysenko sounded nervous. 'I have to tell you that just before Zarov left for West Germany his superior reported he was showing signs of stress. He went into the Serbsky Institute for examination.'

'And the result?' Tweed demanded in a hard voice.

'Three psychiatrists said he was fit, two others diagnosed incipient megalomania. There was a bureaucratic delay. These reports reached me after he'd left Russia.'

'Any other tiny item of information you left out?'

'We thought you should know now . . .'

'You were damned right. You were also damned late.'

Tweed slammed down the phone and looked round the table. Four faces stared at him expectantly.

'It's a race against time – maybe with no time left,' Tweed informed them. 'I have just heard that Igor Zarov may be on the verge of insanity.'

'Jesus Christ!' reacted Bellenger. 'And he has that explosive arsenal?'

234

'I think so, yes. It may be as well the PM has decided in view of what I told her to have an SAS strike force standing by – ready to fly to any part of the continent.'

Hipper arrived in Bouillon after dark and Marler, who was registered at the Panorama as Lambert, a common Belgian name, had to interrupt an excellent dinner.

'What is happening?' he asked as Hipper drove him out of town along wooded deserted roads. 'You've given me Newman's photograph.' He waved the envelope Hipper had handed him.

'Soon you will have to move on,' the pasty-faced Luxembourger said in his slow deliberate manner which irked the Englishman. 'Have your bag packed ready for instant departure.'

'Where to?'

'I will tell you when the time comes.'

'Really?' Marler regarded the plump little man with distaste. 'You will tell me now. Klein knows I don't work completely in the dark. Unless, of course, he'd like his advance back now – minus expenses.'

'He said you would be getting restless . . .'

'Restless be buggered. I'm browned off, mate. Hanging around this one-eyed town pretending to be a huntsman. Up to you. And I hadn't finished my meal. Turn round here and drive back. Tell Klein to stick it.'

'Brussels,' Hipper said quickly, performing a three-point turn at the intersection they had reached. He began driving back to Bouillon. 'Soon after you've completed your commission tomorrow at the Dames de Meuse.'

'That's better. Next time be quicker off the mark – answer a question when I ask you.'

Hipper reached into his pocket, handed Marler an envelope. 'That contains your reservation at the Hilton on the Boulevard de Waterloo. The room will be held until you arrive. An executive suite.' He sniggered, glancing sideways at his passenger. 'Nothing but the best.'

'And you keep your bloody eye on the road – or I'll drive.'

'Lara Seagrave speaking.'

'You know who this is,' Klein's voice answered on the phone. 'Note this address. Boekstraat 198. Got it? Good. Have you a map of Antwerp? Good. Find the address and walk to it as soon as we've finished speaking. Don't be put off by the street. Ask for Mr Knaap at the desk . . .' He spelt out the name. 'Come at once.'

She realized the line had gone dead. She checked the index of streets in her map, found Boekstraat. It was less than five minutes from the Plaza Hotel. Wrapping a scarf round her head, she took the elevator to the lobby and walked out into the streets of Antwerp.

Boekstraat was little more than a sordid alley. A drunken seaman staggered out, stared at her and she walked on. Behind her The Parrot, also clad in seaman's clothes, followed cautiously.

Lara didn't like the look of No. 198. It was a small hotel with a neon light over the doorway. She mounted the steps, entered a bleak lobby. The bright red-haired woman behind the counter looked like a madame. My God, she thought, it's a place where prostitutes bring clients.

'Mr Knaap is expecting me,' she said firmly.

'I'm sure he is, dearie.' The woman spoke French with a heavy Flemish accent. 'My, we're going up in the world, aren't we?'

'I did say Mr Knaap . . .'

'Room 14. Up those stairs. First floor. Fourteen is on the right. No need to give yourself airs and graces.'

'Oh, stuff it,' Lara told her and hurried up the greasy-stepped stairs.

Klein opened the door to her, gave a little bow, gestured for her to enter, closed and locked the door. He waved a hand round the sleazy bedroom.

'I apologize for the accommodation. Security. This place

236

has a secret back exit. For obvious reasons. You'll do better in Brussels.'

'Brussels?'

'That's your next destination. Tell me quickly. What about Antwerp?'

The room was illuminated by a forty-watt bulb inside a bedside table lamp. The pink shade was tattered. Lara remained standing and she sensed Klein was in a hurry to leave. Big deal.

'I don't like the look of Antwerp port,' she said. 'It's a long way up the river Scheldt – a long way from the North Sea. I can't find any safe escape route – the city is dense. It's a trap – rather than an opportunity.' She took a package from her shoulder bag and handed it to him. 'There is a collection of pictures I took. Sorry to be so negative again. In fact, some of the French ports are far more accessible. Is Hamburg the next port to look over?'

'Not yet. I want you to go by train to Brussels tonight – a room has been reserved for you at the Mayfair in the Avenue Louise. You'll enjoy yourself there. It's expensive . . .' He handed her a sheaf of notes held by a paper band. 'For your expenses. I'll contact you there in due course. And now I must leave.'

He took her by the shoulders, pulled her to him. They embraced and he pulled away suddenly. 'Not in a place like this. Wait five minutes after I've left, then leave yourself. And if you have trouble with some man in Boek-straat, use this on him. Aim for the eyes.'

He gave her an aerosol can, kissed her again on the check and left the room. She timed five minutes and hurried down the staircase, past the counter without a glance at the leering madame, and walked rapidly back out of Boekstraat. The Parrot, concealed in a shadowed doorway, frowned as he began to follow her. He felt that he had missed something.

*

The atmosphere was tense as the meeting went on at Park Crescent. Tweed had deliberately created the mood of a 'council of war' to impress on everyone present the seriousness of the situation. The phone rang again, Paula took the call, then looked at Tweed, handing him the instrument as she spoke.

'It's Olympus for you.'

'Tweed here. Any news? Time could be running out . . .' He listened. 'What's that? Please repeat. Thank you.'

He handed the phone back to Paula, picked up a pencil and began tapping it on the table. Paula was beginning to read his gestures. He was worried. He looked round the table.

'Don't ask me how I know. It looks like Belgium. Maybe Brussels itself. HQ of NATO.'

'That doesn't make sense,' Bellenger protested. 'You have been talking about a huge number of sea-mines.'

'I know. I agree.' He glanced at the wall map. 'But it could be Antwerp – the pistol pointed at the heart of Europe, as Churchill once called it in World War One.'

'Makes more sense,' Bellenger agreed. 'What about time running out? You used that phrase.'

'We may have very little of it left.'

'And what, I am curious to know,' Howard enquired, 'is this Olympus business?'

He had said very little up to now, listening instead of talking, which wasn't his style. Paula lowered her head, began doodling in her notebook. How would Tweed deal with this one?

'Oh, that,' Tweed replied casually, 'is just a codeword so I know who is making the report. We change it daily.'

'I'm still puzzled,' Bellenger said. 'Could you briefly sum up the history of this problem – and tell us what progress, if any, we've made?'

'Hear! Hear!' commented Howard and straightened his tie.

'I'll cut corners to make it brief,' Tweed began. 'A bomb was placed outside Miss Grey's house at Blakeney. The bomb disposal team only survived because of information earlier provided by Commander Bellenger. Explosive used was TNT.'

'What about the thirty sea-mines . . .' Howard began.

'Assumed to be armed with the same deadly Triton Three. Colossal explosive power. Plus twenty-five bombs . . .'

'Probably twenty-four now,' Bellenger pointed out. 'One already used at Blakeney.'

'All smuggled out of Russia,' Tweed continued, 'by Igor Zarov, master planner, expert at deception operations, who walked away from the Soviets. Definitely not your normal defector. Lone wolf type. Wants to make a huge fortune while he's still young . . .'

'Don't we all,' said Howard, but no one laughed.

'Zarov may be using the name Klein. He persuaded a top Swiss watch designer to make him special timer devices and control boxes . . .'

'The one crude aspect of the sea-mine we grabbed,' Bellenger remarked.

'Zarov murders the Swiss as soon as he gets his hands on the timers and boxes. A Turkish Nestlé driver is used to transport this lot from Switzerland to some unknown destination. He ends up at the foot of a precipice with his truck. More of Klein's work. Leave no one behind who could help us.'

'The bullion stolen in Basle,' Paula interjected.

'Coming to that. Prior to obtaining the timers Klein plans a raid on two Basle banks, uses Triton Three – confirmed by Bellenger's experts from debris taken from the bank vaults. That's converted into ready cash – I'm guessing here – to pay for the very large team of professional cutthroats he's hired.'

'Any idea of the size of that team?' Butler asked.

'From what Lasalle told me, those recruits include Frenchmen, Luxembourgers and maybe other nations. I can only guess – but I'd say that team numbers between twenty and thirty . . .'

'Oh, my God!' It was Howard who had jerked upright. 'I had no idea it was on that scale . . .'

'Which,' Tweed pointed out, 'indicates a target of some very great magnitude. And that's the two hundred million pound question.' He glanced at the wall map. 'Where is the target? As you see, Klein *appears* to be moving steadily north from southern Europe. He's also recruited The Monk, the top marksman on the continent. And as Bellenger has emphasized, a huge amount of high-explosive is involved. Also a unit of scuba divers. A curious combination. So, can anyone look at that map and make a stab as to what the target might be?'

'Why two hundred million pounds?' Howard enquired. 'That is a gigantic sum.'

'Because a dubious banker – I won't name him – has arranged to have that sum available in gold bullion for some other purpose I don't believe in. Our friend, Klein, has a love of bullion, as you may have gathered.'

'What on earth could he be planning to persuade anyone to hand over money like that?' Howard sounded sceptical.

'Oh, a major catastrophe,' Tweed told him. 'He specializes in organizing them.'

'So what action do you propose to counter this horrendous danger?'

'First, I'd like Commander Bellenger to fly with his experts tonight to SAS HQ in Hereford where the SAS unit is assembling. He can explain to their bomb disposal men about what he's nicknamed the Cossack mines and bombs.'

'Happy to oblige,' Bellenger replied. 'We can be ready to move in one hour. Transport?'

'Two choppers are waiting for you now at Heathrow.' Tweed's tone became grave. 'I must stress to everyone in this room the vital importance of total security. Nothing told you must be even hinted at to anyone else.' He looked at Bellenger. 'The SAS commander at Hereford has no idea of what I've been talking about. So it must remain.'

'You said "first",' Howard pointed out. 'What else have you in mind?'

'Tomorrow I'm flying to Belgium to meet Bob Newman – who at the moment is staying underground . . .'

'Exactly where?' asked Howard, staring at the map.

'If I told you with five of us sitting round this table he'd no longer be underground.' He stood up and walked over to the map, pointing to a certain area. 'We have to make a trip to a stretch of this river known as Les Dames de Meuse. I think there may be interesting developments.'

'Of what sort?' Howard persisted. 'You say you're short of time. I don't see the point.'

'What I have to do,' Tweed explained patiently, 'is to find a link between the banker who handled the bullion stolen from Basle – and Klein himself. I hope to find it there.'

'Why?'

'Because if I'm right the same banker has arranged to have two hundred million pounds more of bullion available. And I am now convinced these waterways – this network of canals from near Basle to the Meuse – is the route along which the bullion travelled. By barge. Maybe the timers and control boxes, too.'

'Sounds like a pleasure trip,' Howard snorted.

'It may turn out to be anything but that.'

28

After leaving Lara, Klein drove north from Antwerp. He crossed the border near Roosendaal into the flatlands of Holland, driving on through the night along Route D. He had changed cars in Antwerp, hiring an Audi and using false papers in the name of Meyer.

It was still dark when he drove through Rotterdam,

north again, to the ancient town of Delft. Dawn was breaking as he moved along narrow cobbled streets lined with ancient buildings. In the middle of the streets flowed canals crossed by hump-backed bridges. The place was deserted as he left the town, drove a short distance further and turned into a large camping site.

Neat rows of campers lined the tracks. In many there were lights as the early-rising Dutch prepared breakfast. Grand-Pierre, alerted by his phone call from Antwerp, ushered him inside a larger camper.

'Coffee?' the Frenchman asked in his own language.

'Litres of it. I've been driving all night. How far is the training advanced?'

'Oh, we're ready when you are. I need one day's warning to assemble the whole team here in Delft.'

'Why?'

Grand-Pierre, ex-French Foreign *légionnaire*, didn't even look at Klein as he bent over the coffee percolator. The Frenchman was huge, six feet tall and heavily built with a mane of black hair. He was an expert safecracker who had never been caught. Those large hands must have a delicate touch, Klein thought as he stood in his dark coat, shuffling his feet restlessly in the confined area of the camper. Just the touch needed for handling timers.

'Why?' Grand-Pierre repeated. 'Because I have over twenty men training in the wilds of Groningen, Holland's northern province. They jog along the beaches, swim in the sea off the Frisian Islands . . .'

'*Under* the sea, you mean?'

'Of course. They attached the dummy mine you gave me to the underside of a Dutch fishing vessel . . .'

'Wasn't that a risk?' Klein demanded, taking his hands out of his pockets and almost at once thrusting them inside again.

Grand-Pierre noticed the gesture as he handed over a large mug of steaming coffee. Restless type, he thought, a bundle of energy, always wanting to move on to his next destination the moment he'd arrived. The slow-moving giant glanced at Klein's chalk-white face as his guest swallowed his coffee. Bloody brain-box with his clever face, wherever he came from.

Not that Grand-Pierre cared. What he cared for was the hard cash paid. As though reading his mind, Klein took a package from his pocket and handed it to the Frenchman with his chamois-gloved hands.

'Help to keep you going. Expenses, plus the equivalent of twenty thousand francs in Dutch guilder towards your fee.'

'No risk,' Grand-Pierre replied to Klein's earlier question, 'and you might as well forget the job. I was there myself, underwater, when they carried out the experiment. They released the mine, swam off, and the fishermen had no idea of what had happened. You said train them, I train them. How far to the target? It's a big team to transport.'

'Not far. Have the locals got curious about your presence?'

'Not a whisper. The men are scattered about several camp sites. They're officially on a package deal holiday.'

'Any problem bringing in supplies? Food, I mean. They don't eat outside, I hope?'

'You said not — so they don't. And always a Dutch-speaking man goes into town for food and coffee. No one drinks. One man disobeyed me. I personally hauled him out of a bar.'

'You disciplined him?'

'Of course.' Grand-Pierre looked surprised. 'I drove him to a quiet spot on the coast, strangled him, weighted him with chains I had in the boot, dumped him in the sea. Is your coffee OK?'

Klein drove back to Rotterdam and inside the city of concrete and glass high-rise buildings, beautiful tree-lined shopping arcades. He parked at a meter near the Hilton, walked along a wide street until he found a public phone box, choosing one where several more stood in a row. It would be a long call to London.

He dialled a number from memory, asked for David Ballard-Smythe, waited. At the other end of the line Ballard-Smythe left his desk at Lloyds of London, walked to the phone.

'Ballard-Smythe here. Who is this?'

'You know who it is. Make a note of this number. Call me back within five minutes. I'm in a hurry. Repeat my number. It's in Holland . . .'

Ballard-Smythe put down the phone, asked a colleague to watch his desk for half an hour. 'A client who is disabled, can't leave his car.'

'OK.' The other man looked at him. 'Something wrong? Look as though you're about to give birth.'

'Well, I'm not. But when you eat an egg for breakfast that's off you don't feel perfect. Be back soon . . .'

Ballard-Smythe, a thin, nervous-looking man in his thirties, hurried out of the building. He'd been paid enough for passing on this information, he needed the money when he had a mistress as well as a wife, but now push came to shove he was wishing he hadn't agreed. The hell of it was he'd spent the advance payment Klein had given him two months ago.

Entering a phone box, he took from his jacket pocket a small leather purse bulging at the seams. Along the top of the telephone directories he arranged a collection of coins. He had an idea he'd be talking for some time.

No need to check the code for Holland. God knew, in his job he was always calling the great port of Rotterdam. He dialled the number he'd written on a scrap of paper and waited.

'Who is this?' a distinctive voice asked in English, a voice Ballard-Smythe instantly recognized.

'Is that you, Klein?'

'Listen. You've kept checking shipping movements in the area I named?'

'Daily. As soon as I reach my desk. My first task . . .'

'Next Thursday. What have we?'

'Well,' Ballard-Smythe began, 'at the head of the list we've got the 50,000-ton German cruise liner, *Adenauer*. Sailing from Hamburg, she stops offshore to take on board other passengers. They come out by lighters from Europort. That will be just before sunset . . .'

'I know. Get on with it. I haven't the time for long calls. What other shipping?'

'Couple of supertankers coming up from the south. Then the usual Sealink ferry will be arriving from Harwich. Oh, and a 10,000-ton freighter, the *Otranto*, from Genoa. Plus three large container jobs up from Africa. There'll be a fleet of shipping approaching Europort. The *Adenauer* will heave to about a mile offshore – giving plenty of free passage for the other vessels to move in.'

'Thank you,' said Klein.

'That's all?' Ballard-Smythe was surprised.

'Not quite,' Klein said. 'You have the key to a safe deposit I gave you – but you don't know where it is.'

'That's right. The one containing the second payment in cash.'

'Take down these details . . .'

Klein gave him the name and address of the bank, very close to where Ballard-Smythe was phoning from. He scribbled the details on the back of the same scrap of paper.

'The third and final payment – the big one – will be delivered to you by registered post in ten days' time . . .'

'Not to my home?' Ballard-Smythe sounded alarmed.

'Of course not. To your office. And in that safe deposit box you will find three packages numbered one, two, three. Take the first two, leave number three.'

'What's inside it?'

'Worthless share certificates. The box is paid for over the period of the next year. It will seem more normal if you leave something in the box. Goodbye.'

The connection was broken. Ballard-Smythe checked his watch. He still had time to go to the safety deposit before he was expected back at the office. He couldn't wait to get at the contents.

At the bank he showed his driver's licence as identification, was escorted down to the vault and the box reserved in his name. He followed Klein's instructions, taking the first two packages, leaving the third.

Returning to the office he went straight to the wash-room and locked himself inside the end cubicle. Envelope One contained one hundred £20 notes. £2,000. The second, heavier package contained a bottle of Napoleon brandy. Funny chap, Klein. Ballard-Smythe remembered discussing drink with him in a pub two months earlier. He'd told Klein how his wife only drank wine, but his favourite tipple was brandy.

At lunchtime he phoned his mistress, Peggy, who worked as a secretary in an insurance office nearby. He met her in a small restaurant not frequented by colleagues. At the coffee stage he handed her a freshly sealed envelope containing the money.

'Keep that safe in your flat,' he told her. 'In the usual place – under that loose floorboard beneath your dressing table . . .'

Ballard-Smythe dare not take the money home. His wife, Sue, had a habit of going through his suit prior to pressing it. And he hadn't been able to think of a really secure hiding place in his own house.

That evening, arriving at his detached house in Walton-on-Thames, he felt nervous. To cover up, he suggested a drink as soon as they sat in the living room, waiting for the meal to be ready. He poured her a glass of wine, then produced the bottle of brandy.

'Must have cost a bit, that,' Sue, a thin-faced brunette observed.

'Present from a satisfied customer.'

He poured a generous snifter, raised his glass and took the first long sip. He dropped the glass, clutched at his throat, gave an agonized gurgle and slumped to the floor. The doctor had the unpleasant task of telling Sue he was dead. The post-mortem confirmed what the doctor had suspected. Death from cyanide poisoning.

In Rotterdam Klein went into a bar and ordered coffee. He never drank alcohol – he hated anything which muddled his brain. He looked round the bar at the polished wooden tables, the spotless quarry-tiled floor, the curtains which were so clean. Very Dutch. As he drank his coffee he checked again over the operation in his mind.

Timers. Scuba divers. Marksman. Lara. Explosives. Banker.

Timers. They were due to arrive within a few hours, hidden inside the load of gravel aboard the barge, *Erika*, Haber would, as arranged, dock his barge at Waalhaven, only a few minutes' drive from where he sat. And Klein would be waiting for him.

Scuba divers. The whole team now based in Delft, a ten-minute train ride from north of Rotterdam. And Grand-Pierre was putting them through their paces – not only training them but keeping them occupied.

Marksman. The Monk was certainly well occupied. By now he'd be on his way to Les Dames de Meuse. His mission should prove good practice for what was coming. He had to kill Newman.

Lara. The sacrificial goat – as he now thought of her – was happily enjoying the luxury of the Mayfair Hotel in Brussels. Doubtless she'd be passing her time exploring the magnificent shops in the Avenue Louise arcade.

Explosives. Safely stashed away. Stored in a very secure place. And only a few hours' travel time away from the target area.

Banker. He would just have time to fly to and consult with Peter Brand. The arrangements the banker had made were the key to the whole operation.

As he finished his coffee Klein thought of the information confirmed to him by Ballard-Smythe over the phone. Everything was working out well. The German cruise liner,

Adenauer, was a key element. It carried a complement of over a thousand passengers bound for a Mediterranean holiday ending at Alexandria in Egypt with a paddle steamer trip up the Nile.

More than half the *Adenauer*'s passengers were American – who had flown to Hamburg from New York. They had been reassured by the fact that the German owners had employed Brinks, the American security organization, to check the ship and everyone who went aboard.

Once sea-mines were attached to the hull of the *Adenauer* – with enough explosive power to blow the liner sky-high – he was confident Washington would play it low key, make no attempt to interfere with his ransom demand. Not with the lives of over five hundred Americans at stake.

Of course they'd have to be convinced he meant business. That meant a demonstration involving a large number of casualties. In Klein's mind he was simply conducting with great precision a wartime-style operation. Now to take a second look at the target.

Klein drove along the tunnel under the river to reach the south bank. Then he turned west and headed for Europoort as the Dutch spelt it.

Europort. The greatest port in the whole world, handling a vast tonnage of goods coming in to feed and keep the wheels of industry turning. The Gateway to Europe. Nothing less.

If blocked off – closed down – whole nations would reel under the chaos. They could, he thought as he drove out of Rotterdam, organize a Berlin-style 1948 air lift. But that had been to help a city under siege survive. A continent under siege could never survive with the aid of only air transport.

The highway ran on and on as he left Rotterdam behind. It was twenty kilometres from the centre of Rotterdam to Europort, thirty kilometres to what the Dutch called the

Nord Zee. He began to pass target points. Shell-Mex oil refinery No. 1. Shell-Mex oil refinery No. 2. The huge Esso oil complex. The bombs would be placed there – and in other places. No oil, no Europe.

Beyond Rotterdam the land becomes very like a desert – with large open areas of sandy stretches of wilderness. Not a tree in sight. He drove on and on along what was now a deserted highway. The salt tang of a strong wind came in through the window off the North Sea. To his right side roads led away to the dock installations. The attack team would be given maps showing their objectives by Grand-Pierre twenty-four hours before the operation was launched.

Certain tradesmen's vans and trucks would be stolen only a few hours before then. The transport to be used had already been located, the habits and timings of the drivers noted.

Klein swung off the road across an area of scrubby grass and sand towards a huge concrete breakwater. He parked the car in the same spot he'd used during his reconnaissance weeks earlier. Buttoning up his black coat to the collar, he rammed his wide-brimmed black hat firmly over his head and stepped out.

No one else was in sight as he climbed to the top of the breakwater and stared out across the endless ripples of the North Sea. Only one vessel was in sight, a huge dredger. He took a monocular glass from his pocket, and focused it on the vessel.

A massive craft with a large crane on deck, it was dredging the mouth to the New Waterway, the entrance to the whole system of communication with the heartland of Europe. He scanned the vessel from stem to stern, lowered his glass, nodded to himself with satisfaction as he returned to the car. The dredger would be the first vessel to be sunk with all hands.

29

Tweed arrived at Brussels Airport the following morning. He was accompanied by Harry Butler and Paula. It was only when Monica walked into his office, cured of her flu, that he asked Paula to join them.

'You take over here at base, Monica,' he had instructed. He spent half an hour putting her in the picture. Paula marvelled at his gift for explaining so swiftly all that had happened. She marvelled equally at Monica's ability to absorb the data.

'Monica takes over as from now,' Monica announced when Tweed had finished. She glanced at Paula. 'Your real baptism of fire is coming up, I sense . . .'

The truth was Tweed had felt – as he had in the past – that a climax was close, that he would need all the back-up he could muster. He hurried off the aircraft in Brussels. He had called Chief Inspector Benoit the night before, asking for certain facilities.

Benoit, a jovial portly man of forty with a great beaked nose, light brown hair and shrewd eyes ushered them into an airport security office which had been placed at his disposal. From his expression Tweed saw the Belgian took an immediate fancy to Paula.

'Don't know how you stand this slave-driving boss of yours,' he commented in English.

'Oh, I just bend with the wind.'

Tweed could understand Benoit's reaction. Paula was kitted out in a suede zip-up and form-fitting jacket, a suede skirt and wore leather knee-length boots. Cups of strong black coffee arrived and Benoit got down to business the moment they were alone.

'A chopper is waiting on the tarmac, an Alouette. As

per your request.' He opened a brief-case and brought out a sheaf of charts which he dumped on the table in front of Tweed. 'Those are from the Navigation Institute of Waterways. They extend down the Meuse across the border into France. I rang Lasalle in Paris as you suggested.'

'His reaction?'

'Surprising. Electric when I mentioned your name. He's flying to Givet just south of Dinant. And we have permission to overfly the frontier if necessary. What are we looking for?'

'A missing Belgian barge. The *Gargantua*. It sailed from Dinant upstream towards Les Dames de Meuse and hasn't been seen since. I want to find it.'

'May be a problem – in the Dames de Meuse – if we don't find it further downstream. The chopper pilot warned me. They get heavy mists in that area. The Ardennes rise to thirteen hundred feet. On either side of the river. Imagine the risk our chopper pilot will face if you want a closer look.'

'I think, Paula,' Tweed said, 'you'd better wait here until we return.'

Paula, her forearms rested on the table, sat very erect, clasping her hands as she stared at Tweed. 'Paula did not come to drink coffee hour after hour in an airport. Remember Monica? My real baptism of fire, she said. When do we leave?'

Tweed glanced at Butler who shrugged his shoulders. 'Better give in now. She's a will of her own, this one has. And a pair of sharp eyes. May come in very useful.'

'Thank you for the vote of confidence, Harry,' Paula said, giving him her warmest smile.

That was when the phone rang. Benoit reached for it 'I told Grand'Place they could get me here,' he told Tweed. He listened, spoke in French, then handed the receiver to Tweed.

'It's Lasalle in Paris – for you. He rang London and they told him you should be at Grand'Place . . .'

'Tweed speaking . . .'

'The Parrot never gives up, my friend,' Lasalle boomed. 'He has followed your girl friend. I have a surprise. Lara Seagrave is on your doorstep.'

'What does that mean?'

'She is staying at the Mayfair Hotel, Avenue Louise in Brussels. She has returned from Antwerp – where she followed her usual routine. Took many photographs of the port area. And watched many ships through her binoculars. The Parrot is furious about one thing. She left her hotel in Antwerp to visit a street of ill fame, the Boekstraat. The Parrot thinks she met someone there – but he didn't know there was a rear exit. Have you traced Klein yet?'

'Unfortunately, no.'

'I have other news, which may mean nothing. Came in on the grapevine through our pal, Calgourli. A communications specialist called Legaud, Jean Legaud, was hired by a stranger recently. Now I hear one of the CRS communications trucks is missing. It may have crossed the border into Luxembourg last night. Report from a frontier post. Similar type of van. A black Citroën truck.'

'Who is Legaud?'

'Had to leave a big telecommunications company suspected of fraud two years ago. No proof, no prosecution. Legaud is a specialist in telephones, radio communication . . .'

'You did say *radio*?'

'Yes. That means something?'

'It might. Thank you for calling, if that is all.'

'For the moment. See you on the Meuse.'

Tweed had just put down the phone when a uniformed security official came in after knocking and Benoit called out 'Enter'.

'A Mr Robert Newman has just arrived from Grand' Place. He is asking for a Mr Tweed.'

'Show him in.'

Tweed was relieved. He'd phoned Newman from London at his hotel in Liège, asking him to meet them at Grand'

Place the following morning. He stood up as Newman came in, introduced him to Benoit, and then Newman spoke to Tweed.

'I need to talk with you urgently. On your own . . .'

'This office next door is available,' Benoit offered, opening a door.

Tweed listened while Newman told him briefly about his visit to the Meuse, what the bargee, Willy Boden, had told him, his encounter with the crusty Colonel Ralston – and his later encounter with Peter Brand at Profondeville.

'This girl friend of his, Carole Browne,' Tweed commented. 'I take it she was positive a man called Klein had visited this palatial villa?'

'Several times. She was quite certain. I believe her.'

'And you mentioned bullion to Brand, you say?'

'Yes, to stir him up. I think I did just that.'

'You do realize that Brand's reference to Les Dames de Meuse is probably a trap?'

'Of course. You think I'm thick? That's why I'm going – to see what happens.'

'I should have assumed that. Bob, we're all going – Benoit has laid on an Alouette – so we can search the river from the air. And all this points to what I've suspected. Now we have a clear link between Klein and his banker, who *is* Peter Brand. More than that, those heavy wheel tracks from Brand's landing stage across the lawn and out into the drive – that could be the vehicle which collected the bullion stolen from Basle on its way to be melted down.'

'My thought too . . .'

'So it becomes very urgent to locate that barge, *Gargantua* – which probably transported the bullion from Basle through the canal complex to Profondeville – and was unloaded during the night.'

'Klein is clever.'

'A master planner. And it becomes even more urgent to locate Haber, the owner of that barge. He's the only one who can tell us what happened. He may even be transporting the timer devices made by that murdered Swiss . . .'

There was a knock on the door, Benoit showed his head, informed them the chopper pilot said they'd have to wait for take-off. Visibility was ten-tenths. Dense fog. Could be clear at any moment. He'd keep them informed.

'I'm in a dilemma,' Tweed confessed as he sat down. 'Lara Seagrave has turned up at the Hotel Mayfair here in Brussels. She's twenty minutes' drive from where we're sitting. And she's just back from photographing the port of Antwerp.'

'I still don't understand this talk of hijacking a ship,' Newman responded. 'Klein has a whole arsenal of sea-mines and bombs. Does that sound like the simple hijacking of one ship?'

'No. Incidentally, in case anything happens to me I think you should know I have someone planted inside Klein's organization. Code-named Olympus. Came about by chance. I get occasional reports – but I think Klein is working on the cell system, that not one single member of his team is told more than they need to know.'

'This Olympus. Man or woman?'

'I'm not telling anyone that. Not even you. Olympus has to have all the protection I can provide. If Klein even suspected, he'd cut their throat. Look at his track record. You know what I fear he's planning?'

'Something pretty big . . .'

'A holocaust,' Tweed replied.

Klein booked in at the Hilton on the Boulevard de Waterloo in Brussels the morning Tweed arrived at the airport. He registered at the Executive Desk on the eighteenth floor in the name Dupont and went up in the elevator to Executive Suite Number 1914. This was the room Marler would occupy when moved to Brussels.

Looking out of the window he gazed at the enormous cathedral-like edifice of the Palais de Justice. Domed, it was the largest building in Europe – larger than St Peter's in Rome. He was staring out of the window when the phone rang.

'Dupont speaking.'

'Legaud here. I called twice earlier. No reply . . .'

'I'm replying now. Where are you?'

'Maastricht. The equipment is in perfect working order. I shall arrive and make delivery by this afternoon . . .'

'I will be in touch. Goodbye.'

Klein broke the connection, took a map from his pocket, unfolded it and spread it out on one of the beds. He carried a detailed map of Europe in his head, but there was no substitute for checking, checking, checking . . .

Legaud, the communications specialist, had done well. Maastricht was just over the frontier from Belgium. Legaud was already inside Holland. He would drive the vehicle to the rendezvous prearranged with Grand-Pierre out in the wilds – where the black vehicle would be fitted with Dutch number plates, the bodywork resprayed from black to cream.

The call had come through quickly. Excellent. His next appointment was with Peter Brand at his residence on the Avenue Franklin Roosevelt. There final arrangements would be concluded for the transportation of two hundred million pounds worth of gold bullion at present held by the Deutsche Bank in Frankfurt. When the time came.

The Alouette lifted off shortly after midday. Tweed, Newman, Butler, Paula and Benoit were aboard as the pilot flew south-east, heading for the start point down the Meuse Tweed had suggested. Namur.

They passed over Namur and Tweed looked down on the citadel, on the fork where the Sambre river entered the Meuse. The pilot then flew steadily south a few hundred feet above the winding river in clear weather. On the port side Tweed used binoculars to check the names of each barge proceeding downstream. Benoit, with his own pair of field glasses, performed the same function to starboard.

They flew above Dinant. Another citadel perched on top of a pinnacle of rock. They were approaching Givet when the co-pilot reported receipt of a message from Chief Inspector Lasalle. Would they land briefly at Givet – on the French side of the frontier – and pick him up from one of the quays?

'Are you feeling all right?' Paula asked Tweed alongside her as the pilot began his tricky descent. 'You've lost colour.'

'Hate ships. They bob about. So does this thing. Think I'd better take a Dramamine.'

'Take it now. Don't think about it. Do it . . .'

Tweed swallowed one of the brown tablets from the packet he always carried. 'It takes effect in less than half an hour,' he commented. 'There could be turbulence over Les Dames de Meuse. Those Ardennes . . .'

Lasalle came aboard with an inspector called Sonnet, a stern-faced slim individual who was a local from Givet. Benoit greeted Lasalle like an old friend and then they were airborne. Tweed left Newman to explain the situation through his head-set. He was entering the pilot's cabin when the machine suddenly climbed vertically, swaying from side to side. Grimly, he held on, staring ahead.

'Ah! Ah!' the pilot called out. 'We are in trouble.'

Tweed didn't need to be told. Approaching Les Dames de Meuse, a bank of solid white fog appeared ahead. Vapour drifted past the perspex window in the pilot's cabin. The river below had vanished. They were flying blind.

'Have to climb,' the pilot continued. 'The hills rise to above thirteen hundred feet . . .'

The machine went on climbing, Tweed caught a glimpse of solid rock on the starboard side, rock which seemed feet away from the plane. He swallowed, binoculars looped round his neck. How the hell could they hope to spot the barge in this stuff? He wished to God he'd insisted on

Paula staying behind. He glanced back into the cabin, caught Paula's eye and she winked. Guts, he thought.

He watched the altimeter climb well above the equivalent of thirteen hundred feet in metres. They should be safe – but the whole exercise was becoming pointless. He peered forward. The fog, rolling in waves, was thinning.

'Where are we?' he asked through his mouthpiece. 'Have you any idea?'

'Directly above Les Dames de Meuse,' the pilot replied. 'I have a wall of rock on both sides. Below us.'

Tweed hardly heard him. He was gazing with intensity at the mist ahead. A great hole seemed to have appeared in the dense whiteness. He peered down. The river was immediately below. He had an impression of loneliness, no water traffic, thick forest descending to the water's edge, a wide belt of reeds spreading out from the bank. He stared at something, leaned forward.

'Pilot! Can you take her down? Now? Land on that towpath?'

'Risky . . .'

'It's clear below us . . .'

'Give it a try, sir.'

Something touched Tweed's sleeve. He glanced up. Benoit, who had heard the exchange, was beside him. Standing behind the Belgian were Newman and Lasalle. The machine began a slow descent as trails of vapour curled round the fuselage.

Tweed had forgotten his queasy stomach. His eyes were fixed on a vast swathe of reeds and grasses projecting from the left bank. Almost like a dense swamp, dark and brooding at a bend in the river. His eyes flickered to the right. Another brief glimpse. This time of forest clinging to the near cliff-like hillside. Again it seemed to be feet away from the machine.

'What is it?' Benoit asked.

'I think I saw something. Down there among the reeds.'

'What was it?'

'Let's wait till we're down . . .'

The pilot was glancing from side to side. More mist had drifted in close to the chopper, mist rising up from the river. He had poor visibility. End up in the bloody river, he was thinking. He said nothing, concentrating on his controls, praying the towpath would appear in the right place as they went down, down, down.

'This,' Lasalle contributed, 'if I'm not mistaken, is where the Ardennes are at their highest. The river is almost walled in by rock and forest. Perhaps your eyes deceived you . . .'

'Perhaps.'

Behind Newman Paula stared fascinated at Tweed. He was crouched forward, like a hound watching a fox, ignoring the chopper's descent. His head was motionless, his stare fixed, gazing at the swamp-like morass extending from the river bank.

She jumped as the machine hit something, settled, lying still. The pilot operated another control, switching off the engine. The whirling rotors began to slow. They had landed on the towpath.

'This is bloody ridiculous. You know that?' Marler remarked to Hipper who sat beside him as he drove on, his headlights hardly penetrating the fog.

They were driving along a curving road above Les Dames de Meuse. Visibility came and went as the fog curtain whirled in front of them. And Marler's mood was not improved by the presence of the soft-spoken Luxembourger.

Hipper turned up early in the morning at the Panorama in Bouillon unexpectedly. He had explained that their 'mutual acquaintance' wished him to accompany Marler on his mission. Marler would have told him to piss off – but he didn't want to draw attention to them in the hotel lobby. The next thing he knew Hipper was in the car beside him, carrying a whacking great Leica cine-camera equipped with a zoom lens.

'Why?' enquired Hipper as Marler drove on along a deserted road.

'Why what?'

'Why is it ridiculous?'

'Oh, God Almighty.' Marler's tone was at its most superior and resigned. 'It is ridiculous because how do you think I am going to locate Newman in this fog? Just assuming he is within a hundred miles of this part of the world.'

'We shall find his car. You will recognize him from the picture I gave you. He will come.'

'How do you know?'

'A friend of our friend pointed him to Les Dames de Meuse. For today.'

'Why don't you say Klein? Your so-called friend is Klein, I take it? Give me an answer or I'll pitch you out of the car.'

'Yes. But you see . . .' That slow pedantic voice. Marler felt he could strangle him. '. . . I have trained myself never to use his name. It is good security . . .'

'Shut up! I heard something. An engine . . .'

'Maybe Newman in his car . . .'

'I said shut up – and I meant it.' Marler stopped the car as the road began running downhill towards the river.

Perching an elbow on the window edge, he listened, one hand cupped to his ear. There it was again. Throb-throb. Louder now. *Above* them. Somewhere in the ceiling of solid fog.

'What is it . . .' Hipper began.

One look from Marler silenced him. The throb-throb was coming closer. Marler craned his neck out of the window, staring skyward. The fog was thinning, a pallid glow which was the sun appeared, illuminating a large break in the veil of mist overhanging the river.

'Chopper,' Marler said. 'Coming down. Taking one hell of a chance in this stuff. And there it is.'

'A police helicopter. Oh, dear. Now-we-must-be-very-careful-indeed.' Hipper was spacing words again, like a ruddy child. 'Do you not think they may well be able to see us?'

'In this fog?' Marler's tone was contemptuous. 'And in case you haven't noticed, the colour of our car is grey. So, the answer to your question is not if we remain stationary. And this happens to be a good vantage point.'

The fog was clearing lower down the steep hillside. Marler had stopped at a point where the road curved round a rocky bluff, hanging over the Meuse which now came into view far below. It flowed slowly, smooth as gliding oil. Pretty wide even this far upstream. A towpath on the bank below them, Marler noted. A sedge-like projection of clumps of grass and reeds appeared spreading from the edge of the far bank.

'Oh, no!' Hipper exclaimed. 'Not here. Not here . . .'

Marler sighed. Hipper was whimpering, almost like a scared puppy. The big Alouette, fuselage gleaming in the pallid sun-light with moisture, descended slowly, a few hundred yards from where they sat in the parked vehicle. Marler could see the pilot was nervous. With damned good reason. A similar bluff of limestone rock projected above the river on the opposite bank.

He waited for the brief clash of metal striking rock, the whirling rotors crashing against a crag. The machine dropped very slowly, landed on the towpath – which was just wide enough to accommodate the Alouette. He reached for the rifle concealed beneath a travelling rug carelessly thrown over the back seat, pulled the telescopic sight free from beneath his seat to which it had been attached by adhesive tape. He asked the question as he cleaned the sight, began attaching it to the rifle.

'Could Newman be aboard that police chopper?'

'I really have no idea . . .'

'And why are you so concerned the chopper landed at this point?'

'Nothing.' Hipper had hesitated before replying. 'Just a fit of nerves . . .'

'Then stop yammering and let me concentrate.'

Marler climbed slowly out of the car, walked to the edge of the bluff. He wasn't worried he'd be seen. People looked everywhere except *upwards*. He adjusted the sight, aimed it at the passengers alighting from the Alouette on to the towpath. Behind him Hipper also alighted from the car, gripping his camera as he joined the Englishman.

'Newman is with that crowd,' Marler observed.

'You can get him?'

Hipper sounded excited. He couldn't keep still. He raised his camera and stared down through the lens at the group moving below.

'Keep your voice down,' Marler whispered. 'Sound carries a long distance in this fog.' He lowered his rifle and glared at the Luxembourger. 'Can't see him now – the fog keeps drifting down there. And get away from me. Climb that hill on the other side of the road. You're disturbing my concentration. What the hell are you doing anyway?'

'Waiting for you to kill Newman. I want a photograph of the body. Our friend will be interested to see that . . .'

Tweed stood on the towpath, sniffing the dank air, moisture clinging to his face like the fingers of an invisible ghost. Down at the edge of the Meuse the atmosphere was creepy. A shaft of sunlight, reflecting motes of the moisture, shone briefly on the opposite bank and was gone. A heavy silence hung over the river and the damp cold was beginning to penetrate their clothes. Tweed adjusted his wide-brimmed waterproof hat and pointed to the congested morass projecting from the opposite bank.

'That's where I want to explore.'

'God knows how,' Newman commented. 'Care for a swim?'

'What a horrid-looking marsh,' Paula said and buttoned up her raincoat to her neck. 'Are you sure that was the place, Tweed?'

'Quite sure. I saw something. Ah, what have we here?'

261

Inspector Sonnet, looking mournful, had disappeared along the towpath round a bend. There was a chug-chugging sound and he reappeared, holding the tiller of a large outboard dinghy as he cruised towards them, steered inshore, stopped the engine and climbed on to the towpath, holding a mooring rope.

'I found it tied up to a rotting landing stage,' he explained. 'Probably belongs to a fisherman. This is one of their favourite grounds.'

'And just commandeered by the police for investigation purposes,' Lasalle announced breezily. 'How do we get out of here if the mist persists? I can't see the pilot agreeing to lift off until it clears.'

'Arrangements have been made,' Sonnet told him. 'A couple of my men are driving two Deux-Chevaux from Givet. They are the only vehicles which can negotiate this towpath. Since they did not know where we would be they started at the end. They should be here soon.'

Tweed glanced at the thin-faced inspector with approval; he seemed well-organized. Almost too good a man for the provinces. He felt the torch he always carried inside his coat pocket, braced his shoulders against the chill.

'Well, who is coming across with me to check over there? I would like Newman with me – if no one objects.'

'I'd like to come to,' Paula said firmly. She saw Tweed's expression. 'At the risk of boring you, someone used the phrase baptism of fire.'

'Three of us so far,' Tweed remarked. 'It's a large dinghy. How many will it hold? Safely.'

'Five,' said Lasalle. 'Benoit, you go too. Sonnet is the helmsman. I'll stand guard here. I could do with a stroll up and down this towpath. I'm stiff. Good hunting, Tweed. Bet you don't find anything . . .'

Tweed thanked God he'd taken a Dramamine as he climbed carefully into the rocking bow of the craft which wobbled madly. He gave Paula a hand to come aboard and then sat down, staring at the swamp.

Sonnet handled the dinghy with great skill, heading

upstream to counter the flowing current, following Tweed's instructions to bring the dinghy to the reed bank at a certain point. Inshore, the power of the current slackened. Sonnet slowed and nosed the dinghy inside the waist-high reeds, stopping so the outboard was not tangled.

It was very dark beneath the overhang of the forest. Paula was looking everywhere and she stiffened suddenly while gazing up at the bank they had left behind. Tweed sensed her reaction.

'What is it?'

'The mist cleared up there for a few seconds. I could have sworn I saw someone on top of a crag.'

'I doubt it,' Benoit called out. 'The mist plays tricks and you see phantoms which aren't there.'

'I suppose so . . .' She sounded unconvinced, then broke off as Tweed stood up and shone his torch. 'My God!' she began. 'What are you doing . . . ?'

Tweed appeared to have stepped out of the dinghy into the squelchy morass. His feet hit solid surface and he reached out to pull at a mass of broken reeds, pulling them away to expose the upper half of a wheelhouse.

Gargantua. The name, a brass plate screwed to the wheelhouse, jumped out in Tweed's torch beam. He had removed a mass of broken reeds piled up against the structure. He shone his torch inside the wheelhouse. Empty. The wheel heeled over at a drunken angle.

'God! You were right,' Newman, close to Paula, called out. 'They sank the barge.'

'Klein's work,' Tweed said. 'I bet six months' pay that when the French forensic people check the hold they'll find traces of gold. Which was why it had to disappear. Better keep back, both of you. The deck's like a skating rink.'

His shoes slopped through a mess of reeds and water, making his way along the inclined deck of the half-submerged vessel. He crouched low, keeping to starboard, holding on to the deck rail. His torch beam picked out a muddled pattern of coiled ropes, oil slicks. It was the port side which had heeled into the swamp, tilting the starboard clear of the deep water.

Sliding his left hand along the rail, he slithered, recovered his balance, continued towards the bow. Following close behind, Paula was amazed at the agility he displayed, moving one foot in front of the other, feeling his way cautiously, checking what lay ahead with the torch.

Paula knew something was wrong when, close to the slanting bow, he stopped suddenly, his posture rigid. He switched off the torch, turned and called out over his shoulder in a brusque but calm voice.

'Paula, go back. Now!'

'What is it?' she demanded. 'I'm not a schoolgirl, Goddamnit. You saw something. What was it? I'm determined to see.'

'Better come back with me,' Newman suggested.

'Oh, do belt up, Bob. Go back yourself, if you must.'

'Very well,' Tweed said. 'Maybe you're right. Look there.'

He switched on the torch again, directed the beam to a point in the swamp just beyond the bow. Paula stared along the beam. She suddenly felt horribly cold. Her legs went like jelly. She gritted her teeth, stiffened her legs, pressed her feet hard against a loop of chain she stood on, forced herself to stand erect.

'Oh, yuck!' She let out her breath. 'I'm all right.'

Framed in the circular beam of the torchlight was the head and shoulders of a man sunk in the swamp. He appeared to be grinning, his mouth slack, his teeth showing. Below his chin his thick neck was slashed with a red wound from ear to ear. The blood had congealed into what looked like a scar. His black hair was matted flat over his head and his eyes stared sightless at the intruders. Just below water level the body had enlarged, bloated like an obscene balloon.

'Haber,' said Tweed. 'He killed Haber, sank his barge.'

Sonnet had come up behind Newman. He peered round

Newman's body to get a better look. Paula distinctly heard in the silence a hiss as Sonnet sucked in his breath.

'That's not Haber. That's Broucker, Haber's employee. The bargee he uses to sail the *Erika*.'

30

Marler peered through his telescopic sight. The mist had cleared briefly and he watched the outboard dinghy returning towards the towpath across the river. Newman's face jumped into the sight, the dinghy continued its passage, Marler had a glimpse of another man, who was Tweed. His finger tightened on the trigger, the image blurred.

He lowered the rifle, gazing down. Another bank of mist had drifted below the bluff, blotting out the Meuse. He waited patiently, glancing behind him. Hipper had perched himself in a rocky crevice above the far side of the road. He also had lowered his camera. He came scrambling awkwardly down the hillside.

'Why did you not shoot? I saw him clearly in my lens . . .'

'Hipper . . .' Marler reached out a hand and clenched the Luxembourger's shoulder, '. . . are you trying to tell me how to do my job?' His grip tightened. 'Because if so it will give me great pleasure to hurl you off the top of this crag. I do need a clear field of fire and the mist came across it. Also, you are not thinking, are you?'

'What do you mean?' Hipper winced. 'And you are hurting me.'

'Hipper,' Marler repeated, 'when the job is done we need a safe escape route. Those are police down there – with a chopper. So, we need two things. Enough ceiling fog to stop the chopper taking off and locating us from the air when we drive off. But, as I said, I also need a clear field of fire. No mist. A difficult combination.'

265

'What are you going to do about it?'

'Oh, it's just me now? That's better. Go back to your rabbit hole.' His tone changed, became very cold. 'And stay there until the job is done.'

He turned away, looked up towards the sky above the Meuse. Dense as cottonwool. No chopper could take off up into that. He smoothed a hand over the crown of his head. The patch he normally kept bald with an electric shaver had grown over – making identification more difficult. The bald patch was his trademark; hence his nickname, The Monk.

He stiffened as he looked down. The river bank was clear of fog. A group of four men and a girl stood chatting on the towpath. The fifth man had cruised back downstream, presumably to the point where he'd found the dinghy.

He raised his rifle, squinted through it. Newman's face and head was bisected by the crosshairs. Very close to him was another man, who appeared to be Tweed. Marler took careful aim, steady as a rock. He pressed the trigger as Newman moved a pace to his right, as Tweed stooped to empty water from his shoe.

The crack of the shot echoed weirdly in the mist. Marler gazed through the sight for a few seconds, then stepped back from the bluff. Hipper made record time reaching him. The Englishman looked amazed.

'Missed him. He moved at the last second. And we'd better get moving . . .'

'A bit close that . . .'

Tweed showed his hat. The bullet had nicked the brim. He stared up towards the bluff and it vanished in a fresh bank of drifting vapour. Lasalle reacted first.

'Someone up there tried to kill one of us. Listen! A car has started. Get that chopper up . . .' He ran to the machine, spoke to the pilot, who slammed the door, started the rotors, began to ascend vertically. He ran back to the others.

266

'The Monk's work, I suspect,' Tweed remarked.

'Is it safe for the Alouette to take off?' Benoit asked.

'The pilot says OK,' Lasalle told him. 'All he has to do is keep rising vertically on the upward course where he descended. He's climbing until he gets above the fog, then he's going after that car.'

'Lord,' Paula said, eyeing Tweed's hat, 'he could have killed you.' She shivered.

'You know what they say – a miss is as good as a mile. And what's this coming?'

Two cars, Deux-Chevaux, orange-coloured, were proceeding at slow speed along the towpath. Sonnet sat beside the driver of one of them. Lasalle took off again, running towards the lead vehicle. He spoke quickly to Sonnet, who nodded as Lasalle gestured vigorously. Jumping out of the car, he ran back to the vehicle behind, spoke to the driver. The vehicle began backing away along the towpath as Tweed watched anxiously. The driver was going to end up in the river.

He didn't. He reached a certain point, turned his wheel and disappeared inside the forest. Sonnet walked back to them.

'I instructed him to find that car. He has driven up one of the tracks which will take him on to the road. He has radio. The Alouette will be able to communicate, guide him. And he is calling for reinforcements.'

Lasalle had been staring up the side of the hill. The mist cleared again, clearly exposing the huge bluff. He pulled an automatic from his shoulder holster, aimed the gun and emptied the magazine, firing at intervals round the crag, varying his aim. Taking a fresh magazine from his pocket, he rammed it in place and holstered the weapon.

'What was that in aid of?' Newman asked. 'He's gone . . .'

'He *appears* to have gone,' Lasalle replied. 'He could have had another man with him, someone who drove away their car. Just a precaution. My fusillade will have frightened him off – if he was still there. Who was he trying to kill, I wonder? How did he know we would be here?'

'I think Newman was the target,' Tweed replied quietly. 'He was pointed to this area by Peter Brand, the banker. Later I think we should have a talk with Mr Brand. Meantime, may I make a request?' he addressed Inspector Sonnet. 'Could I have a brief chat with Newman in that car?'

'Of course, sir. I kept it so we have transport back to Givet. Another car is on the way.'

'We have things to talk over, Bob,' Tweed said and led the way to the car.

'Can't you drive faster?' yelped Hipper. 'You were wrong about that helicopter. I heard it taking off. And why are you turning off the main road? You can't drive fast along here . . .'

'Hipper, shut your mouth. I crave silence. If you do not mind – even if you do.'

They had turned on to a winding country lane which was climbing. Overhead the trees on either side met, forming a tunnel of foliage. Marler slowed the car, then stopped. Hipper clutched the camera in his lap.

'You must drive on – as fast as you can . . .'

'My dear Hipper.' Marler paused to light one of his rare cigarettes. 'That is exactly what they will expect us to do. Belt like mad along a main highway. Listen.'

The chug-chug of a helicopter came closer. Hipper took out a soiled handkerchief, wiped sweat dripping from his greasy forehead. The machine passed overhead, the sound faded into the distance.

'You see?' Marler yawned. 'We wait until things have settled down. They can't search every road in the Ardennes. So, we wait.'

At the last moment Tweed decided to take Butler with Newman to the Deux-Chevaux which was now empty, the driver having joined Sonnet and the others opposite the sunken *Gargantua*. Harry had typically remained silent since their excursion across the river, but he sometimes noticed something in a narrative which escaped Tweed.

'Bob,' said Tweed when they were seated inside the Deux-Chevaux, 'tell me again briefly what you reported about your adventures on the Meuse. Especially anything about those bargees . . .'

He listened intently as Newman recapitulated what had happened. His interview with Willy Boden and his wife, Simone. His later experience aboard Colonel Ralston's *Evening Star*. He had just finished recalling his chat with Ralston's girl friend, Josette, when Tweed interrupted.

'You say Josette told you Haber has a family, a wife and a son called Lucien, living near this tiny village, Celle?'

'That's right. Not relevant . . .'

'I wonder. I think we've got this thing the wrong way round – that Klein has again been diabolically clever. I thought the *Gargantua* might well be used to transport the timers made by the murdered Swiss watchmaker. But it was the *Erika*, the other barge, which Boden and his wife saw moving downstream towards Namur?'

'Right again.'

'We'd better get back to Lasalle and Benoit. I'm worried stiff about the time element.'

'What puzzles me,' Butler broke in for the first time, 'is why would Haber agree to pull the plug on his own barge? Money? I doubt it.'

'And there,' Tweed agreed, 'you've put your finger on the whole business. Let's move.'

'Inspector Sonnet,' Tweed said as soon as they reached the waiting group gathered on the towpath, 'I gather that since you identified the corpse as Broucker, not Haber, you must know something about Haber?'

'Know him well.' The thin Frenchman was terse in speech. 'There may be a frontier beyond Givet. It means

269

little. We are all part of the Meuse. The lifeline of this part of Belgium and France.'

'Is Haber a greedy man? For money?'

'He is ambitious. For his family, his son. Which is why he fights to build up a fleet of barges. To that extent, yes, he is greedy for money.'

'What does he value above money?'

'His family, of course. He worships them . . .'

'So if someone wanted to force him to do something he didn't want to do – a very ruthless man – where would he apply the pressure?'

'Oh my God, you don't mean . . .'

He broke off. The sun had broken through, was burning the fog off the Meuse. The sound of a helicopter approaching became louder and louder. As they watched, the Alouette appeared above them, descending more rapidly this time, only slowing a few feet above the towpath before landing.

'I told the pilot to come back for us,' Lasalle said. 'Unless he spotted the car quickly. Sonnet has used the radio to throw out a dragnet across all main roads. Drivers will be stopped, questioned.'

He ran to the machine and talked briefly with the pilot through the open door. The rotors had whirled to a stop. Lasalle ran back.

'Pilot reports he checked all main roads. No sign of any car. Traffic is non-existent. It was the fog. He says there are scores of country roads through the forest. The killer could be anywhere.'

'Gentlemen,' Tweed intervened, addressing Benoit and Lasalle, 'I request two things. From the navigation instructions I was given with the charts at Brussels airport, I gather each lock-keeper is linked by phone with the next. Further that they keep a record of all vessels passing through their own lock?'

'That is so,' Sonnet confirmed.

'Then we need to trace the barge *Erika* as a matter of international emergency. At the earliest possible moment.

270

When found it must be intercepted with care – by armed men. Then it must be thoroughly searched. Especially its cargo of gravel. Haber must be interrogated.'

'Sonnet, use the radio on that car to start checking all locks. It could be a long business,' Lasalle warned Tweed. 'How many locks between here and Namur?' he asked Sonnet.

'Sixteen between the frontier and Liège, seven between where we stand and the frontier, plus the tunnels . . .'

'Tunnels?' Tweed pounced. 'The barges pass through tunnels? Where is the nearest to here downstream?'

'At Revin, only a few kilometres away.'

'And that, I'm sure,' said Tweed, 'is where Broucker had his throat cut by Klein while Haber navigated the barge through the tunnel. It puzzled me – that he would take a chance on killing a man in the open.'

'Who is this Klein? Haber would never stand by while that happened,' Sonnet objected.

'He might have to – if his family had been kidnapped.' He looked at Benoit and Lasalle. 'That is the second request. I want the chopper to fly me now as close as possible to this village, Celle – where Haber's family lives. And if Sonnet could accompany us – to guide the pilot?'

'Of course . . .'

'Agreed . . .'

Both men spoke at once. Sonnet excused himself while he ran to the car to radio through the instruction to check with all lock-keepers in the search for the *Erika*. Tweed looked at his watch, began to take short paces back and forth.

'You're worried we're going to be too late,' Paula said.

'Exactly. Oh, Lasalle, one more question. That CRS communications van which went missing. What equipment does it carry? What makes it so special?'

'The normal radio stuff – as a mobile HQ for riot control. But it also has the most advanced transceiver and a transmitter just received from America. With that – it has a great variety of wave-lengths – the vehicle gives you a range over thirty miles.'

'A command vehicle,' Newman said grimly. 'Just what Klein needs to control the whole diabolical operation.'

'And what do you lot think you are doing?'

The voice, indignant, intimidating, a woman's, called out to them in French as they stood outside the front door of a small cottage on the edge of a hamlet near Celle. Tweed, Newman, Benoit, Sonnet and Paula swung round to stare at the owner of the strident voice standing by the open gate. Butler merely glanced over his shoulder and continued examining the outside of the building. He sensed it was empty.

It was Paula who stepped forward with a smile. The woman was large, in her fifties, had a hooked nose and a prominent jaw. She stood with her arms akimbo, her stance challenging.

'I am Madame Joris,' she went on, 'and I am looking after the cottage while the owner is away. Who are you people?'

'We are worried about Martine Haber and her son, Lucien. You say they are away? Where have they gone?' Paula enquired.

'None of your business . . .'

'Oh, yes it is.' Benoit walked past Paula, his mood anything but jovial. 'Police Judiciaire.' He waved his warrant card at her. 'Answer the young lady's question.'

'They've gone on holiday, haven't they? She phoned me just before they left, asked me to keep an eye on the place.'

'How did she sound? When she phoned you? They take a regular holiday?'

'Which question first? I'm not on a quiz show. No, they'd never taken a holiday before. Not away. She sounded peaky on the phone – as though she needed the holiday.'

'Peaky? Nervous, perhaps?' Benoit pressed.

'Come to think of it, yes. Short conversation. For her.

272

In a rush to get off to Majorca. Two days ago that would be.'

'Have you a key? Did you *see* her before she left?'

'No! Told you, she phoned. When I came round they'd gone. And no key. What's this all about?'

'One good heave would open the front door,' Sonnet called out. 'Newman has been round the house, says it looks empty. The kitchen is a mess . . .'

'How dare you!' Madame Joris stormed up the path. 'Martine is a clean and neat housewife. I don't believe it.'

'Unwashed dishes piled up in the sink,' Newman whispered to Sonnet.

'One good heave. These locks are useless . . .'

Sonnet pressed a shoulder against the lock side of the door and pushed. It held for a moment, there was a click, the door swung inward. Sonnet recovered his balance.

'You can't do that!' screamed Madame Joris.

'My impression,' Benoit told her amiably, 'is we have just done it . . .'

'I'm coming in . . .'

'I was about to ask you if you would be so kind as to do just that.'

Paula tiptoed in behind Sonnet, gestured to the rug in the small hall which was askew. Madame Joris pushed past them after Sonnet and followed him into the kitchen. She stared at the piled-up unwashed dishes.

'Something's wrong.' She sounded alarmed for the first time 'Martine would never go out shopping leaving things like that. Let alone on holiday.'

'Could you check her clothes, please?' asked Benoit.

Madame Joris came hustling down the tiny staircase in less than a minute. She was agitated and held a pair of shoes in her hand.

'Her best shoes. Bought in a sale. She'd never leave those, her Sunday shoes. Something's terribly wrong. You do realize that, I hope?'

She made the statement as though she were the first to

273

raise the alarm. Tweed stood watching her, hands thrust inside his raincoat pockets. His mind went back to his days as a detective, when he'd stood just like this, confronting a new witness, deciding the best way to handle the unknown quantity.

'Madame Joris,' he began, 'may I congratulate you on your excellent powers of observation?'

She seemed to grow even larger, her full breasts sagging inside her flowered dress. 'I don't miss much, I can tell you that.'

'I'm sure you don't. You know this house. Would you take me over it, see what else you can spot?'

'Of course.' She mellowed visibly under Tweed's flattery, so delighted to be the centre of attraction. 'Shall we start upstairs?'

Tweed followed her up the tiny staircase, just wide enough for Joris to squeeze her bulk between banisters and wall. They went into a small bedroom. Joris began opening drawers. She spoke over her crouched form. 'Wouldn't do this normally, of course . . .'

'I understand, but Martine may be in great danger.' Tweed understood only too well; Joris was revelling in the opportunity to poke among her neighbour's things.

Tweed noted the neatly arranged items on Martine's dressing-table, the few carefully placed pots on window ledges. He looked at the bed, which was made up but had a rumpled appearance.

'Is that the way Martine would make up the bed?' he asked.

'It is not! An apple pie mess, I call that. She was very tidy in her habits.'

Another signal the girl had left behind to alert the police if they caught on to her disappearance. A clever girl, this Martine. And she must have been scared stiff, knowing she and her son were being abducted. The counterpane draped to the floor. Tweed caught sight of a piece of white paper protruding from under the counterpane. He looked round, saw Joris' ample buttocks facing him as she burrowed in a lower drawer. He bent down, took hold of the paper and dragged out a coloured brochure.

Luxair. The Luxembourg airline. The folder had three pages joined together. It had been folded back to a page headed *Cargolux*, the cargo-carrying branch of the airline. At the bottom, in black ink and scarcely legible script one word had been written. *Rio*. Tweed slipped the folder into his pocket.

'What about that wardrobe?' he suggested.

'Can't find anything in the drawers.' Joris marched over to the wardrobe, opened the double doors and stared inside as Tweed joined her. She stood with her arms akimbo, checking the hanging clothes.

'Didn't take her best dress, the one she also wears Sundays.' Her beady eyes dropped to the floor. 'And her travelling case is missing. Never used it. Never went anywhere. But she hoped to one day, when they were rich. That case was her hope for the future.'

'Try the dressing-table,' Tweed suggested.

'If you say so. Mind you, I'm only doing this under police orders.' She looked up as Paula appeared in the doorway. 'Didn't know they were getting such good-looking Belgian policewomen these days. Brussels, I suppose?'

'That's right,' replied Paula.

She looked at Tweed as Joris bustled over to the dressing-table. Paula had a flair not only for languages; she had an acute ear for local pronunciation. With Tweed she now realized for the first time she could pass for a Belgian.

'More trouble.' Joris made her statement with a tinge of satisfaction. A touch of drama, even at a friend's expense, was livening up her dull life. 'She left her best undies,' Joris went on. 'What woman would go on holiday and do that. I've checked in there,' she said sharply as Paula separated the dresses inside the wardrobe, then went on checking the dressing-table drawers.

Paula beckoned behind her back to Tweed. He joined her and she pointed at the rear wall behind the dresses. 'She used lipstick,' she whispered. Scrawled hastily in thick red on the wall were two half-finished words. *Peug. Jaun.*

'He – or they – came for her in a yellow Peugeot,' Tweed whispered back. 'We simply must save this girl and her son.'

'If they're still alive,' Paula responded sombrely.

'What made you think of looking at the wall?'

'Because it's the place I'd have chosen if I was being kidnapped. She must have concealed the lipstick in her hand. While she was taking down a few dresses she scrawled that message.'

'Nothing else,' Joris called out to Tweed. 'Are you feeling all right?'

Tweed, glassy-eyed, had gone into a trance, thoughts flashing through his mind. He blinked, smiled at Joris. 'Lack of sleep, nothing more. Incidentally, shouldn't the boy, Lucien, be at school?'

'I asked that when she phoned. She said she'd phone to the school and tell them Lucien had the flu.'

It took them only a few minutes to check the rest of the upper floor and they descended the staircase. Joris burst out with her discoveries to Benoit with an air of triumph. He listened, lips pursed at her attitude. Tweed waited until she'd finished before he asked the question.

'Did you notice a car pass your house? You're further down the road, nearer the village from the direction you came. I'm referring to the day when Martine phoned you. Perhaps half an hour or so before the phone call?'

'I heard a car, yes. But I couldn't get to . . .' Joris broke off, her eyes shifting round the kitchen . . . . *the window before it had gone up the hill*. Tweed mentally completed her sentence. She was the local busybody.

'Did you hear a car return past your house later – say within another half hour?' he pressed.

'No! There is very little traffic all day.'

'Excuse me a moment.' Tweed took the arm of Benoit, who was chatting in undertones with Paula, and led him to the front room, nodding for Paula to follow. 'Benoit, we're looking for a yellow Peugeot . . .' He described what Paula

276

had found inside the wardrobe. 'And when the car took Martine and Lucien away it drove on uphill – away from the village. Otherwise Miss Nosey Parker would have seen it – she obviously keeps a close eye on what's going on. And she didn't even *hear* it coming back.'

'Makes sense.' Benoit peered out of the front window where a police car with three uniformed men had stopped. 'The locals have arrived. We can get them moving on the search.'

Paula had been standing with her right hand crooked, studying her fingernails. A mannerism Tweed had already become familiar with: an idea had struck her. Paula frowned as she recalled the *A Vendre* estate agent's board outside another cottage in the village. She caught Tweed's eye. He nodded again.

'Excuse me,' Paula said, 'but I've been thinking of the sort of place they might be holding Martine and her son. Not too far away, I'd guess – the risk of being spotted by a local in a car would be too great.'

'Makes sense,' Benoit agreed. 'Do go on.'

'I've often thought the ideal place to hold a kidnapped person would be in a house for sale. The kidnapper could find a suitable empty house, call on the agent, say he agreed the price, pay a deposit, but it would take a while to get it surveyed. It's then completely at the kidnapper's disposal.'

'Ingenious. Very.' Benoit looked at Paula with admiration, turned to Tweed 'If Miss Grey ever wants a job with us here in Belgium I'm sure I could oblige.'

'Thank you. There's something else,' Paula persisted. 'It has to be a suitable place, I said. By which I mean a property remote from the road – and preferably already equipped with facilities to turn a part of it into a prison. Maybe a room with a child's nursery – with bars already on the windows. Or perhaps something even more specialized – some property that's been on the market a while.'

'Better and better.' Benoit rubbed his hands. 'I'll just go and instruct those men coming down the path. Back soon.'

Tweed waited until they were alone. 'Quick, ask Newman to join me. And tell Butler to hold that Joris woman's attention in the kitchen. I'm sure she doesn't understand English. Speak rapidly . . .'

Sonnet had followed Lasalle into the front garden where they were talking to the new arrivals. Tweed held the Luxair brochure in his hand when Newman arrived with Paula. 'This is what I found almost under the bed upstairs. I think the abductor dropped it out of his pocket, Martine saw it, kicked it under the bed. One thing I'd bet money on – Klein sent one of his thugs to do the job.'

'What makes you think that?' asked Newman as he studied the brochure.

'Klein would never have let Martine get away with the signals she left us. The unwashed dishes in the sink, the rumpled bed, this brochure. He's sharp as a knife . . .' He grimaced at the simile. 'Well, we know how he uses knives.'

'This brochure points to Luxembourg City . . .'

'And Peter Brand has a branch of his Banque Sambre there. We haven't the time – but I think we'd better go there now. Benoit may let us use the Alouette . . . Talk of the devil.'

Benoit came into the room, spread his hands. 'Good news and bad. Sonnet has heard over his radio a forensic team arrived aboard the *Gargantua*. But it could be days before a report lands on my desk in Paris. The corpse of Broucker is glued in by heavy mud. At least they've made a start.'

'And the bad news?'

'Telephone strike here in Belgium – overtime ban offici- ally. Which makes phoning from lock to lock difficult – to locate the *Erika*. I've organized a team of police cyclists to ride the towpaths. It slows down the check.'

'Why not start at the far end?' Tweed suggested.

'Which is the far end? Where was the *Erika* bound for?'

'You have a point,' Tweed admitted. 'I have a favour to ask. Could we borrow the Alouette to fly us to Luxembourg City?'

'Ah! You're on to something. Only on condition I fly with you. There's close cooperation between the Luxembourg and Belgian police. I might even come in handy.'

'You're most welcome. Has the search started for that poor girl Martine and her son? You do see how it all begins to link up? Haber had carried out some commission for Klein – transporting the stolen bullion, I'm sure. Then he'd had enough – possibly when Klein asked him to transport those timers aboard the *Erika*. But Klein, the clever bastard, had foreseen Haber might kick up. So first he arranges for one of his minions to kidnap Haber's family. With that hanging over his head Haber *has* to do anything Klein demands – even including standing by when Klein murders his employee, Broucker. Someone else had become expendable – this time Broucker. The track record shows how Klein deals with anyone he no longer needs.'

'He must be a fiend incarnate,' Benoit mused.

'Oh, he's all of that. Can we get moving? One of those cars could take us back to Dinant – where the chopper is.'

Klein was livid with rage. In Brussels he had just visited the Banque Sambre headquarters in the Avenue Louise to see Peter Brand.

'Mr Brand is in Luxembourg City,' the attractive receptionist informed him. 'He flew there in his executive jet this morning. Can I take a message for . . .'

'When is he expected back?'

'He will be at his office in Luxembourg City all day. You could phone him . . .'

'But I can't because there is a phone strike,' Klein said harshly.

'I am really very sorry, sir. Who shall I say called?'

She was talking to the air. The visitor, wearing a smart grey business suit had walked off to the entrance with long strides. Klein had changed from the black outfit with the wide-brimmed hat he had often worn in France. There he had frequently been mistaken for a priest. Which had been his intention; like a postman, he merged with the landscape and was forgotten within minutes of being noticed.

He hailed a cab in the Avenue Louise, told the driver to take him to Brussels Midi, and forced himself to relax. In his mind he was recalling from his phenomenal memory the times of the trains to Luxembourg City. If the cab kept moving he'd just be in time to catch the express which went on to Basle.

Arriving at Midi, he hurried to the ticket counter, bought a first-class return, checked the departure board and ran up the steps. He sank into the seat of an empty compartment as the express began to move.

He never made advance appointments with anyone – they were dangerous because they forecast your movements. But Brand had told him he would be available at the Banque Sambre. It had never occurred to Klein he might mean the branch in Luxembourg City. And he was puzzled what Brand was doing in that part of the world – the last place he wanted attention drawn to.

31

The Alouette flew in brilliant sunshine on a south-easterly course bound for Luxembourg City. Tweed sat with Newman, a map spread across their laps, while Benoit chatted with Butler in front. Butler stared down through the window at the corrugated landscape of wooded ravines and ridges which were the Ardennes.

'According to your markings on that map we're flying in the wrong direction,' Newman observed.

'So it would seem,' Tweed agreed.

The unfolded map of Western Europe carried route markings in felt-tip ink, markings which ended in bold arrows pointing north, always north.

One route began at Marseilles and proceeded north direct to Paris. From where Klein had hired the explosives expert, Chabot – and where Chabot's girl friend, Cecile Lamont, the bar girl, had been dragged from the sea with her throat cut.

A second route started at Geneva, went on to Basle, continued to Dinant and up the Meuse to Namur. Tweed had added a dotted line from Namur, following a circuitous route to Antwerp. Newman pointed to this.

'What does that suggest?'

'It looks like *Antwerp*. You want facts? Lara Seagrave ended her photographic expeditions in Antwerp – before returning to Brussels – only a short train ride from the port. I am also convinced that missing barge is carrying the timers to the target. Follow the Meuse, see how you can branch off it north of Liège along the Albert Canal – direct to where? Antwerp.'

'So why are we flying south – away from the possible target area?'

'Because of that brochure I found in Martine's cottage. It was folded to the Cargolux page – as I showed you. There is a huge fortune in gold bullion being held at the Deutsche Bank in Frankfurt – only a short flight from Findel.'

'Findel?'

'The airport we are heading for – only six kilometres from Luxembourg City. And the word *Rio* was written on that brochure. Rio de Janeiro. In Brazil. A country with no extradition treaty. I asked Lasalle before he left to return to Paris to check with Interpol on Brazil. A long shot.'

'What was? Stop being so cryptic.'

'I remembered the infamous Ronald Biggs, the Great Train Robbery villain. We couldn't extradite him even with the most solid evidence. Why? Because he had made a Brazilian girl pregnant. Interpol will try to check whether a man with a German-sounding name – Klein, whatever – has fathered a child by a Brazilian mother. Then, whatever crime he commits he will be safe.'

'And you think he'll try and fly to Rio from Findel?'

'I think he might fly the gold bullion obtained by a terrible terror threat to Brazil via Findel.'

'As you said, a long shot.'

'The one thing that keeps nagging at me is the explosives. I simply can't see that they were transported by barge. Far too big a consignment, far too dangerous.'

'And every time you mention them,' Newman commented, 'I feel I know something I haven't told you and can't recall. Why is Harry Butler coming with us?'

'To watch the Banque Sambre in Luxembourg City. You give him a description of Peter Brand when we reach Findel, he hires a car and drives to take up watch on Brand's bank in the Avenue de la Liberté.'

Lara Seagrave was becoming bored by the luxury of the Mayfair Hotel in Brussels. She had explored the shops, visited the famous Grand'Place where medieval buildings of different periods walled each side of the square. She'd also noticed a uniformed policeman leaning out of a window and had located to police headquarters.

She sat in front of the dressing-table mirror, brushing her long hair. She picked up the envelope which had been waiting when she arrived. The outside simply carried her typed name. On a blank sheet of paper inside was typed a message.

It won't be long now. Have patience. No long absences from the Mayfair. K.

Klein had foreseen there was a limit to the time she could be kept dangling – that she would grow restless. Hence the letter.

Lara was thinking about something else. She was not convinced by Klein's apparent rejection of Antwerp. The fact he had given her no fresh port to explore she felt was highly significant. Giving her appearance a final check, she left the hotel.

*

Hipper noted the deserted country lane ahead, looked in his rear view mirror to make sure nothing was in sight behind, then swung off along the tarred track. The old windmill – which had long ago lost its sails when converted into a private house – reared up behind the trees like a mis-shapen Martello tower.

He parked the car inside the trees, collected the package of tinned foods, bread and thermos of coffee from the back seat, and walked to the solid wooden door at the base of the tower. In his right hand he carried a bunch of keys on a ring. Selecting a large old-fashioned key, he unlocked the door, went inside, relocked it.

A musty smell of a building unoccupied for a long time met him as he climbed the circular staircase to the next floor. On the landing he again selected another key as he stood in front of a heavy wooden door.

He took a minute or so arranging himself. The package of food was tucked under his left arm, his left hand held the key while the right gripped the Walther automatic, safety catch off. He unlocked the door and pushed it wide open.

Martine Haber sat on a chair in front of a crude wooden table, one hand behind her back. No sign of the boy, Lucien. The Luxembourger pursed his lips. His soft voice was slow and menacing as he aimed the gun.

'Tell the kid to come out from behind the door. Tell him to stand behind that table or I will shoot you within the next ten seconds.'

Crestfallen, a sullen look of frustration on his face, the lad emerged from behind the door, dropped the leg of the chair he had wrenched from it, and walked to the other side of the table.

'Don't try that again,' Hipper warned. 'And you, woman, put your other hand on your lap.'

With a sigh Martine brought her hand into sight, dropping the container of pepper. She would have risked it when Hipper came closer, but she couldn't risk Lucien's life.

The Luxembourger came closer, the gun now aimed at Lucien. Martine sat very still as Hipper dropped the package on the table. Still pointing the gun at Lucien, he examined the strong padlock which locked the closed shutters over the window.

'The Elsan bucket needs emptying,' Martine protested.

'Next time . . .'

'How much longer . . .' she began, then stopped.

Hipper had backed to the door, slammed it shut, relocked it. At the foot of the staircase he checked the telephone cord he had detached from the wall socket. There was an extension phone in Martine's room.

Klein had foreseen at some stage Haber would insist on proof that his family was alive, that they were well. He had called La Montagne, arranged with Hipper to be at the mill at a certain time, then permitted Haber to have a brief conversation with his wife from a public call box.

It was Hipper who had kidnapped Martine and Lucien. He drove back at speed to Larochette. Chabot, the explosives expert from Marseilles, was becoming a pain in the arse. Too restless for Hipper's liking. At least he had accomplished the kidnap well, leaving behind nothing to give the police a clue.

Arriving back at La Montagne, Hipper entered the derelict hotel beneath the cliff face and was immediately grabbed from behind. A vicious knife touched his throat. He froze as he heard Chabot's voice. An almost empty bottle of red wine stood on the sideboard. Chabot's voice was slurred. Oh, God! Chabot was drunk.

'No more screwing around,' Chabot snarled. 'I want to know the target. Now! Or I'll slit your gizzard . . . '

Hipper's mind blurred. 'Antwerp,' he gasped. 'Have you gone mad?'

'No, just lost patience with hanging around.'

Chabot released the Luxembourger and his voice was normal. No trace of being the worse for drink. The bastard had tricked him. Hipper stared in fury at the Frenchman who tossed the knife with a twirling gesture. It landed beside the bottle, the point stuck in the wood, the blade quivering.

'And I'm going out for a walk. This bleedin' place is like being in prison. Worse – with only you as company . . .'

'It's not quite dark,' Hipper protested.

'It's not quite dark,' Chabot mimicked and rubbed his swarthy chin. 'I'm still going for a walk. See you, little one.'

Hipper waited until he had gone, realizing it was an excellent opportunity to make the urgent call Klein had told him to deal with late in the day. He took a grubby notebook from his pocket, checked the number of the Hotel Panorama in Bouillon, made the call. He asked for M. Lambert, the name Marler was using.

'And who is calling?' Marler's terse voice enquired after a moment.

'Your friend. You can recognize my voice . . .'

'Yes. Get on with it.'

'Leave tomorrow for the meeting in Brussels. We hope to complete the business deal. Three o'clock in the afternoon would do nicely.'

'Goodbye.'

Marler slammed down the phone and stood in his bedroom, musing on the message. Tomorrow he'd take up residence in the executive suite at the Hilton Klein had told him about. He took out a map, spread it on the bed and studied it for a few minutes, whistling to himself. Then he folded up the map, shoved it in his pocket and left the hotel.

'No news. No developments.'

Back at Park Crescent in Tweed's office Monica gave the same reply to Howard's question she'd given nine times previously. The SIS chief strolled round the room, brushed a hand over the sleeve of his spotless suit, removing an imaginary speck of dust.

Go away! Monica almost screamed to herself inwardly. He stood by the window, gazing towards Regent's Park. Like a lost soul, Monica thought. Lost because he hasn't Tweed to badger.

'The PM also enquired,' Howard remarked. 'Phoned herself.'

'Ten times?'

'Well, actually no. Once.'

'And how did she react?'

'Said that was all right, that Tweed would report back in his own good time,' Howard admitted reluctantly. 'Better get back to my own office. The "in" tray is practically piled up to the ceiling. Keep busy, Monica . . .'

Condescending so-and-so, she thought. The phone rang within thirty seconds of Howard leaving her in peace. She grabbed for it, expecting Tweed on the line. A muffled voice asked for Tweed.

'He's not here. This is Monica. Can I help?'

'Olympus here. The target is Antwerp. I think.'

'Could you repeat that? The line is bad.' Sounded as if the caller were speaking through a silk handkerchief. 'I did catch the Olympus bit . . .'

'The target is Antwerp. I think.'

'Thank you. I got it that time . . .'

The line went dead before she finished speaking. Monica replaced the receiver slowly. Tweed had told her any message from Olympus was top priority, and for his ears only. Now she had to work out how to try and track down Tweed.

Had it been a man or a woman she was talking to? She had no idea – no inkling of sex or age or nationality. Only that the caller had spoken in English. She decided to try Chief Inspector Benoit in Brussels first.

32

'That's the Avenue de la Liberté where you'll find the Banque Sambre,' Tweed told Butler. 'Leads up from the Place de la Gare. And there is the station. A train is just coming in from the Brussels direction.'

'It's a weird city. Spectacular,' Newman commented, peering over Tweed's shoulder.

The Alouette was flying at a height of several hundred feet, the whole city lay spread out below, the pilot was in touch with Findel control tower as he continued his descent, and the sun shone brilliantly.

Seen from the air, the site of Luxembourg City looks as though in ages past some pagan god wielded an immense axe and clove the ground, leaving behind a vast and deep gulch like a small Grand Canyon. In places the gulch approaches a quarter-mile in width, over a hundred feet in depth.

Possibly the greatest fortress city in Europe, the precipitous walls of the gorge provided a natural defence against armies which roved this part of the continent – a defence enormously reinforced by Louis the Fourteenth's brilliant architect of forts, Vauban.

The Alouette turned east, following the broad highway which leads through open country to the airport. It landed close to the modern building which houses all the facilities associated with airports, a building whose walls seemed to be constructed of glass.

'I want Cargolux,' Tweed told the pilot as they stood on the tarmac. 'If you want refreshment, we won't need you for a little while.'

Harry Butler had already left them, striding towards the

airport building to hire a car. As he walked he folded a copy of an Identikit picture Tweed had given him, a facsimile of the photocopy of Igor Zarov given to Tweed in Switzerland. Tweed had simply told him this was probably a portrait of Klein.

'I need a car urgently,' he told the girl behind the desk. 'The make doesn't matter.'

'Would a Citroën suit you?' she asked in English. 'One of our clients has just left a car before boarding a flight.'

'I'll take it.' He began filling in the form as he spoke. 'How long for me to reach the Avenue de la Liberté?'

'At this time of day, no more than twenty minutes. I have a local map. I will mark out the route . . .'

Klein had leaned up to look out of the window of the compartment he occupied by himself. The express from Brussels was approaching Luxembourg City. It was the sight of the helicopter which caught his attention, flying several hundred feet up and almost parallel with the train.

He took out his monocular glass – the twin of the one he had given to Lara – and focused it on the machine, steadying the glass by perching his elbow on the window ledge. A police job. The word was clearly visible on the fuselage. With Belgian markings.

It appeared to be keeping pace with the express. Probably on traffic patrol. Klein pocketed the glass. No, that couldn't be the reason for its presence. Not in Luxembourg. Not with Belgian markings.

The express slowed, the platform of the station was gliding past, the train stopped. Klein took the light case he always carried off the seat beside him, stood up and prepared to alight. He was going straight to the Banque Sambre to find out what the devil Brand was up to. It was only a short walk from the station exit. Two minutes later he emerged from the booking hall into a blaze of sunshine.

*

288

Before boarding the Alouette at Dinant, Paula had asked Tweed for a private word. They strolled along the waterfront while the others went to where the machine was waiting on a section of open land on the opposite bank.

'I'm worried about Martine and Lucien,' she said. 'Could I stay here and see if I can locate them? If I can we'll have broken the hold Klein has over Haber.'

'Good idea in theory,' Tweed agreed. 'How are you going to set about it in practice?'

'Visit all the local estate agents. Have a look at all the properties on their books – especially any bought recently but where the deal hasn't been completed. Some place not too far away from here, but with a remote situation and which has been on the market a good while.' She frowned. 'I'm not putting this very well, but I've a feeling I'll spot the sort of property Klein would choose when I see it.'

'You could give it a try. After I've made certain enquiries at Findel Airport we'll be flying back here. It's a bit vague though – your specification.'

'Oh, it has to have a telephone which is still in use.'

'I don't follow you.'

'What is the usual sequence of events when a kidnapping takes place? The victim still free – in this case Haber – demands proof from the kidnapper that his family is safe and well. The kidnapper gets over that one by letting him have a brief conversation with whoever has been kidnapped. That means telephone communication must be available. See what I'm driving at?'

'I should have thought of that myself.'

'You have got rather a lot on your mind,' she pointed out.

'Come with me. Before we board the Alouette I'll ask Benoit to liaise with the local police. You'll need one of them with you to have the authority to question estate agents . . .'

And so Tweed had left Paula in Dinant. While the helicopter was flying them to Findel Airport Paula, accompanied by a uniformed policeman, made a tour of the

289

estate agents. She discovered several properties which were promising and was driven to each of them in turn.

It was dusk when they walked away from a property way out in the Ardennes, a large empty house which had once been a clinic for mental patients – and thus had bars on the windows. Paula was disappointed.

'I had high hopes of that place,' she said to Pierre, the handsome young policeman who was enjoying himself hugely in her company.

'Never mind, Miss, we can try again tomorrow. You still have several left for us to explore. I think we should get back to Dinant before dark.'

'I'm tired out,' she admitted. She studied one brochure before getting into the car. 'I'm wondering about this old mill. It looks pretty remote, was on the market for months before being bought by a Mr Hipper. And the phone is still working. How far away is it?'

Pierre checked the address. 'About fifteen miles from Celle. On a lonely country road which doesn't really lead anywhere. We could try that first tomorrow.'

'Let's do that. Now, back to Dinant.'

At the Cargolux counter at Findel the assistant manager was reluctant to provide any information. Benoit took over the conversation from Tweed, showing his warrant card.

'This is an emergency. Get me the chief of police in Luxembourg City on the phone, a man called Fernand Gansen. Then let me speak to him.'

Tweed glanced round the empty reception hall, its floor gleaming like glass. It was very quiet. He liked small airports. Beyond a window he could see a Luxair machine, its tail painted blue with a large white 'L' symbol. The grassy plain spread out into the distance; no sense of being within miles of a city.

Benoit, after conversing with his colleague, whom he obviously knew well, handed the phone to the airport official. 'Talk to him,' he snapped without a hint of his normal joviality. The conversation was brief, the official replaced the receiver.

'I'm authorized to answer any questions,' he said without enthusiasm.

'I want to know if a large cargo-carrying plane is due here – probably from Frankfurt – within the next few days. And its destination may be Rio do Janeiro,' Tweed suggested.

'Let me check.'

The official examined a large folder filled with large forms already filled in. 'Nothing for Rio,' he said. Tweed sensed he was being cagey and Benoit had the same reaction.

'Look here.' He leaned across the counter. 'Gansen gave you instructions. Don't play with me. Answer my colleague. Any large transport machines?'

'Several . . .'

'One from Frankfurt?'

'Actually, yes. A Hercules. During the next three days. A detailed flight plan is awaited . . .'

Extracting the information was like trying to get a loan from a miser. Tweed sensed Benoit was going to explode. He nudged him and stared at the official, his tone pleasant.

'Yes, a Hercules is a big job. Do you handle many shipments of that magnitude?'

'No.'

'But they'd have to give you some rough idea of destination. What is it?'

'South America. Details to follow . . .'

'Name of the consignee?'

Tweed's eyes held the official's. There was a pause. Tweed waited, standing motionless. 'It is police business,' he reminded him.

'The Zurcher Kredit Bank of Basle.'

Keeping an eye open for traffic patrol cars, Butler pressed his foot down, exceeding the speed limit along the deserted highway. Soon he was inside the city, crossing a bridge which spanned the gorge, turning left up a hill. Fortress walls began to appear.

He drove just inside the speed limit through the old city and green lights were with him all the way. He recrossed the canyon over the Pont Adolphe, at a much greater height than the previous bridge. The gorge was far wider, a great depth and the walls had become immense.

He was now driving slowly down the Avenue da le Liberté, the home of so many Luxembourg banks. He saw the Banque Sambre on his side of the broad avenue, cruised past and stopped by a parking meter. Using coins he obtained when he changed money at Findel Airport, he dealt with the meter, then settled down behind the wheel, leaving the engine running.

He adjusted the rear view mirror to give him a perfect view of the entrance to the bank. Checking the Identikit photocopy of Klein, he folded it and put it in his pocket. Brand he would recognize from Newman's description, newspaper reporters were good at that sort of observation.

Butler was now in position to watch anyone who entered – or left – the Banque Sambre. Further down the street was the Place de la Gare where several streets met in front of the old station. He pretended to read the newspaper he'd bought at Findel, giving a convincing impression of waiting to pick up someone.

Klein stood outside the station in the Place de la Gare, in a rare state of indecision. To avoid the sun glare he stood with his back to the taxi rank. He had just come out of a café on the far side of the street where he'd consumed a sandwich *au jambon* and drunk some excellent coffee.

His mood was edgy. He sensed danger and was trying to identify what had alerted him. That Belgian police helicopter? No – he had experienced this phase just before he was mounting an operation.

He couldn't imagine that he'd left behind him anywhere

a clue. Not in that weird watchmaking town up in the Jura; not in Geneva; not in Marseilles or Paris. And not on the Meuse.

It was the imminent launch of the vast operation, he decided. He always became even more cautious at this stage. He had planned to walk straight up the Avenue de la Liberté, to catch Brand off guard at the Banque Sambre. Change of plan.

He went inside a telephone booth and called the bank, dialling the number from memory. Data written in notebooks was dangerous. The operator took a minute or two to put him through to Brand. The banker *had* been caught off balance. Klein would continue to keep him in that frame of mind. There was surprise in Brand's voice when he came on the line.

'Klein? Where are you?'

'Luxembourg City.'

'You might have warned me . . .'

'No reason to. I hope? Meet me half an hour from now. At the Hotel Cravat. Ask for my friend, Max Volpe. Arrange for one of your secretaries – someone you can trust – to come to the same place a quarter of an hour after you've left. She also is to ask for Max Volpe. My friend's room. See you . . .'

'Wait a minute!' A hint of annoyance in Brand's upper crust voice. 'I have a full engagement book. I can probably squeeze you in . . .'

'Check your watch. Thirty minutes from now.'

Klein replaced the receiver. Discipline. Instant obedience. The only way to keep the upper hand. And Brand was about to make another fortune. Or so he thought . . .

He walked out of the booth, climbed inside a cab.

'Hotel Cravat, if you please.'

Klein asked for a double room, registered in the name Max Volpe – another advantage of operating inside the Common Market. The Swiss were meticulous (pedantic was the word Klein used) about hotel registration and often asked to see your passport.

He was given a room on the first floor overlooking the Place de la Constitution and a panoramic view of the curving chasm beyond. Locking the door, he dumped his case on the bed, took out his make-up box and went to the bathroom.

Standing in front of the mirror over the wash-basin he applied foundation cream and then the light-coloured face powder. The face which stared back at him was now chalk-white. Returning to the bedroom, he took a black beret from his case, pulled it well down so it concealed all trace of his black hair.

He next took a pair of horn-rimmed spectacles from the case and perched them on the bridge of his nose. The final item which completed the transformation was a curved pipe, the bowl already filled with tobacco which he'd tamped into the pipe aboard the express.

Stripping off his jacket and trousers, he substituted an old and worn sports jacket and a pair of grey slacks. He repacked the suit and closed and locked the case. Taking a label from his wallet, he penned in capitals the name Max Volpe and attached the label to the case. The make-up box he slipped inside his raincoat pocket.

He stood for a moment, checking over in his mind the sequence of events he had planned. Yes, everything was ready. He walked back into the bathroom and double-checked his appearance. The smartly-dressed businessman who had walked into the Cravat was now replaced by a professorial type.

And there would be no trouble at reception when he left. While registering he had insisted on paying two days in advance for the room, explaining he might have to leave urgently to attend a conference.

He was standing by the circular corner window, looking down into the rue Chimay, when the phone rang. Reception calling. A Mr Brand had arrived, asking for Mr Volpe.

*

In the rear view mirror Butler saw Newman's word picture of Peter Brand emerge from the Banque Sambre and climb into the red Lamborghini. He dropped his newspaper and waited, knowing Brand had to drive past him. Avenue de la Liberté was a one-way street – except for the buses.

Brand wore a small-check suit and a deerstalker hat. Flashy type. Plus the car. One of the boys. Played hell with the women. Butler had him summed up in seconds. He pulled out and followed the Lamborghini.

Brand turned left at the bottom of the Avenue and before he reached the Place de la Gare. Butler had a rough mental plan of Luxembourg City in his mind – after a few minutes' study of the street chart the car girl at Findel had provided. It looked as though Brand was heading back – along the one-way system – by the same route Butler had entered the city. Was it Findel?

Brand streaked across the Viaduct spanning the gorge, past the British Ambassador's residence perched on a projecting plateau above the gorge, past the Cathedral, was then stopped by lights. Which enabled Butler to drive up closer one car behind the banker.

Brand then turned off into the rue Chimay, braked savagely, waited for a girl to leave her slot. Butler drove slowly past, spotted another empty slot, parked his car and was in time to follow Brand walking back down the street.

The banker walked past the ground floor restaurant of the Hotel Cravat, disappearing inside the main entrance. Butler arrived as he left the reception counter and entered a waiting elevator.

The lobby was medium-sized, had a sitting area from where the two elevators and the staircase could be observed. Butler settled into an armchair, took out his newspaper and saw by the lights over the elevator that Brand had alighted on the first floor. A rendezvous?

He checked the layout of the place as he slowly turned the pages of the paper. Almost opposite the staircase was the entrance to the downstairs restaurant from the hotel. On his way down rue Chimay Butler had noted there was a separate entrance to that restaurant direct from the street. Obviously a place used by the locals as well as guests. He crossed his legs and prepared to wait. Butler, a patient man, was good at waiting.

'Something damned peculiar going on,' commented Newman.

'What is that?' asked Benoit.

Tweed had led the way to the canteen at Findel Airport and the three men were sitting at a table by themselves, the only customers in the whole place.

'The Zurcher Kredit Bank – the consignee for that huge transport aircraft – is one of the two Swiss banks a load of bullion was stolen from a few months ago,' Tweed explained.

'Of course! I should have remembered. I don't understand.'

'Neither do I,' Newman agreed, 'but we are on to something. No doubt about that. Just what, I'm not sure.'

'We may be on to the smooth Colonel Romer, the director of the Zurcher Kredit I saw in Basle. I never could understand that bank raid business.'

'Understand what?' Benoit enquired.

'How any gang could take out ten million in bullion from two banks in the centre of Basle and move the loot. Eventually I suspected one of Haber's barges might have been used to spirit it away. That would mean only a short journey for the trucks used to transport the bullion – down to the Rhine. But still it seemed tricky – unless it was achieved with the help of an insider. And now I think we'd better move fast – with the aid of your Alouette once more, Benoit. Back to Brussels. From there I can call Arthur Beck, chief of the Swiss Federal Police, and warn him about Colonel Romer. I think Klein's operation is just about to start.'

'And the target?' queried Newman.

'Wish to God I knew.'

'What about Harry Butler?'

'I arranged with him while we were flying here that he caught a train back to Brussels – or drove there. Depends whether he finds anything at the Banque Sambre. I wonder how Harry is getting on? Still, he's quite capable of running his own show.' He drank the last of his coffee, stood up.

'Can we get moving?'

'The Alouette is at your disposal,' responded Benoit.

'Beautiful weather this, sir,' the concierge remarked to Butler as he stood by the door. He was a friendly soul who obviously liked a chat, a short man with an ample stomach.

'It is, indeed,' replied Butler.

A girl in her early thirties with raven black hair came in from the street, rushed up to the empty counter and stared round. The concierge walked over and asked if he could help.

'I've come to see Mr Max Volpe. He's expecting me.'

'Let me just call his room first . . .'

Butler studied the girl while the concierge used the phone. She wore long black pants, a white shirt under her black jacket and a man's bow tie. Her whole style of dress was mannish, which Butler disliked. The concierge said something to her after replacing the receiver and she hurried inside an empty elevator. Butler noticed she got off at the first floor as the concierge came back.

'Funny way for a girl to dress,' Butler went on in English.

'I don't fancy the type much myself, sir – between you and me. She's from the Banque Sambre. I've seen her there when I've been in to make payments. I gather she's personal assistant to Mr Brand.'

'Really?' said Butler as though the remark meant nothing.

'What is it?' Brand asked testily as Klein locked the bedroom door. This time he was going to assert himself. 'I do know what I'm doing.'

'Just what are you doing here?'

Klein had removed the spectacles before opening the door and the pipe was inside his pocket. His voice was cold, his tone clipped when he asked the question in English. He stared at the banker.

The eyes again worried Brand. He felt his assertive manner slipping. Klein had addressed him like the chairman of the board questioning a director's ability.

'I came here specially to check the arrangements for movement of the bullion from Frankfurt. The Deutsche Bank is getting restless. They want to know details of the collateral to safeguard the bullion.'

'I thought you were going to form a consortium of bankers to guarantee that. And to contribute a small fraction yourself?'

'It's proved more difficult than I expected . . .'

'Because you can't produce your own contribution. You gamble it all away at Monte. And you're paying interest on loans out of capital – just like that swindler, the Swede Kreuger, did in the 1930s.'

'How did you know that?' Brand's face was ashen.

'I check out the people I deal with – *before* I deal with them. No more chatter. What is the position now?'

'The Deutsche Bank is holding the bullion for ten more days. How close is the operation?'

'Transport arrangements?' Klein demanded curtly, ignoring the question.

'The Hercules machine is reserved for our use. What about the air crew?'

'They will be taken over when the aircraft is in mid-air on its way to Findel – by my own air crew.'

Klein thought it unwise to tell Brand the original crew would be shot out of hand, the bodies dumped in the Atlantic. A bit too strong for the Englishman's nerves.

'I'll want to see you again quickly in Brussels,' he went on. 'How long are you hanging about here?'

'I fly back to Brussels aboard my executive jet later this afternoon . . .'

'See you stay at the Avenue Louise until I contact you. Better push off now – you have that heavy engagement book to deal with.'

'No one else knows about those loans?' Brand asked as he moved towards the door.

'Of course not. And no one knows you're using capital to send money to your wife in New York. The Belgian woman who thinks it's interest, that you're a whizz kid banker. The woman who is hopping in and out of bed with all and sundry. As you well know.'

He locked the door when Brand had left. No point in telling him Klein had used him to obtain the bullion – after using him to sell the earlier consignments from the Swiss robberies – because he knew Brand was in a financial mess.

Terror and money were the two factors which influenced men. It was a favourite maxim of Klein's. Carrot and stick, as the English put it. There was a knock on the door. He opened it and a girl wearing a peculiar black outfit stood outside.

'I met Mr Brand on his way out. He said I should come to see you.'

'Come inside.' He locked the door again, saw her expression, shook his head. 'Your virginity is safe. Now, listen. Take this case down to the restaurant at street level. Give it to the head waitress. Tell her to keep it until I come down for a meal. Then go back to the bank. Clear?'

'Yes. I mention your name?'

'Why not? It's on the label.'

Alone once more, Klein put on his glasses, clenched the pipe stem between his teeth, took the black beret from a drawer and rammed it on his head. He checked his watch.

Timing perfect. He'd worked it all out standing in the Place de la Gare. He would arrive at Findel, buy his ticket and board the flight for Brussels.

Something funny was going on. Seated in the lobby Butler finished off the glass of beer the concierge had brought him from the restaurant and checked over the sequence of events he had witnessed.

The bow-tie girl from the Banque Sambre had gone up to the first floor. Shortly afterwards Brand had emerged from the elevator. He looked furious as he marched out. Butler had to take a quick decision.

He stood up, strolled after the banker and stood in the sunshine. Brand was walking back to where he'd parked the Lamborghini, his pace brisk. Should I follow him? Butler thought. That had been Tweed's general instruction.

But Tweed allowed his staff a lot of latitude, expected them to act independently. Bow-Tie worried Butler. Brand had clearly visited a guest at the hotel. A Bow-Tie didn't strike Butler as the sort of girl Brand would loan to a friend for a quick roll on the bed. He went back inside, sat down. Who was this guest on the first floor?

A minute later the elevator door opened, Bow-Tie stepped out, carrying a small suitcase with a label attached. Butler watched her walk straight into the restaurant. More and more peculiar. She came back quickly and walked out of the main entrance. He followed casually, standing again as though enjoying the sunshine.

He saw her hail a passing cab. He heard her sharp voice tell the driver, 'Banque Sambre'. He walked back inside, picked up his empty glass and took it into the restaurant. A middle-aged waitress thanked him as he placed it on the counter. Beside the glass was the small suitcase. The label read *Max Volpe*. Butler went back to the lobby, sat down and hid himself behind the newspaper.

Yes, something funny was going on. Why would a girl come all the way from the Avenue de la Liberté to collect a suitcase and take it into the restaurant? Then shove off straight back to the bank?

He heard footsteps coming slowly down the staircase alongside the two elevators. A stooped man wearing a beret, an unlit pipe in his mouth, appeared, walked straight into the restaurant.

Butler frowned. A chalk-white face. Which didn't fit the

description Tweed had given him of Klein verbally. Face ruddy. He called back in his memory the photocopy Identikit picture. Butler had not merely studied it – he had imagined it with a moustache, a beard, any form of disguise. The stooped man had looked familiar.

He stood up, said goodbye to the concierge who had reappeared, walked back inside the restaurant. The first thing he noticed was the case had disappeared from the counter. He glanced round the almost empty room. The stooped man sat at a table at the far end, the suitcase tucked under the table.

Butler sat down, ordered coffee, paid the bill when it arrived. He read his newspaper while the other man drank his own coffee, checked his watch, paid the bill and walked into the street carrying the case. Butler followed.

Volpe walked up the side street towards the Place d'Armes. Butler reached his car, slipped behind the wheel and cruised up the rue Chimay some distance behind Volpe. The man he was following hailed a taxi, got inside and the taxi headed north. Butler followed and within five minutes he guessed Volpe's destination. Findel Airport.

The Luxair machine took off into the cloudless sky. Volpe sat near the pilot's cabin. Butler was eight rows behind him. At Findel he had bought a ticket, standing immediately behind Volpe. The other passenger had not given him a glance.

Butler still took precautions to change his appearance. Running back to his parked car, he took his small case out of the boot, changed his check sports jacket for a suede version. He took a trilby hat, punched it, put it on his head. After handing back the car he boarded the aircraft. Destination: Brussels.

33

Tweed changed his mind when the Alouette was airborne. He had gone over in his mind everything Newman had reported. Turning round in his seat, he spoke to Benoit who sat behind them, using his headset. The rotor vibration was like a concrete mixer.

'I told you about that Colonel Ralston Bob encountered on the Meuse – travelling aboard his power cruiser, *Evening Star*.'

'Yes. A curious character.'

'On our way back to Brussels could we try and locate that craft? If we can find her I'd like a talk with the colonel.'

'Let us hope it is in Belgian waters – then I can use my authority to back you up if necessary . . .'

Benoit proceeded to instruct the pilot to change course. Newman began to look out of the window after changing places with Tweed. He was confident he'd spot the cruiser if they flew over her. A short while later the river appeared below. Newman tightened his mouth as they flew well above Les Dames de Meuse. He was recalling the unpleasant sight of Broucker's corpse, throat cut, buried to his chest in mud.

'They had a crane aboard a huge floating platform which has hauled up the *Gargantua*,' he told Tweed later. 'Men swarming over it, cars parked nose to tail along the towpath.'

'The forensic team, I expect,' Tweed answered absentmindedly. He was thinking about how he'd tackle Colonel Ralston – if they found him. 'It will take days to check the barge. Too many to help us, I suspect.'

'You think Klein is close to launching his operation?'

'That communications vehicle stolen from the CRS bothers me. He wouldn't hang on to that too long. And from what Lasalle told me about its range of radio signal equipment the operation must be vast.' He tightened his mouth. 'Where the devil could he be hiding that huge armoury of explosives he stole? If we could solve that one we might nip him in the bud. Fat chance of that.'

'Maybe we already know – but don't know what we know.'

Newman was pressing his face close to the window all the time he carried on his conversation. Tweed frowned at his remark. Something rang a bell at the back of his mind but he couldn't latch on to it.

'A cryptic comment if ever I heard one.'

'I wonder how Paula is getting on,' Newman mused, staring down. 'That was a pretty bright theory of hers.'

'Just a theory . . . What is it?'

'I'd like the pilot to lose more altitude. Now!'

They were just passing over Dinant. From that height the pinnacle of rock topped by the citadel looked like a toy. Over the inter-communication system the pilot heard Newman and began to descend lower before Newman spoke again. He'd already lost a lot of height once he'd cleared the heights of Les Dames de Meuse.

'There's the *Evening Star*. Just entering a lock north of Dinant. I'm sure that's it. Wait till we get a bit lower . . .'

'Moving upstream or down?' Tweed asked.

'Downstream – towards Namur. Odd, that. When I disembarked at Namur he said he was going on to Liège. It's almost as though he's patrolling the Meuse – up and down.'

'Where's the nearest point you can land?' Benoit's voice asked the pilot.

'Football field. I can see it now. No one playing on it.'

'Land there, then.'

'A radio message for you, sir. They want you to call headquarters.'

'To hell with Grand'Place   They can either cope – or wait.'

Marler drove up the Boulevard de Waterloo and was glad to be back in Brussels. He passed the Hilton on the far side of the highway, paused for the lights to change at the top, then swung round and drove back in the direction he'd come but down the narrow street leading to the hotel.

The city was a fascinating mix of ancient and modern buildings. Opposite the Hilton an old church stood next to a small bistro-style restaurant. Beyond were high-rise office blocks. About to turn in to the Hilton's underground garage, he changed his mind. Bad security. Having your transport trapped where you were staying.

Ten minutes later, his Volvo parked in an above-ground park, he walked into the huge reception hall-cum-lounge area. He marched straight up to the desk, carrying a sports bag in one hand, a suitcase in the other.

'Dupont,' he addressed the dark-haired girl receptionist in French. 'Room 1914 . . .'

'Oh that's an executive suite, sir. You register on the eighteenth floor.'

'Of course I do.' Marler was very bluff in manner. 'Stupid of me to forget.'

A porter relieved him of the suitcase but Marler hung on to the sports bag. On the eighteenth floor he stepped out into a pleasant room with a blonde girl facing him behind a large desk. Good looker.

'Dupont,' he repeated when she had offered him a seat. '1914. The suite's been reserved for a while.'

She looked puzzled as she pushed the registration pad towards him. 'A man with the same name occupied your suite for a few hours, sir. I hope that was all right?'

Marler gave a broad grin as he filled in the form. 'Quite all right. My brother. Nice view from up here.' He nodded towards the window where the lights of Brussels were coming on as dusk descended, like stars sparkling close to ground level. He tipped his passport towards himself as he filled in a French passport number.

'Your key, sir. I hope you will really enjoy your stay with us.'

'Can hardly fail to in Brussels.'

He gave her another dazzling smile as he stood up. She was eyeing him speculatively. He winked, turned back to the elevators and pressed the button.

Rid of the porter, he explored the suite. Luxurious. Plenty of space. The vast bulk of the Palais de Justice loomed beyond the window, which appealed to his sense of humour. He made a systematic search of the room, found a large drawer which locked, opened it, laid the sports bag inside.

It contained the dismantled sections of his rifle and the telescopic sight, plus ammunition. He placed the sports bag carefully at a certain angle, took a pen from his pocket and made a mark on the base of the drawer at one corner of the bag. He'd know if someone had been fiddling with the padlocked bag. He closed the drawer, attached the key to his ring.

On a table was a basket of fresh fruit, a printed card – *with the compliments of the manager*. Alongside was a sealed envelope with M. Dupont typed on the outside. He opened it. Brief message.

Dinner at the Sky Room. 9 p.m. K. He put the sheet of paper in his wallet, picked up the brochure of the hotel, a de-luxe production. Three restaurants. *The Sky Room. 27th floor. Music and dancing until dawn. The Maison de Bœuf. 1st floor* and the *Café d'Egmont. Entrance hall floor.* The last was the coffee shop.

He glanced again through the Illustrated brochure. The *Maison de Bœuf* attracted him. Stuff Klein and the Sky Room. He'd have to come looking.

He unpacked his suitcase, went into the bathroom for a wash. Marler was wearing a natty blue pinstripe suit, blue striped shirt, plain blue tie. An outfit he hadn't worn out in the country in Bouillon, waiting for Godot. Satisfied with his appearance, he left the luxurious suite. There were beautiful women in Brussels.

Several of them in the lobby glanced his way as he walked out of the hotel and up the street.

Lara Seagrave walked back off the Avenue Louise into the Mayfair Hotel and took the elevator to her room. She had the key in her shoulder bag. It gave you that extra bit of mobility in an emergency.

Inside her room she lit a cigarette, paced restlessly. She was going spare. No word from Klein. If the bastard thought she was going to hang around waiting on his whim all evening he had another think coming. She was going out on the town, maybe meet some interesting man. Just for the evening and dinner. Nothing heavy.

Lara had learned to do everything quickly. She had a ten-minute bath, changed into a navy blue gaberdine suit and a white blouse with ruffles. She carefully chose court shoes with *medium* heels: in case she had to run for it.

Two minutes in front of the dressing-table mirror for a touch of blusher, powder, lipstick and eye shadow. She was ready for anything – anyone. 'I want some new place to-night,' she thought. 'Somewhere close. I'll try the Hilton.'

Behind the wheel of the Renault station wagon Chabot was driving into Brussels. A silent and sullen Hipper sat beside him. There had been a row when the Luxembourger told Chabot without warning they were leaving immediately for Brussels in the newly hired Renault.

'I'll drive,' the heavily built Frenchman had told him.

'No!' Hipper had squeaked in the kitchen at La Montagne. 'I am in charge . . .'

'Not of me, you're not. Klein pays me. Klein is my boss – and if I don't like something *he* says I tell him. So, let's not bugger about. I'm driving. Got it? And I'll be bloody glad to leave this prison . . .'

He'd glanced back as he moved out of the drive at the bleak shuttered stone hulk of a building lying under the cliffs. Bloody glad. And although Hipper wouldn't talk about it, Chabot guessed the operation must be pretty close, thank God. Earlier, with a knife at his throat, Hipper had said the target was Antwerp. Now they were heading for Brussels – only a short train ride from Antwerp.

Entering Brussels, Hipper guided the Frenchman. He drove up the Boulevard de Waterloo, following the same route Marler had taken earlier, turning round at the top and coming down the side street past the Hilton.

'Where are we staying?' he asked. 'And if you don't answer I'll drive this frigging car round Brussels till dawn.'

'The Marolles,' his plump companion, sagging in his seat, replied. 'Turn right at the bottom past the Palais de Justice. It's a poor quarter they are renovating. We stay at the Café Manuel, a Spanish place. The owner has rooms he lets out. No registration.'

Hipper guided Chabot down a curving street behind the Palais de Justice which emerged into a rabbit warren of old streets. Chabot peered up at four-storey buildings which had an abandoned look. The wooden doors padlocked. Roofs collapsing, exposing crumbling rafters like ancient bones. Other buildings were newish, seven- and eight-storey apartment blocks. He grimaced at the old quarter.

'Renovation, you said. They're pulling down the comfortable old places, putting concrete blockhouses up instead.' A minute later. 'That's the Café Manuel.'

'Park the car round the back.'

Chabot didn't bother to ask how long they'd be stuck in this dump. The operation had to be pretty soon – now they'd moved him into the open.

Disembarking at Brussels Airport, Butler followed Klein through Passport Control and Customs, hailed the next cab after the one Klein had entered. He climbed in quickly.

'That cab just leaving. Please follow it. And please don't lose it. I'm sure the passenger is going to meet my wife. I want to be there when it happens.'

'Understood.' The driver looked at Butler in his mirror as he pulled away from the kerb, gave a knowing grin. 'Life is full of problems. What would we do without them?'

'I could do without this one,' Butler replied and subsided into silence.

Over half an hour later Klein's cab stopped at the Sheraton and Butler's pulled in a few yards behind. Butler tipped him generously and followed Klein inside. He moved close enough to the counter, hatless, to hear a reservation had been made in advance. The reception clerk addressed him as M. Andersen.

Klein glanced round as the porter took his case. Butler was studying a brochure he'd extracted from a display piece on the counter. He didn't think he'd been spotted; four more taxis had pulled up behind his own outside. He waited until the elevator had closed, then wandered over and watched the lights. Klein got off at Floor 12.

Butler went into the street to find a public phone booth, to call Park Crescent.

Klein sat in his bedroom, drinking mineral water, his case untouched. He wouldn't be staying here for more than a short time. He was going over his mental check list in his mind.

Chabot and Hipper. They would soon be in Brussels staying at the Café Manuel in the Marolles. A safe enough spot for a short time. He just hoped Hipper would be able to control Chabot – who would undoubtedly wish to explore the city after being penned up at Larochette. Probably looking for a woman.

The Monk. Marler would soon be installed at the Hilton. There would be no problem with him. He could look after himself in any situation. Independent as the devil. A little too much so for Klein's liking.

Legaud and the stolen CRS command truck. Already in Holland at the appointed rendezvous outside Delft. By now the vehicle should be resprayed – unrecognizable and equipped with Dutch number plates stolen with a car – a car owned by a man away from his apartment on business.

Grand-Pierre's team of scuba divers. They would be coming back from their training in the remote north of Holland, assembling at Delft.

Spread out over the continent for weeks, even months, Klein was now concentrating his forces close to the target. Europoort.

34

Jumbo jets were still flying into Hamburg Airport – each carrying a number of American passengers bound for the cruise liner *Adenauer*. The stately 50,000-ton ship with its twin squat funnels dwarfed the dock where a steady stream of taxis and limousines deposited men, women and children eager to start the great adventure.

Unlike other cruise liners plying the world the *Adenauer* was not one class. It had been designed on the model of pre-World War Two transatlantic leviathans. There was *de-luxe* class – with the most expensively furnished state-rooms afloat. Below came first class. Below that second class. Each level had its own restaurant and was sealed off from other classes.

Texas millionaires, wearing Stetson hats, stood by the rails, watching the other passengers file aboard. The Captain had informed his First Officer there was even some of the 'quiet' money from Philadelphia. From these he'd chosen those honoured to sit at his table.

And even when the majestic queen of the seas sailed from Hamburg down the Elbe she would not yet have taken aboard her full complement of passengers. She would heave to in the North Sea to pick up from lighters further passengers. From Rotterdam.

The 500,000-ton tanker, *Cayman Conqueror*, fully loaded with oil for Europe, had left behind the balmy winds blowing off the shores of Africa. She was now proceeding north off the coast of France, heading for the English Channel.

Her master, Homer Grivas, had been warned he would arrive at the moment the *Adenauer* would be lying offshore, taking aboard passengers. It would take some skilful man-œuvring to bring his giant vessel into port but he was confident there would be no problem. He would make Europort at the agreed ETA.

Twenty miles astern of the *Cayman Conqueror* the 350,000-ton tanker, *Easter Island*, also proceeded on a steady course for the English Channel. Its master, Captain Williams, had given orders to keep a sharp lookout on the sophisticated radar system.

He had been informed not only about the *Adenauer* but also of the presence of the *Conqueror* sailing ahead of his vessel. It was important that the distance between the two tankers should not close any further. Apart from that he was quite confident all would be routine. Europort could handle an incredible number of large ships.

Captain Luigi Salvi, skipper of the 10,000-ton freighter *Otranto*, out from Genoa, was sweating with anxiety. His radar operator had the *Easter Island* clearly on his 'scope, moving ponderously ahead of his own ship. He knew he'd have to keep 'in line' – allow the tanker to pass up the

310

channel first, but this would mean late arrival, a fact he'd already reported to the Dutch authorities.

The trick was to stay as close to the tanker as regulations permitted, to cut down the delayed arrival to the minimum. He was carrying a cargo which bore a penalty clause for every hour of the delay.

On top of that, the *Otranto* was equipped to carry ten passengers, one of whom was a director of the line with his wife. The woman expected constant attention. Salvi was therefore constantly moving from his seat at the dinner table to check with the radar operator. He mopped sweat from his forehead. Keep cool, he told himself, you will only arrive at Europort a few hours late. Then he remembered that damned cruise ship, the *Adenauer*. This trip would require all his seamanship.

Trailing behind the *Otranto* three large container ships up from Africa steamed across the oil-like sea, leaving astern three fan-shaped wakes. Visibility was excellent at this point and their masters could see each other's vessels. They carried soya bean meal and were racing to be first to offload. Their three masters were equally annoyed by the presence dead ahead of the *Otranto*. If nothing changed it would be up to the harbour master at Europort to decide which would come ashore first.

The British Sealink ferry service was in normal operation plying between Harwich and the Hook of Holland – the port downriver from Rotterdam and opposite Europort.

The number of passengers varied with each ferry. But it never fell below two hundred souls. Often a ferry would be crammed with up to three hundred passengers. Sealink continued its shuttle, going about its lawful occasions.

*

The Dutch marine controllers at Europort – and the Hook of Holland – were well aware of the number of vessels approaching. They were in radio communication with each ship, they regularly received up-to-the-minute reports from their computers, they had no doubt at all they could handle the situation. This was Europort. The gateway to Europe.

35

Butler had to walk some distance to find a public phone box. He dialled the Park Crescent number. Monica came on the line. Butler sensed immediately she spoke she was in a state of tension.

'Harry, where is Tweed? I have to contact him urgently.'

'No idea. I'm calling from a street phone in Brussels. The last I saw of him he was in Luxembourg City. Findel Airport to be exact. With Bob Newman and Benoit . . .'

'I've tried to locate Benoit. No success. I have two very urgent messages for him.'

'Care to tell me? I'm pretty sure I've located Klein . . .'

'You have! Tweed will want that information, too. Give me a moment to think. You've enough money for the phone?'

'Bags of coins.'

Stupid question, Monica thought. Of course Butler would be prepared for any occasion. His quietness concealed a brain which was always looking ahead.

'Don't tell me if you'll regret it,' Butler warned.

That decided her. She first took the precaution of making absolutely sure who she was talking to – although she recognized his voice clearly. How? Her mind was fogged – she'd not slept in twenty-four hours, holding the fort.

'Who is your usual partner, the man you often work with – and how does he dress?'

'Pete Nield. Snappy dresser. Smart business suits. Has dark hair and a neat moustache . . .'

'OK, Harry. I knew it was you. I've had two calls today reporting the target is Antwerp. "I think," the caller added the first time. Not the second. Now I'll try Grand'Place again. See if they've located Benoit – and Tweed.'

'I'll inform Grand'Place of where I'm staying when I've taken a room. If Tweed contacts you, I've tracked Klein to the Sheraton. I think.'

'Again! That man's a shadow. Take care, Harry.'

Butler walked quickly back to the Sheraton, carrying his bag. He hadn't liked leaving the place unwatched – but you couldn't phone Park Crescent from an instrument which went through a hotel switchboard. He sat down in the lobby to wait a while. He had no way of knowing Klein had just left.

There was an irksome delay after the Alouette had landed on the football field. The co-pilot had to radio police HQ at Dinant for a car.

'Too far to walk to the river,' Benoit explained. 'And Ralston will be on the move. By now his cruiser will have passed through the lock.'

They caught up with the *Evening Star* proceeding down-river near a landing stage. The driver stood at the tip of the stage with a bullhorn and hailed the vessel.

'Police! Moor your vessel here. Brussels CID are coming aboard.'

'That should put the wind up him,' Tweed observed. 'Just the mood I need before I grille this phoney colonel.'

'Why phoney?' Benoit enquired.

'Oh, there's something not pukka about the bastard,' Newman replied. 'As he himself would phrase it. I travelled with him. I wouldn't loan him five quid.'

The cruiser had changed course, was heading in for the landing stage. By the rail Ralston stood staring at the group waiting, hands gripping the rail. To Newman his face seemed more brick-red than ever; as he came close he seemed flushed with fury.

'What the devil is going on?' he barked. 'Who the hell are you to interfere with the passage of my vessel?'

Crew members had jumped fore and aft on to the stage with mooring ropes. A gangplank was shoved on to the stage with a heavy thud. Newman recognized Sergeant Bradley standing a few paces behind his master. Josette strolled along the deck until Ralston saw her.

'Get below!' he shouted.

Alfredo, cook and dogsbody, peered from lower down the companionway, then vanished. 'The gang's all here,' Newman whispered ironically.

The colonel had planted himself at the head of the gangway, blocking the way. Hands on hips, he glared at the intruders. He held up a hand as Benoit, followed by Tweed and Newman, moved up the gangplank.

'I asked what the hell this is all about. You can't come aboard. Say your piece from there.'

'Brussels CID,' snapped Benoit, showing his warrant card. 'Move aside – or I'll move you.'

'Goddamned impertinence,' the colonel raved. He stepped back a few paces. 'Got a search warrant, have you?'

'Do I need one?' Benoit enquired.

They were all standing on deck. Half way down the companionway Josette looked back and Newman winked at her behind Ralston who had turned to Tweed. 'And who, might I ask, are you?'

'Tweed, Commander, Anti-Terrorist Squad.' He also showed his warrant card. 'We can't talk out here,' he continued. 'I suggest we adjourn to the saloon.'

'Do you now? How very civil of you. On my own vessel.'

'I have questions to ask . . .'

'Which I may not be prepared to answer. In case you have overlooked the point, you carry no authority in Belgium.'

'I can always get an extradition order within hours and

take you to London. The charge? Consorting with terrorists.'

'And,' Benoit added, 'I can have you taken to Grand'
Place HQ in Brussels for questioning – pending your extradition.'

'The saloon,' Tweed said grimly. 'Kindly lead the way.'

Bringing up the rear, Newman glanced to the end of the
saloon, saw a whisky bottle three-quarters empty on the
bar counter, a glass half-full beside it. The colonel had
been going it a bit. Hence his loss of judgement. Tweed
also noted what stood on the counter. The colonel walked
to the bar, stiff-legged, turned round.

'I suppose you'd better sit down. What's all this nonsense
you gabbled about terrorists?'

'You know a man called Klein?' Tweed began. 'Before
you reply think carefully. You know Bob Newman – he
was a passenger aboard this cruiser.'

'A spy, you mean?' Ralston sneered. 'He questioned
someone behind my back? Who? Hardly the conduct of a
gentleman – and a guest.'

'A paying guest,' Newman reminded him mildly. 'For a
good fat fee. Your crew are a garrulous lot,' he added,
protecting Josette who sat opposite him close to the companionway, graceful hands clasped in her lap.

Conduct of a gentleman . . . Ye Gods, Tweed thought,
what have we here? He prodded harder.

'Klein was the name I mentioned. Has a man with that
name been on board?'

'I seem to remember someone of that name.' Ralston
smoothed down his hair with one hand, then used the other
to swallow the rest of the whisky.

'This isn't good enough.' Tweed stood up, walked down
the saloon and stood close to Ralston. 'I think Klein
travelled with you more than once. He's a very dangerous
terrorist. Many people's lives are at stake. A description,
please. Where did you pick him up? Where did he leave
this vessel?'

'Difficult to recall details . . .'

Benoit intervened. 'This is useless. I'll fly him in the chopper to Grand' Place, you get your extradition order moving . . .'

'Hold hard, it's coming back to me.' Ralston grasped the whisky bottle and Tweed fully expected him to refill his glass. Instead he marched quickly round the end of the counter, planted it on the shelf, took down a bottle of mineral water, poured a glassful and drank the lot. His movements had suddenly become brisk and Tweed suspected he'd been putting on an act.

'Filthy stuff, that.' Ralston dabbed his mouth with a handkerchief. 'Now, this sod, Klein. Six foot tall, slim build, face white as chalk. Funny eyes.'

Tweed took a photocopy of the Identikit picture from his pocket, unfolded it, handed it to the colonel. 'Recognize him?'

'That I do. Klein. Bit sketchy, but the eyes come out well.' He walked steadily over to Josette. 'You didn't like him either. That him?'

'Yes. Creepy. Couldn't stand him.'

She handed the picture back to Tweed. Ralston stood very erect, one hand in his jacket pocket, the thumb protruding. Tweed had the impression he'd made up his mind about something.

'Took him aboard each time at Dinant. As a favour to a friend. Not my fault he turned out to be a bad lot.'

'No one is suggesting it is.' Tweed's manner changed, adapting to Ralston's own change of mood. How often, it flashed across Tweed's mind, he'd played the chameleon in his earlier role of detective. 'Who is the friend? We need to know, I assure you.'

'Brand, the banker. Peter Brand. Got a place fit for a king downstream. Near Profondeville. Newman knows all this – he visited Brand with me.'

'How much did Brand pay you for this service?' Benoit demanded, his tone brusque.

Ralston stared at him with glaucous eyes. 'I'm not going

316

to have two of you at me. I normally like Belgians. I'll make an exception in your case.'

A wintry smile. Newman stared in surprise. He'd never have associated the colonel with such wit. Benoit, Tweed sensed, was about to explode. He spoke quickly to Ralston.

'Can you tell me anything about a bargee called Joseph Haber? He's gone missing.'

'Has he now? I've seen Klein hobnobbing with him – aboard his barge *Gargantua*. Again, back at Dinant. Twice, as I recall it. Once several months ago, the other time within the past few days. Dour chap, Haber. Kept himself to himself. You implied this Klein is a terrorist. Couldn't make out what nationality he was. Spoke almost perfect English. Thought he was until he tripped himself up. Queer incident, that.'

'What incident?'

'He said something I didn't agree with – can't recall all the details. Doesn't matter. I accused him of talking Double Dutch. He stared at me for a moment with those weird eyes. Then he flew at me, asked what I was hinting at. Sergeant Bradley came in by chance and pulled him up short.'

'Can you remember,' Benoit interjected, 'whether Klein ever had anyone with him when he visited Joseph Haber on his barge?'

'Always on his own. Bit of a lone wolf type . . .'

'A few minutes ago,' Benoit reminded him, 'you called Klein "this sod". You've said you disliked him. Why?'

'Because he acted as though he'd taken over the *Evening Star*. Arrogant as blazes. Ordered Bradley to make him coffee – little things like that. He wasn't popular, I can tell you.' Ralston looked at Tweed. 'Any of this help?'

'Yes. Thank you for your cooperation. Could I ask where we could locate you if the need arises? It's unlikely, but in case . . .'

'I'll tell you exactly what I'm going to do. After what you told me I want to distance myself from Peter Brand as far as possible. First opportunity I'm turning round, sailing back upstream and across the French frontier. Take a bit of a joy ride down the Canal de l'Est. No objections?'

'None as far as I'm concerned,' Tweed replied.

They left the cruiser after refusing Ralston's offer of tea or a drink, climbed back into the waiting car and drove off to where the Alouette waited. Tweed told Benoit he wanted to reach Brussels at the earliest possible moment. The crisis was imminent.

36

Leaving the Sheraton, carrying his bag, Klein headed for a public phone box near the Porte Louise. It was almost dark. Car headlights whipped up the Boulevard de Waterloo, the neon signs had come on, casting a weird light in the dusk. He entered a phone box, dialled a number in Germany.

He was calling the Hessischer Hof Hotel in Frankfurt. Kurt Saur, the Austrian helicopter pilot, answered the moment he was put through to his room. Klein spoke in German.

'Klein here. Are you ready to make delivery?'

'We await your instructions. Both machines are available.'

'Fly at once to Schiphol. You will be met by my agent, Grand-Pierre. Got the name?'

'Grand-Pierre. We will arrive roughly two to three hours from now.'

'Do it.'

Klein put down the receiver, lifted it again, called Delft and passed on the information to Grand-Pierre. The pilots speak French, he told him. Grand-Pierre said he would drive to Schiphol at once.

It was news to the Frenchman that two large Sikorsky

helicopters were coming. Once again Klein had kept the different members of the assault force in separate cells. On arrival at the Dutch airport near Amsterdam Saur would tell the airport officials both machines were in need of maintenance. They would be held in reserve at Schiphol until required.

Standing in front of a shop window, Klein went over in his mind the Sikorsky element. Unlike the CRS command vehicle – which had to be stolen because it couldn't be bought on the open market – the Sikorsky machines had been legitimately hired for cash. And he could rely on Saur who led the four men of the helicopter team.

Kurt Saur, from Graz in the Austrian province of Styria, was forty years old. He'd spent his life hiring himself out for smuggling operations. So far he hadn't been caught. But he felt his luck was running out. He needed one big 'score' to give him the money for a life of leisure. Klein had provided that opportunity.

Klein was in an edgy mood – and knew why. Several members of his team were now in Brussels. The concentration at this moment was inevitable – they had to be close to the target.

But it went against all his instincts for security to do this. He was very close to the Mayfair where Lara Seagrave waited. He'd better go and have a word with her, see whether she was becoming restless.

First he took a cab to Midi station. Here he left his case in a luggage container – which reminded him of the bag he'd deposited at Geneva Cornavin, the bag containing the blood-soaked raincoat after murdering the Swiss, Blanc. So long ago, it seemed.

He took another cab back to the Porte Louise, paid it off, then walked up the opposite side of the Avenue Louise to where the Mayfair was located. He stood for a while behind a file of cars, deciding the line he would take with Lara.

He stiffened suddenly as he saw Lara leave the entrance to the Mayfair. Dressed up to the nines in a gaberdine suit. Where could she be going at this hour? She had strict instructions to wait in her room, to eat at the Mayfair.

On the far side of the street she walked towards the Porte Louise, clasping her shoulder bag. Klein followed at a discreet distance. When the lights were green she crossed the Boulevard de Waterloo. Turning right along the sidewalk, she walked up the Boulevard, stopped briefly to look in a shop window, walked on and entered the Hilton.

Inside the spacious lobby Lara walked briskly past the long counter for the concierge, reception and cashier. She was seething inwardly. Not one damn word from Klein. Would she ever set eyes on him again? Had the swine cut her out of the operation. Anxiety mingled with fury as she pressed the button for Floor One.

A tall American guest arrived as the elevator doors opened. 'Please, after you. Kinda warmish this weather . . .' She smiled her thanks, stepped inside. The American followed and Klein stepped after them a second before the doors shut.

Lara stared at him, then looked away. He'd been following her. She was livid. The lift ascended, stopped at the first floor, the American again ushered her in front of him. Klein caught up with her as she entered the *Maison de Boeuf*, a large room with an air of luxury, quiet and with only a few tables occupied. An open grille behind a serving counter faced her; behind the counter a young man with a chef's white hat looked up.

'What the hell do you think you're doing?' Klein whispered.

He gripped her by the forearm. He needed somewhere quiet without people to sort her out. Discipline. Control . . .

'What does it look like?' she snapped. 'Coming out to have dinner . . .'

'Who with?'

'Let . . . go . . . of . . . my . . . arm,' she demanded, letting her rage show. 'I'm not your serf.'

'We'll go back to the Mayfair.'

'No!' This was like dealing with her bloody step-mother, Lady Windermere. 'I'm eating here. The Mayfair can wait.'

Smoking one of his rare cigarettes, seated in a cosy corner next to the grille, Marler watched the encounter with half-closed eyes. The last man on God's earth he'd expected so soon was Klein. It was only eight o'clock. And who was the girl? It was hardly a friendly meeting.

Lara gave Klein the mockery of a beaming smile. 'If you don't let go of me I'll create one hell of a scene.'

'Later then, at the Mayfair.'

Klein released his grip. The last thing he wanted was a scene drawing attention to himself. He turned abruptly and went back to the elevators.

Marler rose from his table, walked over to Lara before the head waiter could reach her. He smiled, still holding his napkin in his left hand.

'Excuse me,' he said, 'but I'm dining alone. Something I never enjoy. Unless you've someone waiting for you, I'd be delighted if you'd share my table. David Ashley. For dinner, I mean – just dinner.'

She was obviously English and he'd deliberately spoken in that language to reassure her. Being careful not to touch her, he gestured towards his table. 'I'm over there in the corner – you can sit nearest the next table. It's all rather convenient.'

'What is?' she asked, sizing him up, liking what she saw.

'The table. Next to the grille. If you order a steak you can watch, shout "stop!" if you like it rare and he's overdoing things.'

'I like mine well done.'

She had joined him as he followed her to the table. A considerate man. That little touch about letting her sit in the outside seat – enabling her to leave easily if she wanted to. He reached for a bottle cloth-shrouded in a silver bucket.

'All girls like champers, so I've heard. Care for a drop while you study the menu?'

'Thank you. I'd love some. It will calm me down.'

'Then here's to a pleasant evening. I'm rather good at chatter. Even if at nothing else . . .'

Klein walked into the bar leading off the lobby of the Hilton. It was dimly lit, which suited him. He sank into an armchair, ordered mineral water, automatically checking the other drinkers.

Lara's outburst was exactly what he had feared. The long wait was telling on nerves. He'd been so taken up with getting her out of the place he hadn't noticed who was dining in the room, a rare oversight.

He sat sipping his Perrier, his mind racing over every aspect of the operation. He'd have moved them all out of Brussels that very night – but he couldn't up-date the operation. It all hinged on the fleet of ships moving towards Europort.

He decided against visiting the Café Manuel to check on Chabot and Hipper. No one could possibly be aware of his presence in Brussels, but this was the moment *not* to move about the city.

Klein had no intention of sleeping anywhere tonight. Without a hotel room he didn't exist. He'd get a quick meal at the Café Henry further up the Boulevard, have a drink while Marler dined in the Sky Room, then spend half the hours of darkness in a night club.

An attractive woman sat in a nearby chair facing him, crossed her legs, and gave him a long look. He smiled briefly, looked away. There'd be plenty of time for that later. He was thinking that the Sikorsky helicopters would at this moment be flying from Frankfurt to Schiphol. An essential element in the enterprise.

The woman signalled her availability, moving one crossed leg up and down. Yes, plenty of time later. When he was safely in Brazil.

*

Marler was puzzled as he ate his steak. What role could Lara Seagrave possibly play in the coming operation? She could be Klein's girl friend, but he didn't think so. He continued to probe gently.

'You have a job? Or is that too personal?'

'Not at all. This steak is perfect. And I love this restaurant. So warm and comforting.'

The tables were well-spaced, the banquettes at the right height and angle for eating, the coverings a mix of brown and beige. The lighting was indirect, but you could see what you were eating.

'I'm a publisher's scout,' she said, remembering a job a girl friend of hers had.

'What's that?'

'Oh, I represent different publishers – in Denmark, Germany, France and Sweden. My languages got me the job – plus the fact I'm an avid reader. I keep a sharp lookout for books I think might interest one of my employers. It means getting in first – before any of my many rivals.'

'So you travel a lot?' he suggested, watching her over the rim of his glass.

'Yes, I do. It's one of the great attractions of the job. I have just come up from France – Marseilles and Paris.'

'What are you doing in Brussels?'

'Enjoying myself.' She smiled impishly, flirting openly. 'I fly home soon. I'm waiting for instructions. From London,' she added.

'What firms do you represent?'

She reeled off a list, again bringing back what her friend had told her about the job. Marler nodded, called for the sweet trolley. He didn't believe one damn word she'd told him. So what kind of an operation would call for her services? Klein had better not know they'd met. Fortunate he'd given her a false name. No, prudent. He'd done that after seeing Klein arguing with her. Tension? Was it very close?

*

323

Marler timed the ending of his dinner with Lara carefully. He insisted on paying. To her relief he made no attempt to arrange another meeting, to find out where she was staying. She left at 8.50 p.m. exactly and went back to the Mayfair.

Marler told the waiter he had another guest joining him, had all traces of Lara's presence cleared off the table. It was 9.15 p.m. when Klein, tight-lipped, walked into the *Maison de Boeuf*, looked round, spotted Marler, walked across and sat beside him.

'Good evening,' said Marler, one hand nursing his glass of cognac.

'I've been looking for you. I left a note. Dinner at nine in the Sky Room.'

'And I got your note,' Marler smiled amiably. 'I prefer this restaurant. I knew you'd find me sooner or later.'

'When I give an order . . .'

'About the operation,' Marler interjected, 'I listen and carry out your wishes. Which is what I'm paid for. I am not paid to be led around like a dog on a leash, eating where *you* think I should dine.' His tone had hardened. 'I think we should be clear about that. Now, what is it?'

Klein told the waiter he'd already eaten in the Sky Room, a lie. He ordered coffee and turned to his companion when they were alone.

'Be prepared to leave at a moment's notice. I will phone you. Have you a car?'

'Yes. Hired a fresh one.'

'Parked in the underground garage here?'

'Of course not.' He made no attempt to enlighten Klein further. 'Where shall I be driving to? How close are we?'

'Close. The destination I give you when I call.' He stood up, reached for his coat which he'd brought into the room dumping it on a chair. Leaving it at the garderobe made for delay in case a swift departure was necessary. 'Tell the waiter when he brings my coffee I had to leave. Later than I thought.'

Marler watched him walk very erect from the room, the coat over his arm. 'Up yours, chum,' he said to himself and drank the rest of the cognac.

37

At Blakeney, the tiny Norfolk port, Pete Nield was proper browned off, as he put it to himself. He'd spent endless days in the pub overlooking the front and the house belonging to Paula Grey where the bomb had been placed on her doorstep.

By now he was a regular, a habitué of the pub, and a close friend of the barman. Wearing a hunting jacket and corduroy trousers, he sat with yet another beer at a table where he could watch the sea front. The barman, cleaning a glass with a cloth, wandered over.

'See Caleb Fox's coaster is taking on board a different load.'

'So I notice. And Dr Portch is hanging round again. Those two seem real buddies.'

Nield was remembering the night he'd followed Dr Portch's car along the coast road in the dark. How Portch had gone inside a cottage which, it turned out, was Caleb Fox's.

'Anything about the sea interests Portch. He's a pal of the harbourmaster here. Knows the Customs people. That cargo they're loading now. It's Portch's bits and pieces – all his furniture from Cockley Ford. Going back to Holland is the good doctor.'

'He's been there before?' Nield asked casually.

He moved restlessly inside the clothes he didn't like because they felt strange. But hanging about Blakeney all

325

this time he'd have been absurdly conspicuous in his normal smart suits. He'd bought the gear in King's Lynn, which was still his base. And he was still staying at The Duke's Head facing Tuesday Market. Again to avoid standing out like a sore thumb in Blakeney.

Before Butler returned on his own to London they'd discussed what Nield should do. 'Stay here,' Butler had decided. 'Keep an eye on the Blakeney sector.'

'What for?' Nield had queried.

'That bomb found on Paula Grey's doorstep. It was the first appearance of that new Soviet type of bomb in this country.'

'And what has that to do with the price of tea in China?'

'No idea,' Butler had admitted. 'But stick around.'

Nield had stuck around, driving to Blakeney each day, drinking gallons of good Norfolk beer. Now, for the first time, the barman's chance remark seemed to give some point to his long vigil.

'Oh, yes,' the barman replied to his question. 'When he first came to Cockley Ford the practice wasn't vacant for a few months. Some cock-up. I suppose Portch needed the money. He took on a locum job in Holland – and took his furniture with him. Said it would make him feel more at home. Then he brings it back again when he takes up the practice. Now, I hear, he's found himself a permanent post in Amsterdam. He liked the Dutch. So off goes his furniture again, like I just said.'

'Think I could do with a breath of sea air.'

Nield stood up, said he'd be back, and wandered out on to the front which was deserted except for the loading activity by Fox's coaster. Dusk was falling, lights in houses had a weird glow, below in the creek there was the sound of water surging in from the sea. Like a tide race.

Nield turned up the collar of his duffel coat against a chill breeze coming across the desolate marshes, thrust hands into his pockets and strolled along the front.

He was within twenty yards of the coaster when the crane hoisted a loading net containing an oblong crate off the quayside. Inside the net something came loose, a hinged side of the crate slid open. Shouting from the group on the quay. The operator in his little cabin atop the crane stopped the hoist, lowered it back to the quay.

Nield was about twenty yards away when the incident occurred. He lengthened his pace without appearing to walk any faster. Under the spotlight shining down from the crane he saw an old-fashioned wardrobe inside the crate. Both doors had also swung loose, exposing its empty interior. Fit for firewood, Nield thought. The junk people lumbered their lives with.

Three of the removal men from the furniture van standing in the shadows started roping up the wardrobe. Dr Portch came forward, shaking his head as he watched them.

'Sorry about that, lads. I should have locked it more securely. My fault entirely.'

In his high-pitched voice Nield, who had an acute ear for intonation, caught a hint of smugness. Behind the group gathered round the net a Customs official was busy chalking other crates.

'Should know your stuff by now, Dr Portch. Back and forth, back and forth to Holland. A right commuter, you be. You'll be with us again, I'll be bound.'

'Wouldn't surprise me one little bit,' Portch assured him.

Nield stood stock still. His mind raced. Butler's remark. *That bomb found on Paula Grey's doorstep . . . the first appearance of that new Soviet type of bomb . . .* Then Newman's account of what he'd seen the evening he visited Cockley Ford – and the church – with Harry Butler.

Then there was the Custom official's comment. *Should know your stuff by now . . .* He was automatically passing all the crates, marking them with his piece of chalk – without examination. He hadn't even bothered to come and have a look at the opened crate inside the net.

Nield received further confirmation of the appalling idea which had flashed through his mind when one of the removal men spoke as he tackled the crate.

'Can't understand how these screws came loose. You crated most of the others yourself, Dr Portch. This one *I* screwed up.'

'Must have worked their way loose during the journey along that bumpy side road from Cockley Ford,' Portch said smoothly. His voice quickened as he addressed the man tightening the screws. 'Foreman, I'd like to give you your tip now. I'll forget it if I leave it until the last minute . . .'

He had his wallet in his hand, taking out banknotes which he handed to the foreman. 'You've done a very good job again.'

'Thank you very much, Doctor. Very generous. Mind you, we're not finished. Only half the van has been unloaded.'

'And you'll take the same care you always do.'

Nield felt himself go cold. Portch had successfully turned the removal crew's attention away from the loose screws. The crate had been *intended* to fly open – a precaution to show the innocence of the cargo. He suddenly realized Portch had noticed his presence, was staring at him.

'A bit late for an evening walk, sir.'

'A necessary bit of exercise,' Nield replied instantly. 'I have been consuming rather a lot of beer . . .' He belched.

Portch chuckled, a sound like pebbles sliding down an iron chute. 'Getting the wind out of his sails.'

There was a polite chortle from the assembled removal men who stood back as the foreman waved a hand and the hoist began to lift the net prior to swinging it over the hold.

Nield was taut with tension. He had to get to a phone, to call Park Crescent. He turned quickly, caught his foot between two projecting cobbles, lost his balance and heeled over sideways. His skull struck the stone wall of a cottage. The world spun, oblivion fell like a curtain, he collapsed.

The barman, who had been watching from a window, came running along the front as Dr Portch bent over Nield, felt

328

his pulse. As he straightened up Nield stirred, one hand groping against the wall. The barman, panting, stood silent for a few seconds, regaining his breath.

'He's drunk,' Portch announced. 'He practically admitted it.'

'No he's not.' The barman, a burly man with ruddy cheeks, had clenched his fists. 'No one gets drunk in my bar. I saw it. He tripped, hit 'is 'ead against that wall.'

'Well, his pulse is normal . . .'

'He needs to go to 'orspital,' the barman hammered on. 'I'll drive him there.'

'Might be best,' Portch agreed with no particular interest. 'I have to catch the tide.'

The barman stooped as Nield struggled to get to his feet and looped an arm round him, hauling him upright. He glared up at Portch who watched with blank eyes from behind the gold pince-nez. Some doctor, the barman was thinking. And now I see him close up I don't like those eyes. Lizard eyes.

'Can . . . walk,' Nield mumbled.

'With a bit of 'elp. I'll take your weight.'

The barman took Nield back to the pub by easy stages, supporting him under the shoulders. Inside he let Nield sag into a chair near the door. He shouted to his assistant. 'Mick, you take over. I'll be gone a while.' He turned back to Nield.

'Your car's parked down road? Usual place? Give me the keys then.'

Nield fumbled under his coat for his jacket pocket. The barman reached into the pocket, his hand came out with the keys. When he backed the car round the corner in front of the pub and went inside Nield was still conscious, sipping mineral water provided by Mick. The glass suddenly tumbled from his hand, rolled across the floor.

'Never mind that, sir. Ups-a-daisy. Car's outside.'

'Get me . . . to King's Lynn . . . Duke's Head,' Nield mumbled, his face ashen.

'You're going to 'orspital. Come on now.'

With the barman's aid Nield stood up, stumbled towards the door. He nearly tripped at the exit but the barman's firm grip saved him. Nield's last clear vision of Blakeney was of the coaster, the crane swivelling another loading net to the hold. He fell into the back of the car, rested his swimming head on the head-rest, then blacked out.

38

'A lot of urgent messages for you, Tweed,' Chief Inspector Benoit said as they settled in his office at police HQ off Grand'Place. He pushed a sheaf of typed notes across his desk.

Newman sat in a corner chair where he could survey the whole room. He lit a cigarette while Tweed sorted through the pile, arranging it in a certain order.

The Alouette had flown them from the football field to Brussels Airport. As arranged over the radio by Benoit, unmarked police cars had been waiting to drive them into Brussels.

No one had eaten for hours and Newman felt very tired. He also detected rare signs of fatigue in Tweed, his face drawn but the eyes behind his glasses were still alert. Tweed looked at Benoit.

'You have a scrambler phone? I have to call Lasalle in Paris.'

Benoit pushed one of the two phones on his desk forward after pressing a red button on the instrument. 'Installed since the growth of terrorism. Help yourself. You know the number?'

'Yes.' Tweed dialled from memory, wondering whether Lasalle would still be at rue des Saussaies. It was nine in the evening. Lasalle himself answered.

'Tweed? Been trying to get you for hours. I contacted Interpol about whether any German in Brazil had fathered a child. Didn't expect anything but a reply came back fast. Bit of a scandal – the woman involved comes from a good family. A man called Kuhn gave her a son a few months ago. They plan to marry. Nothing on present whereabouts of this Kuhn. Best I can do.'

'Thank you very much . . .'

'Getting anywhere?'

'Nothing definite. Be in touch.' Tweed put down the phone, looked at the other two men. 'Man called Kuhn had an affair with an upper-class Brazilian girl. Result, a son. Supposed to be going to marry her. He's disappeared. Klein. Kuhn. The names are similar.'

'Not conclusive by a mile,' Newman objected. 'Any description?'

'I gather not. It's a miracle Interpol extracted that much information.'

'But if Klein were Kuhn,' Benoit pointed out, 'it would give him a bolt-hole you'd never penetrate. No extradition from Brazil if he has an offspring by a Brazilian girl – even out of wedlock.'

'It's a long shot,' Newman insisted. 'What positive evidence have we got about anything? None. Klein, as someone said earlier, moves like a phantom.'

'I have to call Monica next,' Tweed said.

He was reaching for the phone when there was a knock on the door, a uniformed officer appeared when Benoit called out and the man whispered in his ear. The Belgian police chief looked at Tweed.

'Harry Butler is outside. Ask him to come in,' he told the officer.

'I found Klein, I'm sure,' Butler announced as he sagged into a chair. 'Then I lost him,' he said in a tone of disgust.

'Where?' rapped out Tweed with a burst of fresh energy.

'Here in Brussels . . .'

He described his recent experiences, starting with following Peter Brand to the Hotel Cravat in Luxembourg, his

331

decision to track the stooped man with glasses and a pipe, ending with his losing Klein at the Sheraton.

'Is he still booked in at the Sheraton?' Tweed asked.

'Officially yes, for two more days. I don't think he will come back. The room is paid in advance. But I chatted up one of the girl receptionists and she saw him leave with his bag. That was while I was calling London, trying to contact you. I mucked it up.'

'I don't think so,' Tweed disagreed. 'You are sure it was Klein despite his changed appearance?'

'Bet my pension on it.'

Tweed looked round the room. 'We *do* have definite evidence on several points. Colonel Ralston confirmed Klein visited Brand several times. Brand, therefore, is the banker for the coming operation. Now we have Klein placed in this city. At long last we've tracked him, we're close . . .'

'And the target?' Newman queried.

'I'll call London. I may be able to answer that question after talking with Park Crescent.'

The air of tension, added to by fatigue, grew in the room while Tweed made his call. Benoit, normally calm and jovial, tapped his desk with the fingers of one hand. The news that Klein was in Brussels had shaken him. Newman stirred restlessly in his chair, staring at a wall map of Belgium. Only Butler remained unmoved, waiting the next development.

Tweed's call to Monica was fairly brief. He let her do most of the talking. Near the end of the conversation he asked if she'd any word from Nield in King's Lynn. He put down the receiver.

'I'm reliably informed the target is Antwerp . . .'

'Oh, my God!' Benoit stiffened.

'But,' Tweed went on, 'I don't believe it. Klein is diabolically clever. When I take a hotel room I prop his Identikit picture where I can see it – rather as I once read Montgomery did with Rommel before Alamein . . .'

'I hope,' Benoit broke in, 'you're not suggesting we're facing another Alamein?'

'With the huge armoury of explosives at his disposal we could face enormous casualties. The man is ruthless – maybe beyond the point of sanity.'

'Why not Antwerp?' Benoit demanded.

'Because Klein is past master at the art of spreading smoke-screens to conceal his true objective. Looking at his picture, I realize he's bound to know that by now we're aware he's planning something. He's too clever not to realize with the number of men he's recruited someone will have raised the alarm.'

'But your reliable source, as you termed it,' Benoit persisted, 'says it *is* Antwerp.'

'They think. I'd hoped for a totally positive statement. I haven't got it.' Tweed leaned forward. 'I think Klein is so clever he's probably fooled his own team – just in case someone lets a clue drop.'

'I can't take a chance on that.' Benoit stood up. 'I have to inform the Minister. We have to alert Antwerp, immediately take certain precautions in that great port. You yourself said Klein is in Brussels . . .' He turned to Butler. 'And I'm convinced you have located Klein.' He shook his head. 'No, gentlemen, I can't risk it. What are you going to do in the meantime? Tonight, I mean.'

'Get a light meal and some sleep,' Tweed replied. 'Fatigue is a bad counsellor and we are all very tired. Also, I want to go back over the whole history of this business with Newman. He said not long ago maybe we know more than we realize we know. That could be the case. Hard thought may give me the clue I'm seeking – to the ultimate target.'

Klein made three phone calls from an outside call box. One to Lara, another to Marler, the third to Hipper. In each case the gist of the calls was the same.

'The conference is now arranged. Please leave immediately for Antwerp. A reservation has been made for you in your name . . .' A false name was given for each member of the team. 'You stay at this hotel . . .' A different hotel was allocated for each of them. 'I will contact you there soon after you arrive. Please have meals in your room. Other people have to be contacted re the sales conference.'

It was Klein's sixth sense which caused him to take this lightning decision. Something about Brussels didn't smell right. And the sudden movement would keep everyone occupied and off balance.

Lara would catch a night train. Marler would drive to Antwerp. Hipper and Chabot would also go by car. Klein himself would travel the short distance by night train. He had his case waiting for him in the luggage container at Midi station – although when he'd deposited it he'd had no intention of ordering the speed-up. He gave a sigh of relief as he settled in the otherwise empty first-class compartment as the train left for Antwerp.

Hipper took the phone call in their room at the Café Manuel as Chabot was leaving. He gestured for the Frenchman to wait. Putting down the phone Hipper began stuffing clothes into his case as he spoke.

'Pack your things. We're leaving at once.'

'Shit!' Chabot was furious. 'And I was going on the town to enjoy myself for the first time in weeks. Where the devil are we going now?'

'Antwerp. Do hurry up.'

'That's the target?' Chabot asked as he began folding his own things neatly. Hipper was a toad, he thought. Messy about everything: couldn't even pack a case decently.

'No idea,' Hipper replied. 'Just our next destination.'

Ten minutes later Hipper had paid Manuel an extortionate sum for the room they'd hardly used and, Chabot behind the wheel, they were driving out of Brussels.

Sagged behind his seat belt, Hipper was lost in thought. The sudden decision of Klein had not surprised him. During his last visit to take food to Haber's wife and his son imprisoned in the old mill he had included the usual thermos of coffee.

But this time the strong coffee was rather different. As instructed by Klein, he had laced it with a heavy dose of barbiturates. The two prisoners would sleep well. They would sleep for ever.

Part Three

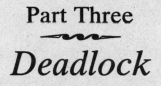

Deadlock

39

'No news of Nield then?' Butler had asked.

Three men were talking in Tweed's room at a small hotel near Grand'Place Benoit had suggested. Tweed, Newman and Butler. Earlier they'd found a small restaurant, dining off omelettes. None of them had felt he could face a large meal.

Tweed had drunk a lot of coffee which had made him more alert. It was two in the morning. He shook his head at Butler.

'Monica said Nield normally reported in daily by phone. He's bought up a load of books, dumped them in a prominent place at the back of his car. Posing as a publisher's representative. He's watching Blakeney – as you suggested, Harry.'

'You said "normally". Has there been a break in communication?'

'Yes. Nothing for the past twenty-four hours. I expect he has his reasons. Now, Bob, I want you to help me – recall everything that's happened since we started this pursuit of Klein. I have the weird idea we've overlooked something. One missing key is the explosives Klein brought out across the Turkish border – before murdering the Armenian truck driver, Dikoyan, and kindly throwing his corpse into the Bosphorus.'

'But what about Klein?' Butler interjected. 'I should be out looking for him. I lost him . . .'

'Don't worry about that. Benoit has thrown out a huge dragnet, recalled men off duty, had copies made of the Identikit picture and distributed them. His men are combing every hotel in Brussels – including some sleazy places down in the Marolles district. Benoit will be up all night.

Including seeing his Minister to persuade him to alert Antwerp – which I still think is the wrong target. Now, you go ahead, Bob. I listen.'

For quarter of an hour he sat silent, watching Newman who, in his terse, reporter-like manner, recalled previous events. At times Tweed leant his head back against the chair, closed his eyes as he saw visually what he'd experienced. Going right back to his visit to the weird village of Cockley Ford. Newman had just finished retailing details of his visit to Brand's luxurious mansion with Colonel Ralston when Tweed sat up straight.

'Just a minute. Those wheel tracks of some heavy vehicle you saw pressed into Brand's lawn – reminds me of something else. The wheel tracks I saw at the church at Cockley Ford – leading to the mausoleum of Sir John Leinster.'

'And now,' Newman said grimly, 'I remember what it was I wanted to recall and tell you. Go back to where all this started. That cargo of explosives – sea-mines and bombs – stolen from the Soviet depot at Sevastopol. OK, Dikoyan was found with his throat cut in the Bosphorus. But there was a bit after that you told me. Something about a Greek vessel sailing from the Golden Horn in Istanbul about the same time.'

'That's right. It was thought that vessel could have transported the explosives . . .'

'The name! The name!' Newman was unusually excited. 'The name of that vessel which disappeared, which has never been seen since. Can you remember it?'

'The *Lesbos* . . .'

Newman turned to Butler. 'That afternoon we drove to Brancaster looking for Caleb Fox's address. Pouring with rain. We met a chap with a walking stick. Military type. He warned us not to walk out to either of the two hulks lying among the sandbanks offshore.'

'That's right,' Butler agreed, wondering where Newman was heading for.

'He said one of the hulks had had its name changed, he took a photo of the thing. He said it was wrecked about six months earlier. My God! I think I've still got the card he gave me with his name and address and phone number. Timms! That was the name. And here is the card . . .'

'What are you up to?' Tweed asked.

'Ronald Timms.' Newman jumped up from his chair, went over to the bed, perched on it and picked up the phone. 'Calling Mr Timms,' he replied as he dialled for an outside line.

'At this hour?' Tweed commented. 'You will get a lot of cooperation. Middle of the night.'

'He lives alone, I think. And the type who doesn't need much sleep.' He was dialling. He waited as he heard the ringing tone in Norfolk. The phone was answered quickly.

'Mr Ronald Timms?' Newman began. 'Very sorry to call at this hour. Hope I haven't got you out of bed. Robert Newman here. I doubt whether you'll remember me but . . .'

'Of course I do. The reporter chappie I warned not to wander out across those creeks. And I'm up, making myself a pot of tea. What can I do for you?'

The conversation was brief. Timms was anything but a waffler. Newman thanked him very much, said yes, he'd certainly call on him when he was next in the area, put down the phone, looked at Tweed.

'That wreck off the Norfolk coast, the hulk whose name had been changed. Timms' photograph brought up the real name under a magnifying glass. The *Lesbos*.'

Nield opened his eyes, stared at a blank white ceiling illuminated indirectly from a light somewhere. He was in bed. Lifting his head he saw the light came through a glass window in the top of a closed door. Where the hell was he?

He pushed back the sheets with an effort, then lifted a hand to his head. It was swathed in bandages. It came back to him. The coaster at Blakeney being loaded. Dr Portch leaning over him, staring down from behind his beak-like

341

nose through pince-nez. A cold, calculating expression. Have to get back to Park Crescent, report what I've found out . . .

He perched on the edge of the bed, realized he was wearing pyjamas. His head swam, there was a pounding at the back of his skull. He saw his watch on the bedside table, picked it up. Two o'clock. He gazed out of the window. Black as pitch. He fastened the watch on his wrist.

Standing up, he nearly fell down, grabbed for the edge of the bed, saved himself. Unsteadily, he walked to the window. Outside a parking area. He saw his own car. He took several deep breaths. A bit better. Where the devil were his clothes?

He stumbled towards a cupboard, opened it, found the clothes hanging inside. Leaning against the wall, he stripped off the pyjama trousers, hauled on his underpants, his own trousers. He wrestled himself inside his shirt, stuffed his tie inside a pocket, sat down on a chair and eased his feet into socks and shoes. He was fully dressed when the nurse flew into the room.

'Mr Nield! What *are* you doing? Get back into bed at once . . .'

'I'm leaving . . .'

A man in a white coat who had glanced through the window came in. He heard Nield's reply. Walking over, he took hold of him by the arm.

'I'm Dr Nicholson. You're suffering a case of mild . . . that is, severe . . . concussion. You must . . .'

'Where is this hospital?'

'The Queen Elizabeth, King's Lynn . . .'

'And . . . what day is it? Wednesday?'

'Thursday. Early morning . . .'

'That's what . . . I meant. How long have I . . .'

'You were brought in only four hours ago. I really insist you must get back into bed. This is a reaction from the concussion. You don't know what you're doing.'

'Want to bet?'

Nield forced himself to grin. God knows how he managed it. He was using up all his willpower to stay on his feet. Couldn't call Park Crescent from here. Too public. He got his jacket on. Fully dressed, his morale rose. He could sort these people out.

'My personal effects. My wallet. Keys . . .'

'At the reception desk, locked away safely.'

'Lay on, MacDuff.'

'I beg your pardon.'

A bit stiff-necked. Stuffy type, Dr Nicholson. Still, trying to do his job. Nield had a terrible thirst. He looked round, saw a jug covered with a cloth, a glass beside it.

'I could do with a drink of water.'

He moved slowly towards the table. The nurse ran past him – as he had hoped. He'd have spilt more on the floor than in the glass. She filled it, gave it to him with tight lips. He drank the lot in four separate gulps, thanked the nurse and looked at Nicholson.

'Which way to reception desk?'

'I'll show you.' Nicholson continued his efforts as they went down a long silent corridor. 'I can't recommend this course of action at all. You're not a fit man.'

'But you can't keep me here. I'm discharging myself.'

'I'd rather gathered that,' Nicholson said drily. 'Here is the desk. Nurse, Mr Nield requires his personal effects. See he signs a receipt.' He looked at Nield. 'I refuse to call a cab. If you must be so foolish you do that yourself. And keep those bandages on. Go straight to your local doctor when you get home. We got your details from your driving licence.'

'Thank you. And Good Night,' said Nield, turning to the nurse.

He told her he wanted a breath of fresh air just outside first and left the building. He had a little trouble finding the car park. No one was about as he climbed behind the wheel, fastened his belt and started the engine.

He soon found himself in a familiar part of King's Lynn and took the turning for London. Nield still felt peculiar. There were moments when his vision blurred. At that time

343

of night the road was deserted but he slowed when he saw an isolated pair of headlights approaching. He wasn't worried about himself, but he had to think of other people.

He had driven through Woburn when the strain began to tell. He found it harder to concentrate. No point in trying to find a public phone box. He gritted his teeth and drove on, knowing he could reach Park Crescent by dawn on the traffic-free roads. That was, if he could keep control of himself – and the car.

'*Lesbos*,' Tweed repeated. 'The ship carrying all those explosives was wrecked off the Norfolk coast. I've been a complete idiot. When Bellenger from the Admiralty told me that bomb on Paula's doorstep was the latest Soviet type I should have guessed. Somehow they transported that hellish armoury ashore, then stored it under our noses.'

'And now you know where?' Newman said.

'Cockley Ford. Those heavy wheel tracks leading from the entrance to the churchyard to Sir John Leinster's mausoleum.'

'Clever bloody Klein,' Newman remarked. 'Hid the stuff where no one would think of looking. So, is the target still Antwerp?'

'No,' Tweed said grimly. 'I've just realized the significance of the strange incident Colonel Ralston told me about aboard his cruiser. Remember he grasped that Klein's English wasn't perfect? Ralston made some remark to Klein about him talking Double Dutch. Klein flew at him. That Sergeant Bradley had to separate them.'

'I'm not following you,' Butler remarked.

'Double-Dutch,' Tweed repeated. 'Klein had never heard the colloquial phrase. He didn't like – was unnerved by – Ralston's reference to Dutch. Because the target is Dutch – not Belgian. It's been staring us in the face. It's Europort, the gateway to Europe.'

'And how is Klein going to transport the explosives across the North Sea?'

344

'Maybe Nield can tell us that. I'll get Monica on the phone. Which means back to Grand'Place and the scrambler. Nield may have found the key we've been looking for.'

'Nield,' Butler commented, 'is usually in the right place at the right moment.'

40

The Met forecast had held. The sea was calm as the proverbial millpond. Inside the bridge of the coaster, midway across the North Sea, Caleb Fox bent over a chart with Dr Portch beside him. The engines were stopped, the vessel drifted gently with the current, no other ship was in sight on radar.

'This is where they meet us,' Fox said. 'We'll wait until we get the signal they're close, then I'll tell the First Mate.'

'Expect any trouble?'

'I'm master of this vessel,' the weasely Fox replied. 'And here they come.'

He had glanced to the port side facing Holland. In the black moonless light a green light was flashing. Three longs, three shorts, two longs. The First Mate came on to the bridge and asked his question.

'Why are we waiting here, Skipper?'

'We're taking on board a group of stevedores. Orders from Head Office. It's a bit secret. Don't tell the crew the real reason, Bates.'

'Which is?'

'After we've unloaded Dr Portch's stuff at Europort we sail up to Hamburg. Some shipyard has a strike. Shipyard owners are taking on this new lot of stevedores, sacking the lot on strike. And we're being well paid for the job.

Bonus in it for you later, Bates. Inform the crew we'll have extra passengers. Handle it in your own way.'

'I'd better go and make preparations. How many steve-dores?'

'A dozen I was told. We'll have to see, won't we?'

Half an hour later four lighters hove to on the port side, two ladders had been slung over the coaster's hull, the first man to swarm up and come aboard was Grand-Pierre. He carried a bedroll and a small case. Other men dressed in seamen's gear climbed rapidly up and dropped on deck. Grand-Pierre made straight for the engine room, slamming shut the steel door behind him, gazing down from an iron platform as a stench of oil hit his nostrils.

Two men in the engine room, he'd been told. He saw them gazing up at him. He dumped his case, tucked the bedroll under one powerful arm, descended the ladder. Reaching the bottom, he walked towards the two men who stood by a mass of dials and gauges.

He reached his right hand inside the bedroll, produced the Luger pistol, shot the first man, then the second. The echoes of the reports resounded round the engine room. He moved close to the first slumped body, pressed the Luger muzzle close to the slumped man's skull, pulled the trigger. He performed the same act with the second sprawled body.

Moving with ape-like agility for a man of his size, he scrambled back up the ladder to the platform. He had the Luger out of sight behind his back when Sadler, who was puzzled about something he couldn't yet put his finger on, opened the engine-room door. Grand-Pierre's bulk blocked his view of the engine room.

'What the hell are you doing here?' Sadler demanded.

The Frenchman peered out. The corridor was deserted in both directions. He aimed the Luger and pulled the trigger in one movement. The heavy slug caught Sadler in the chest and slammed his body back against the wall.

'*Merde*,' muttered Grand-Pierre. Why had he come snooping round at this moment. He hoisted the body over his shoulder, walked back on to the platform, using one hand to shut the door. Perching on the edge of the platform, he dropped his burden. It hit the metal floor thirty feet below with a soft thud. No need for a second bullet there.

Opening the door again, he looked out and saw one of his men carrying another member of the crew towards the engine room. Someone shouted from the other end of the corridor. A crewman was hurrying towards the man stooped under the weight of his dead burden.

'What's the matter with Callaby?' the crewman shouted.

Grand-Pierre waited until he was close, then shot him twice. Gesturing towards the platform to his team member, he picked up the fourth corpse and, as arranged beforehand, dumped that over the edge.

He took a grubby piece of paper out of his pocket as his own man hurried away. Four dealt with out of a crew of nine. An extra name was on the list. A good preliminary exercise for his team, Grand-Pierre thought, a minor trial run for what was to come at Europoort and Rotterdam.

'I tried to contact Nield,' Monica told Tweed over the phone as he sat in Benoit's office for the second time that night. 'When he didn't report in I called The Duke's Head. That was at eleven-thirty in the evening. They said his key was still with reception, that he hadn't returned. I'm worried.'

'Don't,' Tweed urged. 'Pete can look after himself. I may be leaving Brussels shortly, but they'll know here where to find me. Better use the code word Ghent to identify yourself. Got it?'

'Yes, Ghent. Are you all right? You're talking fast – the way you do when you're tired.'

'Perfectly OK. Next thing. I want Commander Bellenger from Admiralty to fly over here at once. He'll react when you tell him I asked for him. Tell him to come to Grand' Place. Also call Number Ten. Say I want the SAS team waiting to fly to Schiphol in Holland now. To stand by for further instructions. I'll try and call the PM myself but I may not get her.'

'You will if you call now. She phoned me a few minutes ago – to ask if I had any news from you. I'd better get off the line. And I'll call when I hear from Nield. Not that much seems to be happening up there.'

'You might be surprised,' Tweed said grimly and rang off.

He looked at Newman and Butler, explained he had to call the PM. They went into the anteroom next door and waited. Butler was not his normal phlegmatic self. He asked Newman for a cigarette although he rarely smoked.

'I'm worried about Nield,' he admitted. 'I was the one who shoved him out on a limb, left him in Norfolk by himself.'

'You heard Tweed say he can look after himself.'

'That's true. But we normally work as a team . . .'

'You are doing right now,' Newman assured him. 'But this time long distance.'

A few minutes later Tweed asked them back into Benoit's office. His expression was grim but before he could explain Benoit came into the room, slammed the door and sat down at the table.

'Coffee is coming. It's going to be a long night. How are things, Tweed?'

'This is confidential. I've spoken to the PM. She agrees with my reasoning that Europort is the target. But she has a problem. She needs evidence to convince the Dutch Government. What I have isn't enough . . .' He recalled for Benoit's benefit his conversation with Newman and Butler in his hotel room. Benoit shook his head.

'I know you, Tweed. I think you could be right. Although it could still be Antwerp. But can I convince my Minister? Like hell I can. The same problem – he wants ironclad evidence before he'll put Antwerp on siege alert. The most I could get is an order for the Antwerp port authority to reinforce security – which means no more than bringing another dozen men back on duty.'

'What about the SAS team?' asked Newman.

'They would be your first thought,' Tweed observed, 'considering you once served with them for a short time.'

'He did?' Benoit was surprised. 'When was that?'

'Oh when I was commissioned to do a series of articles on the organization. To get the proper flavour I asked to be put on one of their courses. It was sheer bloody murder, but I survived. Largely due to the prodding I got from the commander, Blade. Not his real name.'

'Blade,' Tweed informed him, 'is in charge of the team flying in to Schiphol tonight.'

'They are going in then?'

'The PM's decision. She's informing the Dutch Government as the team is in the air. They can always fly back if she can't persuade The Hague of the appalling danger they face. Which brings me to a further request I have to make,' he said, turning to Benoit. 'Would you loan us that Alouette again – to fly me to Rotterdam tonight with Newman and Butler? Another pilot is available, I hope?'

'You need the same chap, Georges Quintin. He took us down the hole in the clouds on the Meuse when you spotted that sunken barge. If Rotterdam gets hairy, he's your man. He ate a meal at the airport and went straight to sleep. He'll be fresher than any of us.'

'Us?'

'I think I'm coming with you. You know Van Gorp, chief of police in The Hague?'

'Yes. Very unorthodox in his methods. Nearly sacked twice for being too tough, for taking decisions on his own in emergencies.'

'A close friend of mine. Together we may be able to convince him. Then he'll act.'

'Talking about that sunken barge, the *Gargantua*, we still have to locate the other barge, the *Erika*, and its owner, Joseph Haber. I'm still convinced he's transporting those timer devices which detonate the explosives. Find Haber, we have definitely found the target.'

'No news yet, I fear. I checked by phone from the

Minister's house. Last seen just south of Liège. Doesn't tell us much.'

Tweed took his charts of the canal system from the brief-case he carried everywhere. He studied them for a moment. 'Just south of Liège,' he commented. 'He could have continued north up the Meuse – to where it becomes the Maas in Holland. Or he could have moved into the Albert Canal . . .'

'Which would lead him direct to Antwerp,' Benoit pointed out.

'I still say Europort,' Tweed insisted. 'And talking about Haber, we've left Paula behind in Dinant trying to locate his kidnapped wife and child. I want her to be able to get in touch with me.'

'Easy,' replied Benoit. 'Leave it to me. She's searching with that competent-looking policeman, Pierre. I'll call Dinant police HQ, leave a message for her to phone here. You leave your own message.'

'Which will say?' Newman asked. 'She's had a pretty gruelling time already.'

'So,' Tweed responded, 'we'll see what she's really made of.' He looked at Benoit. 'Where shall we be staying in Rotterdam?'

'The Hilton. It's central.' He stood up. 'I'll go and get an assistant to deal with it, book us rooms there, including one for Paula. Also, I'll warn Chief of Police Van Gorp we're on our way.'

As he left the room Tweed scribbled a note for Paula. Newman was shaking his head when he glanced up. 'All right, Bob,' he said, 'you like the girl. So do I. She'll never forgive me if she isn't in at the death.'

'Depends whose death it is,' Newman snapped.

Klein left the night train at Antwerp Central. The car he had phoned the hire people for was waiting for him outside the station. A black BMW. He showed identification in the name Peter Conway in the form of a forged driving licence. He paid the fee for the special service involved, climbed behind the wheel and drove to the Plaza Hotel.

He parked a short distance back from but with a good view of the entrance. At Brussels Midi he'd seen Lara board a coach of the same express he'd travelled on. He sat waiting, knowing she would arrive soon. Taxis had been scarce at Antwerp station in the middle of the night. But sooner or later she would arrive. Then he would have to move quickly.

'One thing I forgot to tell you,' Benoit said when he returned to his office. 'That French ferret who never lets go – The Parrot – reported Lara Seagrave left the Mayfair Hotel earlier this evening. She had dinner at the Hilton. A restaurant called the *Maison de Bœuf*, he thinks. He nearly lost her. She was on foot and he had to park his motor-cycle. He walked into the lobby just in time to see her enter an elevator in the distance. It stopped at the first floor and came down again empty. That restaurant is on the first floor. He sat it out in the lobby until she reappeared and walked back to the Mayfair.'

'Doesn't he ever give up?' asked Tweed.

'Never. We've offered him relief, to put one of our own officers on the job. He agrees – for a few hours. Then he's back again. Highly irregular – a French detective operating here. But his sheer doggedness has impressed the hell out of us. Says that he followed her from Marseilles!'

'He did just that,' said Tweed. 'Ferret is the word. Now, I need to keep in close touch with Park Crescent.'

'All arranged. When that Monica of yours phones we'll give her your room number at the Hilton, Rotterdam. And we can take a message while we're airborne.'

'The Alouette is ready?'

'Quintin, the pilot, phoned me. He'll take off the moment we reach Brussels Airport.'

Klein watched Lara get out of the cab in front of the Plaza. She took her time paying the fare and while she did this a second cab appeared in his rear view mirror and crawled to a stop about thirty yards behind him. Klein waited for someone to alight from the second cab. No one did.

He cursed inwardly as Lara disappeared inside the hotel. At the last moment she was being tracked. How the devil could that have happened? He waited several minutes and then a small man alighted from the cab and trudged along the sidewalk.

Hands in pockets, The Parrot walked past the BMW. Glancing inside he saw a man wearing a trilby hat slumped behind the wheel, head turned away, obviously fast asleep. Probably resting after an evening's hard drinking. The Parrot went inside the hotel, approached the receptionist behind the counter. He spoke in English.

'I have a message for a young lady I believe has just arrived. A Miss Smith.'

The sharp-eyed night clerk shook his head. 'No one of that name registered here.'

'I thought I saw her walk in just a few minutes ago,' The Parrot persisted.

'You must be mistaken. No one of that name here.'

The Parrot walked back to his cab. He'd hoped to extract the name Lara was using. He climbed inside the cab, settled down to wait. He must be losing his grip. He felt incredibly tired. Eyes pricking, every limb aching.

Klein, watching him in the mirror, cursed again. He took one of his quick decisions. Starting the engine, he revved it up several times as though he'd had trouble starting it. Which would explain his parking at the kerb in the middle of the night. Then he drove off.

Arriving at Boekstraat, he parked at the entrance, put on a pair of dark glasses and walked to the sleazy hotel where he'd met Lara during her earlier trip to Antwerp, the hotel where Chabot and Hipper were staying.

The same sordid woman was sitting behind her counter. He gave the names his men were using, obtained the room numbers and went up and woke them in turn. He handed Hipper an unmarked map of Delft, the ancient Dutch town a few miles north of Rotterdam. His index finger pin-pointed the location of a camp site.

'It's near Delft-Noord. Get dressed at once. Drive straight to this site. A man called Legaud will receive you. Did you deal with Haber's family at the mill?'

'They'll be dead by now.'

His next stop was at the hotel where Marler was staying under an assumed name. Unlike Hipper and Chabot, Marler was fully dressed.

'I had a hunch you'd turn up tonight,' he drawled.

'Why?' There was a whiplash in Klein's tone, his suspicion surfacing instantly.

'After hanging about forever in Bouillon you suddenly start moving me about like a chess piece. Obvious conclusion? We are about to start the operation. Where to now?'

'You leave at once. You've had bad news . . .'

'Maybe that's true . . .'

'I don't like jokes. Drive to Rotterdam. A room has been reserved at the Hilton. In the name Harvey Miller. I want you there by morning.'

'Piece of cake . . .'

Still fuming, Klein left and drove back to the district where the Plaza was located. Marler always managed to irk him. He drove round, studying the layout until he came to a one-way street – traffic to come the other way only. A straight street and deserted at that hour. He checked his map. The ideal place to shake off whoever was watching Lara.

He pulled in by a call box, got out and dialled the Plaza's number, asking for Lara by the name she'd registered under. She sounded surprisingly alert. He began talking about nothing in particular, like a boy friend calling, then his voice changed.

'Stop listening to our conversation. Get off the bloody line or I'll report you to the manager . . .'

There was a click. On the switchboard the bored night operator swore. How the hell had the caller guessed?

353

Klein then gave her specific instructions as to what to do. He rang off, went back to the car.

He reached the Plaza earlier than he'd expected, pulling in at the kerb a distance behind the cab which was still parked in the same place.

His eyes narrowed as he saw Lara, carrying her case, walking back up the street and going back inside the Plaza. Checking his watch, Klein saw he was five minutes early. Why was she wandering about?

Precisely five minutes later Lara reappeared, walking down the street in the opposite direction, again carrying her case. The cab started up, crawling after her. Klein tapped fingers on the wheel, waiting. She was almost out of sight when he started the car, drove forward at speed.

The Parrot saw the BMW pass his cab at high speed. It pulled in alongside Lara, who hauled open the passenger seat door, jumped inside, and the BMW sped off. 'Don't lose that car!' The Parrot called out to his driver.

'All right, all right. He's exceeding the limit . . .'

'There's a big tip to keep up.'

The cab driver increased speed. The BMW was still in sight. It braked suddenly, swung left into a side street, accelerated. Arriving at the entrance the cab driver stopped.

'Can't follow him up there. One-way street . . .'

'Follow him! Here . . .' The Parrot shoved a handful of banknotes at the driver. 'That makes it worth your while . . .'

'Nothing makes it worth my while to lose my licence. Meet a patrol car and . . .' The driver glanced down the street. 'In any case, he's gone.'

The Parrot followed his gaze. The street was empty. Yes, blast it, he'd gone.

A short while earlier at Park Crescent the call had come through to Monica. In the middle of the ruddy night. She'd hauled from a cupboard Tweed's camp bed, fixed it up

354

with blankets and a pillow. She'd just laid her head on that pillow when the phone rang.

Switching on the table lamp she'd perched against the back of a chair, she reached for the phone. Sitting up straight she suppressed a yawn, then came awake suddenly. It was Olympus.

'Monica? Good. I'm in a rush. It isn't Antwerp. Could be Europoort, Rotterdam. *Could* be. Got it?'

Then he – she – Monica couldn't even guess at the sex of the caller, was gone. She stood up, lifted the phone, padded over to the desk in her stockinged feet and sat down. She had to call Grand'Place, Brussels. Urgently.

Grand-Pierre stood on the bridge of the coaster with Portch and Caleb Fox. Eight of the crew were dead, bodies dumped in the engine room. He watched from the window on the port side where one of his team was operating the deck winch, swinging over the side the last load in its net down to the waiting lighter.

The other two lighters had been loaded and had left, on their way to the Dutch coast with their deadly cargo. Grand-Pierre was sweating. He'd had a busy night.

Earlier he had driven from Delft to Schiphol Airport to meet Kurt Saur, the Austrian pilot, when he landed the two Sikorsky helicopters, now safely tucked away at a remote corner of the airfield. Saur and his co-pilot, with the two-man crew of the second machine, were sleeping at a hotel near the airport.

Grand-Pierre had then driven – often exceeding the speed limit – along the magnificent highway to Rotterdam where he had boarded one of the three lighters. They had immediately put to sea. Before unloading started the huge Frenchman had descended to the coaster's hold. With the aid of a torch he had searched for a small crate marked with a minute blue cross at one corner. While Portch chatted with Fox on the bridge he had taken the small crate from the hold and made his way to the engine room.

Stepping over the huddle of corpses at the foot of the ladder, he had placed the crate in a certain position in the hold. Using a screwdriver and chisel, he had eased off one side of the crate. Inside it was packed with straw.

Locating the bomb, he had turned a switch which activated the radio waveband. The control box he carried concealed in a pocket of his windcheater was already adjusted to precisely the same waveband.

'Easy this time compared to the *Lesbos*,' he said to Portch on the bridge.

'Yes, indeed,' Portch replied in French. 'That was a . . . messy business . . .'

Again they had transferred the explosives in the middle of the night well out in the North Sea. Earlier, in Rotterdam, Portch had laced the British crew's bottles of drink with a mild dose of sedative, enough to put them all to sleep. He had diagnosed food poisoning and they had been put to bed in a seamen's hostel.

A waiting crew of Algerians collected by Grand-Pierre took over duty on the coaster for that crossing to Blakeney. In the middle of the night the rendezvous had been made with the *Lesbos*. The Greek crew had packed the bombs inside the empty crates supposed to contain Portch's furniture – already packed in as few crates as possible.

Grand-Pierre had opened the stop-cocks of the *Lesbos* after being lowered over the side to change the name of the ship. Earlier he had shot the Greek crew, bound the bodies in heavy chains and thrown them overboard where the waters of the North Sea were deep.

The only thing which had gone wrong was the *Lesbos* had refused to sink, had been washed ashore on a sandbank near Brancaster, driven there by one of the sudden storms which blow up in the North Sea.

Here again Klein's meticulous attention to detail had paid off. He had instructed Grand-Pierre to lower all lifeboats into the sea and then hole them. It was later presumed the missing crew had perished in the same storm which had driven the *Lesbos* on to the sandbank.

'What happened to those work-shy Algerians?' Fox asked. 'The authorities accepted our story that all my crew had been taken sick – especially when it was backed up by Dr Portch.'

'What do you think?' Grand-Pierre lit a small cigar. 'They went back to Marseilles.' He paused while he puffed the cigar. 'They're all twenty fathoms down off the coast of Cassis – with concrete boots to keep them there. Can't trust the bastards.'

'And now,' Portch suggested, seeing the third lighter had completed loading, 'isn't it time we left this ship? For the last time.' Behind Fox's back he exchanged a look with Grand-Pierre.

'And where will you be ending up, Doctor, when it's all over?' enquired Fox. 'Buenos Aires? Or shouldn't I . . .'

He broke off as he felt something hard and metallic press into his left shoulder blade. Grand-Pierre pulled the trigger of the Luger. Fox was hurled against the chart table, fell forward, lay still, hands and arms sprawled over it

'He really thought he was coming with us,' Portch said and he giggled.

'Can't afford loose ends,' replied Grand-Pierre, who had picked up the phrase from Klein. 'Let's leave. After you, Doctor. No, on second thoughts, give me a hand to carry him to the engine room.'

'Is that necessary, seeing that . . .'

'Klein's orders. Leave them all in the engine room, close to the bomb. Very tidy man, Mr Klein. You look thoughtful.'

'Seeing Fox lying there like that I was remembering the night that American, Lee Foley, killed those people at Cockley Ford who wouldn't agree to our plan – no matter how much money they stood to make. Then, of course, Klein had to deal with Mr Foley. I wonder if anyone will ever discover the secret of the seventh grave in the churchyard.'

'Let's move the body,' the Frenchman said impatiently.

They carried it between them, Grand-Pierre lifting the shoulders while Portch carried the legs. The helping hands were welcome to the Frenchman, who was feeling tired after his night's exertions. Standing on the platform above the engine room, they swung the body outwards, let go. It fell on top of the others.

'I'm glad that's over,' Portch remarked. 'Amazing how heavy a corpse can be.'

'I agree,' said Grand-Pierre. 'To be avoided wherever possible.'

He pulled out his Luger, rammed it into Portch's chest, fired twice. Portch grunted, doubled up, fell backwards.

Grand-Pierre waited until the lighter had sailed at least two nautical miles from the drifting coaster. It was still dark but his eyes had become accustomed to the night as he took out the control box. His thumb paused over the button. Were they far enough away? Of course they were. He was fatigued. He pressed the button.

There was a muffled boom. Nothing dramatic. Like the sound of a train approaching through a tunnel. Then the world blew up. The coaster exploded into a myriad fragments. There was an ear-splitting roar. A red flame shot into the sky like a rocket. The flame was extinguished by a giant fountain which hurtled vertically, a plume of surf rising upwards. The sea boiled where the vessel had floated. A vibration struck the lighter. For a few seconds, hanging to a deck rail, Grand-Pierre thought the lighter was capsizing as a massive wave rolled it.

Silence. The crew was awestruck. They gazed at each other, thankful to have survived. And that, Grand-Pierre reminded himself, was the smallest of the bombs and sea-mines.

41

It was when Lara was sitting alongside Klein in the BMW that she realized she'd lost interest in him. All passion spent – wasn't that the phrase? Strange how suddenly all feeling was gone, leaving a vacuum. But in the case of Klein it was good to be free of him emotionally.

The trick now was not to let him know she thought as she gazed at the flatlands in the headlight beams. They had crossed into Holland without any problems and were now beyond Roosendaal; well on the way to Rotterdam. As though reading her mind, Klein glanced at her, his complexion drained of colour.

'In Rotterdam you stay at the Hotel Central on Kruiskade – just down the street from the Hilton. It's as central as its name implies, and not far from police headquarters.'

'That's a good idea?'

'Yes. The police never expect to find suspects under their noses. And by the way, you register as Miss Eva Winter.'

Klein smiled to himself as they crossed a reclaimed polder. Miss *Winter*. It rather suited the grisly role he'd allocated for her to play.

The Alouette was just crossing the frontier into Holland as Benoit returned from the pilot's cabin. Tweed sat by the window with Newman alongside and Butler in front. Tweed was restless, Newman sensed, although he sat like a graven image. He looked up as Benoit stood by Newman, holding a sheaf of papers in his hands.

'Several radio messages. Van Gorp, The Hague police chief, welcomes you to Holland. He's meeting us at the

Hilton. He says if you're coming something must be up. And we've had a report of a large explosion in the North Sea between Norfolk and Europort.'

Tweed glanced at Newman. 'What kind of explosion?'

'No one seems to know. A Nimrod aircraft setting off on a patrol saw it from a distance. When it got there it could find nothing to explain it – no sign of a ship's wreckage. Which is strange. They thought at first a vessel's boilers must have blown.'

Benoit handed the messages to Tweed and went back to the pilot's cabin. Tweed read the signals, handed them to Newman.

'Don't like the sound of that,' he said. 'A normal explosion, there should have been plenty of wreckage . . .'

'Whereas a Triton Three bomb might leave nothing behind?'

'Exactly. I do wish we had news from Nield. Not like him to leave us in the dark. And still no news of that bargee, Haber. We'll just have to wait.'

Nield was nearly at the end of his tether as he drove through the deserted streets of London. Thank God he'd arrived before traffic built up. His head was pounding like a bass drum, his vision blurring. With a sigh of relief he pulled up outside Park Crescent.

George, the all-night doorman, let him in, stared at his bandaged head. 'My, been in the wars, sir?'

'Something like that.'

He hauled himself up the stairs, saw a light under the door to Tweed's office, pushed it open. Monica, now fully dressed, also stared at him. He sagged into Tweed's armchair, began talking quickly while she made coffee. She made him keep quiet until he'd drunk the first cup, then went on listening.

'That's it,' he said eventually. 'You know where Tweed is?'

'In Brussels last night. I'll send a message via police HQ in Brussels after I've called a doctor . . .'

'Send the message first.'

'As soon as I've called the doctor,' she said firmly.

The Alouette had just landed when Benoit hurried from the pilot's cabin with more signals. He handed them to Tweed who scanned them quickly. He pursed his lips and stared outside where several cars were drawn up.

'Van Gorp sent them to meet us,' Benoit explained.

'What's happened?' asked Newman.

'I think we were right about that explosion at sea. Nield drove through the night to Park Cresent. In Blakeney last night he watched that coaster of Caleb Fox's being loaded with so-called furniture belonging to Dr Portch. Portch has left Norfolk to take up a post in, guess where – here in Holland.'

'You think something went wrong? That the coaster carried the whole Triton Three armament and blew up?'

'No. I see the hand of Klein behind that. I'm sure he offloaded all the bombs and sea-mines except one. He couldn't leave the coaster's crew behind to tell the tale. So he liquidated every man jack of them. A massacre. Fiend is the word for Klein. But it follows the same pattern. The one that started in Marseilles and Geneva. Leave no one alive who has any knowledge. Those bombs and sea-mines have been landed somewhere in Holland by some method. I'm really afraid, Bob.'

Newman stared at him. He'd never heard Tweed say anything like that before. 'That's it?' he enquired.

'No. Van Gorp reports they've found Joseph Haber. Don't too much like the sound of that either. Just that they've found him.'

'So, that's it.'

'Not quite. Monica has transmitted another brief message from Olympus.' He kept his voice low. 'My contact inside Klein's organization. The message is that it's not Antwerp – it's Europort. Probably.'

'Olympus never seems sure . . .'

'Which is because I'm certain Klein is working on the cell system. Maybe only two or three members of his team actually know each other. And no one except Klein will know the target until the last moment. He's a devil – his security is very professional. But then, considering his background and training, it would be. And that may be the last message I receive from Olympus. I'm very worried about my contact.'

'Why?'

'Because Klein is so clever. Olympus is now in mortal danger.'

Klein dropped Lara at the entrance to Kruiskade opposite the Hilton. She walked the short distance to the Hotel Central, an old five-storey building with a façade which had survived the wartime bombing.

Reception was expecting her, a room had been reserved, she registered and went up to her room on the second floor. As the door closed on the porter she sank on to the bed. Was this the objective at long last?

Lara felt unsure – Klein had led her such a dance. There were other potential targets further north. The German ports of Bremen and Hamburg. On the way Klein had given her the usual instructions.

Check Europort after hiring a car. Check the security. And check the potential for a safe escape route – more than one if possible.

She checked her watch. 7.30 a.m. Better get on with it. She unlocked her suitcase, opened the lid, undid the inner straps to save her clothes from being too compressed. Taking out her camera and binoculars, she went downstairs and had breakfast in the dining room.

She was dressed in her smart gaberdine suit – chosen deliberately before she left the Antwerp hotel. She felt good in it, which helped her keep up a front of still being besotted with Klein.

After breakfast she decided she needed a breath of fresh air to take the ache out of her limbs from travelling in the BMW. She turned left out of the entrance and soon entered a large spacious shopping precinct.

Rotterdam was different from what she'd expected. She'd anticipated a congested mass of concrete blocks. They existed, but the precinct was beautiful. Paved in stone, it was decorated with raised troughs containing evergreen shrubs. Pergolas projected from modern shop fronts. Hanging baskets of flowers were suspended from the overhead beams. She sat on a seat, taking in the beauty of the place. Was it Europort? she kept asking herself. After ten minutes' rest – Lara had enjoyed very little sleep – she walked to the car hire agency whose address she'd obtained from the directory in her bedroom, aided by the street plan obtained from the concierge. Near the agency was a row of phone booths.

'There is the barge, *Erika*, and there is the late Joseph Haber,' said Van Gorp.

Poker-faced, Tweed stepped aboard the barge, followed by Newman and Benoit. They had been driven from the airport to the Hilton. They had dumped their bags. They had driven straight to the huge docking basin of Waal-haven.

It was almost an exact replica of the horror Tweed had seen in the Dames de Meuse – where the other bargee, Broucker, had been buried up to his chest in mud. The *Erika*'s hold still carried its load of gravel. Near the bows two shovels lay where men had carefully started removing gravel – until they unearthed what Tweed now stood staring down at.

Haber was buried up to his chest in gravel. His head flopped back, exposing the rim of dried blood which curved from ear to ear. His mouth was open, slack, and he appeared to be grinning. His skin had a deathly pallor.

'Found him in the middle of the night,' Van Gorp explained. 'Benoit called me, extended the search across the border. We checked and it was reported the barge had been seen in Waalhaven.'

'So,' Tweed said slowly, 'Klein now has the last instruments he needs to organize his catastrophe. The timer devices which will explode the bombs and the sea-mines. Have you issued a general alert? Declared an emergency?'

'No.'

Van Gorp was an impressive-looking man. Towering over Tweed, six feet one tall, in his forties, his hair was greying and he sported a trim moustache. There was a natural air of command about the man, softened by a hint of humour in the eyes. Slim in build with a longish face, he stood in a grey overcoat and a grey trilby hat.

'For God's sake why not?' Tweed rapped out. 'Klein has been here. Haber is wearing his trademark. He carried the timers aboard this barge, I'm certain.'

'I've already spoken with the Minister of the Interior at The Hague. Benoit sent me a long radio message giving me the information you've accumulated.'

'With what result?'

'He's not convinced . . .'

'The same problem I had in Brussels,' Benoit intervened. 'A lack of solid evidence.'

'There's your evidence.' Tweed nodded to Haber, then turned his head away.

'The Minister is attending a cabinet meeting this morning,' Van Gorp continued. 'He promised to bring the matter to their attention. His exact words.'

Tweed glanced at him suspiciously, detecting a touch of irony. Van Gorp stared back, his grey eyes motionless.

'The Dutch Government won't close down Europort without an overwhelming case.'

'Then Klein will close it down for them. You've taken no action at all?'

The Dutchman's eyes twinkled. 'I didn't say that, did I? I believe you. I have cancelled all police leave. I have brought in extra units from The Hague. We are combing the city – looking for any unusual activity. The trouble is you are Secret Service. The Minister made great play with that. Not your scene, man. Tracking bandits.'

'My omission,' Tweed apologized. He produced his warrant card. 'Temporary appointment. I'm a Commander of the Anti-Terrorist Squad.'

Van Gorp grinned. 'Thank you. Now I may have the Minister by the balls. Let's get back to the Hilton fast.' He called out to detectives waiting in a group near the stern. 'Do something about this horror in the gravel. And hurry it up.'

They made their way round the tall white cloth screen erected to shield the barge from public gaze. On their way back in the car Tweed thought about Paula searching for Haber's wife and son.

The car pulled up outside the mill in the middle of the Ardennes. Paula jumped out, followed by her police escort, Pierre. She studied the old stone tower, the shuttered windows, then walked all round it.

'I think this is a very likely prison,' she told him. 'You have the spare set of keys the agent gave you?'

'Yes.' Pierre puckered his lips doubtfully. 'Strictly speaking I need a warrant from a magistrate.'

'Why? We checked the other places yesterday.'

'This one has been bought. Paid for outright.'

'Suppose they're starving inside? A woman with her child?'

'You are very persuasive. After all,' he joked, 'I can only lose my pension.'

The heavy door opened with a groaning creak. Paula followed him inside. Creepy. Pierre switched on his torch. It was Paula who mounted the old circular staircase to the door on the first floor landing. She took a deep breath as

Pierre studied the labels attached to the keys, selected one, thrust it inside the keyhole and turned it.

Taking hold of the ancient handle, he paused, turned it swiftly and entered, his automatic in his hand. Paula followed. At the far circumference of the circular wall a woman with bedraggled hair stood, her arm round a boy.

'Martine Haber?' asked Paula in French.

'Yes. Thank God. Who are you?'

'Paula Grey. Pierre and I have been looking for you, searching empty houses from lists supplied by estate agents. Are you all right?'

'Yes. Perhaps because we didn't drink that.' She pointed to a thermos standing on a crude wooden table. 'It is coffee supplied by the kidnapper, but it tasted odd. So we did not drink any . . .'

'I'll take that,' said Pierre, 'for analysis . . .'

'My husband, Joseph. Is he all right? Do you know where he is? Who are these madmen?'

'We'd better get you both back to Dinant,' Paula said. 'Then I can enquire further.'

Entering the Hilton, Tweed was approached by the concierge who told him there was a gentleman waiting for him in the breakfast room, a Commander Bellenger. Tweed hurried to the room.

'Hello, Tweed. Thought I'd have a spot of breakfast while I waited. Flew over as soon as I'd got the message. Luckily we checked with Brussels before I took off. They told us you were on your way here. Are you on your own?'

'No.' Tweed lowered his voice. 'The Dutch Chief of Police is waiting in my room when you've finished your meal . . .'

'Finished now, old chap. Duty calls.' Bellenger stood up, wiping his mouth with a napkin, leaving his half-eaten meal. 'Get used to sudden calls to action in the Navy,' he continued as they made their way to the elevator. 'Snatch a bite to eat between watches – and before you've swallowed two mouthfuls there's an emergency. There's one here, isn't there?'

'Let's talk with everyone present. And thank you for flying over so quickly. I want you to impress on these people what we're facing. That armoury of explosives – Triton Three – is now hidden somewhere near here, I'm convinced. Target – Europort.'

'Oh God,' Bellenger said as they stepped out of the elevator. 'They could shut down a continent . . .'

In his room Van Gorp waited with Newman, Benoit and Butler. Tweed made quick introductions, then poured another cup of coffee for the bluff, ruddy-faced Bellenger who perched on the arm of a chair.

'Tell them,' said Tweed. He looked at Van Gorp, standing with his back to the window. 'But first you should know a huge quantity of new type of explosive was stolen from a depot inside Soviet Russia . . .'

He phrased the next bit carefully, embroidering to keep his promise of secrecy to Lysenko not to mention Igor Zarov.

'Klein organized the theft of thirty sea-mines and twenty-five bombs of a very advanced type. He used the so-called Free Armenian Movement and others he bribed. That armoury was transported aboard a Greek ship, the *Lesbos*, which vanished into thin air. Only very recently did we realize it is now a wrecked hulk which has lain off the Norfolk coast for months. The armoury was smuggled ashore, hidden inside a hundred-year-old crypt. The whole operation was brilliantly organized – because in Klein we are up against one of the most ruthless men I've ever encountered. I've lost count of the people he's murdered personally to cover his tracks.' Tweed addressed Bellenger. 'I've just returned from viewing his latest victim – Joseph Haber, a bargee from Dinant. He's lying in his own load of gravel aboard a barge in Waalhaven near here, his throat slashed from ear to ear. That was how the timers and control boxes – designed by a Swiss – came to be smuggled into Holland. We've reached today.'

'Very bad news,' Bellenger commented, 'that bit about Swiss-made timers and control boxes.' He looked at Van Gorp. 'I can't tell you how, but I do know the one crude element used in the Soviet mines and bombs is the detonating device.'

'These mines and bombs,' Van Gorp commented, 'must be pretty large – difficult to hide so many.'

'Not at all. It's a great technical breakthrough – achieved, I suspect, with East German scientists. Both bombs and mines will be very light in weight, exceptionally small in size.' He cupped his hands. 'One no larger than a pineapple could entirely destroy a small ship.'

'What about a seven hundred ton coaster?' Newman enquired.

'Wipe it off the face of the earth. You'd have trouble finding any bits left.' He glanced at Tweed. 'I've heard reports there was a mysterious and huge explosion in the North Sea off the Dutch coast last night.'

'That was the coaster – bringing across the armoury. We're sure the armoury was off-loaded on to smaller vessels in the middle of the sea passage from Norfolk to here. Then a bomb was used to eliminate the coaster.'

'Entirely possible,' Bellenger agreed. He looked at Van Gorp. 'And a frightening prospect for you.'

'Just how powerful are these miniaturized mines and bombs?' the Dutchman asked. 'I mean I'd like some idea of the explosive power of this new stuff.'

'Very crudely put, midway between conventional high-explosive and an atom bomb.'

'I see.' Van Gorp's expression was unusually grim. 'As you say, I might have a problem. Where do we start?' he asked Tweed. 'You've been in on this business from the start. You know more than any of us about this Klein. Incidentally, I've informed the Minister of your status with the Anti-Terrorist Squad. You know what he replied? "Well, that regularizes the situation." Just that . . .'

He broke off as the phone rang, picked it up, spoke a

few words in English, then handed it to Tweed. 'For you. A Paula Grey, speaking from Dinant.'

'How is it going, Paula?'

'Fine. Marvellous news!' She sounded jubilant. 'We've found Martine and her son, Lucien.' Her voice became guarded. 'I'm speaking from Dinant police HQ – over an open line.'

'Understood.'

'They're both OK. A bit stressed after their experience – we found them locked up in an old mill tower. I'll be catching a train to Namur, then another from there to Brussels. I'll catch the first flight to Rotterdam. See you at the Hilton.' Her voice changed again. 'Any news of Joseph Haber?'

Tweed braced himself. 'Are Martine and Lucien in the room with you?'

'No, I'm alone, but they're here. Why did you ask that?'

'Bad news, Paula . . .'

'Oh, no. He's not . . . ?'

'Dead. Yes. Found by the Dutch in the middle of the night aboard the *Erika* in a docking basin here. His throat was cut. More of Klein's work.'

'I'll have to tell them – Martine and Lucien . . .'

'Get that policeman, Pierre, to break the news. Police are used to it.'

'I'll leave out the part about his cut throat.' Her tone was firm. 'But I'm going to tell them. Don't try and argue me out of it. See you at the Hilton. I'm going now.'

There was a click at the other end. Tweed replaced the receiver. Gutsy, very gutsy. He told the others the news. It was Newman who reacted first.

'She shouldn't come to Rotterdam. She's had enough. Hell is going to break loose here.'

'It goes with the territory,' Tweed said tersely. He opened his brief-case, took out the Identikit sketch of Igor Zarov and handed it to Van Gorp.

'That's Klein. You might want to make copies and distribute them to your men. And you asked where do we start before I took that call. If you can supply transport I'd like to go out to Europort with Newman – and maybe you, too, Benoit?'

The Belgian nodded agreement as Tweed continued.

'I'm getting to know how Klein's mind works. I might just see something useful. In any case . . .' He gave a grim smile. '. . . it always helps to survey the battlefield before the war starts. Incidentally,' he asked Van Gorp, 'what about the SAS team my PM was flying to Schiphol?'

'I was going to tell you. They've arrived. I offered to provide a room at the airport where they could all kip down while they waited. Their commander, chap called Blade, had other ideas. Insisted they should be scattered in two's and three's. They've left their kit in the chartered plane which flew them in. They're dressed like tourists. Some are sleeping in chairs in the departure lounge.'

'That sounds like Blade,' Newman observed. 'Just as I remember him. Security comes before God with him.'

'Blade is anxious to see you, Tweed, when he can,' Van Gorp went on. 'It's about twenty kilometres to Europort, thirty to the North Sea if you want to go all the way.'

'All the way.'

'Then you could meet Blade here in about three hours' time.'

'Fix it for me.'

'Mind you . . .' Van Gorp hesitated as if embarrassed. 'The Minister was grateful to your PM for SAS support – but he pointed out if we face an emergency it will be up to our own Marines to make any assault on their own. They've already been confined to their barracks. Just in case, he said.'

'Still not convinced?'

'By no means. I doubt if he'll put a strong case before the Cabinet which is now in session. I did my best.' He shrugged, looked down at the Identikit sketch he was still holding. 'At least I can get copies made of this and they'll be distributed within the hour. Excuse me while I attend to it.'

He phoned the desk and shortly afterwards a plainclothes man joined them. Van Gorp gave him the Identikit, speaking in rapid Dutch. When the man had left the room he picked up his trilby.

'The cars are ready. Let's get moving. If Klein is skulking round Rotterdam one of my patrol cars may well spot him with that picture.'

42

In room 904 at the Rotterdam Hilton Marler sat reading *The Times* when the phone rang. Reception informed him that his car was ready, his chauffeur waiting in the lobby. He said thank you, put down the phone.

His car? His chauffeur? What the hell was going on? Slipping on his Aquascutum coat, he unlocked a wardrobe, took out the sports bag containing his dismantled rifle and ammo. No point in leaving that behind.

He pressed the first floor button inside the elevator, got out and slowly descended the staircase for the last flight, his eyes scanning the lobby. A tall slim man in chauffeur's dark uniform and peaked cap stood gazing out of the entrance, gloved hands clasped behind his back.

Marler frowned, wandered over to the reception counter, asked the girl behind it about the call. She pointed to the man by the door.

'There is your chauffeur, sir.'

'Stupid of me.' Marler gave her a beaming smile. 'I missed seeing the chap. Thank you so much.'

As he strolled over the chauffeur swung round, staring at him from behind the tinted glasses so often affected by chauffeurs. Marler paused, still puzzled. The chauffeur spoke.

'Your car is ready when you are, sir,' he said in English.

Only then did Marler realize he was looking at Klein. Bloody clever, he thought. Who notices a chauffeur? Klein stood aside to let Marler walk out first, followed and led him to a BMW parked a few yards up the street.

Opening the rear door, he ushered Marler inside. Glancing up as he settled himself, Marler said, 'Thank you, my man.' He saw for a split second behind the glasses a flash of rage and then Klein got in behind the wheel and drove off, glancing at his passenger in the mirror.

'We are going for a tour of the city,' Klein informed him, 'a tour of the *strategic* sights.'

'So, at long last, we've reached the target?'

'Only if certain information reaches me. Otherwise we will be moving on again.'

'Oh, come off it, Klein! You used the word "strategic". I've got to know whether to take this seriously. I'm a professional – in case you've forgotten. If I know where I am I can be certain to be effective.'

'The first item on our itinerary is Euromast. Remarkable nation, the Dutch. Some of their engineering feats are without precedent. You're carrying your rifle in that bag?'

'I'm not leaving it behind where some curious maid with a duplicate key can open up a wardrobe and start sniffing about.'

The conversation ended on that sharp note and Marler, taking out a street map, opened it up to follow their route. Details of layout, the first essential in any operation. Soon they were driving alongside a wide stretch of water off which stretched a complex system of endless docks. There were freighters, ships of every type, barges berthed everywhere. From his map Marler identified this as the New Waterway or New Maas (Dutch for the continuation of the Meuse into Holland) – the great lifeline of Europe joining up with the Rhine.

Ships' hooters whistled, great barges cruised across its

surface, immense dockside cranes loomed in the distance. Klein slowed down as they drove alongside a large green park on the landward side. He turned a corner where the road ran by the edge of a basin. Marler leaned forward. At the far end of the basin several police launches were moored. Klein had stopped the car, parking it by the kerb.

'We have arrived. You may as well know this is the command centre for the attack.'

Marler alighted, carrying his bag, then stared upwards. It spired vertically towards the clear blue sky, an enormous and shapely circular tower of concrete, a thick column at its base, widening far above his head to a viewing platform, continuing above that – forever it seemed – as a narrower needle to a second viewing point at its distant summit.

'Euromast,' said Klein. 'We go inside. I am the chauffeur you have kindly taken with you to see the view. Check every aspect. This is where you will operate.'

The two unmarked police cars drove along the Maastunnel under the river – a stone's throw from Euromast. Van Gorp drove the first car with Tweed beside him and Newman and Bellenger in the back. The naval commander had immediately accepted the invitation to join them.

'Never seen the biggest port in the world before,' he'd commented. 'The trip will complete my education.'

The second car was driven by a detective who had as passengers Benoit and Butler. Benoit asked the driver a lot of questions. Butler remained silent, listening and observing.

They had left the city behind when Tweed began to take a close interest in the view to his right – towards the river they had passed under. They were now moving along the southern bank.

To their left the view was bleak and monotonous. Like a desert, an impression increased by the sandy plain scattered with scrubby grass, a plain which ran for miles towards the horizon.

373

Gradually Tweed became more and more appalled as he studied the string of industrial and oil complexes bordering the New Waterway. They passed Shell-Mex One, Shell-Mex Two, Esso, Mobil and Gulf.

Each was a vast sprawl of storage tanks like giant white cakes, cat-crackers, refineries festooned with a spider's web of pipes. Each was like a small colony on its own separated from the next by open barren space. By the time they reached Gulf they were, Van Gorp informed them, coming closer to the sea. They passed another Esso depot.

'What do you think, Bellenger?' Tweed asked.

'A bomber's paradise,' the naval commander replied tersely.

'Like to look at the open sea?' Van Gorp suggested.

'Yes, I would.'

The Dutchman swung left round a sharp curve across a canal, turned right off the main highway on to a side road. They were now crossing a kind of no-man's land beyond Europort where the scrub ran away to a distant breakwater. Beyond the hard line of concrete a belt of blue sparkled in the sun. No living soul was in sight and through the open window Tweed felt the whisper of a breeze, smelt more strongly the tang of salt.

'How can you hope to protect all that lot?' Newman asked. 'I haven't seen a single patrol car since we left Rotterdam.'

'Ah!' Van Gorp lifted a hand from the wheel and made an expansive gesture. 'You have just paid me a compliment. My men are there but you don't see them – neither will the bandits, if they come.'

'Bandits? Odd word.'

'I object,' the Dutchman went on, 'to the way these days the term "terrorist" has almost assumed respectability – often the men with flabby minds say they have this cause, that cause. They are ruthless and murderous bandits. Now, I think we'll stop here, Tweed. Maybe have a little walk.'

The soft breeze had faded as Van Gorp led them towards a distant lighthouse alongside the breakwater. Tweed scrambled to the top of the breakwater, stared across the North Sea as calm as the proverbial millpond. In the lee of another arm of the breakwater a man sat in a large outboard dinghy with a fishing rod. Van Gorp, who had joined him, pointed out the lone figure.

'A favourite Dutch pastime – fishing. And out there the catch can be good.'

Tweed was staring at the entrance to the New Waterway where a large dredger with a scoop was working. Taking out his binoculars, he swept the vessel slowly. It was even larger than he had realized, a vast floating platform.

'We need to clear the channel constantly,' Van Gorp remarked. 'We cannot afford to let it get silted up. Those men are always working. Have you seen all you wish to?'

'I think so, yes.'

He strolled back with Bellenger and Newman to the cars parked some distance away. Van Gorp's long legs took him ahead with great strides accompanied by Benoit and Butler who hurried to keep up.

'What do you think?' Tweed asked. 'About the protection he's had the nerve to organize.'

'Undoubtedly he's done his best – probably better than most.' Bellenger paused. 'But from what you've told me about Klein I'm not happy – not happy at all.'

On their way back to Rotterdam they passed a chauffeur-driven BMW heading out towards where they'd come from. Tweed noticed the single passenger in the back, a man slumped with his hat tipped over his eyes. Obviously fast asleep. Some oil executive.

Inside the BMW Klein drove along the highway while from under his hat Marler peered at the vast installations. Ten minutes later Klein followed the same route over the canal and along the side road towards the breakwater.

'You are getting the picture?' Klein enquired.

'It's rather large.'

Marler, observing the road ahead was traffic-free, sat up

and pushed his hat back over his head. He yawned. From Klein's expression in the mirror behind the tinted glasses he gathered his comment had not been appreciated.

'It is the biggest target on the European mainland,' Klein responded. 'And we have the power to destroy the whole thing.'

'Good for you. I wouldn't mind stretching my legs when we can.'

'Which is exactly what we are going to do.'

Klein pulled off the side road and bumped over the scrub land. He stopped close to the breakwater, switched off the engine, got out and opened the rear door. 'Just in case we are watched,' he explained, 'although it is unlikely.'

'Thank you, my man.'

Pushing his hands inside his coat pockets, Marler ran agilely up the slanting wall of the breakwater, standing very close to where Tweed had perched earlier. Klein joined him after collecting a pair of high-powered binoculars. He glanced to where a huddled figure sat motionless with a fishing rod in a dinghy.

'Crazy waste of time. The Dutch are a dull nation.'

He focused the binoculars on the dredger, sweeping the lenses slowly from stem to stern. He handed the glasses to Marler. 'You might care to take a look while I check the boot.'

Returning to the car, he unlocked the boot, removed a sheet of canvas and picked up a length of rope he'd purchased from a ship's chandler. Another length lay looped in the corner. The rope he was holding had been tied at one end into a noose like a hangman's. He tested the knot to make sure it slid easily. The noose was roughly of the diameter needed to place round a human neck.

Satisfied that it worked, he replaced it inside the boot. He covered both lengths with canvas, relocked the boot and waited as Marler ran down the side of the breakwater. He handed the binoculars back as he made the remark.

'Big job, that dredger.'

'It will be the first to go – blocking the channel to larger shipping.'

'How many crew aboard? They'll go, too.'

'A crew of eighteen.'

Marler shrugged. 'It's your ball game. Remarkable the way you have the whole plan inside your head. But supposing we died in a car crash on the way back to Rotterdam?'

'The operation would go ahead.' Klein smiled bleakly. 'I have one other man who knows as much as I do. A formidable Frenchman you haven't met yet. I suggest we drive back now, you've seen the vast location of the operation.'

'But why do I need to see that?' Marler pressed. He lit a cigarette as Klein paused. 'Come on, I have to know what I'm doing.'

'A situation could arise when your services could be called for out here. Doubtful, but not impossible.' Klein's natural impatience showed. 'Now, let's move. We'll eat at a small place on the way back. It may not be Cordon Bleu but it will fill our stomachs.'

'And when does the operation start?'

'Soon,' Klein assured him. 'Soon . . .'

The 50,000-ton cruise liner *Adenauer* was at sea off the West Frisian Islands, sailing steadily south on course for its rendezvous off Europort. Just before leaving Hamburg there had been a few minutes of excitement for passengers lining the rails.

A stretched black Mercedes limousine – accompanied by police outriders – had pulled in to the dockside. A late middle-aged man and a woman had emerged and boarded the ship quickly. One of the Americans looking down on the gangway grabbed his wife by the arm.

'Jesus, honey! That's the US Secretary of State, Waldo Schulzberger.'

'I do believe it is,' she'd replied with a note of awe.

The Secretary of State had been ushered by the captain

himself to their most luxurious stateroom. The wire services were already buzzing with the report filed by an eagle-eyed German reporter on the dockside. Schulzberger was taking a brief respite from his arduous duties.

Approaching Europort from the south the 500,000-ton tanker had received from Rotterdam Marine Control a further signal warning that there might be a delay before it could dock. The master of the *Cayman Conqueror* acknowledged receipt of the signal, gave the order for a slight reduction in speed.

Twenty miles astern the 350,000-ton tanker, *Easter Island*, also received the same warning. Its skipper issued the same instruction to lose speed. Captain Williams shrugged and gave his First Officer a wry grin. 'It's going to be Piccadilly Circus at Europort. Business as usual. Keep an eye on that freighter astern . . .'

Captain Salvi aboard the 10,000-ton freighter *Otranto* reacted to his signal with resignation. It probably meant a further addition to the penalty clause for delay in delivery of his cargo. Well, that was not his problem. Let the lawyers sort it out when the time came. That was what they were paid their fat fees for. A uniformed waiter rushed on to the bridge and paused. Salvi asked what was the trouble now?

'The Director's wife is wondering where you are. She likes to have you at the dinner table.'

'Is that fat cow in love with me? All right, I'm coming . . .'

Astern of the *Otranto* the three large container vessels from Africa were manoeuvring for position, each trying to get ahead of the others to offload at Europort first. To get the best price for their cargo of soya bean meal. The signals caused a furious reaction from all three skippers, but they stopped the race, slowing down reluctantly.

*

Klein drove back under the river through the Maastunnel, passed through Rotterdam and speeded up outside the city on the way to Delft. He glanced at Marler who had not said a word since they left the North Sea breakwater. The Englishman was gazing out of the window.

'See any signs of unusual activity?' Klein asked.

'Exactly what I've been looking for. Negative. I thought we were going to eat.'

'We are. They have no idea we're here.'

'I should damn well hope not.'

Klein glanced at his watch, saw they were early for his rendezvous with Grand-Pierre, changed his route. Instead of by-passing the town of Delft he turned into its maze of old cobbled streets lining the canals. Crossing a hump-backed bridge, he headed north out of the town and past a series of camp sites crammed with camper vehicles. He pulled up outside a single-storey building with a crooked roof and a view of tables laid for meals beyond the windows.

'We eat here,' he announced.

'About bloody time.'

They were half way through the main course when a large man wearing denims and a windcheater strolled past. Klein said he'd be back shortly and went outside. Grand-Pierre stood by the entrance, lighting a cigarette.

The street was deserted. Beyond the restaurant was a handful of small shops which served the camp sites as their main customers. The sun shone down out of a cloudless sky.

'Is everything going according to plan?' Klein demanded. 'I presume everyone is in position?'

'The scuba divers who will attach the mines to those ships are scattered along the coast, waiting in their dinghies.'

'I saw one fishing at the end of the breakwater near the dredger. The others join him later?'

'As planned. I still think we should have used underwater sleds to carry the divers and the mines to their targets – it would be quicker, less risk of being spotted.'

'We've argued that out earlier,' Klein said coldly.

Grand-Pierre showed an unusual trace of excitement. 'Have you seen the papers? A stop press item reports Schulzberger, the American Secretary of State, is aboard the *Adenauer* with his wife.'

'Yes. Which is good news and bad.'

'I don't understand . . .'

'Good because it will put more pressure on Washington not to interfere. Bad because there's likely to be extra security aboard the *Adenauer*. American security – and they may use sonar. Which shows I was right not to use those sleds – sonar would pick them up. Dinghies they'll miss. What about the fishing boats?'

'Two are marked for our use. In each case the skippers' wives have been located. They'll be grabbed just before we seize the fishing boats, taken on board. With a knife at their throats the skippers will do what we want. One is allocated to take the dinghies close to the *Adenauer*, then drop them overboard. Later it deals with the *Cayman Conqueror* tanker. The second fishing boat mines the other vessels.'

'And the sea-mines are aboard these dinghies?'

Grand-Pierre checked his watch. 'They will be within the hour.'

'And Legaud's CRS command vehicle?'

'Tucked away inside that garage we hired in Rotterdam.'

'What about the team which will assault Euromast?'

'Inside another resprayed van on the camp site. They will be leaving soon now.'

Klein frowned. 'A bit early, surely?'

'My idea. It will park close to Euromast. The driver and one of the team inside will pass the time apparently changing a wheel.'

'Not a bad touch, that,' Klein admitted grudgingly. 'And they all have their weapons and plenty of ammo?'

'Uzi machine-pistols, grenades, rifles – automatic. All we took from that raid on the Herstal armaments depot in Belgium a couple of days ago.' Grand-Pierre went on quickly before Klein could ask the question. 'And we dropped that piece of paper with the faked details for robbing a bank.'

'I think that's it. I'd better get back.'

'You have someone with you – I saw him as I passed the window.'

'A man you may have heard of – coming from Paris. The Monk.'

'You have him?' Grand-Pierre couldn't keep the surprise out of his voice. 'My God! You must be paying him a fortune.'

'He's a key figure in the operation.' Klein ignored the implied question as to how much Marler was being paid. He was watching the Englishman over Grand-Pierre's shoulder as Marler tucked into his meal.

'I'll go now then,' the Frenchman said.

'Do that.' Klein clapped a hand on his shoulder. 'One more thing. The bombs for the refineries?'

Grand-Pierre was used to this ploy. Klein had a habit of finishing a conversation and then throwing him a leading question.

'That team is already inside the oil complexes. They slipped in when the security guards changed duty rosters. We intercepted the new guards before they reached the gates, grabbed their uniforms and our men explained the normal guards were ill with flu. There's a lot of it about.' He grinned wolfishly.

'What about the passwords?'

'Obtained at knife point – before the knives went home – as I'd planned. Bodies dumped into a waiting van and dropped into the sea later. Weighted with chains as you instructed.'

'And the two Sikorsky helicopters at Schiphol?' Klein went on.

'I met Victor Saur, that Austrian pilot. He's flown them to Rotterdam Airport. They're supposed to be waiting to pick up top Royal-Dutch Shell executives.' He put a large finger to his hooked nose. 'Very hush-hush.'

At his table inside the restaurant Marler was cramming himself with noodles. He worked much better on a full stomach. The man Klein was talking to had his wide back to him so he hadn't seen his face. A huge brute. The formidable Frenchman Klein had referred to? Maybe, maybe not. He went on eating.

'Back in that restaurant,' Klein was saying, 'I heard a couple of soldiers talking. Something about all Dutch marines being confined to barracks.'

'True. Just a precaution. Probably caused by that mysterious explosion at sea. So everything is going our way. Our little opening shot at that barracks will coincide with the storming of Euromast. All watches synchronized to the second.'

'No problems at all?' Klein persisted.

'Only Chabot.' He shrugged. 'I come back to the camp site and see him wandering through the entrance. Hipper tried to stop him leaving – with a gun. Chabot took the gun off him. He'd been out for an hour's walk. He did that frequently at Larochette, Hipper said. He's restless for action. Aren't we all? But now we're in business.' He grinned again.

'Just don't get over-confident,' Klein snapped. 'Our advantage is the element of surprise. No one knows we're here.'

43

'I've been sacked. At least, suspended from duty pending an enquiry,' Van Gorp announced to the assembled company inside Tweed's room at the Hilton.

His statement added to the atmosphere of tension and gloom. Seated in chairs, on a settee, were Tweed, Bellenger, Butler, Newman and Benoit. The reason for the pessimistic mood had been a report Van Gorp had received from a previous phone call from his deputy. No trace of anything suspicious had been found from the fleet of patrol cars touring the city and Europort. Now this from the latest phone call.

'Well,' Van Gorp continued cheerfully, 'it's happened twice before – and twice I've been reinstated.'

'For what reason this time?' Tweed asked.

'The Minister discovered I'd cancelled all police leave. As if that wasn't enough to upset the entire Ministry of the Interior, I've given the SAS team permission to fly here from Schiphol. That was the Minister himself on the line. I was told to cancel the order. I had pleasure in telling him the team was already in the air, would soon land at Rotterdam.'

'My fault,' Tweed said, 'for urging you to take the decision.'

'But I agreed with you, my friend.' For a moment his air of bravado slipped. He looked pensive as he poured himself a small drink. 'My responsibility entirely.'

He doesn't think it's going to be third time lucky, Tweed thought. He believes he's out for good. And maybe he is – the Minister doesn't like him.

'Why did you want that team here when the Dutch marines are available?' asked Bellenger.

'Sixth sense. Can't explain it more than that . . .'

He broke off as the phone rang for the third time. Van Gorp took the call, then held out the receiver. 'For you, Tweed.'

Identifying himself, Tweed listened for a brief time, asked the caller to come to his room in three minutes, replaced the phone and looked round the room.

'Would you think me impolite if I asked everyone except Newman to return to their rooms for a short while? Thank you, gentlemen.' He waited until he was alone with the foreign correspondent. 'Blade, commander of the SAS team is on his way up. What's his rank?'

'Major.' Newman looked quizzical. 'You have a treat in store.'

Tweed opened the door after a sharp rapping and invited the visitor inside. Blade was about six feet tall, in his late thirties, his face lean and bony, his blue eyes cold, his nose aquiline. He reminded Tweed of a predatory hawk.

He had brown hair, very thick and cut short without a parting. He was wearing a pepper and salt sports jacket and sharply creased grey slacks. A bulky trench coat was neatly folded over his arm.

Tweed looked at Newman. 'I suppose there is no doubt this is Major Blade?'

'No doubt at all. There's only one.' Newman grinned. 'Fortunately.'

'That's because I put him through the wringer.' Blade sat in a hard-backed chair when Tweed suggested he made himself comfortable. 'Mind you, he survived,' Blade went on in his crisp, no-nonsense manner. 'Which, coming from me, is a compliment. Can I raise a point, get down to business?'

'Do, please. We're short of time.'

'I'd have thought in an emergency the Dutch Government would call in their Marines.'

'They would – will.'

'Their marines are good – very good. But my men are trained to work strictly on their own. By the way, what's the problem?'

Tweed sketched in the situation in five minutes. He spoke tersely, telescoping events since he first arrived in Switzerland. Blade sat erect, cupped his squarish jaw in his left hand, his eyes never leaving Tweed's.

'That's about it,' Tweed ended.

'As brilliant an appreciation as I've heard in a long while. You've had military experience?'

'Once. Military Intelligence.'

'Thought so. This Klein sounds a murderous so-and-so. It strikes me he's had top-flight training with some professional organization.'

'He has,' Tweed said, 'but I can't tell you where.'

'My guess would be the French. They're a pretty tough lot. Still, mustn't guess. Any questions?'

'Where is your unit? How quickly could it get here – say to this hotel?'

'The Sabre Troop. Scattered in twos and threes round the airport. Flew here in a chartered aircraft, dressed like a bunch of football supporters – the well-behaved type. Our kit – uniforms, weapons – is inside the aircraft. Two men on guard. Van Gorp organized four plain vans which are standing by at the airport. One phone call from me – give them eight minutes to get kitted out. Another twelve minutes to get here. Answer to your question. Twenty minutes. Less if the lid blows off. As I see it, you don't know where or when Klein will strike. So we have to wait, let him make the first move. Par for the course with us.'

'Your equipment,' Tweed remarked. 'I did warn he has scuba divers . . .'

'All my men have underwater equipment. What do we do now? I studied a map of Rotterdam and this Europort waiting at the airport. And flying in to Schiphol we were diverted – flew over this area pretty low. It's what we call dense territory. Could end up as a street fight. My impression from the bird's eye view.'

'Talking about a bird's-eye view,' Tweed commented. 'The place I want a look at is Euromast. Driving around I kept seeing that dominating tower. Come with us?' he suggested to Blade. 'I'll introduce you as my associate.'

'That's OK. We never let anyone see our ugly mugs . . .'

He broke off. The phone was ringing. Tweed answered it, his voice became cheerful, he said come up now, put down the phone.

'Paula has arrived.' He looked at Blade. 'One of my new staff. I'm breaking her in.'

'Breaking her in half,' Newman muttered.

She came into the room, carrying her case, looking fresh as paint. Tweed introduced her to Mr Blade. Her manner changed, became businesslike.

'Have I interrupted something?'

'No, but you must be tired . . .'

'Not really. Just off the flight from Brussels. I'm a bit of a mess, was going to tidy up, but that can wait – I sense something's happened . . .' She glanced at Blade and Tweed assured her she could talk freely. He poured her a cup of strong coffee while he brought her up-to-date and she sat listening intently, her shapely legs crossed. She drank a whole cup while Tweed was talking.

'I thought Rotterdam was the target,' she said, 'after you told me about poor Joseph Haber. He'd delivered the timers so – like the others before him – he was someone with dangerous information, someone this swine, Klein, no longer needed. What's the significance of Euromast?'

'I haven't a clue,' Tweed confessed. 'Maybe I'll find one when we get there.'

'Where have you been?' Klein asked as he sat at the table in the little restaurant outside Delft.

Marler's expression turned bleak as he sat down, glanced at the other tables, saw no one was near enough to hear him. He leaned forward.

'I've been to the loo. Let's get one thing straight between us now. You're paying me to do a job. You'll get value for services rendered. But I'm damned if I'm going to have you breathing down my neck when I go for a pee.'

'No need to get worked up . . .'

'I'm a good deal cooler than you are – to judge from the expression on your corpse-like face. End of discussion. Next?'

'I see you took your bag with you,' Klein remarked as Marler tucked it between his chair and the wall. 'Does that contain all the equipment you need for the job?'

'It does.'

'What about your clothes back at the Hilton? Could they be left there? For good? Your room is paid for. I assume you paid for meals as you had them?'

'I did. And the clothes are surplus to requirements. They

carry no maker's labels. And two suits are the wrong size – crumpled to look as though they've been worn. That way no policeman can estimate my exact height and weight. Why?'

'Because when we leave here we're on our way.'

'Would it strain your security to the limits if I asked you where we are going?'

'No call for sarcasm.'

Marler's reply was to wipe his mouth carefully with his napkin, crumple it and leave it on the table. Independent bastard, Klein said to himself. But that, he reflected again, was what had made The Monk so effective.

'To storm Euromast,' Klein replied.

The call from Paris for Tweed came through just before they left his room to drive to Euromast. Paula was talking with Newman, telling him how she'd broken the news of her husband's death to Martine Haber. 'Pretty grim,' she said, 'but I did my best . . .'

Benoit was talking to Van Gorp and Butler. Blade stood alone by the window, gazing down at the traffic circling the large road intersection below.

'Lasalle here,' the voice on the phone informed Tweed. 'I've been checking up on the whereabouts of The Monk. God knows how many calls I've made to various countries but I got lucky. I know where he is – or supposed to be.'

Tweed's grip on the instrument tightened. 'Where, René?'

'Shut away in a clinic in Lucerne, Switzerland. Suffering a major nervous breakdown. No visitors allowed. Beck, chief of police in Berne just phoned me back. He was able to get a description of the patient. Fair-haired with a bald patch on the crown of his head.'

'So, he again has his alibi. He's somewhere here in Rotterdam. Maybe within a mile of where I'm standing. If he slips through our fingers he's in the clear again. I must go now. Thank you.'

The assembled group stopped talking as he put down the phone. Tweed again sensed the atmosphere of frustration, depression. He smiled broadly, spread his hands, his tone jaunty.

'The Monk is supposed to be ill in a Swiss clinic.'

'You said he'd be here,' Blade barked. 'The deadliest marksman in Europe you called him.'

'But that proves to me he is here. He always provides himself with an ironclad alibi. You are coming with us, Van Gorp? Despite your suspension from duty?'

'Oh, that.' The Dutchman grinned. 'I told the Minister I needed the instruction in writing before I could accept it. Didn't you know? The Dutch are great ones for the formal procedures being observed? Drives me mad at times. On this occasion the tradition has its uses. The cars are ready – when you are.'

'Just before we leave . . .' Tweed's manner was exuberant. 'I don't think you realize we have one big ace up our sleeves.'

'I'd like to know what that is,' rapped back Newman.

'Klein has no idea we've caught up with him – that we have found the target, that we are already here.'

As they piled into the three waiting cars Tweed noted there was a change of atmosphere, morale had soared.

For Tweed it was a nightmare.

He stood with the others at the foot of the steps leading up to the entrance. He gazed up at the structure which reminded him of the most gigantic periscope in the world. The sheering tower, the overhanging viewing platform far above his head. And above that the slimmer needle of concrete spiring its way endlessly to the final observation point at its tip.

Vertigo.

Only Paula noticed the way he stood stock still, as though hypnotized by the horrific height of the thing. Oh, my God, she thought, I'd forgotten. It's his ultimate terror. Vertigo.

She squeezed his arm. He shook his head to stop her saying anything. He'd realized that she'd understood. He took a deep breath as Van Gorp emerged from the entrance and waved for them to come on. What were they waiting for?

They were waiting for Blade who had wandered off on his own. The Sabre Troop commander was studying the tower from every angle and position. Tweed obviously thought it might be important. He had checked it with a critical eye. He joined Van Gorp and the others mounted the steps and went into the spacious reception hall.

'I've bought tickets,' Van Gorp announced breezily. 'The lift is over there. I think we can all just squeeze in if we have it to ourselves . . .'

The lift – with no view of the outside world – ascended faster than Paula had expected. They had all managed to cram themselves in but they were pressed together and Tweed was hidden behind Blade's tall straight back. He caught Paula looking at him anxiously and winked. There were several levels he noticed from the button panel he could see in a gap between Newman and Van Gorp. One for the restaurant. Who the devil could get any food down – keep it down – up here?

The lift doors slid back. Van Gorp led the way. 'We're on the viewing platform,' he called back cheerily.

Fresh air met Tweed as he stepped out and for the fraction of a second he paused, then forced himself to keep moving, stiff-legged. The platform running round the tower was open. A rail no higher than his waist circled it. Christ! Paula touched his elbow as though by accident. He walked to the rail, grasped it with both hands, stared down. Like gazing over an abyss. Straight down. Sheer drop. Paula stood close on one side, Van Gorp on the other. In the basin barges like match-boxes were moored four abreast. Tweed saw his knuckles were white, gripping the rail like a vice. He forced his hands to relax, holding the metal rail lightly. He concentrated, made himself observe.

Several police launches berthed at the inner end of the

basin. He raised his level of vision. The Maas stretched away, a wide river flowing towards the distant sea. Crammed with shipping. Barges, freighters, tourist boats returning with their living cargo.

It was late in the afternoon, early evening. The sun was setting, a wave of purple dusk darkening the clear sky. Lights coming on all over the miniaturized city. He felt a little giddy. The drop was drawing him over the rail. He looked up quickly.

'Glorious view,' said Van Gorp. 'Most spectacular in Holland.'

'Must be,' Tweed said. 'Think I'll walk round the platform. You stay with our friend, Paula.'

He moved away before she could protest. He had a strong urge to stay close to the circular tower, away from the rail. He compelled himself to put one foot in front of another, staring out at the panoramic view.

Blade had disappeared. Continuing his slow walk, Tweed found him leaning out over the rail, far out, gazing down as though estimating the possibility of scaling the tower. God, if he slips . . . Tweed walked on. The platform was deserted. He changed direction, crossed to the rail to see what was below.

A large green park with toy trees. No one inside it at that hour. The pulling sensation began again. He walked on. It seemed a hell of a long way round. Then he saw the others. Butler, Newman, Benoit and Van Gorp with Paula who stared in his direction, gave him a warm smile but stood her ground.

'Fantastic tower this,' Van Gorp began again.

'How high are we?' Tweed asked.

'A hundred and four metres – three hundred and forty feet. The restaurant is just below us. Then there's the crow's nest up there. That's closed in with glass . . .'

Then why the hell didn't you take us there? Paula thought. This is agony for Tweed, but he won't let on. And I can't do a damn thing.

'Look up,' Van Gorp urged. 'See the tower going on

higher above the crow's nest? Spectacular is the only word.'

'Great. Just great.'

Tweed looked up and the vertigo seemed worse. The immense height of the needle made him feel dizzy again. He looked up for what would seem a normal length of time, then dropped his gaze. The Dutchman was pointing now, one long arm raised, index finger extended.

'Like to take a look at the Space Tower, Tweed? This down here is nothing compared with up there. Right at the very top. Take you to the lift. Come on. Your ticket covers the trip . . .'

'Have we the time?' Paula asked.

'Only take a few minutes. See half Holland from up there. Almost. The North Sea, too. Not to be missed.'

'I'm getting rather thirsty,' Paula persisted.

'We can go to the restaurant while Tweed makes the trip on his own. It's a much smaller lift. See the diameter up there? Very narrow. This way, Tweed.'

'The round trip, as the Americans say,' joked Tweed.

He followed Van Gorp who led him to another lift at a higher level, pressing the button. Paula was nearly going spare. Tweed saw her expression, shook his head.

'Go get a drink. Be back soon. No time at all . . .'

Newman came alongside her as Tweed entered the lift. They watched the doors close on him. 'Why didn't you go up with him, you thoughtless idiot?' she hissed. 'It will be a terrible ordeal – suffering as he does from vertigo.'

'Oh, my God! I'd forgotten – absorbed by the view. You're right . . .'

'I doubt if you've any idea what vertigo's like,' she went on.

'Paula,' he whispered, 'vertigo takes different forms. Once I went up by lift to the top of the Duomo in Milan – the Cathedral. Only a hundred feet up. I came out into the open, walked down a flight of steps at the front, then noticed I could see between the stone balustrade pillars down into the street. I was paralysed. Luckily no one was about – I *crawled* back up those steps.' He raised his voice, called out to Van Gorp waiting to lead them down to the restaurant.

'How high up is that Space Tower?'

'One hundred and eighty-five metres – six hundred feet.'

'Charming,' Newman muttered.

'Oh, one point I forgot to mention,' Van Gorp said. 'That Space Tower is a small glass cabin which revolves.'

'Jesus!' Newman muttered again. 'Now he tells us. Maybe I'd better go up . . .'

'Not now,' Paula snapped. 'Too late – it will be noticed. He'll cope. Somehow.'

Penned up inside the much smaller elevator Tweed was tempted to press the button for the crow's nest. Briefly. He pressed his thumb firmly against the top button and stood motionless.

The elevator shot up much faster than he'd expected, climbing like a rocket. He felt he'd left his stomach behind on the platform. The ascent – up nearly another three hundred feet – took only a few seconds. It will be better at this height, Tweed thought. Like looking down from a plane which never bothered me. The doors slid open, he stepped out.

It wasn't better, it was worse. The elevator doors closed behind him. He was alone inside a small circular cage with glass walls. The light was a glare. He took out a pouch, attached his clip-on tinted glasses over his spectacles, moved close to the glass window.

The sun was setting behind the distant horizon of the sea, a blood-red disc sliding out of sight. Blood. Lots of blood. Why did he think of that now? The sun sank from view. He removed the tinted lenses. He looked down and shuddered. He was gazing down the sheer side of the precipice-like column with a bird's-eye view of the platform so far below. He blinked, feeling disorientated. It felt as though the floor was moving. An illusion . . . God, no! He looked up again and saw the view had changed. The floor was *revolving*.

He felt giddy. The world began spinning slowly. He was going to faint. *Never!* Extracting a tube of mints from his pocket, he popped one in his mouth. The bitter taste revived him. Must get on with the job.

Tweed took the binoculars from another pocket, adjusted the focus, aiming them at the mouth of the Maas. The giant dredger was still working, the scoop bringing up muck from the bottom of the river entrance. He raised a little the angle of the glasses, slowly scanned the sea.

Some distance offshore a large liner was approaching from the north, moving very slowly, speckled with lights. He swung the glass further south. Much further away another vessel coming in, a ship which had to be very big – from its silhouette he guessed it was a supertanker. Directly opposite the mouth of the Maas his glass picked up a tiny speck. The Sealink ferry sailing in from Harwich? Some idea twitched at the back of his mind, then it was gone.

He stood very stiffly, sweat forming on his brow, his legs like jelly. If only the damned thing would keep still. He forced his body to turn round, to look in another direction. Two large helicopters were flying in from the north, about to land at Zestienhoven – Rotterdam Airport. A couple of Sikorskys. He watched them drop out of sight.

From that height he could see the spires and towers of The Hague, the home of that stupid Minister of the Interior. Still, he thought, we have enough of those back home.

He popped another mint in his mouth, took one last look down at the layout below. Rotterdam was studded with lights – more coming on every second. What the devil was that idea he'd had at the back of his mind? He pursed his lips, pressed the button for the elevator.

'Are you all right?'

Paula strolled forward as he stepped out on to the

platform level. She had been waiting for him, pretending to be taking another look at the view. No one was about as she took his arm. ·

'I'm OK. How high was I?'

'Six hundred feet!'

'Felt a bit like it. Oh, and they move the floor around to give more excitement. You get used to it . . .'

'You've lost colour. The others are in the restaurant. A drop of fresh air – just at the entrance to the platform – would work wonders.'

They stood for a minute or two and Tweed took in deep breaths. He suddenly felt better, almost normal. He lifted one leg, then another. The strength was coming back into them. Thanking her, he said he was ready for a cup of coffee.

The restaurant had tables at two levels – those perched up further away from the windows. Van Gorp, sitting next to a window with Butler alongside him, waved. No one else occupied a table near them.

Tweed saw the huge windows which slanted *outwards*. Again he experienced the being-pulled-over-the-edge sensation. Paula sensed his disquiet. 'Let's take one of the tables higher up,' she said brightly.

'No, we'll join them.'

Paula went ahead, sat down in the window seat and Tweed took the chair beside her. He ordered coffee for both of them and stared out of the window. The congestion of shipping inside the basins, moving up and down the Maas, was enormous.

'Enjoy yourself on top?' Van Gorp enquired breezily.

'A unique experience. Quite unique.' He leaned forward. 'Why do I feel this place should be watched?'

'Just asked the very same question myself,' said Butler.

'It is,' the Dutchman replied, lowering his voice. 'You see those two men sitting at a table by themselves? My men. Armed. I could only spare a couple – I'm stretched to the limit checking the river and the docks.'

'Where are the others?' Tweed asked.

'Touring round the place. Especially Blade and Newman. That colleague of yours, Blade, wants to see everything. Even had a look at the toilets. Some kind of specialist?'

'He does my leg work.' Tweed kept his voice low. 'Sea-mines. Thirty of them, as I mentioned. What do they suggest to you?'

'A plan to block the Maas. I have men swarming among those docks and basins – looking for the unusual. And we're watching the oil installations you saw. Nothing so far. I'd know.' He picked up his heavy raincoat, pulled something a short way out of the pocket. A walkie-talkie.

'So still we wait,' Tweed ruminated.

'When the others get back we'll take a drive along the Maas – see if anything's stirring. Ah, here they come.'

Tweed swallowed his second large cup of coffee. The experience of his recent battle with vertigo had dehydrated him. He felt parched as the Sahara, refilled the cup as Blade and Newman arrived, followed by Benoit.

'They had coffee before you came down,' Van Gorp explained. He seemed restless, anxious to move on. 'All except Mr Blade,' he continued. 'Care for some coffee before we go?'

'Not for me, thank you.'

Tweed glanced at Blade sharply. The SAS leader's mind seemed far away; instead of sitting down he stood by the window, staring down.

They descended in the elevator, walked to the parked cars and got inside. Tweed sat alongside Butler in the rear seat of the vehicle driven by Van Gorp. An orange-coloured helicopter was flying downriver, a hundred feet or so above the Maas.

'We ought to be able to work out how Klein will launch an assault,' Tweed said, worrying away at the problem. 'How would *we* launch it? Remembering he has a team of scuba divers.'

'As I said earlier,' Van Gorp replied, 'by using the mines in the Maas – blocking the entry to all shipping. See that chopper which just flew over? No police markings – but it has my men aboard. We are watching from the land, from the air.'

'But not underwater?' queried Paula who sat beside Van Gorp.

'We can hardly have skin-divers permanently swimming around under the Maas,' he told her gently.

'But what I don't understand,' she persisted, 'is they will have to change into wet suits before they plant the mines. Where on earth can they do that – without risk of being seen?'

'No idea.' He started the engine. 'Let's cruise around – this time, Tweed, along the north bank towards the Hook of Holland.' He glanced in the mirror. 'You look thoughtful.'

It was something Paula had said. Tweed suddenly realized the police chief had spoken to him. 'Nothing,' he replied. 'The Hook of Holland, you said. While I was in the Space Tower I saw a dot on the horizon, could have been the Sealink ferry.'

Van Gorp checked his watch, switched on his headlights. 'It would be. She's due to dock soon. Always on time.'

As he pulled away from the kerb Butler turned in his seat to look at Euromast through the rear window. The car containing Newman and the others was following. Tweed also turned in his seat, gazing up at the immense structure.

'Something about that place that worries me,' Butler remarked. 'What it is I can't pin down.'

'It worries me, too,' said Tweed.

44

The Dutch fishing vessel, *Utrecht*, which should have reached its home port, was stationary. A quarter of a mile astern of the stately floating glow-worm which was the *Adenauer*.

The huge liner was almost stationary on the dark sheen of the smooth sea, waiting for the lighters to come out with passengers. Two large dinghies with outboard motors slid across the water, midway between the *Utrecht* and the *Adenauer*. Painted black, they were invisible.

One dinghy was directly astern of the liner – less than four hundred yards away. The second dinghy, launched from the *Utrecht* earlier, was approximately a quarter-mile ahead of the liner, its motor turned off, drifting gently with the current.

Four scuba divers slipped over the side of the first dinghy, paddled water as two specially-constructed nets were handed down to them. Each net was grasped by two men who then went under the surface, hauling a net between them.

Each net contained two sea-mines with the switches tuned to a specific radio band. They swam on under water with ease – the contents of the nets were light in weight, shaped like large eggs, painted a dull metallic non-reflecting grey colour, with squat clamps like suckers protruding.

The first team reached the liner, swam deeper under the vast hull, and paddled on until they were just beyond amidships. Here they stopped paddling, bobbing up and down beneath the dark shape above them. With practised hands they opened the net, released the mines which floated upwards, attracted by the fumes inside the engine room.

The swimmers followed their cargo upwards, each man attending to one mine, swivelling it until the suckers contacted the hull. He pressed a switch. Metal legs shot out, thudded into the hull. The mines were attached. Immovable.

The second team swam in under the enormous twin propellers, performed the same actions at a point half way between the propellers and the location where the other mines had been attached.

Their mission completed, the two scuba divers swam on under the hull of the *Adenauer*. Clad in wet suits, face masks and feet flippers with oxygen cylinders strapped to their backs, they glided through the water, their deft movements almost balletic in their grace.

Emerging beyond the massive bow, the lead man checked the compass attached to his wrist, changing direction by a few degrees. Like his comrades ahead of him he was making for the second dinghy.

He surfaced briefly, looked swiftly round in the night. A pinpoint green light – visible only at sea-level – located the waiting dinghy. He dived under and swam on. Ten minutes later both teams had been hauled aboard the dinghy. They had left behind four sea-mines – armed with enough explosive power to destroy the 50,000-ton liner.

Once Klein pressed a certain button on his control box the four mines would detonate simultaneously. Most of the fifteen hundred souls aboard would die in the first tremendous blast wave – a thousand passengers and five hundred crew. The blast would rip open the hull, surge upwards through the engine room, the explosive wave continuing through the five decks above. Those who survived the blast would be immolated in a sheet of flame with a temperature of over one thousand degrees.

*

On the curving bridge of the *Adenauer* Captain Brunner stood at the port side, surveying the drifting fishing vessel in his high-powered glasses. His First Officer was – as per his instructions – using a signalling lamp to convey Brunner's message to the *Utrecht*.

'What is wrong? You are too close to my ship. Please make way. Reply immediately.'

Aboard the *Utrecht* its skipper, Captain Sailer, stood immobile on his own bridge. Behind him stood Grand-Pierre, a Uzi machine pistol aimed at the skipper's back. On the deck of the small bridge Sailer's wife, Ansje, a small slim woman with long dark hair, lay with her ankles and wrists trussed with rope. A man wearing a Balaclava helmet knelt beside her, holding a knife at her throat.

They had come aboard from the dinghies just after the nets had been hauled in, the catch stored. Grand-Pierre had shouted up in English that their engines had broken down. Wearing dark glasses and a polo-necked sweater pulled up over his chin, he had climbed up the dropped ladder, produced the Uzi.

When Sailer saw a second man come aboard, carrying his wife, he had almost grabbed for the Uzi in his fury. Then he had seen the knife held close to her throat. From then on he obeyed them.

The dinghies, containing four men in each, had been hauled up over the side. Grand-Pierre had then ordered Sailer to make for the *Adenauer*. Now he stood watching the flashing light of the signalling lamp.

'What do they say?' he asked a third man wearing a Balaclava helmet?

'They're asking what's wrong, saying we're too close to them, ordering us to move off.'

'Now listen to me, Sailer,' Grand-Pierre said, ramming the muzzle of his weapon hard into the skipper's back. 'This man is an ex-seaman, knows about signalling. Tell them you have broken down, engine trouble. That it's nearly repaired but you have a man overboard, that you're searching for him. Get on with it.'

The bit about man overboard covered the faint possibility that the two dinghies might be spotted. Sailer took the lamp from his First Mate and began signalling his reply.

Aboard the *Adenauer* Captain Brunner was annoyed. An intruder had just invaded his bridge. Cal Dexter, the chief of the American security team which had boarded at Hamburg to protect the Secretary of State. A tall, lanky, energetic man, Dexter was understandably worried.

'Captain, what is that Goddamn boat doing out there? It's too close.'

'That, Mr Dexter,' Brunner replied, switching to English, 'is what I am now finding out. Please to let me concentrate.'

'It's fishy.'

'Yes, Mr Dexter,' the captain replied with unexpected humour, 'it is a fishing boat. Ah, here we are. Boiler overheated. Repair work will be completed shortly. Also a man overboard. We hope to sail shortly. End of message.'

He lowered his glasses, walked to the front of the bridge as the American followed him. Dexter's tone was terse.

'And where is the Dutch cutter which was supposed to patrol us while we took the rest of the passengers aboard?'

'A technical hitch. It is unable to leave port at the moment. And now, Mr Dexter, please stay on the bridge but again allow me to concentrate. I want to watch that fishing vessel.'

A technical hitch. The cutter was indeed still in port. When it had started up its engines the propeller had turned several slow painful revolutions, making a terrible grinding sound. It had then stopped, refused to move again. Divers were now investigating the cause of the trouble.

In due course they would find a mixture of grit and waterproof grease had been applied to the bearings. No one had seen the scuba diver who had committed the sabotage. And it had been child's play for Klein to locate the vessel. A newspaper reporter had dug out the fact that this cutter would patrol the sea while the *Adenauer* stood offshore. The paper had printed the story because the

Adenauer had become newsworthy the moment the US Secretary of State boarded the ship in Hamburg.

No other cutter was available to replace it. The Dutch Navy was occupied with a NATO sea exercise taking place off Iceland. Marine Control at Europort had just decided to request police launches be sent out to take its place.

The mining of the supertanker, *Cayman Conqueror*, lying offshore less than a mile from the *Adenauer*, proved to be a straightforward operation. The same technique was employed but five sea-mines were attached to the hull. The vessel was fifteen hundred feet in length from stem to stern.

The only moment of danger came when a seaman, trudging along the raised catwalk between the extensive piping systems located on the centre line of the tanker, thought he saw a small green lamp flashing to starboard. He stopped, rubbed his sore eyes, looked again. No green lamp.

He was fatigued, aching for bed, and about to come off duty. He put the light down to eye strain and continued his endless walk to food and sleep. The vague silhouette of a fishing vessel a quarter of a mile or more away meant nothing to the lookout. A boat crawling home to port . . .

On the bridge of the *Easter Island* Captain Williams took more interest in the lone fishing vessel which seemed stationary. His supertanker was waiting for entry permission from Marine Control, drifting a safe distance from the *Conqueror*.

From his position inside the navigating bridge at the stern and abaft the single squat funnel Williams swept the fishing boat with his night glasses. He could see its name clearly. *Drenthe*.

Williams was notorious for his caution, his curiosity about anything *unusual*. A fishing boat offshore well after dark was unusual. With the night-glasses screwed to his eyes he called out to his First Officer.

'Parker. Flash that vessel a signal . . .'

He asked very much the same questions which Captain

Brunner had to the skipper of the *Utrecht* a few minutes earlier. Then he leant his elbows on a ledge and waited.

Inside the cramped wheelhouse of the *Drenthe* Hipper had taken on the role of Grand-Pierre. He held a Luger pistol rammed into the skipper's back. He wore pebble glasses and a handkerchief over the lower half of his face. Curled up on the floor lay the skipper's ten-year-old son, his feet and hands bound with rope, another Luxembourger bent over him with a knife at his throat.

'Signal back that we have a fire on board. That we are getting it under control. No help needed,' Hipper ordered in English. He added the same warning Grand-Pierre had issued.

As the skipper started flashing the reply Hipper took a walkie-talkie from his pocket, raised the antenna, and spoke to one of his men waiting at the stern.

'Mosar, start the fire now. Immediately.'

He spoke in Letzeburgesch, the strange Luxembourg *patois* which is a mixture of French and German – and understood by neither nation. Putting the walkie-talkie away, Hipper pulled the beret he was wearing further down over his forehead, concealing his hair.

The deck under Mosar's feet at the stern hardly moved, so calm was the sea under the moonless sky. A large man with mongrel features, wearing seaman's gear, he carried the bucket to where it would be visible from the super-tanker – at least its contents would be shortly.

The large bucket was three-quarters-full of rags soaked in turpentine with a little petrol added. Stepping back behind the wheelhouse, Mosar picked up the rolled newspaper held with elastic bands, used his lighter to set the tip burning, dropped it inside the bucket and ran back.

There was a flare of flame, a dense cloud of black smoke which climbed into the windless night. The reply signal flashed to the tanker had just been received by Williams on his bridge. He saw the burst of flame, the coil of smoke.

'They have a problem,' he remarked to Parker. 'But

they are expecting to deal with it. Better keep an eye on them – just in case it spreads.'

His attention fixed on the fire, Williams had no idea this was the moment when five sea-mines were attached to the underside of his huge vessel laden with oil. The unseen scuba divers – instructed by Klein who had studied the structure of this type of tanker – had avoided the coffer dam.

This was the space which separated the engine-room from the cargo tanks. The mines had carefully been attached beneath both tanks and engine-room. The scuba divers made their way underwater to the waiting dinghy lying astern of the *Easter Island*. They were not seen.

Aboard the *Drenthe*, Mosar fetched buckets of water already lined up on deck, doused the flames. He left the bucket which continued to send up clouds of black smoke and informed Hipper over his walkie-talkie his task was completed.

'Now we can move on,' Hipper informed the skipper. 'So start the engine. Next objective, the freighter, *Otranto*. She's not far away. After that, those three container ships. Then we can all go home,' he concluded in his soft, sibilant voice.

The *Drenthe* began moving, trailing a white wake, leaving behind the *Easter Island*, another floating death ship.

45

'We'd better get back to the city,' Van Gorp said as he swung the wheel. 'No sign of anything. No reports of unusual activity. No nothing.'

He sounded subdued. He'd received regular reports over his radio from the patrols scouring the city and the docks along the Maas. Tweed sat hunched up behind Paula, a glazed look in his eyes.

'Something's wrong,' said Paula. 'Very wrong. We've missed some key element. I don't think it is the docks.'

'Can't agree,' Van Gorp responded. 'Haber's body was found in that barge. Tweed said Haber transported the timer devices. This has to be the target.'

'What makes you so sure?' Paula argued.

'One point I forgot to mention. My men found a scuba diver's outfit near Haber's barge. That suggests the river . . .

Tweed sat up straight. 'Where exactly was that outfit found?'

'On the deck of a barge next but one to Haber's. It had a large rip in it. Useless. So it was abandoned there. Proof scuba divers are interested in the Maas.'

'*On the deck?*' Tweed sounded incredulous. 'So you had no trouble finding it at all?'

'No. What's wrong with that?'

'Everything.' Tweed was vehement. 'Don't you see? Klein is meticulous in his planning. I've just realized that it's odd Haber's body was left exposed in that way. A few shovels of gravel would have covered the corpse. They'd also have hidden that ripped scuba diver outfit. So, it was left there deliberately. Klein is a past master at laying smokescreens.'

'I don't follow that,' Van Gorp objected.

'He wins either way. Case One. We don't get anywhere near Rotterdam. Haber's body discovered. Just another murder. Case Two. By some mischance we get on to him, track him to Rotterdam . . .'

'*You* did that,' Van Gorp pointed out. 'With very little to go on . . .'

'We trace him this far,' Tweed continued. 'We find Haber's corpse. Nearby a ripped scuba diver's suit is found. Obvious conclusion? Watch the Maas. Too obvious for my liking.'

'Have you checked the hotels?' Paula asked. 'Your men have copies of that Identikit of Klein.'

'A large team has been checking for hours. Showing the picture – especially to the concierges. Those are the chaps who notice things. Result? Complete blank. So what next?'

'Drive back to Euromast,' Tweed suggested. 'How far away are we?'

'Some distance yet.'

On the roof of the high-rise building Prussen, the Luxembourger hand-picked by Klein, stood staring through binoculars. He was alone on the flat rooftop which was rarely visited by tenants of the flats below except in high summer.

Prussen was watching the progress of a large laundry van along a straight street leading to the entrance to the Dutch marine barracks. The driver, delivering laundry to the barracks, was completely under Prussen's control. He was very fond of his mother, now in the hands of Klein's men. When given his instructions by Prussen he had been assured that if he failed to make the expected delivery look normal his mother's head would be severed.

Prussen, a squat, large-headed man, checked his watch. Timing was essential. The driver had synchronized his watch with the Luxembourger's. He had to arrive at the depot at exactly the right moment. Prussen felt in the pocket of his windcheater, took out the control box and waited, still holding the binoculars with one hand. A short time yet before he had to press the button. The extra cargo the driver had no idea he was carrying had been smuggled in among the laundry while Prussen had kept the driver talking at the front of the vehicle.

At Park Crescent Monica's phone rang. She lifted the receiver and immediately recognized the muffled voice. Like talking through a silk handkerchief this time.

'Yes, this is Monica . . .'

'Olympus speaking. It's Rotterdam. No doubt this time. Got it?'

'Quite clearly. I'll pass the message . . .'

There was a click. The caller had been in even more of the devil of a rush this time than during earlier calls. Again she'd no idea whether she'd been talking to a man or a woman. Had she detected a trace of foreign accent? Probably sheer imagination. She picked up the phone again, dialled Grand'Place.

'Police headquarters have a message for you, Tweed,' Van Gorp informed him as he replaced the phone. 'Very urgent.'

Tweed hesitated. He wanted to reach Euromast as quickly as possible. But the message could tell him something vital. Van Gorp watched him in the mirror, waiting for his decision.

'It will only take an extra few minutes,' the Dutchman added.

'Police headquarters then . . .'

The two fishing vessels, *Utrecht* and *Drenthe*, were left drifting a short distance offshore. Under the supervision of Grand-Pierre and Hipper their crews were tied up, roped by their wrists and ankles.

Humanity played no part in Klein's earlier instructions to spare their lives. It would only be a matter of time before a Coastguard ship found them and the crews told their stories of what had happened. Thus providing the authorities with ironclad confirmation that the fleet waiting near the Maas mouth had been mined.

The outboard dinghies brought the assault teams ashore to a quiet part of the coast. Chabot was waiting with three four-wheel drive covered trucks. Within minutes the men were aboard, leaving behind the punctured dinghies to sink.

Chabot led the way, driving the first truck over the rough terrain of scrub and sand. He turned on to a main highway and pressed his foot down, heading for the centre of Rotterdam.

Klein drove past the Hilton and along the Kruisgade while Marler sat beside him. He slowed down and cruised as he stared ahead. A girl walking from the direction of the precinct was hurrying towards the entrance of the Hotel Central. She passed under a street light. Lara Seagrave.

Klein pulled in to the kerb, left the engine running, caught hold of her by the arm seconds before she went inside. She stared at his uniform, his tinted glasses without recognition. She was tugging her arm to free it when he spoke and she knew it was Klein.

'You were supposed to stay in the hotel. Where have you been?'

'For a short walk,' she snapped. 'I'm not staying cooped up inside any hotel hour after hour . . .'

'Your bill was paid in advance. You're coming with me now.'

'I'm going up to the loo first. *If* you don't mind . . .'

'I do. There's a toilet where we're going.'

'I said I was going to the loo. I'll be down in a minute.' She tugged loose from his grip, her eyes flaming. 'My case is packed. Do I bring that?'

'Leave it . . .'

Before he could say another word she'd dashed inside the hotel. Klein was furious. Independent little bitch. He calmed down, began striding slowly up and down past the entrance, a chauffeur waiting for his client. Twice he checked his watch. When she emerged, wearing a camel hair coat, he escorted her to the BMW, opened the rear door and waited while she slid into the rear seat.

Marler stared as he saw her coming, the girl he'd dined with at the *Maison de Boeuf* in Brussels. He decided it would be wise to pretend he'd never met her. She had glanced at him as she reached the car and looked away.

Klein closed the door, went round the back of the car, made sure the boot was locked, the boot which contained the two lengths of rope, one tied into a hangman's noose. Climbing behind the wheel he paused before starting the engine.

'This is Martin Shand,' he told her. 'Martin, this is Lara. Just Lara . . .'

He turned the ignition, and drove off through the night. The traffic had slackened to almost nothing as he made for the Euromast.

Inside the garage Klein had hired Legaud, the communications expert, sat behind the wheel of the resprayed CRS truck. He checked his watch for the third time in half an hour. Beside him sat a Luxembourger clad in windcheater and denims with a small rug spread across his lap. Beneath the rug he held a Uzi machine gun. The Uzi fires at the rate of six hundred rounds per minute.

Legaud was slim with a clever face which slanted down to a pointed, fox-like chin. He wore rimless glasses, which gave him a professorial appearance. In the main compartment behind the cab was a complex of dials and switches with metres indicating wavelengths. It was also occupied by four men dressed in the same garb as the guard beside Legaud. They were equipped with machine guns and Browning pistols.

Again Legaud checked his watch. He nodded to the guard who descended from the cab, pressed the button on the wall which operated the automatic door. The moment it elevated Legaud backed carefully into the quiet darkened street, turned and headed for his objective. Euromast.

'How long does Euromast stay open?' Butler asked as Van Gorp drove close to the river front.

'Until ten at night. People go there for dinner in the restaurant – and to see the view at night. Why?'

'I just wondered,' Butler replied and lapsed into his normal silence.

Tweed had been sitting gazing out of the window, not seeing the river, his mind squirrelling away. It was a mood Butler was used to and Paula, glancing back once, was careful not to say anything.

'Stop the car!' Tweed said suddenly. 'I've been a complete idiot.'

'What's the matter?' asked Van Gorp, parking by the kerb.

'If you wanted to send a top security message could you do it over your radio – or would it be more secure from police HQ?'

'From police HQ. Amateur radio hacks often tune in to police wavebands. Why?'

'It was staring me in the eyes when I was inside the Space Tower. I failed to grasp its significance.' He didn't mention that it had been his feeling of disorientation which had clogged his brain. 'Paula was right when she queried whether it was really the Maas . . .'

'Still don't follow you,' the Dutchman commented.

'Those thirty sea-mines. *Sea*-mines! What are they used for in wartime?'

'To sink ships . . .'

'Exactly. And from the Space Tower I saw God knows how many of them approaching Europort. There was even a large liner.'

'The *Adenauer*. Stopping to take on board more passengers before it sails for its cruise in the Mediterranean. It also has the US Secretary of State aboard – with his wife.'

'Lord help us. Don't you see? Those ships are the objective, the main one anyway. Klein is going to use those sea-mines to hold them to ransom. That's how he will get his two hundred million pounds in gold bullion. I've puzzled over that a lot – what could be worth such a king's ransom? All those ships must be warned. They're in great danger.'

'Police headquarters,' said Van Gorp and drew away from the kerb, accelerating.

Hipper, driving the Fiat he had transferred to after leaving one of the four-wheel drive trucks at an isolated spot, pulled in by the entrance to Rotterdam Airport. He now wore a plain grey business suit and carried a brief-case.

Inside the reception hall he walked across to a small bullet-headed man with black hair plastered close to his skull. The description fitted and the man dressed in pilot's clothing was standing by the bookstall, looking at a paper-back.

'Excuse me, sir,' Hipper said in German, 'but would you by any chance be Victor Saur?'

'I would. Who are you?'

Cold brown eyes like glass marbles stared back at the Luxembourger. A cigarette dangled from the Austrian's thin lips.

'Hipper. You have transport to Brussels for me?'

'Benny will fly you there. That bloke in flying kit over at the drinks counter with an orange juice.'

'Thank you most kindly, sir.'

Creep, thought Saur as he watched Hipper waddle towards Benny, a heavily-built man several inches taller than Saur. There was a brief conversation and the two men went off together as Saur walked outside where he could see the night sky. A few minutes later a Sikorsky helicopter rose above the building, described a half circle and flew off south for Brussels Airport. Saur checked his watch. Dead on time.

A lot of people were going to be dead on time.

On top of the high-rise building overlooking the barracks of the Dutch marines Prussen also checked his watch. Through his night-glasses he saw the laundry van pass through the gates after showing his pass. The van proceeded across the parade ground towards the side entrance where it would park.

Prussen took the control box from his pocket and held it in one hand while the other pressed the glasses to his eyes. The van seemed to crawl. Prussen felt beads of sweat forming on his forehead. He licked his lips once.

Then he remembered his dark glasses. He nearly panicked. He forced himself to remain calm. Placing the binoculars and the box on the wall-top, he took out the glasses and put them on. He raised the binoculars again. The laundry van was just pulling up outside the entrance.

Prussen took hold of the control box, his thumb half an inch above the button. He took a deep breath as he saw a marine emerge to collect the laundry. Now was the moment. His thumb jammed down hard. He braced himself.

There was a brilliant flash of light. Night briefly became day. A thunderous roar almost deafened him. A cloud of vapour obscured the whole barracks area. As it drifted away he saw the building had vanished, leaving behind a scatter of rubble across the parade ground. The van had disappeared and there was a great hole as though a meteorite had landed.

As he made his way towards the staircase, towards the motorcycle waiting in the street, Prussen was trembling.

46

Closeted with Newman only in a room at police headquarters, Tweed used the scrambler phone to call Park Crescent. Monica relayed the message she had received, repeating it.

'How is it going?' she asked.

'Not perfect yet. We still haven't located Klein. I have the feeling we shall soon.'

'One more thing. Cord Dillon arrived from Washington. Since you weren't here he talked with Howard. Don't think he liked his reception. He's flying to Rotterdam to see you. Howard told him you were there. I'm sorry.'

'Not to worry, I'll cope. 'Bye for now.'

Tweed repeated to Newman the gist of the message that it was Rotterdam. No doubt this time. 'And that,' he said grimly, 'I think is the last message from Olympus before the balloon goes up. I'm very worried about Olympus.'

'Who by some chance is inside Klein's organization. Hence these reports?'

'In a nutshell. If Klein ever suspects Olympus that will be the end of my agent. Still, there's not a thing I can do about that. Oh, and Cord Dillon, Deputy Director CIA is on his way over here. I think he's heard those rumours there is an American mixed up in this business. We'll just have to see when he gets here.'

'A rugged type,' Newman commented.

'You could say that . . .'

Van Gorp came into the room and did not look happy. With a sigh he straddled a chair and waved his hands in a gesture of frustration.

'I've been in touch with Marine Control, issued the warning. They refuse to pass it on to the various ships' masters – unless the warning is confirmed by the Minister who is attending a late night Cabinet meeting. The Minister, I'm sure, will refuse.'

'On what grounds?' demanded Tweed.

'The usual ones. Lack of positive evidence. The man I spoke to at Marine Control said he had little doubt the whole thing was a hoax. Couldn't convince him.'

'Jesus,' said Newman.

'Yes,' Van Gorp agreed, 'we may need *His* help before long.'

He looked up, called come in as someone rapped on the door. A uniformed policewoman entered, holding a sheaf of papers. Tweed noticed the papers were quivering.

'You're needed very urgently, sir.'

412

'Excuse me. Back in a minute.'

'Now what,' Tweed mused as they waited. 'That girl's hands were trembling.'

'Maybe Van Gorp is a harder taskmaster than we realized,' Newman joked. Anything to lighten the atmosphere of tension he sensed was building up. He lit a cigarette. He had taken only a few short puffs when Van Gorp reappeared, his face ashen. He closed the door carefully.

'What's wrong?' Tweed asked.

'Something terrible, really appalling. You remember that I had the marines confined to barracks – with the Minister's approval?'

'Yes.' Tweed stood up. 'What has happened?'

'A tremendous explosion – unprecedented power – just took place at the barracks. God knows how many marines are dead. Others badly injured. The entire unit has been wiped out. It must have been several very big bombs . . .'

'No, just one,' Tweed told him. 'And this is Klein's first opening strike. Clever – fiendishly. He has eliminated what he thinks is the one assault group which could cause him trouble. I'm terribly sorry to hear your news. It's a tragedy. But I must also point out it gives us the measure of what we are up against . . .'

The uniformed policewoman appeared. 'The Hague is calling you,' she told Van Gorp.

Before he left he asked Tweed a question.

'I'm still stunned. What was that you meant by the one assault group, etc.?'

'Klein doesn't know there's an SAS unit waiting at Rotterdam Airport . . .'

'I'll remember that when I deal with this phone call.'

He was away longer this time. Tweed unfolded a map of Rotterdam extending to Europoort and the coast and studied it. Newman stood alongside him as Tweed drew a circle with a felt tip pen round Euromast.

'We should be sending men there now,' he was saying when Van Gorp came back.

The Dutchman had recovered his normal poise, stood

erect and pulled at his moustache before he spoke. His manner was crisp, commanding.

'Guess what? The Minister has reinstated me. I asked for it to be put in writing.' He grinned cynically and then became businesslike. 'The warning to all shipping lying offshore is being transmitted at this moment – with the full backing of The Hague.'

'It may be too late,' Tweed warned.

'We'll take it as it comes. More important. The Dutch PM is calling your PM, asking for permission to use the SAS force if necessary. I suspect the Minister of the Interior is taking full credit for that general alert I sent out earlier – even in an emergency like this politicians never lose a chance to gain kudos.'

'In that case,' said Tweed, 'I'd like a private word with my colleague, Blade. I can send him out to the airport to alert the SAS team.'

'Do it. He's waiting downstairs with the others.'

Tweed was talking to Blade in a small room on their own when Van Gorp appeared. During their few minutes alone Tweed had told Blade about the destruction of the Dutch marine unit.

'Ruthless type of bastard, this Klein,' Blade had commented. 'Still, with us it's always no holds barred. I'll drive at once to the airport, get the lads to kit up inside the charter aircraft. We'll need three plain vans backed up to the machine. That way we can leave unseen the moment you tell me where to head for . . .'

Van Gorp was terse. 'Permission granted to use the SAS unit. Your PM laid down one condition – which was accepted. The unit takes its orders from you, Tweed.'

'I'll pass on the message to the troop commander,' Blade said and left.

'It's carnage out at the marine barracks,' Van Gorp told Tweed. 'Pure carnage. Reports keep coming in, every one worse than the last.'

'In that case we'd better get to Euromast fast. With

plenty of armed men. I want Newman and Butler with me. Benoit will come, too, I'm sure . . .'

Alighting from the Sikorsky at Brussels Airport, Hipper told the pilot to wait, found the hired car he'd phoned ahead for, and drove straight to Peter Brand's headquarters in the house of Avenue Franklin Roosevelt.

When the front door was opened after he'd used the speakphone, Brand's secretary, Nicole, a Belgian brunette, found herself looking at a small plump man wearing a trilby pulled down over his forehead which did not quite conceal shocks of red hair. He also wore a handkerchief tied below his eyes and dark glasses. His right hand held a Luger pistol.

'Oh, my God! I thought you were Mr Hipper . . .'

'That's because I'm a good mimic.' His voice was gravelly.

As he replied Hipper shoved the Luger muzzle into her midriff, backed her into the palatial marble-floored hall, slammed the door shut with his right foot.

'Who else is in the house?' Hipper demanded. 'Fool with me and I'll blow a hole right through you.'

'No . . . one. The servants have been given the day off . . .'

'Except Peter Brand. Take me to him.'

He followed her up the broad winding staircase and along a landing to a heavy mahogany door. She rapped on it automatically with a shaking hand. A voice called out, 'Enter.'

She opened the door and was propelled inside by the muzzle of the Luger. Peter Brand was sitting behind a vast desk whose surface was empty except for three telephones in varying colours.

'This gentleman . . .' She felt silly as soon as she had spoken. '. . . forced his way in and asked for you. I thought it was Mr Hipper.'

Brand jack-knifed upright out of his chair.

415

'What the bloody hell is going on . . .'

His right hand reached for an alarm button concealed under the desk. Hipper placed the muzzle against the side of the girl's skull.

'One mistake and she's dead. That's better.' He reached inside his trench coat pocket and produced a length of strong twine, threw it on the desk. 'Tie her hands behind her back. She lies on the carpet on her stomach while you do it. Then lash her ankles. Try anything funny and she goes first.'

'I'm sorry about this, Nicole,' Brand said as he came round the desk, 'but we'd better do what he says.'

'What about you?' Nicole bleated.

'Don't worry. It will work out in the end. It's a kidnapping, a ransom demand will follow, I expect . . .'

Brand knelt by the prone girl holding the two strands of twine. He bound her wrists, then her ankles as Hipper stood well back, the Luger aimed at Nicole. On his knees, he looked up at Hipper.

'What happens next?'

'Open that wall cupboard over there.'

'It's my private bathroom . . .'

'Open the bloody thing. That's better. Now carry her inside and dump her on the floor. Get on with it. We're leaving in a minute.'

Brand hoisted up the girl, carried her inside the luxurious bathroom, placed her gently on the floor, resting her head on a bathmat he rolled into a makeshift pillow.

'Hurry it up,' snarled Hipper. 'Now shut the door.'

Brand closed the heavy door, walked to the far side of his spacious office as Hipper lowered the gun and pulled the handkerchief down over his neck. He joined the banker.

'Can she hear us?' he whispered.

'No chance. That door is inches thick. I tied her loosely so she'll free herself within the hour. Now she's a witness to the fact I've been kidnapped. How is everything at Rotterdam?'

'Marine barracks blown up on schedule. It's the talk of

the city from something I overhead at Rotterdam Airport. All the marines wiped out . . .'

Brand was startled. 'I didn't bargain for anything like that. Klein said the minimum of force would be used. I don't like this . . .'

'But then there's nothing you can do about it now. The machine is in motion, can't be stopped. Hadn't we better get moving? How did you get rid of all the servants?'

'Gave them the night off . . .' Brand sounded nervous as he slipped on his coat. 'Told them I was holding a confidential conference of bankers.'

'And were you doing that?'

'Of course. To cover myself. Don't worry. They won't start arriving for another hour. We hold these nighttime meetings to avoid publicity. I'm ready. You have a car?'

'Of course.'

Before he alighted from the car at Brussels Airport Hipper, still wearing his outsize dark glasses, pulled up the collar of his trench coat to hide the lower part of his face.

He walked very close to Brand as they walked across the reception hall on their way to the helicopter. He had a nasty shock when one of a pair of policemen patrolling called out to the banker.

'Good evening, sir. Off on your travels again?'

Brand, who rarely smoked, took a cigarette out of his pack and lit it slowly as Hipper stood shoulder to shoulder with him. The cigarette incident would be remembered later, would indicate he'd been in a nervous state. Nicole would confirm he had given it up, that he only smoked at times of high tension.

'It's a fact,' he called back in French. 'Sometimes I think I spend more time in the air than I do on the ground.'

They walked on and Hipper let out his breath through moist lips. The pilot was waiting, reached up and lowered the stepladder leading inside the Sikorsky. A few minutes later they were airborne. Destination: Findel Airport, Luxembourg City.

'How many marines were killed?' Brand asked as the Sikorsky flew on through the night, red and green lights flashing. He had lit another cigarette.

'No idea.' Hipper had lost interest. 'We have this ready to put up outside your bank in the Avenue de la Liberté.' He opened up the brief-case he had propped against the seat.

This was a notice in French, German and English. It announced that the Banque Sambre was temporarily closed owing to an electrical breakdown. Business would be resumed as soon as possible.

'Klein doesn't miss a trick,' Brand snapped after a glance at the notice.

'He is a great organizer,' Hipper agreed in his normal soft voice.

Brand puffed at his cigarette. The Sikorsky dipped and pitched for a few seconds. Brand felt the sweat on his hands. All those Dutch marines killed. There would be a tremendous outcry. He was wondering whether Brazil would be remote and safe enough for him when this was all over. As for his Belgian wife, owner of the bank and frolicking about in New York, he didn't give a damn. Be glad to get rid of the bitch who never stopped yacking away. But this marine business . . . Hipper seemed to sense his misgivings as the Sikorsky flew over the lights of Namur below. Maybe it was that second cigarette, Brand thought later.

'No turning back now, Mr Brand,' Hipper remarked. 'Only one way. Forward. According to plan. You are going to be a very rich man.'

'Do shut up. Let me think.'

*

Chabot sat behind the wheel of his parked van, pretending to read as he watched people walking up and down the flight of steps. Above him loomed Euromast, a blaze of lights shining from the restaurant windows three hundred feet up. He wore a boiler suit, the type of garment favoured by a plumber or electrician. Beside him on the seat was a large bag which might have contained the tools of his trade.

'What's the situation?'

Chabot stiffened, looked out of the side window into the face of Klein who was now wearing a military-type leather overcoat and a peaked cap of the type often liked by German students. He had changed from his chauffeur's uniform in a back street.

'Two minutes to go.' Chabot had checked his watch. 'Situation normal. A number of people dining in the restaurant – no sign of security. But those launches at the end of the basin have police aboard. No more than half a dozen. They are taking no interest in Euromast.'

'Your men are ready? And those in the vehicles parked just a short distance away? I don't see Legaud and his command vehicle.'

'Just pulled in behind me,' Chabot commented, looking in his wing mirror. 'Everyone is ready.'

'And Faltz knows what to do when you reach the restaurant.'

'I've told him enough times. He's dressed like a certain kind of American. Behind me in this van.'

A cluster of visitors, leaving, appeared at the entrance. They moved slowly on full stomachs, spreading across the steps as they began to descend to the street. Klein took one last look round.

'Now!' he said. 'Storm the tower.'

'A pleasure . . .'

Klein moved back, carrying an executive case, as Chabot got slowly out of the car after beating a tattoo on the rear of the cab. The rear doors opened, men climbed out, also clad in boiler suits, carrying bags.

The driver of the vehicle behind Legaud saw the movement and hammered the same tattoo signal. The rear doors of his vehicle opened and five men wearing sports clothes and carrying various cases emerged.

They converged towards the crowd of visitors as the third vehicle spilt out more men. Marler walked alongside Klein, carrying his sports bag as Lara followed them. There was a muddle on the steps. Visitors stood aside, apologizing and nodding their heads.

Inside the entrance a Luxembourger went straight up to the ticket counter, walked round it, thrust an automatic hard against the collector's hip. The weapon was below counter level and could not be seen by other visitors leaving the elevator.

'Stay cool,' the Luxembourger advised. 'Why get killed for what they pay you? Just keep your eyes down, go on counting the money. Act normal – you may live . . .'

Faltz, wearing a loud check sports jacket and light khaki slacks, carrying a large holdall, entered the empty elevator. A heavily-built man, he squeezed close to the control panel as Klein, Marler, Lara, Chabot and three other men crammed themselves inside. Faltz pressed the button for restaurant and was the first to step out of the lift. Carrying the hold-all in his left hand he walked into the restaurant, looked round.

It was half-full of diners eating, drinking, staring out at the lights of the city. He walked across to an empty table at the far side where he could cover the whole room. Perching his hold-all on a chair, he unzipped it.

Three masked men burst into the restaurant through the entrance, armed with Uzi machine-pistols. The leader stood in the centre of the trio and shouted his command in English.

'This is a raid. No one will get hurt unless they resist. You get up slowly from your tables, hands stretched out in front . . .'

There was a stunned silence for several seconds. In the sudden silence the only sound was the clatter of cutlery dropping on to plates.

'Get moving!' the leader shouted. 'Assemble by the lift. Now!'

The scrape of chairs being pushed back, the shuffle of feet as men and women stood up and extended their hands in front of them. Two men stood up suddenly from one of the elevated tables. Each held a pistol, gripped in both hands, aimed at the intruders.

Faltz whipped out his own Uzi, took quick aim, shot them both in the back. One crashed forward on the table, scattering plates on the floor; his companion slumped back and disappeared below the table. A woman screamed. Everyone turned to look at Faltz. The leader of the trio at the entrance shouted again.

'Nothing will happen to you if you move fast. Come on – into the hall by the elevators . . .'

'No more casualties,' the masked Klein whispered. 'We just want them out of here – out of the building.'

The diners were filing forward now, hands extended, threading their way between the tables, women clutching handbags under their arms. The trio parted on either side of the exit, their weapons aimed at the crowd. Klein backed into the hall, watching over the black silk handkerchief tied round his face. Other men were below at ground level, one man in a boiler suit at the door stopping other people entering, telling them there was a fault in the elevator system. His companions would be out of sight, waiting to escort diners from the building as they left the elevator.

Klein pushed his way inside the restaurant. Yes, they had remembered: waiters and staff were being hustled out of the kitchen. Faltz, holding his Uzi, slipped across the room to where Klein stood.

'The bodies – two of them. I checked their pockets. They were police. They're dead. What do we do with them?'

'Later.' Klein's tone was abrupt. 'They'll come in useful.'

Marler had disappeared. Leaving the elevator, he had made straight for the outside platform. Carrying his bag, he walked slowly round, close to the rail, staring down. No sign of hostile activity. Yet. The restaurant windows –

plus their height – would have muffled the shots from the police launches at the end of the basin.

He didn't know it but inside the launches the river police were eating a quick meal prior to their turn to patrol the Maas. He continued his tour until he reached a point in the shadows out of sight of anyone. Opening his bag, he assembled his rifle, screwed on the infra-red telescopic sight and shoved the stock hard against his shoulder.

He was looking down into the deserted park. Small shrubs came up so close in the lens he felt he could reach out and touch them. Holding rifle and bag below rail level, he completed his circuit of the platform and stood back from the entrance to the interior.

The first elevator load had gone down, the cage had returned, more customers and staff were being escorted inside. They moved silently, slowly, fearfully and shuffled their feet.

Klein checked his watch. The marine barracks would have been destroyed. Prussen would be on his way to Euromast – and soon the alarm would be raised. The crowd of diners hurrying down the steps outside would be seen, would find someone to tell about their ordeal.

He walked out on to the platform past Marler and peered over the edge. From Legaud's control van a man was reeling out a cable. He had already reached the top step and as Klein watched he disappeared inside the building. Communications were almost established.

The cable would be plugged into the phone system at ground level. At the right moment Legaud would elevate the van's antennae. Klein would have local communication through the van's amplifiers, long distance via radio. Faltz came out on to the platform.

'Those bodies – the two policemen – I leave them where they are?'

'No. Haul them out here. Dump them near the rail. Later we shove them over the edge – just to show them we mean business.'

47

Tweed sat beside Van Gorp who was driving with Paula and Newman in the rear seats. They were on their way to Euromast. Paula noticed Tweed kept smoothing his hair with his hand, a sure sign he was uneasy.

'Something wrong?' she asked.

'He'll have synchronized the whole operation. That's the way his mind works – and we're up against a brilllant mind – diabolical but brilliant.'

'Synchronized?' she queried.

'That horrible massacre at the marines barracks. Something else will have happened. It's going to be an ordeal of pure terror.'

Van Gorp picked up the car phone as it began buzzing. Listening for a few moments, he said he understood, that he was on his way. His expression was grim in the mirror Paula saw. The Dutchman accelerated as he spoke.

'You were right all along, Tweed. He's seized control of the Euromast. Or someone has.'

'It will be Klein. How detailed was the report?'

'Garbled fragments – as so often happens warning a crisis is in the making. A large group of men – and one woman – invaded Euromast. Armed with machine-pistols, they think. Everyone in the restaurant was bundled outside . . .'

'You said you had two of your men in that restaurant,' Tweed recalled.

A bitter note entered Van Gorp's voice. 'They tried to repel the intruders. They were shot in the back . . .'

'Something odd there,' Newman interjected. 'Why didn't they hold the people dining as hostages – to guarantee their own safety? Normal procedure . . .'

'Klein isn't normal,' Tweed replied grimly. 'I suspect we'll find he already has hundreds of hostages – aboard those ships waiting offshore. We'll soon know, but I fear the worst.'

Van Gorp picked up the phone again, pressed a number and then spoke in Dutch. The conversation lasted several minutes and he reduced speed. Replacing the phone he glanced in the mirror and pulled in to the kerb alongside the Maas.

'We're close to Euromast. We walk the rest of the way. The area is cordoned off. Too dangerous to drive closer.'

The first thing Tweed noticed as they walked along the pavement by the river was the silence, the absence of any sound of traffic. They passed several couples hurrying in the opposite direction. None of them were speaking. They glanced at Tweed and his companions. One man with a woman stopped as though about to speak to Van Gorp who was on the outside. The woman tugged at his sleeve and he walked on without saying anything.

Out on the river three barges were turning in mid-stream very slowly. Tweed watched them as they headed for a large basin on the far shore. A police launch, blue light flashing, came up behind them, at speed, then cut its engine and began drifting with the current.

Soon they were quite alone as they approached the large park below Euromast. No traffic on the river, none on the road, no more pedestrians. An uncanny silence which had a sinister atmosphere descended on the area. In the distance a wide red and white tape was stretched across the road, extending over the sidewalk.

'What is happening?' Tweed asked.

'Two cordons have been set up – one there in front of us and another half a mile further back. The whole area is being sealed off – including the river. Traffic helicopters have been forbidden to fly anywhere near the tower. We are moving into a zone of total isolation.'

*

'What is the position, Inspector?' Van Gorp asked a small wiry man who appeared to be in charge of the police gathered by the barricade.

'A large group of men have seized Euromast – armed men. You should not proceed beyond the tape, I suggest. A temporary HQ has been set up in a building on West Zeedijk at the end of Parkhaven.'

'What is Parkhaven?' Tweed asked.

The inspector glanced at Van Gorp. 'It's all right,' the Dutchman replied. 'This is Tweed, Commander of the Anti-Terrorist Squad in London. He probably knows more about those people inside Euromast than any of us.'

'Parkhaven is the docking basin Euromast overlooks.'

'And why should we not proceed beyond the tape?' Tweed pressed. 'Has there been trouble already?'

'Two of my men made their way towards the entrance steps. A man inside the entrance fired two bursts of machine-gun fire. Warning bursts, I believe. He could hardly have missed had he intended to hit them. Since then there has been an unnerving silence.'

'Klein tactics,' Tweed whispered to Van Gorp.

'So how do we reach this HQ? Quickly. Even at some risk,' Van Gorp said firmly.

'You could take that path across the park and past the church. But keep an eye on the tower. We don't know what maniacs we may be dealing with.'

'I was told all the diners and staff were herded out. Is that correct?'

'Yes, which is rather strange. Almost as though they cleared the decks for action, so to speak.'

'They did,' Tweed told him.

'I had two men inside the restaurant,' Van Gorp said stiffly to the Inspector. 'I know they were shot. Any further news?'

'None. We questioned a number of the diners – a police patrol car happened to be cruising close by and saw something was not right. The descriptions of the weapon used differ – but we believe it must have been a 9 mm Heckler and Koch or a Uzi . . .'

'I see.' Van Gorp's tone was clipped. He turned to Tweed. 'I am forgetting my manners. This is Inspector Jansen. Now, we'd better make our way across the park.'

'I will come with you,' Jansen said, 'then I can take you to the HQ. We shall not be very close to Euromast but we shall be exposed if there is a marksman up there on that platform.'

'There probably will be,' Tweed remarked. 'The best in Europe. So I suggest we don't talk, that we spread out.'

'Several rifles have arrived but none of our marksmen yet.'

'I can use a rifle,' Newman said.

'And,' Tweed added, 'he's had military training and was a crack shot at Bisley.'

'Give him a rifle,' Van Gorp ordered. 'I will take full responsibility. This situation is unprecedented . . .'

There was a very brief delay while Jansen fetched a rifle from a van, handed it to Newman, who examined it by the light of a street lamp. He checked the weapon to make sure it was unloaded, tested the mechanism, accepted a magazine from Jansen and nodded.

'I'm ready.'

The walk across the park along the winding footpath was an eerie experience. Jansen led the single file and Tweed had Paula in front of him so he could throw her to the ground if shooting started. Although a distance away the Euromast seemed to loom over them. The lights were on in the restaurant windows but there was no sign of life.

Newman walked on the grass a few yards away from the file and closer to the tower. He held the rifle across his chest, the muzzle slanted upwards. He glanced ahead frequently but most of the time he was watching the tower. He didn't expect to hit a target if an emergency arose but he knew he could fire with close enough accuracy to hit above the rail, to force any marksman to keep his head down.

The silence amid the grass and the trees became more oppressive. The path seemed to wind forever. Newman was relieved when his night vision became accustomed to the darkness. He thought he saw movement, stopped instantly, took the aiming position, his finger round the trigger. He resumed walking slowly when he decided it had been an illusion.

They left the park, crossed a wide street by a church, made their way round a complex and deserted intersection of streets, then Jansen led them to the back of a building. A uniformed policeman stood on guard. They went inside.

They were climbing a stone staircase when Tweed asked Jansen the question.

'Was a girl seen among the intruders?'

'Yes, quite young. Early twenties. Had her face masked with a coloured handkerchief. Again, descriptions varied to the point of futility.'

'Was she also carrying a gun?'

'No one asked that question. I think one of the guests who were thrown out would have mentioned it. They mentioned a girl – as though surprised. These days!'

'Could she have been taken in under duress?'

'I don't think so. One witness – a woman, of course – said she marched in as though she owned the place.'

'Why are you so interested in this girl?' Newman asked.

He had caught up with Tweed on one side while Paula joined them on the other. Jansen was climbing nimbly higher to yet another floor.

'I am thinking of Lara Seagrave, the girl I cross-examined in Smiths' tea-room in Paris, the girl whose bitch of a step-mother – Lady Windermere – I visited in London. The girl The Parrot was following all the way from Marseilles, watching her take photos of different ports. The girl whom, I'm convinced, set out on this thinking it was all an adventure. Why Klein still needs her I can't imagine.'

They had arrived. Jansen paused before a metal fire door

which was guarded by a uniformed policeman. He waited until they had reached him before he issued his warning.

'We're going out on to the roof. Crouch low, move slowly. We don't want those people inside Euromast to spot us – someone may be scanning the whole area with binoculars . . .'

The roof was a flat concrete surface surrounded by waist-high walls. Stooping low, Tweed followed Jansen. The silhouettes of a large number of men were scattered in different positions. The majority close to the wall nearest Parkhaven.

Jansen led him to where a tripod had been erected. A telescope was mounted on the tripod. Further along the wall stood a second tripod supporting a cine-camera with a zoom lens. A man crouched behind the camera.

'This observation point is the nearest we can get,' Jansen explained. 'The telescope gives us a clear view of the platform.'

'But hasn't there been any communication from them?' Tweed asked, squatting on his haunches. 'And how would you respond?'

'No communication at all.' Jansen sounded depressed. 'Except when a couple of my men approached the tower and they reacted with a machine-gun burst. As a warning to keep away. Since then an awful silence.'

'Klein tactics,' Tweed repeated, turning to Van Gorp who was crouched beside him. 'It's the prelude – to unnerve us.'

'Answering your second question,' Jansen went on, 'we have brought in a police van with an amplified speaker. Parked behind an empty truck to shield it from the tower. No reaction to that – except for a call to speak to someone in high authority.'

Tweed looked at Van Gorp who flexed his hands before he spoke. 'I'd better go out there and try to get Klein talking – if he is up there.'

'Oh, he's up there, all right.' Tweed's tone was brisk. 'But I think I'm the one to attempt it. I'm beginning to know how his mind works. I've had secret reports on his background and character. Before I go I'd like to call my colleague, Blade, at the airport, arrange for the SAS team to be brought near here. They'll need quarters on their own – with no contacts with the police.'

'We may have just what you need,' said Jansen. 'I'll show you . . .'

He waited while Tweed took a quick look through the telescope. The platform appeared deserted. He swung the lens a few degrees and the restaurant came into view. All the lights were still on but over a number of windows there were hangings obscuring the interior. Either curtains had been drawn or they'd used table cloths. Figures moved beyond the clear windows and vanished.

'Don't go,' said Paula. 'It's too dangerous. Klein is crazy.'

'Maybe a little, but I'm going.'

'And I'm coming with you,' Newman said, still holding the rifle. He gave Paula a wink of reassurance.

The quarters Jansen suggested for use by the SAS team were one floor down, at the back of the building. Four rooms – with a bathroom – separated from the rest of the building. Over the windows blinds were drawn down. Tweed agreed they were suitable, Jansen produced a street plan, marked the route the team should follow, said he would send a motor-cycle outrider to escort them and then left Tweed alone to use the phone perched on a rough wooden table.

'Blade,' he said when he got through, 'situation here at Euromast serious. An armed group has taken possession. No, they didn't take hostages – just threw everyone out. A motor-cycle outrider is coming to guide you here with your team. I'll give him a note signed by me. It will include the word Olympus.'

'I'll get the lads geared up ready now. Somewhere we can wait? Discreetly?'

'Attended to.'

'Be with you shortly . . .'

429

Tweed sat motionless at the table for a few moments, thinking of his approach when he reached the tower. Then he dismissed the idea. Always best not to rehearse in advance. Play it off the cuff. He went outside where Newman was waiting for him.

Tweed walked with a steady tread beyond the barrier cordoning off Parkhaven. He couldn't remember when he'd last slept but now the moment of crisis had arrived fresh adrenalin was pumping through his veins.

Hatless, he wore an overcoat, both hands in view, arms swinging gently. He was damned if he was going out there with his hands in the air. As he headed towards the police radio car parked behind the truck he slowed his pace, studying everything in sight at ground level.

Below Euromast the four rows of barges berthed alongside each other were still there, the barges he'd noticed looking down from the platform. The atmosphere was weirdly silent and deserted. No traffic movement on the Maas. He glanced at the three police launches moored at the end of the basin. From inside motionless figures watched him as he kept up his pace. He reached the police van.

Through the open window he saw a man behind the wheel on the side furthest from the tower. He leant his forearms on the edge of the window.

'Let me have the mike. I'm here with the authority of Inspector Jansen . . .'

'I know. You're Tweed. He's called through over the radio.' He handed over the microphone and Tweed saw it had a long cord. That was helpful. He gripped the mike, turned, walked to the foot of the steps and looked up. Two figures peered at him over the rail from the platform, one aiming a rifle, both masked.

Newman braced himself against the wall of the building where he had stayed when Tweed went into the open. His rifle was aimed at the waiting figures three hundred feet above.

Klein stood by the rail alongside Marler who held his rifle aimed at the figure below. Klein had a pair of night-glasses trained on the tiny figure at the base of the tower. The face was clear in the lenses and Klein sucked in his breath.

'God! What's *he* doing down there? How could he have got here so fast?'

'Who is it?' Marler enquired in a languid tone.

'Tweed. The last man on God's earth I expected to confront.'

'Who is Tweed?'

'Deputy Director of the British Secret Service. One of the most wily and dangerous men in Europe. Time to scare the guts out of the bastard.' Klein switched on the throat microphone linked to Legaud's command vehicle and its amplifiers.

'Who are you?' Klein demanded in English.

His voice blasted out of the amplifiers on the roof of Legaud's van. Distorted, it had the weird echo of a ghost as it carried to Newman, to the watching police on top of the HQ building.

'My name is Tweed. I have the full authority of the Dutch police to talk to you. We want you to evacuate Euromast at once. And if your gunman pulls the trigger you are both dead within seconds.'

His own voice, broadcast by the speaker on top of the radio van, sounded normal, calm, as though this was a normal situation.

'Do not threaten me. You hold the lives of thousands of people in your hands.'

The voice was confident, chilling. Almost as though Napoleon were issuing orders for the battle of Austerlitz Klein raised his other hand, holding a black box.

'Do you know what I am holding? The radio control to liquidate all those people aboard the ships waiting outside

431

the Maas. If you shot me my thumb would depress a button – sending out a signal which would detonate the sea-mines.'

'What are you chattering on about?' Tweed asked, attempting to throw Klein off balance – to reveal too much.

'A large team of scuba divers has attached sea-mines to many ships. The *Cayman Conqueror* and *Easter Island* supertankers. The freighter from Genoa, the *Otranto*. Three container ships.' A pause. Tweed heard Klein suck in his breath before he went on. 'And above all, the *Adenauer*.'

'So you say . . .'

'*Tweed!*' Klein's voice was ice-cold. 'Let me explain what I can do. This control box was designed by the Swiss. They are very good with sophisticated mechanisms. You have heard of the Swiss?' The tone was mocking.

'I believe so. Yes.'

It was a duel of nerves. Newman grasped that immediately as he watched the erect figure on the platform through his telescopic sight. Hatless, thick dark hair, wearing a leather military-type coat with broad lapels, Klein was determined to dominate the tiny figure at the foot of the tower. And Newman could hear every word of the exchanges. Could Tweed hold his own? A man almost dropping with fatigue.

'The box I am holding – which will be in my hands at all times – has a number of buttons. Each attuned to a different waveband, each linked in this way with the sea-mines under a particular vessel. Take your hand out of your pocket.'

Tweed, gripping the microphone at the end of the cable leading to the police van in his right hand, had thrust the other hand inside his coat pocket.

'I'm not here to pander to your whims,' he replied. 'Get on with what you have to say.'

'So, by pressing, say number one button, I can sink the *Otranto* by itself. The freighter will vapourize. The other vessels remain afloat. There is another button for the *Cayman Conqueror*, and so on. You understand what I am saying?'

'Highly ingenious.'

'Tweed, you had better take me seriously . . .'

'Oh, I'm doing just that. The reverse applies. You are surrounded, isolated, and Euromast can be stormed at one word of command.'

'I still do not think you have grasped the situation. On the control box I hold there is a red button. The one my thumb is poised over now. That is tuned to a different waveband – a waveband with a signal common to every vessel which has been mined. I press the red button and all the mines detonate, all the ships go down, including the *Adenaeur.*'

'Highly ingenious . . .'

'Two hundred million pounds in gold bullion is the price. My researches tell me that gold is now held at the Deutsche Bank in Frankfurt for a South American loan. Have it loaded aboard the chartered Hercules transport waiting at Frankfurt Airport. I will later give you its destination. The crew for the plane is also waiting. Understood, Tweed?'

'Government sanction will have to be . . .'

'I haven't finished.'

Above the distortion of the amplifiers Klein's voice came like a whiplash.

'I can't hang about here all night,' Tweed informed him.

'Hang? Hanging. Yes, that is part of the scenario you will see unfold.'

The hairs on the back of Tweed's neck crawled. The cruelty of this man was limitless. What was he talking about? Klein was talking again.

'A warning. The majority of my men are not inside this tower. They are watching those ships. Do not try to find them. They are in radio communication all the time. Do not attempt to disembark one passenger or crewman from any of the ships. Do not attempt to smuggle out naval bomb disposal scuba divers to any ship. Do not attempt to interfere with my communications with jamming equipment. Do not let anyone go near the cream command vehicle a few yards from where you stand. Do not interfere

433

with the lighting or power of Euromast. If any of these instructions are disobeyed I press the red button.'

'Any more suggestions?'

'Tell the Dutch to search for two fishing vessels abandoned offshore west of the mouth of the Maas. The *Utrecht* and the *Drenthe*. Their crews will confirm I have done what I have told you. And no craft of any kind must move on the Maas. The go-between who will arrange for the bullion to be loaded aboard the transport aircraft at Frankfurt is Peter Brand, the Belgian banker. Banque Sambre. Understood?'

'Seems clear enough.'

'You will come back here in precisely four hours from now. At 3 a.m. You will then be told the destination of the Hercules carrying the bullion.'

'Governments have to be consulted . . .'

'One thing more,' the chilling voice continued. 'The British Sealink ferry was delayed docking at the Hook of Holland by the presence of so much shipping. It waited off shore. That ferry is also mined. It must not move from its present position.'

'If you say so. You could be bluffing.'

Tweed maintained the same casual, offhand tone he had kept up during the long deadly dialogue, still hoping to provoke Klein into saying the wrong thing. He appeared at long last to have irked his enemy.

'Tweed! You still do not seem to have fully grasped the enormity of what faces you. Before you go, perhaps this will help to convince you.'

Klein stepped back from the rail, nodded to two of his men who crouched below the rail. They heaved up the bodies of the two detectives shot in the restaurant and heaved them over the edge, dropping them three hundred feet.

The first body hit the steps a dozen yards from where Tweed was standing. Hit the concrete like a sack of cement with a soft thud. The second corpse sailed out a few feet further, sank like rock, head first. Tweed clearly heard the crack of the skull splitting open. He felt sick, then a cold fury.

'One final demonstration,' Klein called out.

The giant dredger, *Ameland*, had continued its work of scooping the bed of the Maas clear of silt late with the aid of lights. Now the eighteen-man crew were snatching a quick meal below as the massive hulk began moving from the middle of the Maas on its way to its berthing dock. It moved very slowly and a mile away two men sat in a dinghy offshore from a breakwater watching.

One man had a pair of night-glasses focused on the *Ameland*, the other nursed a compact powerful transceiver in his large lap. Both Luxembourgers were dressed as seamen. Beyond the breakwater onshore a Saab was parked in the wilderness of scrub and sand. The man with the transceiver checked his watch by its illuminated face and gave his companion a nudge.

'Soon now. Any moment . . .'

He never finished his sentence. There was a muffled thump – it was a small sea-mine. A brief flash of light which lasted seconds. The dredger shuddered as though struck by a giant's hammer, listed, tilted at a more extreme angle. The scoop at the tip of the metal arm performed a slow arc. The dredger upended, held its distorted angle for a moment, then the whole vessel split in two and sank beneath the surface. Thirty seconds had elapsed since the mine was detonated. No survivors.

'The demonstration has taken place,' Klein announced. 'Near the mouth of the Maas the dredger *Ameland* has just been sunk in mid-channel.' He removed his thumb from button number two, moved it above the red button.

Tweed stood very still, staring upwards. He recalled watching the dredger at work when they had driven out with Van Gorp to the North Sea.

'What about the crew?' he said into the mike.

'I imagine they are enjoying life with the fishes – twenty fathoms down.' His voice became more piercing through the amplifier. 'The Maas is now partially blocked to shipping of any size. If necessary, other mined ships inside the river will also go down. The gateway to Europe will be closed. You have until three in the morning, Tweed. Any more questions?'

Tweed walked back to the police van, handed back the microphone to the driver, then at a brisk pace made his way back to where Newman still waited, rifle aimed at the Euromast platform.

48

'It happened,' Van Gorp informed Tweed. 'The *Ameland* has been sunk in mid-channel. A danger to the largest ships wishing to reach Europort.'

They were sitting round a table in the HQ building. Newman, Paula, Butler, Jansen and Benoit. The room was bleak and sparsely furnished. Van Gorp had explained it was in the process of renovation. Coffee had been brought in from an improvised kitchen.

'How many crew on board the dredger?' Tweed asked.

'Eighteen. All drowned.'

'And those two bodies lying at the base of Euromast are your men?'

'Yes. The two detectives I placed in the restaurant. I asked over the phone via the police van for permission to collect them while you were on your way back up here. Permission was refused, the brutal bastard.'

'Tactics again,' Tweed said quietly. 'I know Klein now. His policy is to show no mercy.'

'And he tried to break your will,' Newman observed.

'Tried very hard. My technique of baiting him with a casual attitude did make him talk too much. The unknown is the most terrifying. Now we know he has the box – that he can sink all those ships. So there must be no overt action. Yet.'

'Your SAS team is due shortly,' Van Gorp reminded him. 'What do they do?'

'Take up the quarters assigned to them. Blade will continue to act as our liaison with them. You'll never see their faces or that of the commander of the Sabre Troop,' he added, covering Blade's real role.

'You know Klein better than any of us. What do we do?' asked Van Gorp.

'We give in. Accept his demands. Let him have the bullion.' Tweed spread his hands. 'What else can we do? He may soon sink the *Otranto* to show he means business. My PM will support me.'

'I thought she *never* gave in,' Van Gorp commented.

'You heard what he said. He can close down Europe – simply by sinking more ships he must have mined inside the Maas. Look at the vast amount of supplies from abroad which come in via Europort – or sail on direct up the Rhine. Germany is very vulnerable. So is Switzerland and Austria. Holland as well. And it's two-way traffic. Think of the huge volume of exports travelling all over the world via Europort. Look at the amount of oil which comes in by this route. Antwerp can't take the extra load – it's working to full capacity already.'

'We could organize an airlift,' Jansen suggested. 'Like the famous 1948 airlift into Berlin.'

'That was to keep one city going. And they only just managed it. We are talking about half a continent. To say nothing of the lives of all those people aboard the ships waiting in the North Sea. No,' Tweed said emphatically, 'we give in. I had better tell Klein briefly now to keep him quiet. Where is this phone linked to your van outside Euromast?'

'In the next room. You just pick it up, speak to the

driver and you're through to the speaker mounted on the van's roof. While you were out there talking to him I've made a number of brief phone calls. Bonn, The Hague, Berne and Paris have been alerted. They're talking already, thinking of calling a conference.'

'No time.' Tweed was abrupt as he stood up. 'Klein will not wait. And there are a lot of decisions to take when I've told him of our decision.'

He left them, went into the next room to use the phone. Newman lit a cigarette. Van Gorp 'borrowed' one from him. It was Paula who made the comment.

'Tweed is now at his most dangerous. He said he's giving in. Don't believe it. He's waiting his opportunity. No one is going to manipulate him.' She looked at Van Gorp. 'Didn't you notice when he said "no overt action" he added "yet"?'

'But I don't see what we can do. The governments will not agree, I'm sure. And if they don't Klein will close down Europe. It's deadlock.'

'I've told him we agree,' Tweed announced when he returned and sat at the table. 'He went on again about how he was in supreme command – the Napoleonic touch again. I just listened and repeated that we agree. He still wants me back at the base of the tower at 3 a.m. What's happened?' he asked seeing the expression on Van Gorp's face.

'I'm afraid there has been a further development.' It was Benoit who answered. 'A phone call from Brussels. Peter Brand has been kidnapped at gunpoint. I also spoke to his secretary who is in a state of near-hysterics. One of the police officers at Brand's house in Brussels told me he was seen at the airport – boarding a helicopter. It flew off in a south-easterly direction.'

'Findel Airport. The Banque Sambre in Luxembourg City.' Tweed glanced at Newman. 'Kidnapped! Another Klein smokescreen – to make Brand feel he's protected.

438

A go-between, as he called Brand, acting under so-called duress. Brand is going to be on the spot when the bullion is flown aboard that transport plane to Findel.'

'What do you suggest?' Benoit enquired.

'I'd like Newman and Butler to be flown at once to Findel. Bob knows Brand, has met him. With your permission, Benoit, I'd like to give Newman carte blanche to act as he thinks fit when he gets there.'

'And I'd like to take that rifle with me if possible,' Newman requested.

'Agreed,' said Van Gorp.

He took one of several form pads which had been placed on the table. Scribbling on a sheet, he signed it, handed it to Newman.

'That covers you for Holland. Benoit will, I am sure, grant you authority for the firearm later.'

'Of course,' Benoit said. 'But how quickly can we get moving on the flight at this hour?'

'I know a Royal Dutch Shell director who has an executive jet at Rotterdam Airport,' Van Gorp replied. 'I'll call him while the three of you are being driven to the airport.'

'A hand-gun might come in useful for me,' Butler suggested.

'A Browning automatic would do?' Van Gorp asked. 'Good. We will supply it, borrow it from one of my men.' He scribbled again on his pad, tore off the sheet and handed it to Butler. Writing something on another sheet, he handed it to Newman. 'That is the number here where you can contact Tweed. Anything else before I phone about the executive jet?'

'Yes,' said Tweed. 'Apart from checking on those fishing boats – as Klein suggested – I strongly urge you to ensure all his other instructions are obeyed. No searching for his men watching those ships, no attempt to use scuba divers to check the named vessels for those sea-mines. They are where he said they were. We just wait. One thing worries me intensely.'

'Which is?' asked Paula.

'His reference to hanging. That it was part of his scenario. I can't figure it out. But I don't like it. Now, I need the use of a scrambler phone to call the PM . . .'

'Just installed. The lines will be burning all night between here and The Hague. To say nothing of Bonn and God knows where else. Through that door. There's an anteroom leading to the quarters your SAS team will occupy. You can use the phone now. Don't forget to press the red button . . .'

Tweed closed the door behind him as a plain-clothes detective came into the room and spoke to Van Gorp in Dutch, then left. There was a lot of activity and Newman was impressed with the way everything seemed under control. No sign of panic. Van Gorp used the phone on the table, had a brief conversation in Dutch, ended the call, looked at Newman.

'The executive jet is at your disposal. The pilot will be at the airport waiting when you get there. And a car is waiting in the side street for you. Also a policeman on the ground floor will give you a scabbard to conceal that rifle. Butler, he will give you a Browning and a hip-holster – if that's OK?'

'Prefer them. Takes forever to haul it from the shoulder type.'

'One point,' Benoit intervened as he stood up with Newman and Butler, 'I'd like to call in briefly at Brussels Airport before we fly on to Findel. First, I can call the local chief of police in Luxembourg City. Second, Brand and another man were by chance seen at that airport. I'd like a first-hand report.'

'Tell the pilot. He is under your instructions to fly wherever you tell him.' He stood up, shook hands with all three men. 'Good luck. We'll keep in touch. This nightmare has to end soon – for better or worse . . .'

Inside Euromast at platform level Klein had finished checking that everything was to his satisfaction. He'd sent Chabot to organize defence at ground level. At this stage he would not risk being trapped in the elevator and out of touch. Everywhere he went he carried the control box.

The elevator doors opened and Chabot stepped out. He nodded to Klein.

'If they try to rush the building they'll be cut down. Furniture has been piled up into barriers. Men with machine-pistols are posted covering the entrance.'

'Expecting a spot of trouble?' drawled Marler who had walked in from the platform, rifle cuddled under one arm.

'Just taking every precaution,' Klein replied coldly. 'It's not likely while I hold this.' He extended his right hand, gripping the control box, thumb poised over the red button.

'And the whole shooting match really goes up if you pressed that little jigger?'

'Every ship I have named floating offshore – and a few more I haven't in the Maas.'

'Good show. You seem to be organized. Think they'll really pay up the dibs?'

'What option have they?' Klein turned away and addressed the Frenchman. 'Go fetch the girl. Time to prepare her.'

'Prepare her for what exactly?' Marler enquired.

'You'll see. In due course. Shouldn't you be watching on the platform?'

'With two of your sturdy lads out there guarding the fort? Incidentally, they're a bit tense. Tell from the way they grip their weapons. Persuade them to relax a bit when you next go out. Trigger-happy characters worry me. I could do with a drink.'

'There's only mineral water or coffee . . .'

'Water will do splendidly. Gets a bit thirst-making during the early hours . . .'

Earlier Klein had personally supervised the emptying down a sink of every bottle of alcohol stacked in the bar. No one was going to have his brain muddled with alcohol while the operation was in progress. Marler stared with vague interest as Chabot and a Luxembourger hauled Lara

Seagrave out of the restaurant kicking and elbowing them in the ribs. She glared at Klein.

'What the hell do these thugs think they are doing?'

'Acting on my instructions. Tie her by the hands – behind her back – and by the ankles.'

A second Luxembourger appeared and grabbed her from behind. Chabot released her and walked towards Klein, his expression grim, his large hands clenched into fists.

'What exactly are you doing?' he demanded.

'I know you're sweet on her. That is immaterial. Go out on to the platform and check the situation. Then come back and report to me.'

Klein turned away and watched Lara as she protested violently. Marler lit a cigarette, tucked it in the corner of his mouth and spoke quietly.

'I also am interested in what you propose to do with her – has she misbehaved in some way?'

'Nothing to do with you.'

'I'll ask you once more,' Marler continued in the same even tone as Chabot disappeared outside. 'Has she misbehaved? I'm talking to you, Klein.'

'Don't you see?' Klein swung round to face Marler, his hand holding the control box at waist level, smiling savagely. 'She's a spy. We caught her entering the Hotel Central. She had been instructed to stay inside. I think she was phoning someone.'

'That's bloody ridiculous!' Lara shouted as her hands were bound behind her. 'I have done everything you ever asked me to . . .'

'And maybe a little bit more I didn't.'

'Klein, I'm inclined to agree with Lara. This is faintly ridiculous. Pure supposition.'

'Then how did Tweed turn up here so quickly?'

'No idea. Maybe he tracked you.'

'My security is meticulous. We will not discuss this matter any further. And I thought you wanted a drink of water.'

'So I did.' Marler grinned. 'Thank you so much for reminding me.'

He walked off in the direction of the restaurant. They were binding Lara's ankles together now. She tried to struggle but the two men held her tight. Klein waited until she was trussed up and then nodded to the man holding a looped rope.

'Now, tie that round her waist. Not too tight. Must allow her to breathe.'

The rope was lopped round her slim waist and for the first time Lara's fury gave way to fear. She bit her lip to stop showing any emotion. When the job was finished there was a length of rope extending from the centre of her back about twelve feet in length. The Luxembourger coiled it, lifted her up and spread her along a deep couch against the wall.

'What about this?' he asked, picking off the floor the rope noose he had dropped while tying the girl up. Like the other length round her waist it extended about twelve feet from the noose.

'Leave it near her feet for the moment.'

'What is it for?'

'Have you never noticed how sentimental the world is over the fate of a single individual as opposed to the lives of thousands? The average human mind cannot encompass the death of whole tribes in Africa. But if one single hostage is at risk it becomes high drama. We must use every psychological weapon to force the governments concerned to obey us. Public opinion will do the trick if all else fails. And it is a three-hundred-foot drop from the platform.'

49

The car taking Newman, Butler and Benoit to the airport followed Route One – a route Van Gorp had worked out carefully on a map and had cordoned off. On the way they passed a small convoy of three vans proceeding at high speed in the opposite direction.

'The SAS team,' Newman said laconically. 'Thank God it was flown over – after what happened to the Dutch marines.'

'You think Tweed will ever use it?' asked Benoit.

'He'll use it. He's just waiting for Klein to make one slip – and Klein will do just that. He thinks he's infallible. No one is.'

'When we get to the airport,' Butler interjected, 'can we find out what type of machine was used to fly Brand and his so-called captor to Findel? It will help us when we get there. I mean Brussels Airport.'

'Good idea,' Benoit agreed. 'Should have thought of it myself.'

'He doesn't say a lot,' Newman commented, 'but when he does it's worth listening to. And if you ever see him coming towards you on a motor-bike,' he joked, 'run for your life.'

'Everyone has to have a hobby,' Butler replied.

'Yes, but not a lethal one.'

Newman was aware of a different atmosphere inside the car as the uniformed police driver approached the airport. Back at the improvised HQ near Euromast it had been claustrophobic. Now he was doing something active Newman felt a lifting of the spirits. He sensed the same reaction in his companions.

'Van Gorp has arranged for food to be taken aboard the jet,' remarked Benoit. 'Suddenly I'm ravenous.'

'I could do with a bite to eat myself,' agreed Butler.

'And I do believe we have arrived,' Benoit said as the car came to a stop. A police escort took them to the waiting machine and no one asked Newman questions about the scabbard he carried with the suitcase he'd picked up from the Hilton en route. Five minutes later the jet was airborne, leaving behind the deserted airport, heading through the night for Brussels.

In Luxembourg City inside the Banque Sambre on the Avenue de la Liberté, Brand and Hipper sat in the banker's office. On their way in they had paused in the empty street to attach the notice announcing the bank was temporarily closed to the front doors.

Hipper had played out his charade of acting as Brand's captor from the moment the Sikorsky landed at Findel. He had walked shoulder to shoulder with the banker to the waiting limousine where a chauffeur opened the rear doors for them.

They were driving along the highway into the city when the Sikorsky took off again, flying back to Rotterdam Airport to join Victor Saur's other machine.

Relaxing in his executive swivel chair, Brand had just called a senior director of the Deutsche Bank in Frankfurt who had already been alerted by Bonn. He picked up a glass of cognac and stared at Hipper, sitting like a sack of potatoes on the other side of the desk.

'They're saying they refuse to release the bullion,' Brand remarked in a lordly tone.

'They must . . .'

'Relax, Hipper. That's the opening move I expected. It's like a chess game. We all go through the motions. But in due course they will release that bullion, permit it to be loaded aboard the waiting transport. Now, hadn't you better do your thing? Call the local police, tell them you

445

have me here with a gun to my head? All that jazz. And if they try to break in here you'll shoot me out of hand. Whatever that weird phrase means,' he added blandly.

'I hope they're convinced . . .'

'Up to you to do just that – convince 'em. Then we wait until the bullion plane arrives and I trot out with you to Findel to check it's all in order.' He sipped his brandy and indicated a closed door. 'Lucky I have an efficient secretary. She has stocked up the fridge and the freezer. We shan't starve. You can cook, I take it?'

'I was once a cook in a restaurant.'

'Splendid! We can eat in the board's dining room. Might as well keep up a decent standard of living while Klein puts on the pressure. Now, that call to the police . . .'

Tweed came back into the room and Paula watched him anxiously, still worried about his lack of sleep. He walked briskly to his chair, sat down and clasped his hands.

'The PM has given me full authority to act in liaison with you, Van Gorp. She's livid about the mining of the Sealink ferry – livid and worried. But she's chirpy, as always. She's already been in touch with the German Chancellor in Bonn, suggesting he permits release of the bullion when I give the word.'

'When will that be?' asked Van Gorp.

'No idea. I've also asked Commander Bellenger to get over here fast from the Hilton. After he's phoned London to arrange for a specialist team of bomb disposal to fly here. Men who know the workings of this new sea-mine and bomb.'

'But,' objected Jansen, 'you've told us not to make any attempt to go near the threatened ships.'

'Correct. But when we've finished off Klein we'll need that team to go out and defuse those mines.'

'You sound very confident,' Paula ventured.

'He's a megalomaniac. He's sure he's got us in the palm of his hand – which he has at the moment. He'll make a mistake through over-confidence. Then we strike. Talking of striking, I thought I heard men arriving in the room beyond the place I was phoning from.'

'The SAS team arrived by the fire escape at the back. They're settling into their quarters. The other door from the anteroom leads into one of their rooms . . .'

Blade came into the room, wearing his civilian outfit. Speaking to Tweed, his manner was urgent.

'The troop commander wants to take his men out on to the roof so they can take a look at Euromast, size it up. It means we need the roof cleared of your men, if that's all right for a few minutes, Van Gorp. They want you to go with them, Tweed – to brief them.'

'I'll attend to it now,' Van Gorp replied.

He stood up and went up the staircase on to the roof. He was back very quickly. 'All clear. Warn them to crouch low – it is probable Klein has men with glasses scanning all the surrounding buildings.'

'They'd do that anyway, but thanks. I've been asked to stay in their quarters while they're away – to guard certain special equipment.'

He glanced at Tweed and disappeared into the ante-room. 'Do we stay?' asked Jansen. 'I've heard no one ever sees their faces.'

'I don't think you will,' observed Tweed, 'so I'd have some more coffee and stay where you are.'

There was a delay of only a few minutes. Only Tweed realized Blade was changing into his SAS gear before he led the troop to the rooftop. The anteroom door opened without warning and Paula gave a gasp, her hand flying to her throat.

A file of men padded into the room, moving past the table at either end. To Paula they seemed incredibly sinister. They moved so silently. Each man was wearing a Balaclava helmet shrouded with a camouflage net so only the eyes showed. They were clad in complete battle gear and most wore a series of canvas pouches attached round their waists. Most carried an ugly-looking squat sub-machine gun but three were armed with rifles. They slithered through the room like ghosts and were gone as Tweed led them upstairs.

'Oh, my God,' Paula said, 'I wouldn't like to have them after me. What was that funny gun most of them carried?'

'A 9 mm Ingram MAC 11. Has a range of a hundred and fifty feet, equipped with a collapsible stock. Fires at the rate of six hundred rounds a minute. The magazine takes forty rounds,' Van Gorp explained.

'Sounds deadly.'

'It is. And some of them had the type of Browning automatic we gave Butler before he left for Findel. That has an effective range of two hundred feet. Those boys are really tooled up for action . . .'

'I counted fifteen men.'

'A formidable force . . .'

Out on the roof Tweed crouched low and ran for the wall with an agility which surprised Blade, close behind in his battle gear. They squatted on their haunches behind the wall as the rest of the troop spread out on either side. Blade had Tweed on his right, his deputy to his left.

'Get the picture, Eddie?' he asked. 'And if anything happens to me you take your orders from Tweed. No move to be made without his sanction. Well, there's the target. How does it look to you?'

Eddie peered through the mounted telescope, adjusted the focus, swivelled the instrument very slowly, stopping, moving on. He lowered the angle to study the entrance at the top of the steps.

'We've tackled worse,' he replied eventually. 'Main problem is it's isolated – no buildings close enough to operate from – and we won't be scaling that tower.'

'How would you go about it then?'

'You've explained the interior. Divide the troop into a couple of sections. One storms the entrance, clears the ground floor. Two heads straight for the elevator, makes for the platform level, cleans out platform and restaurant. Any idea how big that elevator is?'

'Eight feet wide, six feet deep. I paced it out when we were going up, when I walked out of it.'

'Six men, I suggest. Three pressed against one wall of the elevator, three against the other. Stun grenades at the ready, of course.'

'Just like that?' Blade snapped.

'Main problem as you told it is this Klein and his little toy, the control box with the red button.'

'You're right,' Tweed whispered. 'No assault can be attempted so long as he's holding that gadget. We have to hope for a lucky break.'

'One more idea,' Eddie said, his eye pressed to the telescope which he'd raised to its original position aimed at the lighted windows ot the restaurant. 'We place a man with the bazooka on this roof, a man linked with a walkie-talkie to one of the team inside the elevator. How fast does it go up?'

'Seconds,' said Tweed.

'Fair enough. Chap in the elevator gives the word the moment he presses the button for the elevator to go up. Our man up here instantly fires a bazooka shot inside the restaurant – that distracts the attention of any Klein men in the lobby at restaurant level. Only for seconds as the elevator shoots up. Seconds are all we need. Stun grenades, of course, to paralyse any men in the lobby. That's just first thoughts. And an important query. Any hostages?'

'They have a girl with them, Lara Seagrave,' Tweed said.

'*With* them?' rapped out Blade. 'What does that mean? One of them?'

'I don't think she knew any of this was going to happen. She is the step-daughter of Lady Windermere, the queen of bitches. I met Lady W in London. She drove her step-daughter out of the family home. So Lara goes out to prove she can make it on her own, looking for adventure. I think she's a pawn in Klein's deadly game.'

'Which is it?' Blade demanded. 'We treat her as a hostage?'

'Yes.'

'But if you're wrong,' Eddie whispered, 'if she has a gun in her hand, we shoot. It's the only way we operate. And would you excuse me a second? I want to check with the lads – see if they've any questions. Be back shortly . . .'

'Blade, I have one special instruction to give you for when you go in. You pass it on to everyone in the troop just before the assault . . .'

He whispered for less than a minute and in that time Eddie was back, crouching beside Blade.

'It's OK,' he reported. 'Everyone is happy.'

Happy? Tweed thought only Newman, who had trained with this troop, would understand the use of that word in these circumstances. He led the way back across the roof and down the staircase.

50

Tweed sensed the tension inside the windowless room as soon as the last SAS man closed the anteroom door behind him. The waiting was getting to them. Van Gorp sat very stiffly. Jansen was doodling meaningless shapes on his notepad and he threw down the pen as Tweed entered. Paula gave him a watery smile.

'The fishing boats – *Utrecht* and *Drenthe* – have been found,' Van Gorp announced. 'Their crews were tied up. They confirm what Klein told you. Scuba divers went overboard from them carrying the mines inside nets. So now we know definitely.'

'I never doubted it for a moment. Thank you,' he said

when Paula poured him a fresh cup of coffee, shoved a plate of ham sandwiches in front of him.

'Eat,' she commanded.

'And,' Van Gorp went on, 'the news is leaking to the outside world. Reuters have sent out a report there is some sort of emergency at Europort. It was inevitable, of course. Some of those people thrown out of the Euromast restaurant have been released. We kept them for questioning as long as we could but there was a limit. They were told not to talk – that lives were at stake. But still some have obviously not resisted the temptation to open their mouths.'

'What about Commander Bellenger?'

'Arrived while you were on the roof. He's now in the anteroom, using the scrambler to have a bomb disposal squad sent here at once.' He tapped his pencil irritably on the table. 'And I have tried to counter the Reuter report by spreading a rumour we've spotted an old sea-mine from World War Two floating near the entrance to the Maas. Might work. For a short while.'

'Clever,' Tweed commented. 'Very clever, that . . .'

He waited as the phone rang and the Dutchman took another call. 'Klein,' he said, putting down the phone. 'He wants to talk to you again.'

'It's only two o'clock. He's an hour early.' Tweed shrugged as he stood up. 'Of course it's deliberate – to keep us off balance.'

'You can tell him the German Chancellor is holding a cabinet meeting at this moment. And the cabinet at The Hague is in all night session.'

'I'll keep that up my sleeve. He's up to something. Let me find out what first.'

'You've hardly eaten anything,' Paula protested. 'Let the bastard wait. Van Gorp can tell him you're on the phone to London.'

'Daren't risk it. Klein isn't normal.' Tweed paused. 'Has anyone noticed the absence of something vital?'

Three blank faces stared back at him . Van Gorp shook his head. 'Nothing I can think of.'

'The bombs. He has twenty-four powerful bombs at his disposal. We've heard from him about the sea-mines. Why nothing about those bombs? I'd better go and perform my act.'

Tweed stood at the foot of the tower, microphone in one hand, the other thrust inside his coat pocket. Above him at platform level Klein looked down. Marler strolled out, wrapping a large red silk scarf round his neck.

'Bit nippy out here. Mind you don't catch cold,' he warned Klein amiably.

'Cover Tweed, for God's sake. That's what you're here for.'

'Anything you say.'

Staring up, Tweed saw the tiny figure beside Klein raise his rifle. In the shadows of the building behind him two Dutch marksmen had taken Newman's place.

'Is the bullion on its way to Frankfurt Airport?' Klein called out through the amplifier on top of Legaud's vehicle. 'If not, I can provide you with a further demonstration.'

'The British, German and Dutch governments are considering your demands. And you are one hour early. Our appointment was for three o'clock.'

'I'm advancing the schedule . . .'

'Say what you like, you know such a decision can't be taken in five minutes.'

'Considering are they?' Klein's voice was icy. 'I believe that was the word you used. They need something to encourage them to decide now. I'm holding the control box, Tweed.'

'I assumed you would be . . .'

'I'm going to press button number eight . . .'

Fifteen odd miles away down the Maas a detective called Beets, wearing a dark suit and holding an automatic, was

treading very cautiously inside Shell-Mex Number Two.
His companion was close behind him. Sent in by Van Gorp
– with orders that they must not be seen – they made their
way in the dark silence close to the river.

Above them a grid of pipes stretched away; close to
them to their left loomed the shadow of a futuristic-looking
cat-cracker. In the near distance Beets could see oil storage
tanks which had reminded Tweed of giant white cakes. The
only sound was the lapping of water against the wharves on
the Maas.

Probably Beets' first warning of danger was the hammer
blow of the shock wave, but this would have coincided with
the deep rumble of the explosion.

Within seconds the complex was a sea of flame and
fire as it engulfed everything. An incandescent sheet
must have swallowed up Beet and his companion –
later their charred and cindered corpses were found,
impossible to distinguish one man from another. A
deafening boom thundered upriver as the complex
became an inferno of high temperature, a red beacon
in the night.

Tweed heard the distant boom. He froze. Resisting the
impulse to turn round he continued staring up at the
platform. Klein was leaning forward, left hand on the rail,
right hand out of sight.

'And that was the first oil complex to go up. Would you
say that might encourage your so-called governments to
consider a little faster. Do look downriver. A spectacular
sight. The sun is coming up early today – but from the
west.'

Tweed turned round slowly. In the distance the sky was
illuminated with a fiery red glow. They would see that
aboard the ships offshore was his first thought. He turned
back to the tower.

'Which one, if I might enquire?'

'Shell-Mex Two. Totally destroyed. Go away, Tweed!

Come back at three o'clock. With news that the bullion has been loaded.'

A new arrival greeted Tweed when he entered the HQ room. Commander Bellenger was standing, wearing a duffel coat. Van Gorp and Jansen, seated at the table, looked grim and Paula watched Tweed intently. Bellenger, bluff and calm, was the first to speak.

'Happened to be taking a *shufti* on the roof when that little lot went up. Heard every word our Mr Klein said. I'd guess he had two of the larger bombs planted inside the oil complex. Judging from the volume of sound, the intensity of the fire glare. He's prodding us, I take it.'

'Something like that.'

Tweed sank into his chair, drank some coffee, ate a ham sandwich. He was surprised to find he was ravenous. Bellenger joined them at the table as he went on reporting.

'The bomb disposal team is on its way. Flying in. A Captain Nicholls is in charge. Says he met you, Tweed. In Norfolk.'

Tweed glanced at Paula. 'Remember him? His squad defused the bomb on your doorstep.' He looked at Bellenger. 'He has experience of underwater work?'

'Bit of an all-rounder, our Nicholls. Answer is yes. He's an expert scuba diver, has defused mines before. Only chap I know who works on land and sea. Bringing in a mixed team – some of his lot, some of my naval chaps. Bit of a sticky situation we've got ourselves into, I gather.'

'Two of my men were probably inside the Shell complex when it was wiped out,' Van Gorp said sombrely. 'And an observer on the opposite bank has confirmed to me the place is a ruin.'

'Sorry to hear that,' Bellenger said. 'Casualties of war.' He turned to Tweed. 'Is there nothing more we can do?'

He looked up as Blade appeared in the doorway to the anteroom. 'The SAS commander wants one of his men stationed on that roof. Is that all right?'

'Of course,' agreed Van Gorp. 'Tweed had best accompany him. Otherwise his appearance will scare the wits out of my men.'

Tweed went ahead of the masked SAS man who appeared, recognized that this was Blade's deputy, Eddie. He came back after a few minutes and took his seat at the table, then he explained to Bellenger.

'I know who Klein really is. He has a background of highly professional military training. He's a master planner, probably one of the most brilliant in Europe. He foresees every contingency . . .'

'A ruddy genius,' Bellenger growled.

'Look at the way he's planned this vast operation,' Tweed persisted. 'He made sure the bullion was easily available. He's got a transport plane standing by at Frankfurt large enough to shift that bullion. He has several thousand lives at his mercy as a bargaining counter for the gold. He's chosen the most strategic target in Europe and laced it with bombs, I'm sure – Europort.'

'And he won't allow us to move the bodies of my two men thrown down from the platform,' Van Gorp commented. 'I requested permission while you were on the phone. Answer? No.'

'Hideous,' Tweed agreed. 'But that's a deliberate display of his total ruthlessness . . .'

'One thing which puzzles me is his escape route,' Paula said. 'How does he hope to get away? He can't even use that beastly box as a threat once he's out of range. And we can't be sure of what the range is.'

'Twenty-five to thirty miles,' Bellenger informed her. 'In London we studied blueprints supplied by Tweed . . .'

'The ones they found in the Swiss research director's safe which Beck gave me in Geneva,' Tweed explained.

'. . . and those blueprints were detailed drawings of the radio mechanism,' Bellenger continued. 'We were able to work out the range.'

'Which gives him control from Euromast of all those vessels he's mined,' Van Gorp confirmed.

'His escape route,' Tweed commented, 'which Paula

raised. I was coming to that. I doubt it will be a number of cars – as Paula pointed out, once he's beyond the range of detonating those sea-mines we'd have him. I also doubt it's the river – for the same reasons. I've been thinking of the air . . .'

'So have I,' said Van Gorp. 'I've had my men check Rotterdam Airport. There's a Sikorsky waiting there, a big job. Pilot is an Austrian, a Victor Saur. Says he's waiting to collect a number of oil executives – on instructions from a Royal-Dutch senior director called Bouwman. I happen to know him. I've put in a call to his home address to check . . .' The phone began ringing. '. . . and this could be him.' He picked up the receiver.

'Chief of police, Van Gorp, here. Sorry to call at this hour. We met once at a reception. I have an important question to ask you . . .'

Inside his apartment, Bouwman, a stockily built man of forty with a fuzz of thick dark hair, was still fully dressed. His wife sat stiffly in an armchair while the masked man held a Luger to the side of her skull.

'This could be the police checking those Sikorksys,' he warned. 'You know what to say. Get it right first time. Make any attempt to warn them and your wife loses her head.'

The phone went on ringing. Bouwman took a deep breath, lifted the receiver, announced his identity. He listened for a moment while the masked man used his left hand to listen in on the extension phone by the armchair.

'Yes, I remember you, Van Gorp. For God's sake why have you disturbed my sleep. My wife's too, for that matter . . .'

He listened, his eyes glued to the gunman's. 'Yes, that is correct,' he replied. 'Those two choppers are waiting to pick up a certain delegation for a conference. I will tell you the conference is very secret so please don't broadcast the fact. Some of the individuals involved don't want any publicity. And one machine may have to fly off to pick up some important papers needed urgently. Is that all? Maybe on another occasion you'd call at a more civilized hour.'

Bouwman put down the receiver. The gunman carefully replaced the extension at the same moment. The oil executive used his display handkerchief to wipe his moist forehead.

'For God's sake remove that pistol from my wife's head. The job's done now.'

Van Gorp put down his own phone. 'False alarm. Bouwman confirmed the machines are being held at his disposal. He also bit my ear off for waking him. Normal reaction.'

'Then how *will* Klein escape?' Paula demanded. 'He'll have a plan. You can bet your life on that.'

'The trouble is we are betting so many lives on this business. Now who is it?' Van Gorp growled.

He picked up the phone again as it began ringing, listened and said yes, he'd pass the message on.

'Tweed. London wants you to call back. Some woman called Monica. She says you have the number.'

'I'll use the scrambler.'

Tweed went into the anteroom, closed the door, sat down and dialled. Monica came on the line immediately. The PM had asked her to inform him that the German Chancellor was on the verge of issuing the order to release the bullion. There had been an emergency meeting of the EEC Commissioners in Brussels. And could he call Moscow at the special number? Tweed said he understood, broke the connection and ran to the door which he opened, speaking briefly.

'Bonn is about to release the bullion. Van Gorp, could you get on to Bonn. Tell them to take as long as possible over loading the trucks. Warn them they may be watched. Pretend one of the truck doors is jammed, won't lock. Anything for a short delay. I've another call to make. And could you find me a green Verey pistol? Must be green. The Coastguard or someone must have one.'

'The police launches are two hundred yards from here,' Van Gorp replied. 'The ones at the end of Parkhaven basin. They will have one. We'll sneak one out for you.'

'And what on earth does he want a green Verey pistol for?' asked Bellenger.

'It's going to be all action soon,' Paula told him. 'I have heard about this change in Tweed from Butler. A long period of waiting, then he moves.'

'He has moved,' said Jansen with a rare flash of humour. 'He has gone back into the anteroom.'

Seated again at the table, Tweed dialled the special Moscow number Lysenko had given him during their clandestine meeting outside Zurich. A girl operator came on the line, he spoke to her in Russian and within seconds a familiar voice began talking.

'Where are you calling me from, Tweed?' demanded Lysenko.

'Somewhere in Europe. By scrambler. What is it?'

'We are getting reports of a big crisis building up in Rotterdam, Holland. I am also getting reports that American mavericks are involved – men with CIA training.'

'You mean you are spreading those reports. If you don't at once stifle those reports I'll reveal the whole story of Igor Zarov . . .'

'But we have an agreement . . .'

'Made invalid by any underhand manoeuvre on your part. I'm supposed to protect *you*. I also intend to protect the Americans. Are you going to keep quiet?'

'Providing you abide by our agreement . . .'

'Which I agreed to do. Stop talking nonsense. Why did you really call me?'

'Have you tracked down our traitor? Have you any clue as to where he might be? What steps are you taking now?'

Tweed sighed aloud. 'Now listen to me, Lysenko. I work in my own way. You should know that by now. I certainly have no intention of reporting every move I make. Leave the whole problem in my hands. And call off your propaganda lackeys or you will regret it. Anything else?'

'Not at the moment. Goodbye . . .'

The connection was broken. Paula came in after tapping on the door and hearing his assent to come in. She carried a tray with a plate of sandwiches and coffee.

'Close the door,' he said when she had put the tray on the table. 'This is the first chance we've had to be alone – to talk privately. And do sit down.'

'Problems? Or shouldn't I ask?' she enquired, seating herself opposite him as he tackled the food.

'The Americans have a saying. Between a rock and a hard place. That is my position at the moment. The Russians are the hard place, the Americans the rock. I have Cord Dillon, Deputy Director of the CIA descending on me any minute. I have Moscow wanting to know what is going on. I have to act to keep both happy – or at least quiet. The American alarm I can understand. I think at the very top in Moscow they understand the position – but the man who communicates with me is a pain. What is the atmosphere out there?' He nodded beyond the door to the HQ room.

'Pretty bloody. It's this waiting for Klein, waiting for a decision about moving the bullion – waiting, waiting – that is telling on their nerves.'

'It's coming up to three o'clock. I feel it will soon be over. Probably in one great thunderclap of action.'

'That sounds ominous. You're worried about someone inside Euromast, aren't you?' Paula suggested.

'I'm worried about all those people aboard the ships waiting offshore. Which reminds me,' Tweed said, standing up, 'I wonder how they've dealt with that problem.'

Van Gorp was on the phone again as Tweed went into the other room and took the same place at the table. The discussion continued for some time in Dutch and then Van Gorp put down the phone.

'That was the Dutch EEC Commissioner speaking from

Brussels. They, also, have called an all night session. The Commissioners make the point that two hundred million pounds in gold is chicken feed compared with the vast sums which will be lost if Europort is wrecked. They're inclined to give in.'

'What have you done about informing the masters of all those ships which have been mined?' Tweed asked.

'The only thing we could do. We sent each of them a signal telling them what had happened, leaving it to their discretion as to how much they told their passengers and crew. We also – through Marine Control – ordered them to stay where they are, to make no attempt under any circumstances to disembark passengers.' Van Gorp smiled bitterly. 'I have seen a copy of those signals from Marine Control. They all end up by saying the situation is under control. Like hell it is. Under the control of Klein they mean.'

'May I ask,' interjected Jansen, 'why you flew Newman and Butler to Findel?'

'Because they may well have a vital part to play at the climax,' Tweed replied and left it at that.

51

The executive jet carrying Newman, Butler and Benoit landed at the deserted airport of Findel. A car drove out to meet them as they descended the small step-ladder the pilot had unfolded.

'This will be the police,' Benoit said. 'If you don't mind I will handle them. We will talk in French so you will know what is going on.'

'Be my guest,' said Newman, hoisting the rifle scabbard over his shoulder with a strap.

Benoit carried on a terse conversation with the Luxembourger inspector of police who alighted from the car to greet him. Yes, Peter Brand had landed earlier from a Sikorsky with a small plump man Brand introduced as his bodyguard. Yes, he had then left the airport in a chauffeur-driven limousine waiting for him. Now there was a crisis in the Avenue de la Liberté . . .

'What about the Sikorsky pilot and his machine?' Benoit asked.

'We only heard from him after the limousine had driven off and reached the Banque Sambre,' the inspector explained. 'The pilot had been forced to take off from Rotterdam by Brand's so-called bodyguard – who was actually his kidnapper. The pilot had been warned to wait twenty minutes before he said a word. If a police car intercepted the limousine Brand would be shot instantly.'

'Of course!' Newman commented ironically.

'Do go on,' Benoit urged the inspector. 'What happened to the pilot?'

'He said he must return immediately to Rotterdam where some VIP passengers would arrive at any time to be flown to some secret destination. Something to do with Royal-Dutch Shell.'

'And this crisis at the Banque Sambre?'

'You had better come and see for yourself. We have a police car which will take you there now.'

'It's a bloody muddle,' Butler commented when Newman translated what had been said as they followed Benoit and the inspector to the airport building.

'Agreed,' Newman whispered back. 'And Tweed would call it a smokescreen. Let's see what's happening first.'

The Avenue de la Liberté, normally deserted at this hour, was a hive of activity. The whole street was cordoned off with barriers and police cars. All side streets leading into it had been closed off. Police carrying arms patrolled somewhat aimlessly.

'That building is the Banque Sambre,' the inspector explained, pointing to the closed doors of an edifice with lights on in the first floor. 'That is Brand's office – up there with the lights on.'

'What exactly is going on?' Newman demanded.

'We have a state of siege . . .'

'Why?'

'The kidnapper phoned police headquarters, said Brand was being held at gunpoint. The gunman warned no attempt should be made to storm the building or Brand would be shot. He also said he is being held to check a gold shipment due to arrive at Findel. I have no idea what he means.'

'We have,' said Newman. 'It's all linked to what is happening in Rotterdam. Is there any way we can get inside that building over the rooftops. Myself and Butler, I mean.'

'It is impossible!' The inspector was appalled and his normal air of stolidity vanished. 'Peter Brand's life is at stake. Don't you understand what I have said? He is a most important person.'

'The cat's whiskers,' said Newman.

'I beg your pardon?'

'Nothing. Have any other conditions been laid down – apart from not storming the building?' Newman enquired.

'Yes, there must be no attempt to interfere with his telephone communications with the outside world. No attempt to tap his lines. Rotterdam has requested us to abide by these conditions. Some man called Tweed . . .'

'We know about Tweed,' Newman told him. 'I think we'll stay here awhile,' he said to Benoit. 'Meantime,' he went on in French, 'I'd like a very fast car made available for my use.'

'Brand has a Lamborghini in a garage nearby,' the inspector said. 'But I don't think he'd like it being used.'

'He's a prisoner,' Newman pointed out. 'What he likes or doesn't like is irrelevant. What happened to the chauffeur-driven limousine which brought him from the airport?'

'Parked in a side street close to the Banque. The chauffeur has been told to stay with the car by Brand.'

'Then get me the Lamborghini now, please. Park it nearby in the street leading across the Viaduct to the airport. With the keys in the ignition and a police guard watching it.'

'May I ask what you foresee?' Benoit enquired.

'Sooner or later Brand is going back to Findel to check the gold shipment coming in. You said so yourself. When that happens I want to reach Findel first. Butler and myself.'

'I know what I'd really like,' said Butler. He looked at a police outrider sitting with his legs straddling a Honda. 'That motor-bike.' He turned to Newman. 'With you inside the Lamborghini and me on the motor-bike it will give us more flexibility for action. And a crash helmet that fits my big head.'

'Good thinking,' Newman decided.

Within a few minutes Butler had his Honda. He tried on several helmets the inspector obtained from other outriders, found one that fitted, left it on his head with the ear flaps dangling.

'You have a plan?' asked Benoit. 'You know what is coming?'

'Just pray that I'm right.'

Aboard the *Adenauer* passengers were dining late, making their meal last. Anything rather than go to bed and not sleep. The liner's master, Captain Brunner, after receiving the signal from Marine Control had taken a strong decision. He would inform everyone of the exact position.

Waldo Schulzberger, US Secretary of State, was the first to be told as he sat in his stateroom with his wife and Cal Dexter, the lanky chief of security.

'I'll signal Washington now,' said Dexter, springing to his feet. 'Find some way of getting you both off this floating bomb.'

'You'll do nothing of the sort,' Schulzberger ordered him. 'I don't mind you contacting Washington, but we're staying aboard.' He turned to Captain Brunner. 'You say you're informing all the passengers of the situation?'

'Yes, sir.'

'Then my wife and I will not take dinner here in our stateroom. We'll eat in the first-class dining room . . .'

The rumour spread quickly – no one found out how it started – that the Secretary of State and his wife would be taken off the *Adenauer* secretly. It caused a sensation when Schulzberger appeared in the dining room. He stopped to chat with guests at several tables.

'It's a load of hogwash that Lucy and I are leaving the ship,' he told one industrialist who posed the question. 'We've paid our fare like the rest of you folks. We intend to enjoy the cruise soon as those people in Rotterdam have sorted this thing out. Which I know they will . . .'

He also declined to sit at the captain's table, joining a group of passengers at a large table. The news spread like wildfire through the ship. Soon the crew heard of his decision. Morale soared. If Schulzberger was staying the danger couldn't be all that great. One boisterous woman said as much to Brunner, who smiled and walked on.

'God help us,' he whispered to his First Officer. 'From that signal I received – reading between the lines – I'd put our chances of survival at fifty-fifty. If that . . .'

Tweed was talking to Blade on their own in the anteroom.

'When do you want to get your troop into position for the assault? The situation could develop very fast from now on. The bullion is being loaded at Frankfurt Airport aboard a transport aircraft bound for Findel.'

'Now. They are ready. And I don't want them cooped up any longer than is necessary. Mainly, I want every man on the ground so he can see for himself the lie of the land. Will you lead the way?'

'We move now then. Down the back staircase. Van Gorp

has warned his men. One thing, I want to try and get aboard one of those police launches – to take a look at Euromast from another angle. Whatever happens, your troop doesn't attack until I fire a green Verey light. Whatever happens,' he repeated.

Five minutes later they were making their way along the side street towards the line of buildings screening them from the Euromast. It was 2.45 a.m. Fifteen minutes before Tweed was due for another confrontration with Klein.

Inside Euromast at platform level Klein watched the elevator door open. Chabot, returning from the Space Tower at the summit, stepped out holding a pair of night-glasses. Klein had sent him up there at regular intervals. He never went up himself since that would have isolated him from what was happening below.

'What is the situation now?' Klein asked.

'Same as before. All the vessels are waiting with their lights on. The *Adenauer* is a blaze of lights from stem to stern. No change in their position.'

'Good. Go up again in ten minutes' time.' He checked his watch. 'That will be just before Tweed comes to meet me again. Make a quick scan next time. No more than two minutes, then come down to report before I speak to Tweed.'

'Klein . . .' Chabot took several paces closer and his manner was aggressive. '. . . a lot of us want to know the escape route – how we're going to get away when the gold is delivered.'

'And I have told you a score of times you will hear later. I will give exact instructions. You will be surprised how easy it will be . . .'

'Surprise me *now* . . .'

He stopped talking as Marler appeared from the platform holding his rifle loosely in his right hand. The Englishman was still showing no signs of the strain which was growing among the rest of the team.

'Bit of activity out there,' Marler remarked. 'Down by those police launches at the end of the basin.'

'Show me.'

Gripping the control box in his right hand, looking like a commanding general in his leather greatcoat, a monocular glass looped round his neck, Klein followed Marler on to the platform, standing by the rail as Marler raised his rifle.

Klein lifted the glass to his eye and gazed down in the same direction. There was movement in the shadows astern of the police launches. He caught a brief glimpse of Tweed, crouched low, who disappeared behind the bulk of the wheelhouse.

'Wasn't that Tweed?' Marler called out.

'Yes. Don't shoot him. Yet. We still need him – to conduct the negotiations.' His voice rose to a high pitch. 'They are testing our willpower. I warned them not to move anywhere in sight of Euromast. Those policemen. Shoot them. That will demonstrate we mean what we say.'

'How many do you want?' Marler enquired.

'All police who move. Shoot them down.'

Tweed slipped aboard the police launch and ran for cover. He was met behind the wheelhouse by the river police chief of the flotilla, Spanjersberg. He gave him instructions as he stood up cautiously, his binoculars aimed at the platform.

The figure of Klein in his military-style outfit stood out in the lens clearly. A few yards further along a figure with a rifle aimed. The Monk.

'Here is the Verey pistol I was going to bring you,' Spanjersberg said. 'Loaded with a green. Now I will tell my men . . .'

They had been confined aboard the cramped launch for hours. Spanjersberg approached each of the four men separately where they had taken up different viewing points. He spoke to them in whispers, retreated back to the safe side of the wheelhouse and made a gesture with his hand, a downward chopping gesture.

The four men began running towards the stern at the same moment, zigzagging as they pounded along the deck. For a second the only sound in the deep silence of the night was the thud of their boots on planking. Then came a fresh sound.

The dull crack of a rifle being fired. In rapid succession. So rapid it was almost a continuous and single sound. Marler was pressing the trigger, moving the muzzle a fraction, pressing the trigger.

Blade saw it from the shelter of the wall where he crouched. Four running men, spread out. The first fell, rolled, stopped. The second cried out, dropped like a sack of cement with a thud Blade didn't hear. The third man nearly made it to the wheelhouse, then threw up his hands and sprawled inert on the deck. The fourth man dived down the steps of a companionway which swallowed him up.

'That bastard,' said Blade, his tone mild.

'We don't move?' Eddie, crouched next to him, asked.

'Not till Tweed fires the green signal. You know that. God, Tweed will be raving inside.'

'I see why you were so keen on my skill with a moving target,' Marler commented. 'Must be out of practice.'

'Why do you say that?' Klein asked in surprise.

'Only three out of four. Should have got the lot. I'll get better as we go on.'

'We've made our point,' Klein snapped. 'When Tweed tries to get back let him go. That little demonstration must have shaken his nerve.'

'Which is the crux of your strategy?'

'Always keep the enemy off balance. Surprise him. Break him down.'

They had moved off the platform when Marler asked his question. First he lit a cigarette.

'This elusive bullion we keep hearing about. Any sign of our getting our hands on the loot?'

'Brand is under guard in Luxembourg City. He has phoned me to say Bonn is weakening. I expect to have good news soon. Has everyone eaten?' he asked Chabot who appeared from the direction of the restaurant, munching a sandwich. 'Full stomachs are what an army marches on. Napoleon.'

'They have taken it in shifts to eat,' Chabot reported. 'The food we brought with us, that is. And, before you ask, they have drunk nothing but the mineral water or the coffee we also brought with us.'

Klein nodded. He had known there would be food and drink in the restaurant food store but inside two of the cases his men had carried in to Euromast there had been canned meats, butter and bread, cans of coffee, condensed milk and bottles of mineral water. Klein believed in relying on his own supplies. Drinking water from the kitchen taps had been banned. The Dutch might get clever and introduce some poisonous element into the water supply.

'Now,' he said, 'we will prepare the major shock for the next encounter with Tweed.'

'It may be some time yet,' Tweed warned Blade as he passed the masked figure crouched behind a wall.

Van Gorp was waiting for him when he entered the HQ room via the back staircase. The Dutchman stood up, his expression bleak. He waited until Tweed was seated.

'I was on the roof when that incident occurred. Three of my men are dead – or badly injured . . .'

'Dead. Spanjersberg said they had to be. He's waiting with them on the launch . . .'

'I am not prepared to stand by while that swine kills off my men one by one. What happened?'

'Spanjersberg indicated they wanted to leave. We thought if all four ran at once there would be too many targets. The marksman on that tower is even better than I thought. It's appalling, I agree.' Tweed looked straight at Van Gorp. 'If you wish to take control of the operation I am in your hands. After all, we are on Dutch soil.'

The Dutchman sat down slowly, spread his hands. 'I realize it is a matter of psychology – dealing with that megalomaniac. You know him better than any of us. Please carry on. And I see you have your Verey pistol.'

Tweed had laid it on the table, exposing his right hand. A blob of blood welled up from the back of the hand. Taking a bloodstained handkerchief from his pocket Tweed dabbed at it.

'That needs attention,' Paula burst out.

'A sharp chip of wood flew up from the deck when a bullet hit it. Nothing to fuss about.'

'I'm not fussing. It needs washing. I've got Elastoplast in my shoulder bag. I'm dealing with it . . .'

While she attended to his hand Tweed went on talking to Van Gorp. 'What's the latest met. report? You have a new one?'

Silently, the Dutchman pushed a sheet of paper across the table. They had been receiving regular weather forecasts at Tweed's suggestion for some time. He read the latest and Paula felt him stiffen.

'What is it?' she asked.

'More bad news,' Van Gorp told her.

'I wonder,' said Tweed. 'Major weather change on the way. A heavy sea mist expected and little drizzle. It's a new factor.'

'You mean Klein won't be able to see what's going on out at sea, that we might be able to move the ships out of range?' Van Gorp suggested.

'Certainly it will eliminate their visibility to the lookout I am sure Klein keeps up in that Space Tower. As to moving the ships, too dangerous. Remember, he said he had men watching on the coast. They'll be in radio communication with him. If they report movement he'll press that button.' He looked at Paula. 'Thank you,' he said as she completed stanching the flow of blood. 'No,' he

469

continued, 'it is here at Euromast the deadlock must be ended. It is conditions here which count.'

He waited as Van Gorp took another phone call. Another conversation in Dutch. Van Gorp swore as he put down the receiver.

'The news is really leaking out. That Reuter report started it of course. Now newspaper reporters, TV crews are trying to slip through the cordons for a view of the tower. Some are bound to get through. And who the hell is this?' He picked up the phone again, listened, handed it to Tweed.

'It's for you. Newman on the line . . .'

'Tweed? This is an open connection. I'm talking from a café near a certain bank . . .' Tweed thought Newman sounded strained, tired. Lack of sleep. '. . . and we're waiting for the banker to leave for the airport. He's being held at gunpoint – if you know what I mean.'

'I do. The expected consignment is on the move. Give me that number so I can call you. Any plan?'

'When the moment comes Butler and I will arrive at the airport first. Ahead of you-know-who. I'll make it up as I go on from there.'

'Bob, when you reach that airport, get Benoit to call me – ask him to keep an open line. I need to know what's going on there as well as here.'

'Will do. Cheers . . .'

Van Gorp put down his coffee cup. 'What's the reason for that? Needing data from both ends?'

'Because Klein will be doing the same thing – synchronizing his operation at Findel with what he does here. We have to outwit him – and it may all hinge on seconds.'

The phone rang again. Van Gorp said yes and no several times, put down the receiver, picked it up almost immediately as it rang a second time. He spoke in Dutch, then ended the call.

'First was from Frankfurt. They're loading the bullion aboard the Hercules transport. Brand can check the consignment when it reaches Findel – but the pilot has instructions not to fly on to any destination until Klein surrenders his control box.'

'That arrangement will test my powers of negotiation,' Tweed said thoughtfully with a faraway look.

'Better you than me. The other call was local. My radio interception people are picking up a lot of strange traffic in a language they don't recognize. I can call them back and they can play you part of a tape.'

'Do that. Quickly please. I don't like the sound of that development.'

'Klein is speeding up his operation,' said Paula.

'Trying to catch us on the wrong foot,' agreed Tweed.

He took the phone Van Gorp handed him and listened carefully as a tape was played back. He couldn't understand one word. He handed the phone back.

'I know what it is. Klein is being clever again. He has a large number of Luxembourgers – and that language, so-called, is their *patois*. Letzeburgesch. Mix of French and German. Understood by neither race. You need a Luxembourger to tell you what is being said. Do you know of one living in Holland?'

'Not off hand. I'll try to locate one, get him to listen to the tapes. I've been thinking about those Sikorskys out at the airport. Something about them bothers me. I'm wondering whether to put guards on them.'

'Don't,' Tweed said quickly. 'Leave them alone. I have my reasons.' He checked his watch. 'And Klein is late calling for me. Bad tactics for me to make the first move. Think I'll go up on the roof, see what's happening.'

'Can I come?' Paula asked.

'Good idea. Give you a breath of fresh air.'

It was drizzling when they emerged on to the roof, a fine sea-like spray. Van Gorp had told Tweed it hadn't rained for weeks. Crouched at the wall, he peered through his binoculars at the huge barges moored close to Euromast in Parkhaven. Four abreast, there were twelve of them altogether, berthed stem to stern.

The weather change had transformed the whole atmosphere. The roads gleamed under street lamps. The decks of the barges had a fine sheen of moisture. Drizzle settled on the oily surface of the Maas.

At that moment Tweed wondered, although he had no way of knowing the weather change would be the key factor when the climax came.

52

'They have given in to our show of force,' Klein said as he paced round the lobby leading to the platform. 'The gold is being loaded aboard the transport plane.'

He seemed as fresh as ever, Marler observed. Still in iron self-control. No excitement showing in his voice which was as cold as ever.

'How can you be certain?' Marler enquired.

'That phone call I took. It was from a man I have watching at Frankfurt Airport. And, of course, the call came via Legaud's van. Legaud reports an increase in radio traffic on the police band. But all routine calls. A prowler seen at such-and-such a street corner, etc.'

'Any conditions before they release the gold?' Marler persisted.

Klein smiled icily. 'Brand, accompanied by my armed guard, is to check the bullion. When he reports it is correct I am supposed to surrender this control box.'

'But you won't?'

'What they don't know is that hidden aboard that transport plane at Frankfurt I have my own armed air crew. Always have an ace up your sleeve, Marler. Now, we will prepare our new shock for Tweed.' He called out to two masked men. 'You know what you have to do with her. Do it!'

The two men seized Lara who still lay on the couch,

bound with ropes. Lifting her upright, they propelled her towards the platform. They had a hard time; she kept fighting. Kicking with her tied ankles she caught one a blow on the shin. '*Merde!*' he grunted and gripped her tighter. They lifted her off her feet, she bent her knees, swung back as though on a swing, supported by her captors, swung forward and almost hammered the other man in the groin.

'You've used me, you lousy swine!' she screamed at Klein.

'If you simply relax it will be much easier for you.'

'What the hell are you going to do with me, you bastard?'

'Provide Mr Tweed with a fresh demonstration that we never let up. It's called keeping on the pressure.' His voice changed. He snapped out the order to the two men. 'Get on with it. Take her on to the platform.'

In Luxembourg City Benoit hurried over to the café opened up by the proprietor who slept over the premises. Police-men came and went, drinking coffee, eating sandwiches. He found Newman and Butler hunched over more black coffee, sitting at a window table where they could watch what was going on.

'A phone message from Tweed. The bullion is being loaded on to the plane at Frankfurt. It is only a short flight here.'

'Any sign of activity at the Banque?' Newman enquired.

'Nothing at all. Except someone we couldn't see closed the curtains over his office window. You may have to leave soon now.'

'I've checked the Lamborghini,' Newman replied. 'Best you come with me. Butler can go ahead on his motor-bike. I certainly don't want him behind us.'

'That's slander – or is it libel,' Butler commented amiably. 'I'm very good on one of those machines. '

473

'But I do wish you'd drive with the wheels on the ground.'

Benoit left them to check the latest position with the inspector. Newman drank more coffee. Anything to keep him awake. His eyelids were heavy as lead.

'If it is a fake,' Butler remarked, 'this so-called kidnapping of Brand, why is he throwing away all he has? One of the top bankers. A luxurious estate on the Meuse. A mansion in Brussels. He's got it all.'

'Except Benoit says he hasn't. He spends money like confetti. Apparently the Brussels Fraud Squad has been waiting for an excuse to move in. Friend Brand has been paying interest out of shrinking capital. Even to his madcap wife in New York. And she could arrive back at any time. Brand's trouble is she can read a balance sheet. Her father taught her. If Benoit should be right Brand is on the verge of bankruptcy. So, he needs a safe country, and a slice of that Frankfurt bullion.'

'The way things are going, he could get it. Klein has got a stranglehold on us.'

'May be up to us to break that stranglehold.'

'Would you believe it,' growled Van Gorp, 'a TV crew has penetrated the cordon and set up cameras on the roof of a building with a full view of Euromast? Just to the west. I'd like to remove it – but we'll get a scream about police interfering with freedom of the media. In any case, newspaper reports are beginning to appear in Tokyo. Soon the world will know.'

'Klein might not like that,' Tweed warned. 'If not, you'll have to send men to shift them. The reason? They are endangering people's lives . . .'

Van Gorp snatched up the phone at the second ring, listened, said something brief in Dutch, put down the receiver and looked at Tweed.

'Over to you, I fear. Klein wants to talk again . . .'

Tweed appeared near the foot of the tower a few minutes later. On the way he had conversed briefly with Blade who had spread out his Sabre Troop into three different groups. 'They're ready to attack,' he'd assured Tweed. 'And one man is now on the HQ roof with a bazooka aimed at the restaurant . . .'

Tweed had stopped at the police van to collect the microphone with the long cable. He walked carefully to the same place at the base of the tower; the paving stones were slippery. He felt moisture damping his face and was glad he'd put on his waterproof hat. He looked up and spoke in a firm voice.

'Before you start talking I have a demand to make . . .'

'No demands . . .'

'Shut up and listen to me. You are on the brink of success. Medics are waiting to come out and remove those two dead men on the steps. The medics are dressed in shirts and shorts. You can see they carry no weapons. Unless you agree I have lost the cooperation of the Dutch authorities. They will not allow those men to lie there any longer.'

'By all means remove them. It would be a humanitarian act.'

Tweed stared up at the platform. Why this change of mood? He was suspicious, uneasy. Klein's voice through the amplifiers sounded jocular.

'I'm going to signal them to come and do their job,' Tweed warned. 'I'm out of it if you play any tricks.'

'Would I play tricks on you, Tweed?' The voice was mocking now. 'Send in the medics.'

Tweed studied the tiny figure of Klein leaning over the rail, one hand out of sight. Holding the control box, he felt sure. Beside him Marler stood, a tiny wisp of blond hair showing in the light from the interior lobby, rifle aimed point-blank at Tweed.

Slowly, Tweed raised his left hand. Four men wearing white shirts and shorts walked rapidly out of the shadows, carrying stretchers. In less than a minute they were moving away, each supporting the body of one of the policemen toppled from the platform. Why this change of mood? Tweed asked himself.

'And now,' Klein called out, 'a different demonstration which will show you we will stop at nothing.' He called over his shoulder. 'Bring her out. It will give those TV ghouls over there something they will really enjoy.'

Tweed froze with horror. A girl was being lowered over the rail. He pulled out his binoculars with his left hand and aimed them upwards. Oh, dear God! No! He felt sick in his stomach, a reaction succeeded by one of cold unreasoning fury. He could have killed Klein with a knife if he'd been up there.

Lara Seagrave had a rope tied round her waist. The only support which stopped her plunging three hundred feet. Her legs dangled over the abyss, her hands tied behind her back. He went on staring through the binoculars, pressed hard into his eyes. The horror had only begun.

A masked man leant forward and looped a noose round her neck. She was literally hanging in space. Tweed could see the rope round her waist was extended back up over the rail and out of sight, a rope holding her tightly. From the noose another length of rope – this one loose – extended back also out of sight. This was macabre, unthinkable.

Klein's voice began speaking. His tone was detached, as though describing some everyday occurrence.

'This is Lara Seagrave, daughter of Lady Windermere, a well-known London hostess. You heard the name clearly? Lady Windermere. She is supported safely by the rope round her waist which we have attached to the leg of a very heavy table. The noose round her neck is also attached to another leg of the same table. We only have to cut the first rope and she will hang from the neck until she is dead. Any attempt to storm Euromast and a man standing by cuts the first rope. She is our hostage – our guarantee of good behaviour on your part, Tweed. Now, do you understand the position clearly?'

Tweed lowered his glasses, unable to look at Lara's face for a moment longer. She looked terrified – fear beyond belief. He swallowed, unable to speak, automatically gripping the microphone, struggling for self-control. Lara . . .

'I said,' Klein's voice repeated, 'do you understand?'

Tweed glanced up again, saw the suspended figure, lowered his head. Oh, Jesus Christ! This was awful. He was aware suddenly of the heavy silence. The medics had gone with their grisly burdens. Couldn't hear a thing. Except for the gentle lap of water against those barges. He took a firmer grip on the mike, on himself.

'Klein we also want medics to remove the bodies from that police launch . . .'

'No! They moved without my permission. They stay where they are. I will ask you again . . .'

'Klein! Haul her back inside or you're finished. I will be replaced by a senior Dutch official . . .'

'Then I will talk to him. Go away. We are waiting for the gold to reach Findel. Next move then.'

Tweed looked up quickly. Klein had disappeared. Only Marler stood there, rifle still aimed. He walked slowly away. Handing back the mike to the driver, he trudged on in a daze. Reaching the entry to the side street his feet slipped on the greasy surface. A hand grabbed his arm, steadied him. A voice spoke. Blade's. 'We'll enjoy sending that bugger to kingdom come.'

'We must still wait . . .'

Tweed used his hand to haul himself up the back staircase. Paula met him at the top. She looped an arm through his. 'Come and sit down. That was terrible, I saw it from the roof . . .'

Arriving inside the room, he sagged into his chair, then he straightened his back. Round the table they watched him without speaking. Bellenger, Jansen, Van Gorp. No one seemed to know the right thing to say. Tweed broke the silence.

'I know the girl. Lara Seagrave. Met her in Paris. She had been spotted photographing ports. I liked her. I'd have liked her as a friend. She's Lady Windermere's step-daughter. Not daughter. That slip was deliberate on Klein's part. Makes her sound more important. Only reason she's up there is the bloody step-mother. Drove her out of the house.' He paused. 'Now, we must put our thinking-caps on. The next stage is Klein's secret escape route. He has to have one. I think I know what it is.'

'Well?' said Van Gorp.

'Let's see what develops. It will be soon now.'

'In the meantime,' commented Bellenger, 'we can do nothing at all. That girl will just have to stick it out . . .'

'How can you be so cold-blooded, so Goddamn callous?' Paula burst out.

'Just getting the thing in perspective. I have a daughter of my own. Not callous at all, I assure you.'

'He's right,' Tweed told her. 'We can only wait.'

'He's got a stranglehold on us . . .' Bellenger paused. 'Not phrased well, that. Sorry.'

'You have a plan, Tweed?' Van Gorp asked.

'I'm playing it off the cuff. Klein ran out of luck long ago. He's going to make a mistake. I've pandered to his ego. I'm banking on that. He'll make just one mistake.'

53

'I want you to bring that Seagrave girl back in here now.'

Chabot faced Klein, a Walther P.38 automatic pistol in his right hand, muzzle pointing at the floor. The Frenchman's face was pallid with fatigue. Behind them on the platform Marler watched, holding his rifle.

'She stays out there, you fool,' Klein rapped back. He extended the control box in front of his waist, thumb poised over the red button. 'Put that gun back into your holster now. This very minute.'

'It's too much . . .'

'Shut up! Listen!' Klein's voice became matter-of-fact as he explained. 'Your knowledge of mass psychology is zero. They now have TV cameras recording the scene out there and soon pictures will appear all over the world.'

'What's that got to do with my request?'

The tense expression on Klein's face, the poised thumb, the steel in his voice frightened him. He slid the gun back inside his hip holster as Klein continued.

'People are stupid, very sentimental. This is something the tiny minds of those watching can take in. One girl on the verge of eternity. One slash of a knife and she hangs from her neck, choking her life out until she is dead. They can take in the fate of a single individual. The idea that two thousand people aboard those ships are at risk is too much for their feeble minds. Using Lara Seagrave as our hostage is my masterstroke. You will see.'

'I still don't like it,' Chabot repeated obstinately.

'Then go down to ground floor level and stay there. Someone else can go up to the Space Tower. You are now in charge of the defences at the entrance. And remember, Chabot, if they should attack they will shoot down every-one in their way – if you let them get inside. So, if that happens, you kill them first. Go to the elevator. Don't come back.'

'The French can be so sentimental,' Klein remarked as Chabot disappeared inside the elevator.

'I don't like it too much myself,' said Marler who had walked in from the platform. 'You could have pushed them a shade too far '

'Ah, that is a point of tactics you raise. You British can be very ruthless in your gentlemanly way. My judgement of psychology is better in this case. Now we are alone for a moment I will tell you your role in the escape plan.'

'Which is?'

'A Sikorsky will take off from Rotterdam Airport where it is now waiting for my signal. It will land on one of those large barges moored below. I shall board it with a team of men – still holding this control box. Your job will be to stay on the platform to cover me. From this height – with your talent with that rifle – you will be able to shoot down anyone foolish enough to try and prevent my escape.'

'Won't work. The moment your chopper is out of range of the ships offshore they'll be after you.'

'My dear Marler, I have thought of that. The Sikorsky will fly downriver above the Maas – *towards* the ships. The range will narrow, not widen.'

'Clever.' Marler leaned against the wall. 'What after that?'

'The Sikorsky flies low, well below radar level. It flies on over the *Adenauer* and heads north for a certain Frisian island. There a large power cruiser is waiting to take us on board. By then they will have lost us. The cruiser takes us to a certain destination where we board a waiting executive jet. Comments?'

'You've left me carrying the can . . .'

'No, carrying this.'

From behind the seat where Lara had lain trussed up he produced an executive case, dumped it on the seat, snapped open the catches with his left hand. He gestured to the contents.

Marler blinked. Holding the rifle in one hand, his finger inside the trigger guard, he stooped over the case. Packed with neat bundles of banknotes. He sorted through several stacks at random. Fifty-pound notes. He made a quick calculation.

'One hundred thousand pounds,' Klein said.

Marler extracted one note, held it up to the light. He examined it carefully then stuffed it in his breast-pocket behind his display handkerchief. Closing the case, he replaced it behind the seat, straightened up.

'Hope you didn't print those yourself. If you have done, I will certainly find you. What about the big balance?'

'In bearer bonds, negotiable anywhere in the world.'

Klein patted his pocket. 'I give you them when the Sikorsky has landed.'

'Very neat. Except it leaves me here to face the music.'

'The second Sikorsky picks you up five minutes later. The pilot knows the route – again along the Maas– to another power cruiser waiting in the Frisians. You take the rest of the team with you. All the time I have you covered – with the control box aboard my helicopter.'

'Communication. In case of a spot of bother?'

'The pilot of the second Sikorsky will be in constant touch with my pilot. Any interruption and I press the button. You can explain the position to Tweed. He's an understanding type of chap, as you'd say.'

'What comes next?'

'The signal from Brand at Findel – confirming the bullion is genuine, the right amount. Then the first Sikorsky arrives.'

'Neat,' Marler said again. 'What could possibly go wrong?'

54

Seated with Butler in the café overlooking the Avenue de la Liberté, Newman stared at the TV screen above the serving counter. The proprietor had left the machine on – even though it showed only a blank screen.

'They get so used to that damn thing,' he said, 'they leave it on when there's nothing on . . .'

He stopped, gripped Butler by the arm, nodding towards the TV. An announcer had appeared. He began talking. 'The crisis at Rotterdam . . .' Pictures flashed on to the screen.

'Oh, my God!' Newman said hoarsely.

'It's bestial,' Butler commented.

The camera had zoomed in close on Euromast. The figure of Lara Seagrave suspended from the platform came up. The camera zoomed in closer. A shot of her face, distraught, stricken with terror. The camera panned slowly up and down the side of the immense tower.

The announcer was explaining the position in detail. The fact that only two ropes held her, the second a noose round her neck. Newman swore, went over to the phone on the counter and told the proprietor this was a security call. The man vanished through a door. Newman dialled the number Tweed had given him.

'Tweed here.'

'Bob. We've just seen Euromast on TV. The girl hanging in mid-air. Klein is a sadist . . .'

'More a brutal psychologist. I was just going to phone you. We're close. Gold loaded at the other end. Plane due to fly off. May have done so now. Don't forget to get Benoit to keep on an open line from Findel so he can contact you. The codeword for taking action is *Flashpoint*. Once you're told that word take any action you like to stop the plane taking off again.'

'You can synchronize it like that?'

'I don't know. I can only hope and pray.'

'Flashpoint,' Newman repeated.

At the house in Eaton Square, London, Lady Windermere was furious as she climbed out of bed and slipped into a peignoir over her night-dress.

'Why have you woken me at this hour?' she snapped at her Spanish maid. 'What's all this nonsense about something terrible, Anita?'

'Please to come and look at the television . . .'

'The TV? Are you mad. It's not on . . .'

'But it is, your Ladyship. Please to come and look . . .'

Tightening her thin lips, Lady Windermere followed Anita down the curving staircase into the study. She paused at the entrance, surprised. The TV screen was showing pictures.

'It's Lara,' Anita said, almost sobbing. 'Look for yourself.'

'Where is this happening?'

'Rotterdam – in Holland.'

With a face like stone Lady Windermere sat in an armchair. The camera was scanning the full height of Euromast as the commentator explained. Then another close-up of Lara hanging from the platform. Lady Windermere clenched her hand.

'The little fool. I said she'd get into some awful scrape. Now this dreadful publicity – and Robin's wedding is on Saturday. It really is too bad of her. She could spoil everything. What a disgusting spectacle.'

'But, your Ladyship, shouldn't we call your husband?'

'No, certainly not. He's in Manchester on business. At this hour he'll be fast asleep.' Thank God, she thought. If Rolly knew he'd be on the phone, making a fuss.

'On no account are you to ring him,' she ordered. 'You've already spoilt my night's sleep. Switch that thing off. I do not wish to see any more. If it goes on it will take the spotlight off Robin's marriage in the papers. I'm going back to bed.'

How perfectly infuriating, she said to herself as she mounted the staircase.

'An American, Cord Dillon, is waiting to see you in a car parked in the side street,' Van Gorp informed Tweed. 'He wanted to come up but the guard stopped him.'

'I'd better go down and talk to him in the car,' Tweed said, standing up. 'Call me instantly if there's a development.' He looked at Paula. 'Like to come with me?'

A crimson Cadillac was standing by the kerb in the dark side street. A uniformed chauffeur opened the rear door and Tweed, followed by Paula, got inside. The Deputy Director of the CIA was a tall, well-built man in his fifties with a craggy face. He had a shock of thick brown hair, was clean shaven had a strong nose, prominent cheekbones and ice-blue eyes.

'Who is she?' he snapped, gesturing to Paula.

'My personal assistant. Totally vetted. Paula Grey. Meet Cord Dillon.'

'This talk with you was to be between the two of us.'

'Paula stays. If you're going to talk about what I think you are she may be able to help.' Tweed waved his hand, indicating the spaciousness of the car. Paula sat turned sideways in one corner, Dillon in the other of the rear seat with Tweed between them. 'Where did you get this wheeled palace?'

'US Embassy at The Hague met me at the airport. What I want to talk about . . .'

'Just a moment,' Tweed interrupted. 'You'll want what I may tell you off the record – so switch off the tape recorder, if you don't mind.'

Dillon reached down below the seat, turned a switch. 'Off the record. I'm in a hurry. So are you. Let's get to it. We have had strong rumours an ex-CIA man is mixed up in this Rotterdam business. I think Moscow is spreading the poison. My worry is it could be true. Remember Lee Foley?'

'Left you – with all his expertise – to set up CIDA, the Continental Detective Agency, in New York. I last encountered him in Switzerland . . .'

'He's gone missing.'

Despite his normal manner of iron self-control, Tweed sensed anxiety under the surface. There was as much tension inside the Cadillac as in the HQ room.

'How long ago was this?' Tweed asked.

'Six months. Boarded a flight for London, left Heathrow and vanished. Foley was good at that trick. We've used good men to track him. They've come up with zilch. A guy doesn't just walk out on a profitable business and disappear. Foley did.'

'Paula,' Tweed suggested, 'tell him very briefly about

your experience at Blakeney and on the road to Cockley Ford.'

He listened, checking his watch several times, while Paula recalled what had happened tersely. Including the bomb on her doorstep. Dillon grunted when she'd finished.

'Tweed,' he began, 'if Foley is involved here, I'm going to ask you a favour. Don't care how you do it. Just make sure any part Foley has played never goes public. The Russians would tear us to pieces. OK? Then I'll owe you one.'

'I'll do my best. Now, fly back to London. Wait for me at your Grosvenor Square Embassy. I'll contact you when I can.'

'I have another problem. Cal Dexter, Schulzberger's security chief aboard the *Adenauer*, reports Schulzberger won't leave the ship.'

'Good for him. You have no problem. Go back to London as I suggested. Now I must get back.'

'What happened?' Dillon asked as Paula reached for the door handle. 'To Foley, I mean.'

'He shook hands with the devil.'

'The bullion is on its way to Findel,' Van Gorp told Tweed as he came back with Paula. 'The governments are putting a heavy burden on you. They're assuming somehow you'll get the gold back. Luckily no hint of this surrender has reached the outside world. Yet,' he added.

'Then Klein will know, too. I'm sure he had someone at Frankfurt Airport watching. Gentlemen . . .' Tweed laid his hand on the Verey pistol. ' . . .we are close to the crunch.' He looked at Van Gorp. 'Don't forget Benoit – and Flashpoint. You have your man on the roof watching?'

'Yes. I don't understand your plan, but he's in constant contact with me through his walkie-talkie.' He picked up his own walkie-talkie off the table. 'And I'll call Benoit myself.'

'He may call you, ask you to keep the line open.'

'What do you plan to do?' asked Bellenger. 'Incidentally, a bit of good news. The bomb disposal lads have arrived at Schiphol outside Amsterdam. Why not fly them here?'

'Not yet. As to my plan, I have very little idea. I will have to react to events as they unfold – waiting for that one unguarded moment of Klein's. He, of course, will have been monitoring all communications through that CRS van, as I said earlier.'

'Don't worry about that,' Van Gorp assured him. 'I worked out a code for the police radio band. You've no idea how many prowlers we seem to have loose on the streets tonight.'

'How is Lara getting on?' Tweed asked quietly.

'Still suspended by that rope. That man is a fiend.'

'But a clever fiend. All along he has held us in a balance of terror. He has done enough to hold us in the deadlock. Sinking the dredger, *Ameland*. Blowing up Shell-Mex Two. Killing five policemen. The Lara thing. All enough to stop us daring to move. But nothing yet so tremendously appalling – like sinking the *Adenauer* – which might make us throw caution to the winds. I warned you – a master planner.'

'So what next?'

'At this moment we are in the hands of Newman.'

Benoit rushed into the café up to the table where Newman and Butler waited. He was breathing heavily and it was a moment before he could speak.

'Brand has asked permission to be driven to the airport. The transport with the gold is coming. He has warned us the man holding him will shoot him dead if we attempt to interfere.'

'You were able to persuade the local police chief to leave the airport free of his men?' Newman asked, standing up, looping the scabbard with the rifle over his shoulder.

'With difficulty, yes. He agreed.'

'Then let's get moving. Pretty damn quickly – to get there before Brand and his so-called captor.'

Five minutes later, with Benoit seated beside him, Newman was driving the Lamborghini across the viaduct, crossing the chasm. No traffic about. He rammed his foot down, exceeding the limit, swerving round corners, then on to the highway direct to the airport. Benoit pressed his tingling feet against the floor, trying to preserve his portly aplomb.

Newman increased speed on the highway. Benoit watched the needle on the speedometer creep steadily higher. Something streaked past them. A motor-cycle. The rider hunched under his crash helmet.

'God! He's moving,' Benoit gasped.

'Butler. Wheels off the ground. Ever seen a motor-bike flying? New experience for you.'

'The whole thing is a new experience . . .'

No sign of life at the airport. Lights on inside the main reception building. Newman drove round the side and parked out of sight. Brand mustn't see the Lamborghini. Benoit levered his stiff limbs out of the car, carrying a large torch in one hand.

'Why did you want me to bring this?'

'I'll be out somewhere on the airfield when the machine gets here. I want you by a window facing the airfield, with the telephone in your hand. The moment Rotterdam gives the go-ahead – Flashpoint – you signal with that torch. On and off six times. That's vital. I'm hamstrung – so is Butler – until Tweed sends his own signal . . .'

Butler had perched his motor-cycle on the side of the building closest to the airfield. He was checking his Browning automatic when they found him.

'Hear it coming?' Butler asked.

'I can see it,' said Newman .

'I'd better get to security, find a phone, the right position,' said Benoit.

The night sky was clear, moonless, star-studded. There were two mobile stars, one green, one red. From the east came the rumble of the approaching transport plane carrying the gold bullion.

One of the double doors of the Banque Sambre opened. Brand – arms extended in front of his body – emerged slowly. Hipper, a slouch hat pulled over his forehead, a handkerchief masking his face, came alongside him, holding the Luger against the banker's skull.

They walked slowly along the Avenue de la Liberté as police marksmen on the roof covered Hipper. Turning down the side street, they approached the waiting limousine where the chauffeur held open the rear door.

The inspector, hidden inside a doorway, spoke into his walkie-talkie to the marksmen. 'Don't attempt it. The gunman's reflex action would pull the trigger. Brand must reach Findel alive . . .'

The limousine drove off slowly past the barriers which had been removed. Reaching the street leading to the viaduct, the chauffeur accelerated. He kept up the same speed until he arrived at the airport. As Brand stepped carefully out, followed by Hipper, the huge transport machine from Frankfurt landed.

'The plane is at Findel,' Klein said as he put down the phone. 'So is Brand. He's just called from the security office. In a few minutes he will check the bullion, then report back to me over the aircraft's radio.' His voice was still detached, calm.

'When do you call up the Sikorsky?' Marler enquired.

'The moment Brand reports he's checked the gold. It is only a few minutes' flight from Rotterdam Airport. Legaud's van will ensure all communications work . . .'

Inside the CRS vehicle the professorial Legaud had sent one of the four men to sit behind the wheel through the door linking the cab with the interior of the van. He felt quite safe as he sat in front of a console of dials and switches, wearing a headset as he listened to the police radio band.

Three more armed men sat in the van behind him. The vehicle was bullet-proof, the few windows made of armoured glass. A telephone receiver lay on its side by his left hand, keeping him in constant touch with Klein. The whole operation had hinged on his expertise, or so Legaud preened himself.

Inside the HQ room Tweed sat with his hand close to the Verey pistol. Van Gorp was talking to Benoit. He put the receiver on the table.

'We now have an open line permanently to Benoit. He says the plane has landed. Brand has arrived. He's going aboard the aircraft. How long to check the gold?'

'No idea. Again, we wait.'

'So drink more coffee,' said Paula.

'I'm swimming in the stuff, but thank you, yes.'

'It will be soon, then?' asked Inspector Jansen.

'Soon,' Tweed replied and drank more coffee.

'There's something very wrong,' Newman said to Butler who sat astride his Honda.

They were near the end of the runway, at take-off point. Newman had suggested they walk the long distance in the dark as he clutched his rifle. Butler was mystified why they were waiting there.

'What's wrong?' he asked.

'That transport plane. When it landed it taxied to the other end of the main runway, then turned slowly through a hundred and eighty degrees.'

'Why did you expect?'

'The control tower would have instructed it to move on to one of the approach paths. It's positioned itself where it could make an immediate take-off. I don't like it. I sense some trick.'

*

Brand had climbed the ladder lowered by the air crew into the plane. Hipper, Luger aimed at his back, had followed. As Brand stepped aboard the pilot pulled him out of sight.

'We are ready when you tell us the cargo is OK. We have now dealt with the air crew which took off from Frankfurt.'

'Dealt with them?'

'Shot them, of course. When we're over the Atlantic we can drop the bodies. Now, we are short of time. You come this way.'

He led Brand into the cargo hold where long wooden boxes roped down were stacked. The ropes had been removed from several boxes. The pilot explained they'd work as a team for speed. He would rope down each box after Brand had checked it while his co-pilot un-roped others for Brand's inspection. The radio op. was at his post in the pilot's cabin, keeping in touch with Euromast.

Brand took a leather pouch from his pocket, unfolded it and extracted from its leather compartment a small glass pipette containing a liquid. Standing over the open box, staring at the large ingot stamped with German markings, he held the pipette over it, let slip a tiny drop. It sizzled as it landed on the ingot.

'Gold,' Brand said. 'Let's keep moving. Next box . . .'

'Klein wants to talk again. Wait while I check we're ready.'

Van Gorp put down the phone, picked up the other one lying on the table and spoke to Benoit. He nodded to Tweed as he lay it on its side. 'Benoit is waiting. Brand still checking that gold.' He picked up the walkie-talkie, its aerial already extended, exchanged a few words in Dutch with his man watching on the roof. 'Communications in order.'

'And your man on the roof understands the signal I told you both in private he would receive – if my plan works?'

'Didn't understand it – as I don't – but he'll recognize the signal, inform me instantly. Then I pass the codeword to Benoit. Good luck.'

Three minutes later Tweed handed the Verey pistol to Blade who was still waiting with his Sabre Troop. 'Keep that for me,' Tweed requested. 'Collect it from you when I get back.'

Standing at the base of Euromast with the microphone in his hand, Tweed stared up. Klein began talking immediately in a brusque manner, giving orders.

'The gold is checked. Sensible of you to carry out my orders. Now listen. Don't interrupt. A Sikorsky is flying in here. It will land on one of those barges behind you. I shall leave the Euromast with a number of my men. Others will stay inside Euromast. When I leave to board the machine I will be holding the control box, thumb over the red button. Shoot me, my last act will be to press the button. Everything goes up. A second Sikorsky will arrive – to take off the rest of my team. My Sikorsky will fly downriver – closing the range with those floating deathtraps. Any interference, I press the button – both Sikorskys will be in constant radio touch.'

'That was not the arrangement . . .'

'I said don't interrupt. That is the arrangement now. All those people's lives are in your hands. I shall remain in communication with Findel. The plane will be allowed to take off. Any interference with that take-off – you know what will happen. And in case you doubt my will to do as I say . . .'

Klein tapped his right leather-soled shoe twice. Marler was further round the platform, rifle aimed at Tweed. Inside the lobby a Luxembourger sawed through the rope holding Lara by her waist. The last strand broke . . .

She fell a dozen feet. The noose tightened round her neck. She swung slowly in space. The TV cameras zoomed in, recording the sight of her extended neck, her bulging eyes.

Tweed gazed up, frozen with shock and disbelief. Chilled

to the bone. His eyes glued to the suspended figure, hanging like a marionette, a broken rag doll. He realized he was in shock, gripping the mike like a vice. His legs felt paralysed. He couldn't move. It wasn't happening . . .

55

Tweed took back the Verey pistol from Blade and crouched next to the troop commander. He was silent for a minute or two, being careful not to look up at the tower. The drizzle was still falling, a moist sheen gleamed on the sidewalks and the decks of the moored barges.

'You're soaked,' Blade remarked.

'Just a bit wet. What's that thing?'

He pointed to a phone handset which lay on the ground next to Blade. A cable stretched from it away into the distance.

'The Dutchman organized that while you were out there. An efficient lot, these Dutch chaps. Don't panic. That will be for you,' he said as the phone started a muted buzz.

'Tweed here.'

'Van Gorp. That was pretty grim . . .'

'Shock tactics. Perfect timing. Klein's about to run for it. That showed he means business with his bloody little red button.'

'Still deadlock then. I'm waiting. So is the other chap at the end of the line . . .'

'Must go. Something's happening.'

Blade had gripped his arm. The growing sound of a helicopter approaching broke the silence. The Sikorksy looked enormous when it hove into view over the river. Tweed gripped the pistol. 'Just one mistake, Klein,' he whispered to himself.

On the platform Klein watched the machine coming, turned to Marler. 'I'm going down in the elevator. Cover me.'

'Will do.'

Klein took five men inside the elevator, holding the control box firmly. Emerging from the elevator on the ground level, he walked alongside a wall and stared out of a window. The Sikorsky had turned over Parkhaven, was hovering above one of the barges. It descended slowly. Rotors still whirling, it settled on the deck, its port side facing towards the end of the basin where Blade's men were hidden.

Klein walked out slowly, hand extended. A file of men holding Uzi machine-pistols followed him down the steps. Klein walked across the sidewalk, stepped off the kerb into the street. A dozen yards more and he would he shielded by the bulk of the machine which kept its rotors whirling, ready for immediate take-off.

On the platform Marler moved round to the far side – away from the buildings where the Sabre Troop waited. Raising his rifle, he rammed the stock into his shoulder and waited, gazing through the telescopic night sight.

Klein stepped on to the barge deck which was sleazy with oily wetness. No one behind the wall with Tweed saw what happened next. Klein moved forward towards the open door of the Sikorsky, his leather-soled shoes slipped, he lost his balance and sprawled forward full length. The control box slid out of his hand, skidding under the chopper's fuselage. Klein hauled himself forward, made no attempt to climb to his feet. His hand reached forward to grip the control box.

Marler saw it clearly through his sight. The hand reaching out desperately for the box. He began shooting with surgical precision. The first bullet tore into the outstretched hand. Klein's arm jerked back in a reflex of pain.

He rolled on his side, closer to the box. Using his uninjured left hand he reached again for the box. Marler saw the hand as though it were inches from his face. The long fingers clawing forward like a spider's legs. He aimed for the centre of the back of the hand, it disintegrated into a bloody mess of mangled flesh. Again the arm jerked back. He aimed for the lower back as Klein rolled in agony, pulled the trigger. The body jerked convulsively, lay still. Marler aimed for a point below the left shoulder blade and fired again. Klein twitched, lay motionless. A figure in the doorway dropped to the deck. Marler shot him in the chest. He was hurled back as though hit by a hammerblow. Inside the Sikorsky, sitting behind his controls, the pilot, Victor Saur, was confused. He had no idea Klein had been shot. Another man appeared at the doorway, saw the body of his companion and retreated inside the machine. 'No sign of Klein yet,' he reported.

On the platform Marler turned as a Luxembourger walked round the side of the tower. He shot him. Then he walked to the rail, held his rifle at a vertical angle, waved it sideways back and forth three times, and reloaded.

Tweed saw the signal, fired his Verey pistol. Above Parkhaven a green light flared brilliantly. Blade's men moved forward in three widely separated groups, crouched low as they ran for the entrance to Euromast.

On the roof of the HQ building Van Gorp's lookout gave the warning through his walkie-talkie.

'*Flashpoint!*'

Inside the HQ room Van Gorp grabbed for the phone which linked him to Findel.

'You there, Benoit? *Flashpoint! Flashpoint!*'

Blade's men had reached the entrance. Several hurled stun grenades over the crude barrier of furniture. The grenades exploded with a deafening crack. Balaclava-masked figures leapt straight over the barrier. They were firing their Ingram machine-pistols as they landed.

Dazed by the stun grenades, nine of Klein's team armed with Uzis attempted to aim their weapons. Swift, short fusillades of bullets hit them. They crumpled, fell to the ground in grotesque attitudes.

On the roof of the HQ building Blade's trooper holding

the bazooka aimed it carefully, pulled the trigger. The missile hammered through the restaurant windows three hundred feet up, detonated inside.

On the platform Marler heard the *whoosh* of the missile coming, dived down behind the railing. The platform shook with the force of the explosion. Most of Klein's men at that level had been inside the restaurant. Marler pulled out his bright red scarf, let it fall over his jacket. He risked a glance over the rail. The Sikorsky was still on the barge, its rotors whirling.

Tweed, waiting by the side of the building the SAS troop had attacked from, also stood watching the helicopter. Someone came up behind him, tapped him on the shoulder. A familiar voice spoke. Captain Nicholls. From the bomb disposal squad at Blakeney.

'Bellenger sent me to join you. I've just arrived. Balloon's gone up . . . '

'Klein must be dead. I'm worried about the control box he was carrying. It can . . .'

'I know. Bellenger explained. Why don't we walk over there?'

The Sikorsky had begun to lift off. Saur had panicked. As the machine climbed higher they had a clear view of the deck of the barge. Tweed saw the two bodies lying there.

'Let's move,' he said.

They walked at a normal pace towards the barge. From Euromast came the sound of desultory machine-pistol fire. A series of sharp cracks. No one else on the waterfront. Tweed kept an eye on the elevating helicopter. It was now turning, heading for the Maas above the docking basin.

On the platform Marler heard the Sikorsky taking off. Standing up, he raised his rifle. He aimed carefully for the section which held the petrol tanks. He waited, seeing Tweed walking with another man, far below – waited for the Sikorsky to get far enough away. It reached the end of the basin, flew on over the Maas. Marler pulled the trigger three times in rapid succession.

495

Nothing happened for a few seconds. Marler estimated the Sikorsky was thirty feet above the water. A tongue of fire appeared, expanded into a flaring flame. Saur, his flying kit on fire, dived from the doorway. The fire enveloped him as he dropped into the river. The Sikorksy exploded, showering the air with fragments. In seconds it was a glowing fireball. It plunged into the Maas. The water sizzled. A second petrol tank exploded. A geyser of water as dramatic as one in Yellowstone Park rose from the river, then collapsed. The dark surface of the Maas became smooth and still as the grave.

Marler walked inside the entrance to Euromast, glanced round the lobby, holding the rifle he had reloaded. No one. He was watching the elevator – which had started to climb from the base of the tower. He sat at a table half-sheltered by an upended couch, took out from his pocket a wad of cottonwool he used to freshen himself up with eau-de-Cologne. Wetting two tufts with his tongue, he stuffed one in each ear.

He sat at the table with his forearms, leaning on it, his hands extended, flat on the table's surface. The rifle he left on the floor. The elevator had arrived at the platform.

The doors opened. Inside, both men pressed against the wall, stood Blade with Eddie. The moment the doors opened they hurled the stun grenades. Despite the cottonwool, the sound was deafening. The two men jumped out, Ingrams aimed. Eddie saw Marler, swivelled his weapon. Blade saw the red scarf. A second before Eddie fired he yelled.

'Don't! Red scarf . . . !'

Eddie automatically approached the platform while Blade, his eyes slits behind the Balaclava, advanced on Marler, Ingram aimed. Marler gestured towards the British passport he had tossed earlier on the table.

'Don't shoot the pianist,' he said. 'He's doing his best.'

Blade flicked open the passport, compared photo with the man seated at the table. 'You nearly had it that time,' he said.

'Nearly is close enough. Look, I have to get down on to the waterfront. Tweed may need a little help. Satisfied? I've a rifle I'd like to take with me. Use that phone to warn the chaps below I'm coming down. And there's still one up in the Space Tower.'

There was a brief rattle of machine-pistol fire from where Eddie had gone. 'The bazooka must have missed a couple,' Marler commented. 'And the elevator went down, is coming up again '

'More of my chaps. I'll send one down with you. No time to use phones . . .'

One of Klein's men appeared from nowhere. Marler nodded but Blade had seen him. He half-turned. The man, ashen-faced, had his hands up. Blade shot him twice.

On the waterfront Tweed waved a hand. The three police-men Marler had 'shot' stood up, raced off the launch ashore.

Tweed and Nicholls stepped on to the barge cautiously. The drizzle was still falling, the deck surface was coated with a greasy sheen. Then the two men froze. The Sikorsky over the Maas had just exploded.

'There's the control box,' Tweed said, pointing.

'I see it. You wait here. I know how it works. Those blueprints from Switzerland you handed to Bellenger in London were shown to me by his naval chaps. Their bomb disposal lot is still waiting at Schiphol. I came on ahead in case you needed a spot of help . . .'

And he had used his loaf, Tweed thought. Nicholls was wearing civvies, dressed in a dark suit under a raincoat, carrying an executive case. He laid it on the deck, squatting on his haunches, opened it, took out a small leather pouch.

'Don't worry,' he assured Tweed.

'A lot of lives are connected to that damned box.'

'I know. Like I said, wait here . . .'

He walked across the deck which pitched slightly, moving to bump against the wharf, then drifting out to collide heavily with the barge moored alongside. Using a torch, Nicholls checked the neck pulses of both bodies, then walked slowly round the control box, which lay about four feet away from Klein's wrecked hands. Bending down, he used the thumb and forefinger of his right hand to lift the box. He walked back to Tweed, asked him to hold the torch.

'You'll be surprised how simple this is . . .'

Tweed stared at the rows of numbered buttons, then his eyes locked on the red button. Using his left hand, Nicholls opened the leather pouch, selected a small screwdriver and shoved the pouch back inside his pocket. He unscrewed the screw at each corner of the top of the box, tucking them inside his pocket. The distant rattle of a machine-pistol drifted down to them from the Euromast platform. Nicholls ignored the sound, lifted the top of the box carefully and slid that into his pocket. A maze of wires led from what looked like a battery. Nicholls substituted a small pair of pliers for the screwdriver, snipped ten wires, including one coloured red. Lifting out the battery, he handed the box to Tweed.

'Press any button you like. Nothing will happen. The box is disarmed.'

'Thanks, but no thanks,' Tweed replied, handing the box back to Nicholls.

He looked up as footsteps, a swift deliberate tread, came across to the barge. Marler. Rifle held loosely in both hands.

'I'd better get back,' Nicholls said. 'Next job is link up with the team waiting at Schiphol, get out to those ships . . .'

'I wonder how this happened,' Tweed enquired, pointing a foot to Klein's dead body.

'Slipped on the greasy deck. Made the mistake of wearing leather-soled shoes. Mine are rubber. If the drizzle hadn't come . . .' Marler shrugged. 'We'd have been up the creek. Gave me the few seconds I needed to shoot him – that control box slid out of his hand. Just the chance I was waiting for.'

'We have one more problem. While we're alone. Klein must not be identified.'

'Think I could help there.'

Marler glanced round, then walked to the other side of the barge. The barges were still bumping up against each other, then opening up a stretch of water about three feet wide before they began closing again. Marler strolled back, looked at Euromast. Deserted outside. He used his foot to roll the corpse of Klein across the deck, a task made easier by the slippery surface. When Klein was wedged against the gunwale he looked round again as Tweed walked to where he stood. Marler placed his rifle on the deck, waited until the gap between the heavy barges was widest, then levered the body into the water.

It floated until the barge they stood on moved against it and pushed the body forward. The two barges met. There was an ugly cracking sound, the sound of bones being crushed between the makeshift vice. Marler peered over as the barges slowly parted company again.

'Skull crushed flat as a dinner plate . . .'

Tweed took his word for it. Marler picked up his rifle. In the distance was the sound of a chopper approaching. They stepped off the barge. It began to move towards the second barge again.

'He'll end up as the original thin man,' Marler remarked. 'I have one more job to do.'

'Which is?'

'Second Sikorsky coming in from the airport. To pick me up. So Klein said. A bullet in the back soon as I went aboard would be my guess. Then the long drop into the Maas. Here she comes . . .'

Marler aimed for the cockpit as the machine came down-river, began to turn in over the Maas, losing height. Later they hauled up the Sikorsky out of the river and found the pilot with a bullet between the eyes. Again Marler fired three times in quick succession. The helicopter, now hovering at the entrance to Parkhaven, began to gyrate as it dropped out of control. The rotors were still whirling as it hit the water. The Sikorsky settled, the fuselage vanished, the rotors whirling to a stop whipped up a foam and then they were gone.

As they walked back along the waterfront Tweed glanced up at Euromast. At least someone had pulled in out of sight the pathetic body of Lara Seagrave, thank God.

'*Flashpoint!* . . . !'

Van Gorp's warning came down the line clearly to Benoit at Findel. He dropped the phone, picked up his torch, went close to the window and flashed the torch on-off-on six times.

Newman had moved to a position midway along the runway between take-off point and where the Hercules transport was still stationary, revving its engines. He stepped off the runway on to the grass and backed a dozen yards.

It was still dark but his eyes had regained their night vision. As he had suspected, the plane was doing the wrong thing: it was revving up to full power. The transport began moving towards him. Slowly at first, then a steady increase in speed. He braced himself, shoved the stock of the rifle hard against his shoulder. He was aiming for the huge tyres on the machine's wheels.

As it came closer a door opened. Framed inside stood a man holding a machine-pistol with a long barrel. Probably a 9 mm Uzi. Forty rounds in the mag. The night was filled with the roar of the oncoming transport. Ignoring the gunman in the doorway, Newman aimed his night sight for the blur of a fast-revolving tyre. The gunman had begun to open up on him. A spray of bullets hit the grass fifty yards from where he stood. In seconds they'd be firing at him point-blank.

The sound of the transport's engines drowned the noise of the motor-cycle Butler was riding, coming up behind the tail of the plane. He held the handlebars with his left hand; in his right he gripped the Browning automatic. He came like a rocket, was suddenly alongside the machine. He raised the automatic, pressed the trigger, firing non-stop at the doorway.

Hipper toppled out of the plane, thudded down on the concrete runway. Newman fired several shots, moving the muzzle a fraction. The transport sheered past. Newman saw the port wheel collapse, metal grinding through rubber. The machine's starboard side swung through an angle of ninety degrees – carried on by its intact starboard wheels. The plane wobbled across the grass, stopped. Butler pulled up a few feet behind the open door, reloaded, aimed his Browning upwards. A ladder was dropped as Benoit arrived in a jeep driven by the chief security officer. Brand alighted first, climbing down with hesitant steps. Benoit was waiting for him. Before the banker could turn round Benoit clamped his hands behind him with a pair of handcuffs.

'Peter Brand, I have a warrant for your arrest . . .'

Epilogue

Two weeks later three men sat in Tweed's office at Park Crescent. Newman sat in the armchair, Marler stood by the window, Tweed occupied the seat behind his desk.

'So you've seen off Cord Dillon,' Newman remarked.

'He flew back to Washington yesterday,' Tweed answered. 'I took him up to Cockley Ford with the order to exhume the seventh grave in the church cemetery. When they opened it they found the body of Lee Foley. Dillon reacted well, said he didn't know who he was. Afterwards he told me he recognized the signet ring on the corpse's third right finger. My guess is Klein couldn't get it off and had the villagers dump the body in.'

'And our nice friend, Ned Grimes, confessed before he died?'

'Talked non-stop. Foley had explained the idea to the villagers with Klein and Dr Portch present. Offered them the earth if they would cooperate – let the tomb of Sir John Leinster be used to store a secret cargo. That was the bombs and sea-mines due for delivery by the *Lesbos*, of course.'

'But not everyone agreed?'

'No, now we come to the nasty bit. Six of them – egged on by a Mrs Rout, the postmistress – wouldn't play. Threatened to report the plan to the police. Enter Lee Foley one evening at The Bluebell, masked in a Balaclava when they'd manoeuvred all the six dissenters to be present. He mowed them down with a machine-pistol. Except Simple Eric. No one worried about him. No one would believe a word he said.'

'Why did the other villagers agree to go along?'

'Greed, pure greed. Foley offered them a fortune,

handed out expensive presents – including a Rolex for Simple Eric. They had no idea what was going to be hidden in the tomb. I doubt if they cared. Portch by then had them in the palm of his hand. He took them off occasionally for holidays to distant places – and escorted them.'

'After they'd buried the bodies of their fellow-villagers,' Newman commented. 'What a macabre business.'

'I gathered from Grimes they were divided into two factions long before Foley and Portch appeared. That's not uncommon considering the isolated lives some of those tiny villages in Norfolk lead,' Tweed remarked.

'And afterwards Portch practically held them in quarantine – with very little contact with the outside world?'

'Again not uncommon – especially round Breckland. Some of them have never seen London. Portch would charter a flight to some lonely West Indian island out of season to stop them getting restless.'

'And what happened to Foley?' Newman enquired.

'He blundered. Panicked when Paula followed him. Decided he had better wipe her out. Hence the TNT – packed inside one of the smallest Soviet bombs. Klein was furious, drugged him at Cockley Ford, then cut his throat. Grimes helped dispose of him. Hence the seventh grave. I think Klein met Foley in New York during his UN posting. Like recognized like. Foley, Dillon told me, had contact with European arms dealers, probably supplied the weapons. Klein would have killed him anyway in due course, I'm sure.'

'And now they're all dead. Again, how macabre,' Marler drawled, 'that they died of anthrax, a rare disease.'

'Contracted, so the Special Branch doctor diagnosed,' Tweed explained, 'from old rags piled in Sir John Leinster's mausoleum. After the explosives had been moved Grimes used it to shelter cattle. If Dr Portch had stayed, had not been blown up with that coaster, I'm sure he'd never have allowed it. Ironic.'

'So,' Marler remarked, 'another touch of irony. Earlier Portch covered up the six murders of Foley's with a fake diagnosis of meningitis. Had the village quarantined. Now the accomplices to mass murder have died of anthrax the place is once again in quarantine. The strange death of a village cleansed with flame throwers.'

'All except Simple Eric,' Tweed reminded him. 'He survived – weak in the head, strong in the body. Now he's living at Cockley Cley. A lady there has given him shelter.'

'No trouble with the coroner?' Newman enquired.

'None at all. Special Branch has moved in. Matter of national security. And no one will believe Simple Eric if he talks.'

'Later I thought your Olympus was poor Lara,' Newman observed. 'Not Marler.'

'Tricky when I had to "shoot" the three police,' Marler recalled. 'I aimed to miss, hoping to God Tweed had fixed it for them to fake death – which he had. Helped my status with Klein. On the Dames de Meuse I also aimed to miss Newman, nearly killed Tweed. He moved as I fired.'

'That was a bit of luck,' Tweed said. 'I'd earlier "created" a skilled assassin called The Monk – Marler's first job for us. With the help of a few friends on the continent we built up his "reputation". He's a marksman, as you now realize, Bob. But he never killed that German banker. We simply spread the rumour in the right quarters it was The Monk's work. The banker wanted to take a long holiday incognito – away from the press – in Honolulu. He agreed to cooperate with the German police. Same with the Italian police chief, who *was* killed, but not by Marler. Again we spread more rumours.'

'What was the idea?' Newman asked.

'We thought that sooner or later Marler would be approached by someone wanting a top statesman killed. Even a Secret Service chief. Marler would have warned us. As I said, it was sheer luck Klein hired him.'

'Trouble was I couldn't tell Tweed much,' Marler remarked. 'For the simple reason I didn't know the target until late on in the game. Then Klein stuck to me like glue. I'd have shot him inside Euromast when I knew his horrendous plan – but he carried his infernal control box everywhere. I nearly had kittens when he shoved that poor girl over the rail.'

'I'm attending the memorial service,' Tweed said. 'I paid a call on Lady Windermere when I got back. Incredible woman. Accused me of being responsible for the postponement of the wedding of her wretched son, Robin. She didn't realize her banker husband, Rolly, was listening from the next room. He walked in and said he was leaving her. She blamed me for that.'

'What did you say?' Newman asked.

'"My pleasure." Then I left the old cat. I must be getting vicious . . .'

He broke off as the phone rang. It was Moscow. Lysenko came on the line, asked if Zarov had been traced yet.

'You can forget he ever existed. Because he doesn't any more. No questions. You said you'd leave it to me. It's called détente.'

He smiled as he put down the receiver. 'I never thought that I could do it. Keep Washington and Moscow happy at the same time. It's been a weird case.' He clasped his hands behind his neck. 'I had both of them on my back. Do it for us. Oh, Bob, while I remember. Marler is joining us as sector chief for Germany. Good at languages. Hasn't been to university – the new breed.'

'Congratulations,' said Newman.

He didn't shake hands. Those two, Tweed thought, will be at each other's throats in future. Solve one problem, create another. He reached for the file on his desk as Newman stood up. 'Howard has already dumped a fresh job on me. Oh, Bob, Colonel Romer of the Zurcher Kredit wasn't involved, Beck has told me.'

'I'll push off,' Newman said. 'I'm going to ask Paula out to dinner. See you.'

Tweed stared at him with a blank expression as Newman grinned, gave a little salute and left the room.

'Pipped you at the post?' Marler suggested.

'Actually, no. Paula has already agreed to join me for dinner at Daphne's this evening.'

Marler had left Tweed alone when Monica came into the office. She sat at her desk, began tidying files, then asked the question.

'One thing I can't understand. Klein must have been amazingly greedy. He already had twelve million Swiss francs from the bullion stolen in Basle. More than enough to set him up for life. Why go on and risk mounting that huge operation to grab even more money? I know it was a huge amount . . .'

Tweed paused, glanced at the door to make sure it was closed. Again he hesitated before he began speaking.

'This is strictly between the two of us. Forever. The PM did tell me what was really at stake when it was all over. Came out in her conversation with the General Secretary. Inside Russia there is a powerful faction which doesn't like Gorbachev and his reforms, a hard-line group which wants to bring him down, take over power. Partly Red Army, partly KGB. Identities unknown – even to Gorbachev. Zarov was their agent.'

'Still don't understand.'

'The conspiracy was diabolically clever. This group realized they couldn't safely organize a coup *inside* Russia. They decided to set up a secret base *outside* the Soviet Union – South America. From there they would organize the coup – probably through sympathizers inside various Soviet embassies. A plan like that takes money, a great deal of money. Hence the assault on Europort. When the coup succeeded, I suspect Zarov had been promised the top KGB job, probably a seat on the Politburo. I think he saw a quick route to become General Secretary in due course. Imagine a man like that ruling Russia. A lust for power was the driving force. None of this was revealed to me until last night. I think the PM decided to tell me because I was lucky enough to foil the attempt. And anyone who succeeded Gorbachev was bound to be a menace to the West. Which is why she decided to help him.'

'What a terrifying thought. A man like Zarov running Russia.'

'Don't let it keep you awake. It's all over now. I hope.'

Time passed. The authoritics had boarded up the entrance from the highway to Cockley Ford. No one ever went near the place. Nature – Breckland – began to take over in its slow relentless way.

Ivy and other creepers invaded the abandoned village. Spreading up the cottage walls, they penetrated the windows, crept into the rooms. The gardens became a jungle, merging with the encroaching forest. The footbridge alongside the ford collapsed. The road through the village disappeared as undergrowth took root.

A small boy vanished and was never seen again. A searching helicopter had great difficulty locating Cockley Ford. Eventually it found the place. From the air humpbacked mounds engulfed in vegetation were all the pilot could see of the scorched village. As though Nature had buried forever the cottages where so much evil had originated.

Colin Forbes
The Leader and the Damned £5.99

In 1943 Hitler was at the height of his power. At his side, Martin
Bormann. And constantly on his mind, the war against the
beleaguered might of Stalin's Russia. After 13 March of that year,
records show a drastic change in the Führer's behaviour and
personality: 13 March 1943 was the date of a bomb attack on the
Führer's private aircraft. If Hitler was destroyed on that fateful date,
who was the man in the Berlin Bunker two years later? And how did
Bormann succeed in keeping the anti-Nazi generals from seizing the
Reich?

'It is easy to forget this is fiction' DAILY MAIL

Double Jeopardy £4.50

A British agent inexplicably murdered on Lake Konstanz; his
replacement, Keith Martel, must move swiftly. The neo-Nazi Delta
organization are fighting dirty, and maybe someone else is fighting
the same way. A nightmare bloodbath in Zurich, a sudden attempt
on Martel's life, and close to midnight on 2 June the Summit
Express takes the top four western leaders to meet the Soviet premier
in Vienna. One of them is targeted. Which one and how to save him
are Martel's problems.

'One of the top half-dozen British thriller writers' DAILY MIRROR

Colin Forbes
Cover Story £4.99

'Adam Procane has to be stopped . . .'

It was the last message his wife ever sent. And even as he read it, foreign correspondent Bob Newman knew she was dead. Soviet Intelligence had sent a film of her murder to London with the warning – *tell other people to keep away from Procane* . . .

Procane, a top Washington official, is about to defect, and with the Presidential election two months away, it's the last thing the Americans want. Trouble is, until they know exactly *who* he is, they can do nothing to stop him.

In London, Tweed of SIS watches and waits. Four highly suspect Americans have already passed through en route to Scandinavia – the Deputy Head of the CIA, the National Security Adviser and his wife, and the Chief of Staff of the Armed Forces. Any one of them could be Procane.

Meanwhile Newman has slipped off to Finland, bent on revenge. So it's time for Tweed to act. To get back into the field. To stop Newman and find Procane – before the dreaded GRU do the job for him . . .

Colin Forbes
Janus Man £5.99

'The wires hum across North Germany. The same message repeated again and again. *Tweed is coming . . . TWEED IS COMING . . .'*

A British agent found floating in the Binnenalster at Hamburg. A murder clumsily disguised as an accident to lure Tweed of the SIS into a killing ground in the borderland of the Cold War . . .

With Bob Newman, foreign correspondent turned minder, to watch his back, Tweed hunts a killer working on Moscow orders from Hamburg and Lübeck to Copenhagen and Oslo and back to the East Anglia countryside.

And he knows that there's an enemy in his own citadel, that one of his four European section chiefs is working for the other side. Codename Balkan, The Janus Man who faces both East and West.

As the body count rises, the command goes out from the East: *Kill Tweed* . . .

Terminal £4.99

When international news correspondent Bob Newman gets a tip-off about a mysterious package smuggled across an eastern border it's yet another link in a chain of sinister incidents that have one thing i common – they are all connected with the Berne Clinic and Terminal. But what is Terminal? And why are British SIS so desperate to find out?

All Pan books are available at your local bookshop or newsagent, or can be ordered direct from the publisher. Indicate the number of copies required and fill in the form below.

Send to: Pan C. S. Dept
            Macmillan Distribution Ltd
            Houndmills Basingstoke RG21 2XS
or phone: 0256 29242, quoting title, author and Credit Card number.

Please enclose a remittance* to the value of the cover price plus: £1.00 for the first book plus 50p per copy for each additional book ordered.

*Payment may be made in sterling by UK personal cheque, postal order, sterling draft or international money order, made payable to Pan Books Ltd.

Alternatively by Barclaycard/Access/Amex/Diners

Card No. | | | | | | | | | | | | | | | | | |

Expiry Date | | | | | | |

_____

Signature:

Applicable only in the UK and BFPO addresses

While every effort is made to keep prices low, it is sometimes necessary to increase prices at short notice. Pan Books reserve the right to show on covers and charge new retail prices which may differ from those advertised in the text or elsewhere.

NAME AND ADDRESS IN BLOCK LETTERS PLEASE:

....

Name _____

Address _____

_____

_____

_____

6/92